...eleven novels for adults, five for young readers and a collection of short stories. Perhaps best known for his 2006 multi-award-winning book *The Boy in the Striped Pyjamas*, John's other novels, notably *The Absolutist* and *A History of Loneliness*, have been widely praised and are international bestsellers. In 2015, John chaired the panel for the Giller Prize, Canada's most prestigious literary award. His latest novel is *A Ladder to the Sky*.

www.johnboyne.com
@john_boyne

By John Boyne

NOVELS
The Thief of Time
The Congress of Rough Riders
Crippen
Next of Kin
Mutiny on the Bounty
The House of Special Purpose
The Absolutist
This House Is Haunted
A History of Loneliness
The Heart's Invisible Furies
A Ladder to the Sky

NOVELS FOR YOUNGER READERS
The Boy in the Striped Pyjamas
Noah Barleywater Runs Away
The Terrible Thing That Happened to Barnaby Brocket
Stay Where You Are and then Leave
The Boy at the Top of the Mountain

SHORT STORIES
Beneath the Earth

The Congress of Rough Riders

JOHN BOYNE

BLACK SWAN

TRANSWORLD PUBLISHERS
61–63 Uxbridge Road, London W5 5SA
A Random House Group Company
www.rbooks.co.uk

THE CONGRESS OF ROUGH RIDERS
A BLACK SWAN BOOK: 9780552776141

First published in Great Britain
in 2001 by Weidenfeld & Nicolson
Black Swan edition published 2011

A CIP catalogue record for this book
is available from the British Library.

Addresses for Random House Group Ltd companies outside the UK
can be found at: www.randomhouse.co.uk
The Random House Group Ltd Reg. No. 954009

Penguin Random House is committed to a sustainable future
for our business, our readers and our planet. This book is
made from Forest Stewardship Council® certified paper.

Typeset in 11/14pt Giovanni Book by
Kestrel Data, Exeter, Devon.

Printed and bound in Great Britain by Clays Ltd, Elcograf S.p.A.

8 10 9 7

For Carol, Paul, Sinéad and Rory

Chapter One

On Lookout Mountain

My great-grandfather is buried on Lookout Mountain, his grave overlooking the Great Plains and the Rockies, far from the Cedar Mountain, Wyoming, resting place that he had requested before he died. This grave, chosen for him by family when he no longer had a say in it, is near Denver, Colorado, where I lived for a year, where I worked, where my son was born and where my wife was murdered.

Standing there, with the white-topped peaks in the distance forming part of the great spinal column that connects the forests of western Canada to the dry-aired flatlands of New Mexico, the senses are struck by the spicy scent of pine needles in the air while the quick breeze encourages brisk movement. The wildlife – the bison, the elk, the great bears – drift from hilltop to plateau, glancing warily at visitors. There is no restlessness here, just slow movement and ongoing life. This is a separate place and although it was not my great-grandfather's desired grave, I feel sure that he would have been able to approve of it.

My father, Isaac – who, like me, was named for his great-grandfather – never visited Lookout Mountain, never in fact set foot outside England during his lifetime, but he always spoke of it with authority, the same authority which he lent to his study of the life of the grave's occupant, who died in 1917, the year before Isaac's birth. My most recent visit to the grave was my third. My first came a few weeks after arriving in Denver in 1998 and then again about a year later. Isaac assumed that I would be here more often – he refused to believe that my wife and I would come to Denver for any other reason than to be closer to Lookout Mountain and it remains much more his place than mine. I could never equal his passion for our family history, his need to have an illustrious past, a celebrated ancestor. He was a storyteller with just one story to tell, but that story was the story of a lifetime. I was interested, I was certainly intrigued, but Lookout Mountain has never been my haven. In fact, it's represented something which has caused me only pain. My most recent visit came about because Isaac had died and there was something that I needed to do there.

I'm a child of the 1970s, born on the first day of the decade, when Isaac was fifty-two and a first-time father. He met and married my mother when he was fifty. From time to time he would tell me stories about his childhood, his youth, but he gave very little away, his own life and history being of little interest to him. In fact, I never really got to know where he had come from or what his own childhood was like. Instead, the stories he told were about his grandfather and he gave me his name, William, which I kept in its full form, unlike my ancestor who opted for the diminutive Bill. I was probably six or seven before I realised that my father was the same age as most of my schoolfriends' grandparents. It confused me a little, and scared them, but I didn't ask many questions. I barely knew my mother. She left home when I was four years old, divorcing my father and marrying a doctor before emigrating to Canada, where she still lives. We rarely speak.

It's hard to know whose story this is. It's partly mine and it's partly Bill's, but in the centre comes Isaac, telling me all he knew about his grandfather and making me who I am at the same time. Three generations of men, separated by long periods of time and place, in some ways none of us really related to the others at all. I spent my life running away from Isaac but now that he's dead, I find myself keeping his memory alive more and more through the stories.

Isaac's prized possession was mounted on the wall of our living room and I knew better than to take it down without permission. It was a Smith & Wesson handgun, manufactured in Kansas in 1842 and given to Bill by his own father as a reward for saving his life when he was a child of nine. An American, Bill's father had been taken as an Abolitionist by some Pro-Slavery men after he gave a speech near the Salt Creek trading post in Missouri where he refused to endorse the admittance of slavery into the new state of Kansas. Having been part of the original settlement of Iowa when it was brought into the union, Bill's father had been entrusted with leading the settlement of the region. As such, his was a voice which was given credence by the local population. When he spoke, his words carried almost the weight of government, a future government, and his policies and ideals could settle plans for the manner in which the new state would be run. He was invited to speak on that day by the men of Missouri who believed, wrongly, that he would endorse their plans for the ratification of slavery. When he did not, and when he spoke

9

vehemently against such a policy, he was stabbed by a local man and although the wound was not fatal, from that moment on his life was under threat.

'Is it loaded?' I asked Isaac, time and time again throughout my childhood, staring at the carved wooden handle and rust-tinged metal. 'Could it kill someone?'

'It might be,' he replied, always refusing to let me know one way or the other. 'The thing about that gun is that it's so old and it's seen so much gunpowder run through its chamber over the course of its life that it's likely to explode in the hands of anyone who takes it down and tries to mess with it without permission. Be warned now.' This was his way of ensuring that I did not touch the gun. 'I'm trusting you now, William,' he said, pointing towards it but staring at me fiercely, fierce enough to make me know that there would be few things he would ever say to me in his lifetime that would carry such a weight of responsibility. 'You're never to take that gun down, do you hear me? Never without asking me first.'

I nodded. I heard him all right. But I was a child at the time and I didn't necessarily listen.

Bill's story, as Isaac tells it, began in an Iowa log cabin in 1846. He was probably one of the first children to be born in the newly settled state but his childhood on those flat plains ended after only five years when the barren land was swapped for the Mississippi River as the growing family moved to LeClair. When I think of his days growing up along those banks – a Mark Twain childhood – it fills me with envy, so far removed is it from my own London upbringing. Only two generations separate us, but Bill's and my life are so different and I can no more understand his life in the nineteenth-century American mid-west then than he could have predicted mine now. And yet I do, I think of it often, I write of it now, for as separated as we are, he is part of my chain and my ancestry, part of my links to a time and place which no longer exist. The west. The settling of the Americas. The basics of Isaac's stories are all my father and I had to connect us and that's where they were set, almost every one.

Although he had enjoyed little formal schooling himself, Isaac was a keen educator when it came to his only child and tolerated no truancy on my part. Playing the role of both father and mother he got me ready for school in the mornings, prepared my lunch and dinners, and sat with me in the evenings to help me with my homework. To be allowed a sick day from school I practically had to be admitted to hospital. I was a solid student and did well; there was no alternative offered to me. When I went to bed at night, Isaac's day also ended for his life was empty without me and so, to fill those hours before sleep, he drank whisky.

It's easy to see why he wanted me to make something of my life and to excel at everything to which I put my mind. For he had led a carefree existence as a child, un-monitored by his father Sam, and left school when he was only fourteen, a reasonable age to begin the career at which he was to prove quite successful for a time. That of petty criminal.

Isaac was a small man, in stature if not in personality, and even in his late twenties he could have easily passed for a teenager. He used his lack of size to assist himself in his career as a burglar and a thief. He was good at it too, it has to be said, managing to make quite a living at his chosen profession until, inevitably, a series of misdemeanours saw him jailed for four years, a period which counted for almost half his thirties, after which he never again laid hands on anything which did not belong to him. Whatever took place when he was inside, he turned his back on his past when he was released and worked in a variety of jobs – labourer, taxi driver, builder – until he met my mother and settled down with a small painting and decorating business which paid little but sufficient to support comfortably enough the three of us, soon to be the two of us.

I think my father wanted a son who would do the things that he had never done. He gave me opportunities but watched over me at the same time and never allowed me to squander the chances which came my way. He felt he had done nothing of substance with his life, unlike his idolised grandfather, and wanted me to be more like the older man than like him.

Bill, on the other hand, received scant education and expected less. His brief studies were prematurely ended when he was nine years old after an incident which led to his sudden exile from Mississippi and near imprisonment. He was bullied at school by an older boy, Stephen Gobel, who was his rival for the affections of one Miss Mary Hyatt. A long-simmering feud erupted into a fight, during which Bill drew a small dagger from his pocket and stabbed Master Gobel in the thigh. The sudden appearance of so much blood, not to mention the squealing of the injured boy like a stuck pig, led Bill to flee the school and join a freight train headed for Fort Kearney, where he spent the summer herding cattle, a far cry from the regular summer activities of the nine-year-olds of my generation.

Like Bill, I too became a steady brawler during my

early years in school. Streamlined and cosseted at home, I sought my opportunities at school to prove myself and to assert my individuality. I made the early mistake of talking about Bill's life and adventures before realising how disbelieving my peers would be and paid for it for some time before I decided that the slightest slur against my alleged ancestry would call for severe action on my part. Unlike Isaac, I was not a small child and was capable of sizing up to anyone in the schoolyard with only a modicum of fear. I never betrayed it though and made sure to get my blows in first, proving my seriousness in a fight almost before it had even begun. Often my adversaries would be surprised by my attitude and back off; at other times they would prove equal to the challenge and beat me senseless. Either way, it infuriated Isaac.

'It doesn't matter who wins or loses,' he said when I came home one afternoon, a little bruised perhaps, a streak of dried blood slashed roughly across my cheek, but nonetheless the victor in my latest playground clash. 'You don't go to school to treat the place like a boxing ring.'

'But they were making fun of—'

'It doesn't matter what they were doing, William, that's not why I send you there,' he shouted. 'Look at you. Look at that cut over your eye.'

'But I won,' I protested, expecting him at least to be impressed by the fact that if I was going to involve myself in fighting then I could come out on top.

'Worse still,' he said however, causing me no end of confusion and self-pity. 'I'd rather see you lose. At least then I'd know how badly the fight ended and feel that you might have learned some lessons from it. What does the other boy look like anyway?'

I shrugged. I wasn't sure how to phrase it. 'He'll be all right,' I muttered, shuffling my feet on the ground and refusing to return his gaze as I recalled the sight of a split-lipped boy sniffling and limping his way back home, one eye beginning to seal in upon itself, throwing curses at me in defeat, threatening what he would do to me the next time that he caught up with me. 'He'll live.'

'You're a disgrace to yourself,' he told me. 'Picking on a bunch of kids.'

'But *I'm* a kid!'

'That's no excuse. When your great-grandfather was a boy, do you think he went around causing fights for no reason? Do you think that's how he went on to achieve so much?'

'Probably,' I said, refusing to be beaten in any argument, physical or verbal. 'He wasn't exactly famed for his pacifism, was he?'

Isaac squinted at me and held back. I could see him working this through in his mind, wondering where I had learned words like *pacifism* and attitudes like sarcasm at the same time. That was the start of it, he must have realised. The point where I was growing up and could slip away from him if he was not careful.

'Don't let me down now, William,' he said eventually in a quiet voice. 'There's a lot expected of you. A lot to live up to. I gave you your name for a reason.'

Sometimes, for no reason other than the fact that I could, I hated and resented my great-grandfather in equal parts.

The first winter that Bill spent in Kansas was a preparatory one. The Enabling Act was before Congress, awaiting ratification, and when it was finally passed it allowed settlers to stake claims on the land, to settle down and earn a living through the farms. The family had moved there some time in advance of the decision, anticipating the bill's approval, and were able to claim a portion of the land, where they built their home and started their working of the soil. They planted crops and reared livestock. Another child was born. Bill became familiar at an early age with the tribes who had lived there before the settlers arrived and learned to speak some of the Kickapoo language which dominated the area. He became fluent quite easily and this helped him become friends with the Indian children who lived nearby.

His friendship with the tribes who would ultimately be driven off their land by the American settlers led to his early initiation into the Mide religion, with which he was enamoured for a brief time during childhood. Traditionally, belonging to the Mide involved initiation through the learning of stories about the Kickapoo past, their slow drift westwards across the continent, and their belief in the value of herbal medicines to counter any illness and mark any significant event in a man's life. They were a peaceful people, given to ritual and tradition, and although they must have been wary of the arrival of the white men, they were at first treated well, and as neighbours, unlike many of the other tribes of the Northern American continent at that time, and the two cultures settled into a peaceful cohabitation.

Famously, the family arranged an enormous barbecue on their new land to cement a friendship with the Kickapoo people. The barbecue lasted for two days and several hundred Indians were fed the slaughtered animals which formed part of their farm. Bill's mother introduced them to coffee, which they had never tasted before; the gradual replacement of one culture with another had begun, masked as kindness, and was being replicated across the new United States.

For the first time Bill had begun a friendship with an Indian boy, whose name was not passed down to us, and some of the skills of the native culture were shared. They spent long afternoons shooting birds from the sky with bows and arrows, no doubt missing more than they ever managed to kill, but it was an education and a beginning into learning the ways of the Indian which would benefit Bill as his career developed.

My knowledge of other cultures, in comparison, was limited to those few students in my class who were black, or Pakistani, perhaps the odd European exchange student. Each was treated with varying degrees of suspicion and each, in general, kept with those who they knew best. Unlike my great-grandfather's early days in Kansas there were not many attempts made in my south London comprehensive to integrate our English culture with that of the immigrant or the foreigner. Fights would break out in the schoolyard based on the simple existence of difference between us, a difference we could not define but which in some strange way threatened us. As a boy, I tried not to involve myself in these confrontations, confused as I was by the differences between right and wrong. Isaac's ongoing stories of my great-grandfather's life and times, both within and without the native people of the west, had created a feeling of ambivalence within me towards other cultures. I knew that Bill had begun his life as a friend of the Indian, but I also knew that he had eventually taken up arms against them in order to fulfil the role which he had created for himself as an archetypal hero, and then he had finally exploited them in his later life by helping to create the kinds of myths which, when properly continued, transpose themselves into history and become the very things which are ultimately taught as fact.

Isaac, on the other hand, would never question either Bill's motives or his integrity, believing that his grandfather's subtly changing attitudes over the course of his seventy years reflected not an alteration in his own point of view for mercenary or personal reasons, but rather a change in the behaviour and attitudes of the Indian tribes themselves. Of course, this was based entirely on his belief in his grandfather, his utter and unswerving pride in that man's achievements and life, and the vicarious manner by which he sought to add splendour and mystique to his own at times unfulfilling existence. Having said that, the integrity of which I speak is one which was matched by my father's own life and value system. He may have tried to dominate both our lives with his overpowering sense of personal history and he may have ultimately paid a high personal price for that perseverance, but by God he believed in it and I'm not sure I've ever found anything to place my faith in quite so strongly as Isaac placed his faith in the continuing momentum of his ancestry.

To the Smith & Wesson gun and the manner in which Bill saved his father's life, some more of Isaac's stories can relate. A plot was hatched by the Pro-Slavery men to murder Bill's father for his voice was becoming too strong in the state to be ignored. He was forced into exile from his home but it was rumoured that he himself was plotting to create a constitution for Kansas which would outlaw, if not the existence of slavery, then at

17

least its promotion and expansion, a small step perhaps but part of a greater eventual plan.

Bill's mother learned that a group of men had discovered her husband's whereabouts and were riding out to murder him and she instantly despatched the child Bill on his pony to Grasshopper Falls, where his father was in hiding. A long ride ensued and, incredibly, in the middle of the night Bill came across these men as they rested and planned the attack they would make when they caught up with their prey.

'Hold there,' called the roughest of the three, an overweight and hirsute farmer whose horse no doubt bore a sorry weight. The man had seen the nine-year-old boy passing in their direction but had been unable to make him out in the distance. 'What's your business there, boy?'

Bill slowed down his pony and cautiously continued at a trot, forcing himself to pull the animal up calmly when he reached the men, immediately afraid that they would understand his purpose. 'Going home, sir,' said Bill quietly, pulling his peaked hat further down his youthful forehead, the long strands of straw-coloured hair flicking out beneath it in wisps.

'And where's your home then?' asked another man, the thinner one, the one whose complexion made it clear that he felt more at home in a saloon with a bottle of whisky in front of him than he did sitting around a campfire in the dead of night with a couple of hired killers by his side and a task of murder lying ahead before his breakfast.

'Not far now,' replied Bill. 'Another mile or two.'

'You know what's a mile or two from here?' he asked suspiciously, looking into the distance as if he could see that very length from his standing point. 'Nothing but what you see around you now, that's what. This is just plains land. It's six miles easy to the next town.' The next town being the very one where Bill's father was no doubt preparing for a night's sleep, even as his son rode towards him. 'You're not lost, are you?'

'No sir,' continued Bill. 'I'll get there. I know where I'm—'

The small fire which the men had built to warm their evening chose that moment to spit out a hunk of red hot wood with a noisy crack and Bill's pony, taken by surprise, reared up in surprise. 'Calm down,' he muttered in the nag's ear. 'Take it easy now, boy.' Something in his attitude must have caused the men to become suspicious, for one reached over now to take the lead of the pony, causing the animal to take a cautious step backwards.

'Why don't you get down from that horse now,' said the man, looking up at Bill and squinting in the darkness in order to get a better perspective on the boy's face.

'I think I ought to keep going till I—'

'Get off the horse,' he repeated sharply. 'You've got too far to go tonight on your own. You can't be headed home, that's for certain sure.'

'I know where I'm going,' repeated Bill, ready to pull on the reins and dig his spurs into the unfortunate beast's side if necessary, in order to continue them on their way. A full moon travelled slowly across the night sky and its progress lent a sudden brightness on to their night scene, causing the thin man to exclaim suddenly.

'Here, Meadows,' he said, pulling on the fat man's sleeves as he squinted in the direction of their new arrival, attempting to make out the features of the face

19

which still lay somewhat hidden beneath the cloth hat that his mother had forced him to wear before leaving. 'You know what I think? I think this is the son of that black Abolitionist we're chasing after. That's it, ain't it boy? That's who you are, say it is.'

'You're wrong,' said Bill firmly, his inexperience and youth betraying him for once. 'I'm not his son.'

'*Whose* son then?' asked the thin man, coming towards him now and reaching up to pull him down. 'Get down here anyway, boy, that we can take a good look at you.'

Sensible to danger, he had to make a quick decision. If he alighted from the horse he could be left stranded there, miles from either home or destination, while the killers rode on to complete their work. He could even find his own throat cut within a minute or two. He blinked, he looked from the face of one man to the other, and deciding that it was better to be foolhardy than trusting, he dug his ankles deep into the sides of the pony beneath him, pulling on the reins so hard that as the beast turned away from the men they were forced to jump back in fright. Meadows missed a step as he did so and fell back towards the fire, where he landed for a moment before scrambling back to his feet in fright, the confusion of the moment causing neither of them to notice as the boy rode off into the darkness.

'I'm on fire!' shouted Meadows, the white cotton material of his left sleeve suddenly darkening beneath a moving stream of flame. 'Put me out, I'm on fire!' he roared again, dancing on the spot before his companion pushed him to the dirt and rolled him over once quickly, smothering the flames immediately.

'He's escaping,' shouted the thin man. 'Get after him.' They ran to their horses and untied them, ignoring the neighing protests of their tired charges and within moments were racing along the plains, following my great-grandfather, who was to prove too fast for them with his lighter weight, arriving in Grasshopper Falls a full thirty minutes before the intended killers. Just as the sun broke through the sight-lines on the corner of the town and before it had finished its ascent and announced the day, my two ancestors had fled and survived their certain murder.

'That was when he got his reward,' Isaac told me. 'There were no phones or messengers in those days. From the minute your great-grandfather was sent away on his horse with the warning, his mother had no idea whether either her husband or son were still alive.'

'Did they go home?' I asked, a boy of Bill's age myself then, nestling against the pillows and my father as I drifted off to sleep. Around me the light threw shadows on the western memorabilia with which Isaac had decorated my room. The contradictions of both a confederate and a union flag, posters of cowboys riding across prairies, on my desk a model of Fort Laramie, where a treaty was once signed between the leaders of the Cheyenne and Comanche people and the government, moving the natives from the Great Plains and into Western Oklahoma in exchange for food, supplies and the possibility of a limited education.

'Eventually, Bill did,' he said. 'Got home and he was the hero of the hour. When the whole family were reunited, his father gave him that gun, which until then he'd been wearing on his own holster, as a reward.'

'I bet he let him use it too,' I muttered in protest at my father's insistence that I leave it alone. 'I bet he didn't just hang it on a wall for show.' Isaac ignored the barb.

'Those times were different,' was all he said. 'Stay there for a minute though.' He left the room and I glanced at the clock. Almost eleven p.m. I was falling asleep but didn't want to give in until he returned. This was the part of these stories that I enjoyed the most, the reason I always stayed awake to their end. This was the punch line, the reward which was mine for allowing Isaac to tell his history.

He returned in a few minutes and I saw his dark figure standing in the doorway, the light from the hall throwing his body into darkness for a moment before he came inside, a small, ageing man with a large gun by his side, a gun twice the size of his own hands, a gun that you could see even he had difficulty holding, let alone a nine-year-old child like his grandfather had been at the time. As he leaned over me, I caught a sudden wave of whisky breath and marvelled at how he could manage a swift drink in so short a time between leaving my room, collecting the gun and returning to me.

'There you go,' he said, sitting down on the bed beside me and massaging the gun fondly, the prized possession that it was, second only in his life to me. For while I was never allowed to touch the gun on my own, or take it down from the wall, he was permitted to finish his stories with some style, displaying for me at their conclusions the rewards which were given to boys who put their own lives at risk to save their fathers. 'Take a look at the side,' he said, flicking on the bedside lamp beside me and I blinked with the sudden brightness before peering down at the tight inscription which I had read there a hundred times before. My father's own name: Isaac Cody.

'My great-grandfather's name, given to me,' he

said, he always said. 'Just like you're named for yours, William.'

I thought about it. For once I had a question to ask. 'But why am I William?' I asked, looking up at him now, my brow furrowed in that little-boy look of confusion. 'Why can't I be Bill too?'

He laughed. 'Now that would be a blasphemy, my boy,' he said, shaking his head as if the very idea was impossible. 'It's one thing to name you in the man's honour. Another thing entirely to be using that same name on a daily basis. Bill Cody?' he asked, thinking about it for a moment before dismissing the whole idea as impossible. 'There'll only ever be one Bill Cody and he's dead and buried now. That's a name you'd have to earn. For now you can stay a William.'

'But Buffalo William doesn't sound as good,' I protested weakly.

'Your great-grandfather's name is his own name,' he said firmly, switching off the lamp and walking slowly towards the door. 'And he spent a lifetime building it. You let him have it and you make your own name. That's what life is all about.' He paused for a moment and stared at me as I pulled the blankets up to my shoulders and rolled over on to my side, exhausted now, ready to close my eyes. 'Tomorrow night I'll tell you another story,' he said, closing the door behind him and leaving me to darkness and sleep. And I knew this was true, because in Isaac's world there was always another story to tell.

Chapter Two

A Society of Men

Bill was only thirteen years old when he first joined a freight trail. Already though, he was hardly a child, having killed his first man – an Indian – earlier that summer, a murder which had lent the boy a certain amount of notoriety which he was known to have both enjoyed and encouraged. It's hardly surprising that he became the showman that he did in later years, considering his earlier inclinations towards publicity and attention. Even faced with a murdered man bleeding at his feet he could see only newspaper headlines and dollar signs.

A freight trail consisted of twenty-five wagons, each of which steered about seven thousand pounds of oxen across the frontiers. Bill was the lowest of the low on these trails, a hired hand, a teamster, but he wore his official title – that of 'bullwhacker' – with pride. There was no private time and precious little sleep but the bullwhackers cared little for such indolent pleasures, content instead to value the freedom of the open plains and the constant potential for danger. They were a youthful bunch and it was not unusual to have a hard-working and eager child among their number.

Bill's first experience of the problems which the

freight trails could encounter, however, took place in the summer of 1859, when he joined the crew of a wagon trail destined for the plains near Salt Lake City, where the armies of General Albert Johnston were preparing for an offensive against the Mormons. The practice of polygamy was one which the government of the new United States was firmly opposed to and as the nation spread further west, expanding the reaches of its executive branch into new territories, it became vital that her people followed one law of a unified land. The Mormons had already been driven from both Missouri and Illinois but had finally established a home and settlement in Salt Lake City. Despite the aggressive tendencies of the government, this time they were not going to give up their homes or way of life without a fight.

Bill was stationed at Fort Leavenworth and had made, two friends in Albert Rogers and David Yountam, boys slightly older than he was but who envied him the brief celebrity which he had enjoyed after killing the Indian. Their duties at the fort were varied and ill-defined; for themselves, they were simply happy to be part of a society of men who could be called upon at any time to undertake an exercise of danger. They had been at the fort longer than Bill and upon his arrival had been torn between their liking for him and their natural inclination to bully a younger boy; almost despite themselves a friendship had formed. Rogers was a Missourian who had not seen his home since the age of seven; now, at fourteen, he was preparing to sign up as a bullwhacker once the next trail was announced. Yountam was a year older again but had lost his left arm when he was thirteen after an unsuccessful argument with a buffalo which had seen the limb ripped off at the elbow. To prevent a potentially fatal spread of disease around his body, the local doctor had simply carved off the ravaged appendage at the shoulder, eventually sealing the hole with fire, an action which had left a misshapen memory at the boy's side, devoid of nerve endings, insouciant to pain. It was Yountam who first broached the idea of their joining the trail towards the camp of General Johnston.

'When does it start?' asked Bill as they lay in their bunks in a small, white-sheeted tent just inside the limits of the fort, where non-commissioned lads such as they made their home while waiting for chance or opportunity to come their way.

'Not soon enough for me,' replied Yountam, scrambling up in bed to look at his two friends; any glimmer of escape from the monotonous, dreary lifestyle of Leavenworth was enough to fill him with excitement, so bored was he with his daily tasks of shining officers' boots and cleaning up after the horses. 'They say that General Johnston is planning an attack on the Mormons late this summer but that supplies have to be brought in so that when they are routed, the army will be able to settle the land. Otherwise the Mormons will just wait for them to leave and go back again.'

'I don't know why they're bothering,' muttered Albert Rogers, a louche lad who questioned all authority just as much as he desired to be a part of it. He had a reputation for insubordination but could think of no life outside the army which would suit him as well. 'What harm have these Mormons done anyway that's so wrong, can you tell me that?' He didn't look at the two boys as he asked his question, merely lay back in his cot, one arm slung across his eyes, blocking out the light from the candle which Bill had lit earlier.

'They're Mormons!' replied Yountam immediately. 'Ain't that enough?'

'Enough for what? Just 'cause you give them a name, that's enough to say they should be driven away from wherever they choose to live? That's a reason, is it?'

Bill sat back and looked from one boy to the other cautiously. Ethical debates were frequent between these two, who had known each other for three years before Bill's own arrival into their lives. He was often torn between feelings of frustration with them – for they argued constantly and over the most ridiculous things – and a sense of hero worship which he found difficult to contain. They had assumed the roles of older brothers to the thirteen-year-old boy and as none of them had any family nearby, their relationships were close. Bill was still new to this centre of military activity; he was a child capable of losing himself in his desire to be part of this dream world. And yet for him, the friendship between Rogers and Yountam seemed not one based on actual affection, but rather on their familiarity. Yountam searched continually for adventure, never questioned anything he was told to do, and wanted nothing more than to be given a direction in which to travel and a hot meal when he got there. Rogers, for all his commitment to remaining part of the daily life of Leavenworth, appeared to see it as little more than a place to eat and sleep. His belief system questioned everything and on more than one occasion, Bill feared that the conversations between his two friends would end in a fight, even bloodshed.

'Mormons go against our way of life,' proposed Yountam, a comment which made Rogers merely snort.

'Way of life,' he muttered disparagingly, spitting out the words like rotten food. 'What's that then, Davy?

Sleeping on a cot in the middle of a field with a quarter loaf of bread inside us, that's a way of life is it? One to be defended and preserved at all costs? God save us if it is.'

'You know what they do,' insisted Yountam. 'All them wives they have. Ain't natural for a man to have so many.'

'I don't know,' said Rogers after a pause, sitting up now and looking at his two companions with a dry smile on his face. 'I wouldn't object to a bunch of women running around after me, ready to satisfy my every need and desire. How about you, Billy? Would you say no to a little bit of pampering?' He looked across at his friend and gave him a large, conspiratorial wink. Bill, thinking of his own growing interest in some of the officers' daughters who passed him by every day without so much as a smile or a nod, sat back nervously and looked away, pleased that the candlelight spared him revealing his blushes. 'Of course, maybe that's not what you're after though, Davy,' he added sarcastically, spoiling for a fight. 'Maybe that's not the kind of thing you go for at all.'

'Don't matter what you think, Albert,' continued Yountam, unwilling to allow his friend's cynicism to alter his plans and ignoring the digs that were coming his way. 'I don't hear them generals coming over here to ask your advice on who we should and shouldn't be fighting. That's what they say is going to happen and that's what we ought to be a part of. You don't want to stay in this tent rotting away for the rest of the year, do you?'

'No!' cried Bill loudly, wrapped up in his friend's enthusiasm, his exclamation coming out so loud and suddenly and with an unexpected falsetto crack in his voice that the other two could not help but laugh.

'There you are then,' said Rogers, lying back again, his hand reaching down with neither self-consciousness nor embarrassment to stroke himself beneath the ragged sheet which lay above him, unwashed for three years now. 'You've got a convert there, Davy. Another one on the trail against those diabolical Mormons, may they burn in hell. What a friend he has in Jesus. So when do you start off on the crusades?' he added sarcastically.

'We have to get permission to be part of it,' said Yountam. 'It's not going to be easy to get in. One of us is going to have to petition Lew Simpson. He's got to approve it.' Simpson had been appointed the commander of the trail and was one of the oldest hands at cross-country bullwhacking, not to mention a fearless, celebrated character in his own right. We have to make our case to him and make it convincing too. They're not looking for many boys of our age and there's a fair number wanting to be a part of it.' He looked across at Bill, who stared back at him blankly. 'What do you say, Billy Boy?' he asked. 'Are you up for it?'

'Me?' cried Bill in alarm. 'Why do I have to ask him? Why can't you? It's your idea.' Secretly, he was afraid of Simpson, a figure of true authority in the fort who inspired fear in all those boys who had yet to encounter real adventure. His legend made him the stuff of both envy and nightmares, while his enormous girth intimidated all.

'Take a look at me,' said Yountam quietly. 'A one-armed boy isn't going to be the best advertisement for our cause, now is he? And if he takes against me, then he's likely to take against both of you as well.'

What makes you think I want to go anyway?' asked Albert Rogers, pausing in his activities for a moment to look across the tent.

'Well you do, don't you?' replied Yountam. 'You don't want to be left behind here on your own, am I right?' Rogers snorted and said nothing. Of course he wanted to go; it was simply his sense of calculated deliberation which refused to allow him to show any enthusiasm.

'You can do whatever the hell you like,' was all he said in a casual voice; neither Bill nor Yountam took his derision seriously. They knew he would never agree to being left behind.

'Here's the thing, Bill,' continued Yountam, looking again at the youngest member of their trio. 'You've got that Indian story to tell, right?'

'I suppose,' said Bill nervously. 'Ain't that good a story though,' he added, playing it down in order to get out of this task, something he had never done before.

'You just go to Simpson, tell him about it, make it sound real good, convince him that you're about the most fearless fellow at Fort Leavenworth and that the trail would be crazy to leave without you and when he agrees you tell him that you've got two friends who are every bit as brave and strong as you are and we come as a team and before you know it we'll all be on our way to the general's camp. What do you say, Bill? Will you do it?'

My great-grandfather closed his eyes for a moment and thought about it. It was true that he was beginning to grow restless at Leavenworth. He looked at the cramped tent in which they sat, could feel the grumblings in his stomach from the lack of rations they were given, and knew that the time had come to move on. He didn't really have any choice in the matter.

'All right then,' he said, resisting a sigh and forcing himself to sound decisive. 'I'll do it.'

Yountam sat back and smiled, satisfied with his persuasive abilities. In the corner, Rogers merely snorted and – spent from his activities – turned over and drifted off to sleep.

Isaac wanted to know whether I told people about my great-grandfather and the life that he had led. I wasn't sure what to say; after all, I didn't particularly want to hurt his feelings but the time never seemed right for me to tell my friends the stories that he told me.

'Well no,' I admitted. 'Not often anyway. It doesn't really come up.'

'It doesn't?' he asked in amazement, looking at me as if it was vaguely crossing his mind to question whether I was actually his son or not. 'Well why ever not, William? When I was your age I told all my friends. They thought it was the greatest thing ever. A man like that in the family? Doesn't seem right just to—'

I shook my head, interrupting him. I'm sorry,' I said quickly. 'I just . . . I can never seem to find the right way to tell people about it. About him, I mean.' This was a lie. I'd been hearing stories about my namesake and supposed ancestor Buffalo Bill Cody for as long as I could remember and as a very young child I felt exactly like Isaac's friends had felt half a century earlier. I thought it was exciting and unusual and I felt proud that I knew tales of my heritage that other boys of my age could never equal. The adventures which my great-grandfather had undertaken, and at an age not so much older than I was then, fascinated me and made me wish that I could travel the world too, making a name for myself to rival his. And so I had in fact told several people about Bill, but these stories, this revelation, had not received the kind of impressed reaction which Isaac would have expected. Which he would have demanded.

I was seven years old when a group of friends began to form around me, the ones who would stay with me throughout my youth and early adulthood. We became close soon after we met, and before long we were inseparable, our friendship stemming from the simple fact that we sat together in the back row of our classroom. Of the three of us – Adam, Justin and I – Adam, the oldest, was the closest thing we had to a leader, someone we all looked up to and who determined one way or another how we spent our days. Justin was quieter and often seemed happy simply to have us as his friends; he was very open hearted and we knew we could rely on him for anything, while I was perhaps more lively and troublesome than either. We all, however, managed to find ourselves in the requisite number of scrapes and mischief that young boys should.

Their family lives were very different to mine. They each had a mother and father and between them a fair number of siblings, while my house consisted solely of Isaac and me. Also, the fact that Isaac was a good deal older than any of their parents made my domestic arrangements curious to them and as children they were, I think, slightly afraid to come to my house. With good reason, as things turned out.

Isaac was never the easiest man to cultivate as a friend. He rarely showed affection and his abrupt manner could be downright terrifying to strangers. Ever since my mother had left, he had grown to live his life increasingly and vicariously through me. He knew my homework and my schooldays better than I knew them myself. He made me account for every moment of my day and grew offended if he felt that I was keeping secrets from him. And, like any child who for the first time manages to cultivate a group of friends his own age, there were many secrets to keep, many small confidences which I had no desire to share with him. There were things that we did together – childish things, mischievous things – which Isaac had no place in, where he could have held no interest, but which nonetheless he felt excluded from and blamed me for.

He manifested the pain of such exclusion through long silences with me and general rudeness to my friends. When they came to our house, which was not often, he would stare at them suspiciously and hover outside whatever room we were in, always finding some excuse eventually to enter it, driving us to another place, a different part of the house, or one of theirs. He would lean over them and they would flinch if it was evening time as the rush of whisky breath could be quite over-powering.

The only thing which my friends liked about my house was the Smith & Wesson gun on the living-room wall. They stared at it with rapt attention whenever they were visiting, but Isaac saw to it that they were almost never left alone in the room with the gun, for as little as he trusted me with his prized possession, he trusted them less. Unlike his attitude to me, however, Isaac refused to tell them his stories, feeling that they were his to hand down to me and mine to deliver to the world, and yet he grew angry at my refusal to do so. He saw it as my betrayal of my heritage and of him.

It was in school that I finally decided to risk telling my classmates what Isaac had been telling me for years, I was about eight at the time and our teacher was asking each student in turn to tell a story about their grandparents. Most of the stories were normal enough, each depicting some pleasant, uncontroversial old person whose life seemed dominated by rocking chairs and allotments, rather than bullwhacking and settling huge areas of North America. When it came to my turn to speak, I decided to take a chance.

'William,' said my teacher, Miss Grace. 'Your turn. Would you like to tell us about your grandparents?'

'They're dead, miss,' I said with a shrug.

'What, all of them?' she asked irritably, as if they had died simply to provoke her.

'All of them,' I agreed. A few of my classmates turned to stare at me, squinting their eyes in despair. It was as if they thought I was just being deliberately awkward.

'Well are there any stories you know about them anyway?' continued Miss Grace. 'Anything at all you'd like to tell us?'

I thought about it. 'I know some stories about my great-grandfather,' I said. 'I could tell you one of those if you like.'

'Wonderful,' said Miss Grace, clapping her hands together in delight. No one had gone back an extra generation yet and she seemed to feel that this was an unexpected treat. She explained to the class just what a 'great-grandfather' was, pointing out that it was not just an extra special one, and the room stayed relatively quiet as they waited to hear what I had to say about him.

'Well,' I began nervously, licking my lips as I wondered about the reception this would get. 'It goes back quite a bit because my father's pretty old anyway. My great-grandfather was born in 1846,' I said, unsure whether I should go for the potted biography or move straight into some tale of daring that Isaac had ingrained on me.

'1846!' exclaimed Miss Grace in excitement. 'Imagine that!'

'And he wasn't born in England either. He was an American.'

'Oh,' she exclaimed in disappointment, as if a particularly bad taste had just come into her mouth. She stared at me as if I had just uttered a profanity and was encouraging others to do likewise. 'An American,' she repeated. 'Are you sure of that, William?'

'Very sure,' I said. 'Isaac told me.'

'Your father told you,' she corrected me, for she disliked the fact that unlike the other children in the class I almost always referred to my father by his given name. Indeed, I was also under the impression that she disapproved of the fact that ours was a one-parent family and, given the slightest provocation, would have reported Isaac to social services for no other reason than the fact that his wife had run off with another man.

'Yes,' I said. 'My father and his father were born in England, but my great-grandfather was an American.'

'All right then,' she conceded with a sigh, agreeing to allow him to be of foreign birth if I insisted it was so. 'An American. Do you know where in America he was from?' Her question struck me as one which was determined to expose my lie so I took some pleasure in taking it in my stride.

'Iowa,' I said and her smile froze. The fact that I, an eight-year-old, knew of a place called Iowa suggested that I might in fact be telling the truth. She just nodded and, opening the palms of her hands towards me, urged me to continue, suggesting that now there would be no more interruptions on her part.

'He was a cowboy,' I said after a suitable pause and the entire room exploded in mirth; even my friends, with the exception of Adam, were laughing. A few people made the sounds of guns being shot and lassoes being waved in the air. Others still pushed their hands forward and away from their mouths quickly as they yodelled, giving a fair imitation of a Hollywood-style Indian. Adam merely looked at me and raised an eyebrow, probably assuming that I was setting the teacher up with some elaborate lie.

Miss Grace quietened the room and looked at me with irritation. 'What do you mean, he was a cowboy, William?' she asked. 'What sort of a cowboy?'

'Well he started out as a bullwhacker, and then he—'

'A *what*?'

'A bullwhacker, miss. He rode in wagon trails across the country, bringing supplies to armies and helping to settle states.' She looked at me open mouthed, amazed that I was saying this in such a matter-of-fact way, as if people like this existed all over the world and were far from unusual. I continued. 'Then he spent some time as part of the Gold Rush before joining the Pony Express.'

'The Pony Express!' she said incredulously.

'Yes. After that . . . I think that was when he joined the railroads, hunting buffalo to feed the crews. That was where he got his nickname.'

'What nickname?' asked Miss Grace and I could see her face grow ever more exasperated as the scale of my story grew. I paused before answering but eventually sat up straight, looked her in the eye, and said the two words which Isaac had said to me on countless occasions.

36

'Buffalo Bill, miss.'

At that the room collapsed in laughter, children literally banging their tables in mirth, and I looked around in dismay and confusion before – almost as suddenly as they had begun – they stopped and rather than laughing, they were staring at me wide eyed and nervous. I was in a daze and wondered why my ear was ringing and my eyes felt stung. Miss Grace had marched down to my seat and slapped me hard across the face, hard enough that I had almost fallen off my seat, and had it not been directed so that I fell towards the shoulder of Adam, as opposed to the empty space on my left, I would have doubtless landed on the floor. I looked up at Miss Grace in confusion and she was wringing her hands now in anger, her thin, bony fingers growing white as she pressed them tightly against each other, as if she had hurt herself as much as she had hurt me. I felt a slight dampness about my ear and reached to touch it – it was momentarily numb – and when I looked at my hand there was a thin line of blood, for a ring on Miss Grace's finger had nicked my ear and cut it slightly at the tip.

'That's enough, William Cody,' she said to me, a little taken aback herself by the injury she had inflicted. Her voice was full of fear now at her actions; there was a tremor there we had all heard on too many occasions. 'I won't have you making a mockery of me in my own classroom, do you hear me?'

'But I wasn't,' I protested, sufficiently recovered from my shock now to be able to feel the first sting of tears behind my eyes and the words break slightly in my throat. 'It's true. My great-grandfather was—'

'Just because you have the same name as some old mythical cowboy does not mean—'

'But he wasn't mythical!' I pointed out over her shouting. 'He was a real man.'

'That's as may be. But he was *not* your great-grandfather,' she insisted. I was confused. In my short life, he had *always* been my great-grandfather. He had always been the person who connected Isaac and me to our shared past, not to mention the only thing which seemed to connect us to each other. I had never known anyone protest so vehemently against his existence and couldn't understand why she would do so. Did she know something that I didn't? 'He had nothing to do with you,' she continued. 'Nothing at all.'

'But why couldn't he be?' I asked her. 'Why do you say that?'

'Because it's ridiculous,' she said. 'For one thing, he died hundreds of years ago.'

'He died in 1917,' I informed the ill-educated old harpy and for a moment I thought she was going to return to my desk and let rip on the other ear.

'You're to stop this, William Cody,' she said in a firm voice, pointing at me with little stabbing motions. 'You're to stop this right now. We're having a perfectly pleasant discussion here and you must ruin it with a bunch of silly lies. I won't hear another word from you for the rest of the afternoon, do you hear?'

'But I—'

'Enough!' she shouted. I could tell that she was a little shaken by her sudden and inexplicable burst of rage but I had seen her inflict damage on children before in the classroom and it almost always came out of the blue and was immediately followed by nervous dismay on her part. She wanted no more of me now, wanted my ear to stop bleeding and for me to change my name and maybe emigrate and only then could she move on.

I sat back in my desk and said no more, unsure why the telling of these stories should cause such anger on her part. I barely listened as another student nervously began a simple story about his jumper-knitting, hospital-visiting, cake-baking old grandmother and lost myself in thought and eventually anger – not against my teacher, but directed towards Isaac, on whose shoulders I firmly laid the blame. It was his fault I was in trouble, I reasoned. Him and his stupid stories.

An hour later, as we poured out of the room to begin our lunch break, I felt a finger pointed into the narrow gap between my shoulder blades and turned my head around slightly to see Justin standing behind me. He leaned forward to my good ear and whispered, with a slight giggle, his hot breath causing me to shiver a little inside: 'Stick 'em up.'

Lew Simpson was one of the earliest frontiersmen and it was said that he was the first person to coin the phrase 'bullwhacking'. At the time of the trail towards General Johnston's camp, he had been at Fort Leavenworth for several months, recovering from an attack which had taken place in the Rockies earlier in the year when a wagon trail he was commanding was set upon by a group of Indians. While unsuccessful in their attempts to destroy their trail, the attackers had caused some serious injuries among some of the forty-niners who were part of it. Simpson had been close to death when he was brought to Leavenworth but, to the surprise of all, he had recovered and had almost returned to his previous fearsome best, although not only had the experience cost him some of his remarkable girth, but his beard had also visibly whitened during his convalescence. He held court in the saloon of the fort most days as he waited for fresh orders – which could often be weeks in arriving – and it was indeed true, as David Yountam had announced, that he had been instructed to lead a trail to General Johnston's armies in order to bring them fresh supplies. The trail was to consist of ten wagons and the pay was high – $40 per month per man – for it was known that this was not going to be a simple expedition and that there were many dangers which could lie along the way. These could come not only from anticipatory Mormons, but also from the Indians of the plains who had seen enough to know that the appearance of more wagons could mean the arrival of yet more settlers and the inevitable wars which would see them driven off their land.

Bill couldn't sleep on the night before he was due to approach Simpson to request a place in his trail. Although his life had not been entirely free of excitement or adventure, he believed there was a difference between the fear of combat and death and the terror which he felt, inside when he thought about approaching a man so fearsome and famous as Lew Simpson. Although he believed Yountam was right when he said that Bill was the best of the three boys to speak on their behalf, it was a commission he dreaded, and rightly so, for Simpson was known to give short shrift to children and mere adventurers.

Nevertheless, he had committed himself to the task and the following afternoon, spurred on by a plain-speaking speech of encouragement from Yountam, and a less enthusiastic but still clearly desirous one from Rogers, he approached the saloon and, pausing only for a deep breath on the outside, pushed open the door and stepped inside.

It was a small, dusty room, no more than one hundred

square feet in total, with a short bar stretch.
its left-hand wall and a filthy mirror behind
were about twenty men gathered inside, all wi
shot-glasses of murky whisky in front of them.
talking, some smoking, some playing cards. I
anyone glanced at the boy as he walked through
gaps between the tables, looking from face to face
find his prey. He discovered him holding forth at
table at the rear end of the room, an ancient, grizzled
warrior with long white hair and a beard of such snow-
white hue that it contrasted visibly with the bulbous
scarlet of the bullwhacker's nose. Above the sprouting
hairs of the beard, a series of red lines tracked their own
trail towards the man's eyes, the broken veins which
testified to a lifetime of drinking and adventuring
settling across his face. His voice carried deeply around
the table and the three younger men who sat with him
listened in admiration as he recounted the story of some
long-vanished glory. Bill stood by his side nervously,
his hands shaking so much that he was forced to put
them in his pockets and wait until he was noticed by
Simpson's three-man audience before daring to give a
slight cough, causing the monologue to end and the
huge head of his potential employer to spin around and
stare at him in surprise.

'What is it, boy?' he asked after taking a moment to
look the lad up and down suspiciously. 'What do you
want? Come to buy me a drink, have you? Well I'll
drink your health with it if you have.'

The three men roared with laughter and Bill stared
at them before giving a brief smile and wondering why
he had not prepared his speech before coming into the
saloon in the first place. In his mind he could picture
Yountam and Rogers sitting outside on a cross-fence,

41

vaiting to hear the result of this conversation, pleased that it was he and not they who had to endure it.

'It's about the trail,' he said eventually in a quiet voice which, to his relief, nevertheless held steady and firm. 'I wanted to ask about the trail.'

'What's that?' asked Simpson quickly, his eyes squinting for a better look. 'Speak up, boy. Got a mouth on you, ain't you? What trail are you talking about then?'

'The trail to supply General Johnston, sir,' said Bill. 'I heard such a trail was due to begin soon. To take over Salt Lake City. The . . . the Mormons, sir.'

'Ha!' roared Simpson, his hand belting down on the table ferociously, causing Bill to jump in sudden shock, although he maintained his position, his toes curling within his shoes as he planted his feet so firmly into the wooden floor beneath him that he feared he might push through at any moment and fall on to the ground below the boards. Where have you heard of this trail then, boy? Been listening at doors, have you?'

'No sir,' said Bill quickly. 'Not at all. It's all around the fort, that's all. I heard some others speak of it.' He had no idea whether it was indeed all around the camp or not but it seemed to appease the older man who looked satisfied that people were speaking of him and this potential exploit already.

'Well what of it?' he asked eventually. 'What do you need to know of it?'

'I wondered whether I could join it, sir,' said Bill. 'That is, there's three of us, me and David Yountam and Albert Rogers. We've been working here for months now and wanted to hope that maybe we could be of some use to you in this trail.'

Simpson stared at the boy and his face broke into a slow smile. He must have been in a good mood that day for at another time he might have swatted the boy about the ear and thrown him head first through the saloon doors and out into the dusty path beyond. 'And what use would a lad like you be to me?' he asked. 'How old are you anyway? Eleven? Twelve?'

'Thirteen sir,' said Bill, immediately regretting that he had not exaggerated his age although his still slight frame and height might have given any such lie away. 'And Yountam and Rogers are fourteen and fifteen apiece.'

'I know that Yountam boy,' said one of the men at the table then, a thin-lipped man in his early thirties, already bald of head but compensating for this with a bushy black beard and moustache that had long since seen a scissors. 'Ain't he the one-armed boy who got into the argument with the buffalo? About which one of their mothers was the ugliest, I reckon.'

Bill opened his mouth and thought about it. A lie would be pointless; the truth would out sooner or later. He nodded. 'That's him,' he said quietly and then, in a braver voice, 'and while the buffalo might have won the fight, Yountam won the argument. The buffalo's mother was the ugliest you ever saw.' Simpson let out an enormous laugh and my great-grandfather took this as an encouragement to continue. 'The thing about Yountam,' he said, 'is that he's indispensable because a braver, more fearless lad never—'

'Ha, you're mad, boy!' roared Simpson. 'What need have I of a one-armed lad in a trail like this?' Bill stared at him crestfallen and the man spoke again, more kindly this time. 'I've no doubt he's a brave lad,' he admitted. 'There's many a one would run from a fight like that and many a one who pays a price for standing his ground, but this is a dangerous ambition ahead of us. I need men who can take care of themselves and not have to rely on others. What about you though? What have you done of any note?'

'I killed an Indian,' said Bill in a quiet voice, answering the question but feeling his mind dominated by a further question, the one of loyalty, the one concerning whether he should pursue his ambitions towards this trail on his own or return outside to his unwanted friend.

'An Indian, is it?' laughed Simpson, settling back into his chair and folding his arms across his chest, delighted that there might be a tale to be told here at last. 'Well go on then, lad. We'll 'ave that one. How did it come about then?'

Bill sighed and told the story. How, on a journey past the South Platte River, resting overnight, he had looked up in his sleep towards the moon drifting slowly past overhead and had been surprised to make out the unmistakable figure of an errant Indian crouching stealthily through their camp. With neither fear nor a second thought he had grabbed hold of the Smith & Wesson gun which his father had given him and for the first time aimed the pistol at another human being and pulled the trigger as much in excitement as in terror. His first shot, a lucky one, had hit the man directly in the forehead, killing him instantly and although he perhaps had posed no threat to my great-grandfather's party, the incident became the basis of an early episode of heroism for which the boy was duly celebrated. In telling the story to Simpson now, he grew more and more animated, exaggerating details, all memories of Yountam and Rogers out of his mind, until he reached the climax, the shooting of the gun, the fall of the brave, by which point the entire room was listening and holding their breaths. And there the story ended in a respectful silence.

'And you killed him?' asked Simpson eventually, his gravelly voice cutting through the atmosphere which Bill had created through his showmanship. He had a gift for holding an audience.

'Stone dead.'

'And your fellows were saved? Every one?'

He blinked and hesitated for a moment; after all, he could never have been sure whether they were in actual danger or not. 'Every last one,' he asserted.

Simpson nodded and turned away from the boy and looked at the table, running his fingers along the top of it carefully, his eyes flitting back and forth as he thought about it. 'All right then,' he said eventually. 'All right. Maybe I can take a chance on you after all. You're young but you're brave enough, by God. A man who can see to it that his partners don't get scalped in their sleep is still a man, it seems to me, even if he is only half the size and ain't shaved the beard from his cheeks yet. You want in, you're in. What's your name anyway?'

'Cody, sir,' replied my great-grandfather. 'Bill Cody.'

'Knew a Cody once in New York, tried for state assembly. Liked to keep company with donkeys and horses, if you know what I mean. You're nothing to him are you?' Bill shook his head quickly and Simpson nodded and gave him the job. 'Well good luck to you then, Bill Cody. Welcome aboard.' Some of the room cheered but Bill knew not which way to go. He considered his options, remembered who had persuaded him to enter this room in the first place and almost against his better judgement shook his head.

'My partners,' he said. 'Yountam and Rogers. They're

braver than I, sir. We stick together, you see. And they're—'

'No one-armed—' shouted Simpson again but this time Bill had the fortitude to interrupt him.

'Surely his bravery in standing down the buffalo and surviving to tell the tale is equal to my killing an Indian in the dark,' he said. 'Please, sir, take them too. You won't regret it. They work hard around here.' He paused before adding: 'And none of us takes up too much space either 'cos we're all short, every one of us. And skinny on it too.' Simpson roared with laughter and shook his head before reaching out and punching Bill in the ear, a gesture intended as a friendly note of acceptance but one which sent the boy reeling and one which made his ear sting for a day afterwards nonetheless.

'All right then,' he cried eventually. 'Get on out of here anyway and gather your band of roughnecks together. Bullwhackers all, if that's the only way you'll have it. This trail starts in the morning. Early!'

Bill's face lit up and he held himself back from reaching up to stroke the already swelling ear. He made to move away, wanting to run outside to tell his friends the news, when Simpson called him back suddenly.

'Come here,' he said and the room went silent. Bill stepped closer, and closer again, until Simpson stopped urging him on. 'Take your hands out of your pockets.' He looked down to where he had put them before the interview began, so nervous had he been about their shaking. 'Show me your hands,' he said quietly.

'My hands . . . ?' he replied, surprised by the request. 'What do you—'

'Show them to me!' shouted Simpson and Bill lifted them quickly out of his pockets before holding them, flat, at eye level. He looked at them himself now, ready to observe how they shook in terror and bit his lip in embarrassment, wishing he could control his childish nervousness. And then his eyes opened wider at what he saw. To his surprise, his hands held steady and they weren't shaking even slightly. He looked up from them in surprise and his gaze met that of Lew Simpson who nodded appreciatively.

'Steady as a rock,' he said in a cheerful voice, winking at his new charge with a smile. 'You'll do.'

It was only the first of two punches to happen that week, but I wasn't on the receiving end of the second one. My claims to having been descended from Buffalo Bill Cody, while given no credence whatsoever by my teacher Miss Grace, were virtually ignored by my classmates who, having never even heard of my great-grandfather, were in no position to call me a liar. Still, for the time being I drew a veil over the story and said no more about it. Miss Grace pretended that her outburst had never taken place and naturally I did not mention it to her again. When Isaac saw my swollen ear he assumed that I had been in a schoolyard fight and thought little more of it, stopping only to ask whether I had won or lost.

'Lost,' I said, knowing that this would hurt his pride a little, something I felt keen to do right then. For the first time in my life I began to wonder whether his stories were actually true or simply a figment of his imagination. I had never had cause to question them before but Miss Grace's actions had made me unsure. Either way, I had felt humiliated in the classroom and blamed Isaac for this. When he came to my room over subsequent nights to tell me his ritual stories I feigned over-tiredness for a while, but he ignored that and continued to talk of scouts and prairies and wagon trails being captured and burned by bands of Indians until I had no longer any choice but to listen, which was when I began to do so in sullen silence, a long way from the enthusiastic adventure stories I had once enjoyed. Isaac told them well, but he was starting to lose his audience.

My two friends made no further mention of the incident either. We had all been involved in scrapes of one sort or another with the diabolical Miss Grace and it would have been strange if I had not found myself the victim of her insane fury at one time or another. It was Justin, however, the quietest and most insecure of my friends, who would be the next victim of a random act of violence, only on this occasion it would come a little closer to home. Once again, however, it would be Isaac who I would blame for it, only now with a little more justification.

It was rare that we were left in the house on our own. Isaac's painting and decorating business did not take up too much of his time and he almost never worked past three o'clock in the afternoon. On this particular day, however, only a few afternoons after the incident in the classroom, he was late home and I was surprised to find the three of us – Adam, Justin and I – left on our own without my father making his presence felt in the next room. And I felt free.

'Where's your dad?' asked Justin nervously, no doubt expecting him to appear out of the shadows at any point, so suspicious were they all of my ancient father and his mysterious ways. 'Is he hiding somewhere?'

'Why would he be hiding?' I asked, a little exasperated by the question. 'What sense would that make?'

'I don't know, but he's usually here somewhere, isn't he?'

I shrugged and grunted a quiet acknowledgement. 'He's out,' I said after a moment, without even having to leave the room to verify this. The house felt different when he was not in it. Somehow I managed to feel more relaxed and at the same time quite tense, for the only reason I could suspect for his absence was an early drinking session, and I didn't like it when he came home drunk. I looked at my friends and could see them grow more at ease as well, their shoulders drooping a little as they became limber and less concerned about their manners. We wandered around for a while, had something to eat, played a little football in the garden until eventually, returning back indoors, we dropped into the armchairs in the living room, racking our brains for something to do.

'Who owns the gun?' asked Justin, looking up at the Smith & Wesson on the wall, Isaac's prized possession.

'Isaac,' I said, barely looking up at it. 'Me. Some day.'

'Can I take it down?' he asked but I shook my head.

'No. I'm not allowed.'

'I didn't ask whether *you* could take it down or not. I asked could I.'

'No.'

'Go on.'

'No,' I insisted, knowing how firm Isaac was about being the only one to handle the gun. I no longer believed what he had told me when I was younger about it exploding in the hands of anyone other than him, but I still felt it was sacrosanct and was predisposed to be afraid of it. My two friends frowned, as having identified it as an object of some interest they naturally wanted to play with it. My refusal only made it all the more attractive.

'Did it belong to that guy?' asked Adam, his brow furrowing as he tried to recall the name.

'What guy?' I asked innocently.

'That guy. The guy you said in class was your grand-father.'

'*Great*-grandfather,' I corrected him.

'That's it. Was it his?'

I shrugged. 'So I'm told,' I conceded. 'It has his father's name on it anyway. Isaac Cody.'

'That's *your* father's name,' said Adam.

'He was named for his great-grandfather,' I explained. 'I was named for mine. He was a "William" too. Apparently it's some kind of tradition.'

'What was it you called him?' asked Justin, trying to recall what I had said in class earlier in the week. 'That nickname you said.'

I threw my eyes to heaven, not really wanting to get into it. 'Buffalo Bill,' I said finally. 'He was some old cowboy.' I could see they were only mildly impressed. They still didn't have a clue who Buffalo Bill was sup-posed to be, but cowboys and guns are still interesting to nine-year-old boys and that in itself was worthy of note.

'Take it down,' said Justin again, desperate to get his hands on it. 'Let's have a shifty.'

'I told you no,' I repeated. 'I'm not allowed. It's only a stupid gun anyway. Who cares.' I slumped off the arm-chair in protest and drifted back to the kitchen for a glass of water. When I returned the gun was off the wall and being passed from one pair of grubby hands to the other. 'What are you doing?' I said, exasperated. 'I told you to leave it alone.'

'We were just looking at it,' said Adam with a sigh and he passed it back to Justin who, having finally got a hold of his prize, was proving unwilling to surrender it. He held it aloft and pointed it at each of us, one at a time.

'Stick 'em up,' he repeated, an echo of what he had said to me as we had left the classroom a few days earlier. Adam, for some reason, put his arms in the air. I simply frowned and walked towards him, demanding that he return it to me. The way that he was waving it gave me pause however and, even though I knew that it wasn't loaded and probably wouldn't work anyway, I grew nervous, unhappy about the careless way that he was handling the gun. His small fingers closed in towards the trigger and slowly, so slowly that even from this distance I could see its action move, it pressed down and the lever at the top of the gun stepped outwards. I held my breath, expecting death at any moment, and closed my eyes but all I heard were two clicks, the sound of Justin's finger pressing on the trigger and the empty chamber rotating, and the sound of the door opening behind my friend.

He spun around immediately and it only took Isaac a moment to see what was happening. Justin was still holding the gun aloft, but now he was aiming it at Isaac and in his nervousness, in the strange energy of the moment, he pressed the trigger again and this time the sound of the gun's release echoed around the room and made us all jump. Isaac blinked in shock and jumped back and at that moment Justin dropped the Smith & Wesson, that most sacred of objects, on the floor where it banged against the floorboards noisily. Isaac looked at it and his face grew red, his lip snarling, and without giving it a second thought he reached back, curled his right hand into a fist and punched Justin directly in the face, sending him flying back across the room, landing in the corner with a start. Adam and I stared at our fallen comrade open mouthed; I looked at Isaac and bit my lip, willing myself not to cry. No one said a word; the whole scene had lasted only a couple of seconds. Isaac looked at the three of us without a trace of remorse.

'It doesn't belong to you,' he said. 'You shouldn't touch what doesn't belong to you.'

I walked towards him and stared up at him defiantly. The smell of whisky was unmistakable. I could hear Justin slowly picking himself up off the floor behind me and the two of them gathering their coats, wondering how they could make their exit with the minimum amount of fuss. I heard whispers behind me that suggested that Justin's nose was bleeding profusely. I stared up at Isaac's face and paused before saying the only thing I could think of which could hurt him as much as he had hurt my friend.

'You're only making it all up anyway,' I said. 'None of it's real. None of it. You're delusional. Full of sad fantasies. You're a joke.'

He stared back at me and for a moment I thought that he might hit me too but instead he just brushed past me with a smile, deliberately hitting my shoulder as he went, as if he was a child himself. He reached down and picked up the gun before setting it back on its rightful perch on the wall. He turned to look at us and shook his head.

'You're lucky you're all still alive,' he said angrily, before turning and walking out of the room and I didn't know whether the luck he spoke of was because the gun wasn't loaded or because all he had done was to punch Justin in the nose. Later that night, while trying to sleep, I heard a commotion at the front door and ran to the top of the stairs to hear what was happening. It was

Justin's father, here to complain that, according to his son, I had punched Justin in the face and had broken his nose. For some reason, possibly through fear of Isaac but a need for revenge nonetheless, he had blamed it all on me. What was Isaac going to do about it, Justin's father wanted to know. There was talk of the police. The phrase 'juvenile delinquent' drifted up to me.

'Leave him to me,' said Isaac eventually, calming down the enraged father. 'Believe me, I'll punish him all right, fighting like an animal in a zoo. He'll be sorry, don't worry. Your lad's got nothing to worry about in the future, I promise you that.'

I didn't mind Justin blaming me; I understood his reasons. I was, however, a little surprised at how easily Isaac absolved himself and took this new version of events as a replacement for what had actually taken place. I frowned and returned to my bed and tried to sleep.

Russell, Majors and Waddell were the company that the government had entrusted with the supplies for General Johnston and they set off early in the morning, ten wagons filled with meat, lard, ammunition and gunpowder and every conceivable supply which might be needed for an extended siege on Salt Lake. Bill, Yountam and Rogers were separated in the wagons, with each of the boys assigned to a different one, and Bill himself was bringing up the rear in the wagon second from the end. They travelled for three or four days and eventually, as they got closer to Green River, decided to hold camp for a day in order to work out the best way to approach Salt Lake. Simpson called all the wagons to a halt and after they ate spoke to them about his plans.

'This is where things can get difficult,' he informed them, watching each face for any sign of panic. 'There are bands of Indians gathered in these parts and depending on their feelings on the day, they may let us pass through unharmed or they may choose to look for a scalp or two. Either way, we have to be on our guard. Now I'm going to take a couple of men and scout ahead a few miles to see the lie of the land and we'll plan our route from there.' He looked around the camp at the various men gathered before him and noted how some were looking back at him anxiously, hoping to be picked to ride out with him, while others were slinking back, preferring the idea of a rest and a respite from any potential dangers which such a scouting expedition might entail. Simpson ignored both sets of men and centred instead on those who looked impassive, those who displayed neither fear nor excessive bravery.

'George Woods,' he called, pointing at his regular second-in-command who was standing by the side of a wagon smoking a pipe, his eyes pressed firmly closed as if he was asleep in his stance. 'You'll come with me for the ride, won't you?'

'Got nothing else to do,' drolled Woods, waving a hand casually in the air as if he neither cared whether he went, stayed or was shot in the head by a gang of marauding Indians even as he stood there. His easy-going nature was what made him a certain man for such adventures.

'And one more,' called Simpson, scanning the crowd with a certain look of disdain before his eye landed heavily on the white-cheeked face of my great-grandfather and his smile returned as his pointed finger cut through the men and singled him out. 'And you, Bill Cody. The famous Indian killer. Braver than the braves, or so you tell me. We'll take you too. What do you say, are you game?'

'Yes!' roared Bill eagerly, jumping forward, the spur in his boot unfortunately connecting with the side of the wagon as he jumped, causing him to topple head forwards into the group standing in front of him, his entire body disappearing from view as he rolled on the ground, the tumultuous laughter of the men causing him no end of embarrassment as he searched for his hat before standing up again and walking sheepishly forward, dusting himself down.

'Shut up, the lot of you!' shouted Simpson, ignoring Bill's stumble as Simpson and his two choices made their way towards their horses. 'Leave the lad alone. We'll be back in a couple of hours and I expect to see all these horses fed and watered by then, do you hear me?'

They rode slowly through the mountains, making their way towards the peaks where they might get a view of the land that lay before them and the distance they would have to travel before reaching their destination. They spoke little at first and Bill took his lead from the two older men; if neither of them were going to begin a conversation then it was hardly his place to do so. Woods looked as bored as ever but Bill knew, even from the couple of days they had already spent together, that he was alert to the slightest movements around him and the boy did not mistake his lack of society for indolence. Simpson and Woods rode together, with Bill a few paces behind, but after an hour or so, Simpson muttered something to his partner, who picked up his pace a little while the other man held back and joined my great-grandfather.

Again, there was total silence for some time as

Bill and Simpson rode side by side and my great-grandfather could feel himself growing more and more intimidated by the older man's presence as they travelled along. He sat up straight in his saddle, pulled the peak of his hat a little further down over his forehead to block out the rising sun and carefully watched the country below him and the road ahead as he waited for some sign that his presence was an asset to their scouting party.

'Don't say much, do you?' said Simpson eventually, looking directly ahead and with only a trace of a smile whispering along his lips. 'Lads your age usually chatter on forever. That's why I can't stand most of 'em, truth to tell. You on the other hand. You never open your mouth.'

'I thought we were too busy paying attention to start talking,' said Bill.

'You saying I should shut up?'

'No, no,' Bill stuttered quickly. 'No that's not what I meant at all, sir. I just meant—'

'Oh relax, Bill,' said Simpson, reaching across and affectionately patting the horse rather than its rider. 'I'm just joking with you. Don't take it all so seriously.'

'No sir.'

'And you can stop calling me "sir" too. That's beginning to get to me. Mr Simpson will do fine for now.' Bill nodded. There were a lot of questions he wanted to ask Simpson and none of them related to their present task. He wanted to know more about the adventures that he had had over the course of his life, the very things which he himself was planning for his future. For now, however, he said nothing, sensing that it was his place to listen and answer questions at that time and not ask any.

'Where's your family, Bill?' asked Simpson eventually. 'They know you're out here or did you run away?'

'They know I'm somewhere,' he replied. 'They're back in Iowa, or were last time I laid eyes on them. I ran away. Not from them as I couldn't do something like that.'

'So what did you run away from then?'

'I was in a fight in school. Near killed a boy.'

'Damn, but you're a bloodthirsty little brute,' laughed Simpson, shaking his head. 'First an Indian, and now some snot-nosed kid.'

'I didn't actually kill him. Just beat on him pretty badly. You see, he—'

'Whatever, it don't matter,' said Simpson dismissively. 'All I'm asking is if you're planning a return to there at some point in the future.'

Bill shook his head. 'No time soon,' he said. 'All that's there for me is a farm and marching around all day ploughing fields. And that's not for me. I want more than that.'

'A country needs farmers,' said Simpson quietly. 'You shouldn't be so quick to dismiss such work. That what your father does?' Bill nodded. 'Well, I suppose it's natural for a boy to want to branch out on his own but all the same . . . this life isn't for everyone, you know.'

'I know it.'

'Can be mighty lonely out here. Can be dangerous too. You know how many people I seen killed over my time on the trails?' Bill looked at him and raised an eyebrow, awaiting the number. 'Damned if I know,' said Simpson with a touch of sadness in his voice. 'All as I know is that if I had two cents for every one of them I'd have made myself King of Mexico by now.' Bill laughed and Simpson turned and frowned at him. 'What are you laughing at, boy? You think it's funny? People getting killed?'

'No,' said Bill quickly, flushing slightly. 'Of course not. I only meant that—'

'It's not funny,' said Simpson looking forward again, knowing that he had meant no disrespect. 'It's not funny at all. I only hope you're ready for whatever does come ahead of you 'cause I seen boys not much older than you—' He broke off suddenly as Woods turned his head and nodded at the road ahead. Riding towards them was a group of ten men, each carrying firearms, and as they approached they slowed down, lifting their guns and aiming them squarely at the heads of the three horsemen. Simpson came to the front again with Woods, and Bill took a central position behind them.

'What's this then?' asked Simpson cautiously, his voice attempting to sound light-hearted. What are you men about today then?'

'I think you should know that, Lew Simpson,' replied one of the men. 'On account of the fact that you're riding on here, a bunch of no-good bullwhackers, looking to kill some of us. Who sent you then?'

Simpson narrowed his eyes and looked at his opponent in confusion. 'I'm sent to kill no man,' he said. 'So you can lower your arms, friend, as I mean none of you any harm.'

'That so?' asked the man in mock amusement. 'And there I was thinking that you were sent with supplies for General Johnston so that he might route us out of our homes. I seen you before, Simpson. I know what you do for a living.'

All three were lost for words now and Simpson, an intelligent man, merely shrugged and agreed to it. 'Well then, you have us now, sir,' he said. 'The only thing left

58

to settle is what you mean to do with us. If you mean to kill us, then have at it and let's not waste our time talking about it. What do you say?'

Bill looked from Simpson to their opponent nervously, gripping the reins of his horse firmly between his hands. He knew the ways of men enough to know that they would shoot all three of them without remorse if they felt like it and he was sure that this would be too early an exit from this world for himself.

'I don't mean to kill you,' replied the man, identifying himself as one John Smith from Salt Lake City. 'But I do mean to show you something which might make you think again about what you're doing. Let's ride on a little ways.'

Simpson, Woods and Bill were escorted, front, rear and sides, by the ten horsemen as they made their way back across the Rockies, but now to another peak in the distance, a point which lent a view over the area where they had left their wagon trail a couple of hours earlier.

'Your army dares to send reinforcements and supplies to take us from our home,' said Smith, the apparent leader of this gang of dedicated Mormons. 'From our home!' he repeated, shouting now. 'Just as they did in Illinois and Missouri.' He pronounced the last 's' of Illinois as if it was not silent, eliding it into the 'and' as if the two states were part of a greater package. 'What right have they of that, can you tell me?' His tone was non-confrontational, almost friendly now, as he and Simpson took the lead, their horses taking the trail across the land slowly and carefully, for the distances beneath them were vast and the canyons no friendly area.

'There was no place for you there,' said Simpson,

loyal to the union. 'Or in Salt Lake City, matter of fact. Your practices are against all that's right and proper in the world, sir. That's why we have at you.'

'Ha!' roared Smith. 'Rather our practices than yours of debasing yourself in every rat-infested whorehouse from northern Alaska to southern Florida, carrying your syphilitic bodies across the nation and infecting all you come across without a care for anyone but your own pleasures. Rather that than your drunkenness and your meanness and your sloth. To think you condemn us when you're what you are.'

'I do condemn you, sir,' said Simpson. 'And not because of who you are or what you do but because I am a representative of the United States government which has given this country a code of honour, a law, a constitution that you and your like flaunt and debase every time you take another wife or centre your godless communities around your illicit behaviour.'

Smith smiled and hesitated before answering. 'And you think your General Johnston will be able to change all that, do you?' he asked.

'Or die trying,' came the reply. 'And if I can play some part in helping him then by God I will have done my duty by this land.'

Smith merely nodded and called his horse to rest, reaching out to take the reins of Simpson's horse too in order to bring him to a halt. They were reaching the edge of the plateau. 'Then look down there, my friend,' he said courteously, pointing at the ground far below where the ten wagons had been stationed earlier on. His tone was smug, as if he had already won any future arguments. Take a look down there and see what you can do to beat us now.'

Simpson, Woods and Bill climbed off their horses

and stepped to the edge, peering below and covering the roof of their eyes with their hands to prevent the sun from blinding them to the scene which was taking place down below. The wagons were still there but their occupants were all huddled in one place now, some distance from their goods, surrounded by a group of Mormons who aimed their guns at the men, ready to fire at anyone who made a foolish bid for heroics. Around the wagons themselves, more men were circling and setting fire to the cloth coverings which surrounded the bent metal of each one, until all below them was a steadying fire, all their possessions succumbing to the flames. Eventually the arsonists drew back from the heat and all were forced to watch as the flames grew, licking into the food and gunpowder within the wagons which inevitably began to explode in all directions now, destroying everything. Simpson's face fell, as did my great-grandfather's, for they knew they had failed now and they would either die or return home beaten, unsure of which fate was worse.

'And what will you do with us now?' asked Simpson eventually. 'Kill us, I suppose?'

'Unlike you, I have no interest in killing,' explained Smith. 'Indeed, you're all free to go. On foot, of course.' Some of his partners took a hold of their horses and down below, the men who had been under fire were beginning to walk away, unsure where they should be going as their persecutors rode off with their own horses in tow.

The three men eventually caught up with those they had left behind and they began their long trek to the nearest station, this time Fort Bridger, defeated, having failed in their efforts. It was not a feeling that my great-grandfather wanted to experience again.

Chapter Three

Separation

I was fifteen years old and no different to any other boy of that age in that I was almost impossible to live with. My relationship with Isaac had developed to the point where we lived together peacefully without ever really speaking to each other. Neither of us made any demands on the other; I silently agreed to listen to his stories as we sat around the dinner table – Bill Cody being the only topic through which he felt he could relate to me; in those tales, he stressed, lay the foundations for my *own* life, for the secrets of honour and success in the world. Other than that, we kept a cold distance from each other. We were polite whenever we spoke, but never eager to be left in the same room together for any length of time. I had grown my hair long and it curled over my collar, the blond strands refusing to stretch down my back in the fashion I wanted. I did it partly to annoy my father, who scowled whenever young people appeared on the television blurring the lines between the traditional male and female identities. Isaac, an old-timer all the way, liked to know who was who and what was what.

By 1985, Isaac had retired, closing down his business and taking instead to a few regular haunts which defined his movements throughout the day: the armchair in front of the television, the local pub, a park where he would sit for hours and scowl at passers-by. He was sixty-seven by then and I noticed that his body was closing in on itself, making him seem smaller and more compressed than the giant I had seen him as when I was younger. We passed each other that summer – I on the way up, he on the way down – as I rose towards six feet in height and my body filled out and grew more muscular. I wore white T-shirts and tight blue jeans and made a point of never smiling. I acquired a girlfriend named Agnes, an ugly name but a prize catch nonetheless. Relations between father and son became purely civilised.

The one concession I made to boyhood was the continuation of my paper round, which I had been doing since the age of ten. Although it seemed slightly contradictory to my friends Adam and Justin when taken in the context of my new teenage delinquent era, I didn't care what others thought and still quite enjoyed the routine. It was an early start for me – I rose at six o'clock every morning – and my route covered about six miles per day, which helped to keep me fit. I liked the feeling of the mounds of papers in my basket growing lighter and lighter as the sun came up, my bike becoming easier to push as the last of the news got delivered in the area closest to my own house. The streets were generally quiet at that time of the day; it was pleasant to be able to cycle along the main road where at other times of the day one took one's life in one's hands, and I liked to veer from side to side, cycling on the wrong side of the road, courting danger, feeling free, letting go of the handlebars and flying down the hills. So when my friends teased me about my childish job, I simply shrugged and carried on, oblivious to their taunts. I was a paperboy and proud of it. And unlike most of them, I had some money in my pocket.

Agnes Cliff was in the same year in school as me and was generally considered to be beautiful but terrifying. She had long blonde hair which, unlike mine, continued straight down her back and she wore dark-black mascara around her eyes. She chewed gum incessantly, even when we kissed, and had that rarest of teenage luxuries: her own car. (Wealthy family.) At sixteen she was about four months older than me, but those four months were all I needed to feel that I was finally learning from an experienced woman. She didn't talk about her feelings – she claimed that she had none – and was content to stand on corners and be stared at, frown at strangers, and sit in the park, kissing me. None of which I had any issue with. She knew that she was beautiful and had barely to make any effort with her appearance to maintain it. She pretended that she resented the attentions of men who would stare at her when she entered a room or walked down a road, but she did nothing to discourage them and probably enjoyed the power it gave her.

Isaac took exception to her at first, such a novelty was a young girl to our small company of men. I didn't talk about her at home but he often mentioned having seen us in the park together, or walking through the town, although he had never come over to introduce himself. She only came around to our house once but it was a troublesome visit. It was shortly after Christmas and we were alone in the living room, Agnes lying on the sofa, me sitting in an armchair, the fire lit, steaming mugs of coffee in our hands. It was mid-afternoon and we were watching daytime television, staring at the box and saying little to each other, having decided that school was simply not acceptable for the day. Eventually Isaac came in and was taken by surprise by her presence. Indeed, he looked at her as if she was something I had dragged in from the streets.

'Why aren't you in school?' he asked me and I shrugged, not bothering to turn around to look at him. I may have granted him an obligatory grunt. 'You'll learn nothing and you'll make nothing of yourself if you don't go to school,' he informed me but I could tell from his voice that he was merely going through the motions. He wasn't bothered whether I was in school or not any more. He never believed that the lessons I needed to learn could come from a classroom. He sat down in his armchair and looked in the direction of the television also, squinting at it as if he had never seen anything like it before. He had still not acknowledged Agnes but she seemed equally oblivious to his presence. 'Get me a glass, William, will you?' he asked politely, affecting a slightly more refined voice, and somehow I felt unable to tell him to get it himself, as I often might. I sighed and went into the kitchen, returning with a small whisky shot-glass, the same one which was virtually an extension of his own hand. I had naturally assumed that this was the type of glass he wanted.

The bottle was already standing on the table and Isaac took the top off carefully. I watched him as he took in the quick rush of scent from the bottle, his eyes lighting up as he poured the liquid into the glass, the sense of calming relief that even the anticipation of the drink could give him. Sitting back he put it to his lips before pausing and I looked in the same direction that he was looking. Agnes had turned her head and was watching him carefully.

'Isaac . . . this is . . . Agnes,' I said casually, waving a hand in her general direction, as if I wasn't too sure either who she was and was even less bothered than he. It was important to appear casual; at fifteen years old, anything stronger might have indicated that I had actual feelings.

'You're staring at me, Agnes,' said Isaac and there was a twinkle in his voice as he spoke.

'It's a little early to be drinking, isn't it?' she asked him in a steady voice. I flinched, wondering how he would respond to this, and not a little surprised that she would make such a rude comment to a perfect stranger in his own house. I barely gave much thought to his drinking myself any more for even though he drank a lot and regularly, he was not an alcoholic. I always had the feeling that if he had to stop drinking, then he could, quite easily. But at that time there was no particular reason why he should. So he simply continued.

'Not really,' Isaac replied eventually. 'Some men say they wait until the sun rises over the yard-arm. Me, I've always said that when school is out, then it's time enough for a drink.' He paused for effect. 'And school is clearly out.'

'Well it's disgusting, drinking at this time of the day,' she said. She turned and looked at the television again and I slowly rotated my head to look at Isaac, who was looking at me now with a bemused smile on his face. I turned away, unwilling to catch his eye.

'I enjoy a drink,' Isaac said, not in the least defensively.

'So do I, but not at two in the afternoon,' said Agnes.

'Surely you're too young to drink?' he asked her and she sighed in exasperation. There was a long pause

66

when no one said anything. I tried to concentrate on the television and wondered how soon I could break the silence by standing up and announcing that we were going out. We hadn't planned on leaving the house though until after four, when school would be out anyway. It was unsafe to visit the town centre or wander the streets aimlessly while playing truant; you never knew who you might bump into. I had been under the impression that Isaac would be on scowling duty in the park until four so thought we would be safe inside for another couple of hours yet. 'Would you like a drink, Agnes?' he asked eventually in a friendly tone of voice. 'Is that what you're saying? That you'd like to join me in a dram?'

She shrugged. 'Nothing else to do,' she said, as if she was doing him a big favour, and I stared at her in surprise. The last thing I wanted was for my father and my girlfriend to begin a drinking session. Who knew where something like that could lead?

'Maybe we should go,' I suggested. 'Do that . . . thing.'

'What thing?' asked Agnes irritably. 'There is no "thing".'

'Fetch Agnes a glass, William,' said Isaac, unscrewing the bottle again, never once taking his eyes off her. 'There's a good lad.' I didn't move and pursed my lips together in irritation. 'A glass, William,' repeated Isaac and this time Agnes gave me a look which said *Now!* and so I got up and did as I was told.

'One drink,' I said to her as I put the glass down, acting as if I had some control over her actions, somehow wanting Isaac to believe that I was in charge of this situation. 'Then we have to go.'

'To do the "thing", I know,' said Agnes sarcastically.

'Don't worry. The "thing" will wait for us.' She made inverted comma signs in the air with her fingers every time she uttered the word and looked at me as if she wondered what on earth she was doing with me in the first place.

They drank a whisky together and then they drank another. Agnes didn't flinch as she tasted it; I had only tried it once or twice but had not as yet grown accustomed to the taste. They carried on talking and seemed to be getting on fine but when Isaac opened the bottle to pour her third and his fourth she placed her hand across the top of her glass.

'Thanks,' she said. 'I've had enough.'

'You'll have another,' he urged, just beginning to enjoy himself.

'I've had enough,' she repeated quietly and pushed the glass away, returning to look at the television as if their friendliness had never even taken place. I turned to glance at Isaac who looked crestfallen; it wasn't every day that a pretty girl wanted to sit and knock back whiskies with him. The fact that she appeared to know when she had had enough irritated him.

'Don't be such a girl,' he said, but the pause between her line and his had been too long; the regular run of conversation had already ended and his comeback seemed needy and slightly pathetic, not to mention embarrassingly silly.

'I *am* a girl,' she pointed out without looking at him. A tense silence ensued and I excused myself for a moment, walking upstairs to use the bathroom. I threw some water on my face and stared at my reflection in the mirror as I dried it, racking my brain for a place we could go in order to get out of the house but also avoid being caught by any authority figures. I spent a little longer upstairs than necessary and when I went back into the living room, Agnes was standing up and brushing her hands down her skirt to straighten out the creases. It stopped just above her knees and was a point of controversy between her and the school, although neither I nor my classmates had any problems with it. 'Come on, William,' she said firmly. 'Let's go.' Isaac was sitting back in his seat, nursing his whisky, and didn't even look at me. The atmosphere seemed strained but I thought nothing of it at the time.

'Right,' I said, reaching for my jacket, pleased to be leaving but feeling as if I could not look at Isaac's face for fear of feeling unkind somehow. He wasn't looking at me, he was pouring another drink, his eyes half closed, his body rigid. I opened my mouth to say something conciliatory, but before the words could come, Agnes grabbed my arm and pulled me towards the door.

'I'll see you later,' I said, shaking free of her grasp but Isaac wouldn't look at me.

'It was just the drink, that was all,' he muttered quietly and at the time, I assumed he was talking to me.

George Chrisman was self-conscious about the red burn mark which covered a good portion of his left cheek, a design which resembled a map of Central America from the wide northern points of Texas and New Mexico to the thin islet of the Panama Canal, where it grew narrow before exploding forth once again into Colombia and Venezuela. The mark was the result of an accident he had had when he was in his teens. While he dozed at the kitchen table, his mother walked past with a pan of bubbling lard and tripped on the wood carving which her youngest son, Denny, had left at the side of the table earlier in the day. As she fell, the pan flew into the air, George woke with a start but not soon enough to escape a shower of boiling grease which disfigured his otherwise good looks for ever. Previously a personable, cheerful character, he took the opportunity then to harden himself and became known as something of a brute and a violent fellow, particularly if anyone was foolish enough to stare too long at the signs of his disfigurement.

Now, at the age of thirty-two, and controlling a ranch in Julesberg, he was at the top of the town hierarchy, a justice of the peace, a non-practising minister, and one of the most important agents for the Pony Express line in the west. His wife Sarah had borne him six children in as many years, six daughters, one of whom would eventually murder him on the eve of her own wedding after he withdrew consent for her to be joined with a man he had originally considered to be her social inferior – he was a Baptist – a point upon which he would relent before changing his mind once again while his daughter was enduring her final dress fitting on the upper storey of the ranch, an hour before she came up behind him as he slept by the fire and slit his throat noiselessly from ear to ear.

On the morning my great-grandfather met George Chrisman for the first time, he was recovering from a hangover, having celebrated long and hard into the night the birth, only hours earlier, of this same daughter. His mood therefore was torn between happiness at being made a father again and misery at the level of pounding which was going on within his head, not to mention the slow churning of his breakfast within his stomach. He was not in the mood for conversation. A few days earlier he had hung a sign on the porch of his office inviting applicants for a position with the Pony Express

Company of America. *'Skinny, expert riders willing to risk death daily,'* said the sign. *'Apply within.'* He had received no applicants so far, which was unfortunate as he wanted to fill the position as soon as possible.

Bill arrived in Julesberg with a carefree attitude, a sixteen-year-old boy who looked no more than thirteen, with a thin, taut body and curly blond hair. He had come from Pike's Peak, where he had been prospecting unsuccessfully for gold. It was one of those rare moments in my great-grandfather's life when he felt unsure of who he was or where he was going. He had left Pike's Peak with the intention of returning to Fort Leavenworth but the combination of a leaky raft and a lack of a sense of purpose found him wandering instead into Julesberg on that hot summer's morning, looking for something to do, hoping for adventure. His white cotton shirt, which he had been wearing for four days, was sticking to his chest with perspiration and he hoped to find a saloon that might serve him a cold glass of iced water before deciding what to do next. As he stood in the centre of the town, taking his hat off his head to wipe his brow, he saw the sign hanging on George Chrisman's window and, never one to miss an opportunity, immediately knew where his next stop should be.

The interview was brief and to the point. Chrisman looked at him with distaste as he sat down before him and sniffed the air without subtlety, urging the boy to go straight to a bathhouse in the future before seeking employment with Christian men.

'I only just this minute arrived in . . . in town,' said Bill defensively, unsure of exactly where he was and unwilling to pluck a random name from the air in case he was wrong and he gave offence.

'Julesberg,' said Chrisman irritably, pointing out the window towards a sign which gave the name of the town and its population (1,439) quite clearly. 'Have the goodness to discover where you are too.'

'I'm sorry, sir,' said Bill, maintaining his usual level of politeness but unsure for how long he could do so. He was not quite the pliant, respectful fellow he had been a couple of years earlier, having seen a little more of the world, and of men, since then. 'An honest mistake. I've been travelling for days now. Liked the look of this town the minute I walked into it though.'

'Did you indeed?' muttered the older man, suspicious of new people, particularly the young. 'Not a Baptist, are you?'

'No, sir,' said Bill, surprised to be asked such a question.

'And where you been before now then? Who are your people? Will I know them?'

'Doubt it,' he replied. 'They're the Codys. Late of Wyoming. Now of Iowa. My father's Isaac Cody. Maybe you've heard of him?'

'Can't say as I have,' said Chrisman. 'Knew an Isaac Delaitre once. You anything to him?'

Bill blinked and his mouth sat open while he wondered how to answer that. He stared at the burn mark on the cheek of the fellow opposite him and had to will himself to take his eyes away from it. Chrisman flinched, aware that Bill was staring at the deformity, and his hand instinctively went to his cheek to cover the mark for a moment. 'No, sir. Never had the pleasure,' said Bill then quickly. 'I'm sure he was a good man though.'

'Ha!' said Chrisman. 'I was sure he was too. Until he stole a hundred dollars from my office and disappeared off on a horse belonging to Ben Kendall over there.' His wagging finger indicated a group of about twenty similar-looking men standing talking outside the general store; Bill had no idea which man his potential employer was identifying. 'You tell me you're related to Isaac Delaitre and I'll see you tell me where he is or you'll hang for it, so help me.'

Bill nodded slowly. He was tired and weary and unable to maintain conversation for long. He wanted to sleep. Recent weeks had not been as entertaining as he wished his life to be. The prospecting for gold had been a worthless endeavour. He had spent a good portion of each day standing in one position of a stream, his feet growing steadily more numb with the coldness of the water, a small pan in his hands which he would fill with water, stone and mud, before slowly sieving through it and carefully discarding every element of non-gold material back into the water until his bowl was empty and he would have to begin again. Each evening at the campfire, both men and women would sit around and tell tales of the men they had known who had struck it rich doing that very thing. No one present ever seemed to have discovered very much but every one of them had known a man who did. It was only that that kept them going, the hope of a sudden rush of gold pebbles rolling into their bowl. The possibility of a better life.

A week had passed, and then another, and Bill had still not made his fortune. He tried different parts of the river each day, but was irritated by the fact that there was almost always another prospector standing not ten feet away from him. They stood, about fifty of them in a line along the river, wishing each other luck but praying that it would be they and no one else who would find the precious objects. On one afternoon the man next

73

in line to him had found a piece of pure gold the size of his thumb and had been surrounded so quickly by the others that he had run immediately to his horse and galloped away to the nearest town to redeem it before an accident befell him. Bill hadn't seen him again. Had he been standing about three or four feet to his left, he thought, that would have been him.

The morning after that incident he had risen a full hour before anyone else and walked far away from their camp, down towards a turning in the river from where he could not be seen by his fellow prospectors. He walked for about an hour until he was sure that there was no chance of anyone catching him up or trying their luck that far down, took off his shoes and stepped gingerly into the water. He made his way carefully over the sharp rocks at the side, for the last thing he needed was to cut himself this early in the day, and stood about fifteen feet in from the shore, at the point where the water was just below knee level. Without thinking he crouched down with his bowl to dig in for his first supply, forgetting that he was deeper than usual and immediately soaked his trousers in the rear. Cursing loudly – there was no one to hear him – he took them off and stood there in his underwear, leaving his trousers stretched out along the rocks in order for the sun to dry them. *This is water*, he reasoned to himself. *You have to expect to get a little wet if you're standing in a river.*

A couple of hours later he was shaking out his bowl, carefully separating the silt of the river's base from the pebbles which were held within it, when his eye was taken by an unfamiliar yellow object lodged within. He gasped and pressed his fingers into the soft mess and pulled it out, holding it up to the sky as he squinted to get a better look. He had found a piece. It wasn't big, no bigger than the nail on his thumb, no wider either, but it was hope at least. It was the first piece he had found and suggested that there might be more. He laughed in excitement and looked around but there was no one there so he placed it inside his shirt pocket and continued to dig in the water for more where that had come from. Within about thirty minutes, no richer but still excited by his find, he realised that he could barely feel his feet any more. The sun had risen and grown warmer and the water had grown more icy as it gushed down his legs. He turned back for the shore and eventually collapsed there, climbing up on a small hillock and lying back to rest for a moment, before sitting up and massaging his frozen feet, a difficult task considering his hands were almost numb from the cold too. It was while he was trying to encourage the blood to return to them that she appeared.

'You're a long way from the others,' she said, a girl a few years older than he, perhaps about twenty, who he had seen around the camp over the last few weeks but given little notice to. He thought perhaps she was the daughter of one of the older prospectors. 'You lost or something?'

Bill looked at her cautiously and shook his head, aware that he was sitting there in just his shirt and underwear but not feeling sufficiently self-conscious to pull his trousers back on. He leaned over to see whether there was anyone else following a few steps behind but she was alone. 'I'm not lost,' he said. 'Just thought I'd try my luck a little further down river, that's all. Get tired working in the same place all the time. Nothing to find down there anyway, if you ask me.'

She sat down on the hill a little below him and watched him carefully. 'What's wrong with your feet?'

she asked, watching as he kneaded them carefully. 'They're practically blue.'

Bill flushed and felt a little naked before her. 'I think I spent too much time in the water,' he said. 'They need to get the warmth back into them.'

The girl nodded and thought about it for a moment before seeming to come to a decision and reached over and removed his hands. 'Here,' she said. 'Let me try. Your hands are probably cold as well.'

Bill swallowed and leaned back, allowing his hands to support him as he stretched out on the grass. The moment she touched him he felt both tired and alert at once; her hands were warm, her skin soft against his, his feet flinched at the gentle pressure of her fingers. 'So?' she asked eventually, her voice lowering a little. 'Did it work?'

'Did what work?' he asked, looking at her carefully as she concentrated on his toes. She had a pale face and dark hair and a small mole just below her right ear. She was no beauty but she was not unattractive either. Her body was what might be called plenteous, even though there did not seem to be an ounce of fat on her. He stared at her and although she had never quite entered his attentions before, he felt their solitude and intimacy begin to make him alert to opportunity.

'Moving down river. Did you find anything?'

'Not really,' he said.

'Not really?'

'Not much.'

'Not much, what does that mean?' she asked, glancing at him briefly with a quick smile before turning away again. 'Does that mean nothing at all or something, but just a little something?' Her hands moved carefully from his left foot to his right and he curled the toes of the former in and out. He was unsure whether he should tell the truth or not but when her fingers brushed the hairs on his leg as she began to manipulate the right foot, he felt himself unable to disappoint her.

'Just a little something,' he admitted and reached into his top pocket, removing the small golden nugget and holding it in the air. The girl looked at it and drew in her breath. To him it remained nothing spectacular, a sign of hope and nothing more, but to her it was still gold. It was what they were all looking for. It was beautiful. And it was his. She had difficulty taking her eyes away from it, but she did so eventually, also taking her hands from his feet. Bill swallowed nervously, disappointed that her attentions had ended, and replaced the nugget in his pocket as she altered her position from beside him to the grass between his feet.

'So,' she said. 'How does that feel? Any better?'

'Much,' he said, nodding enthusiastically. 'I think the feeling's coming back.'

'That's good,' she said carelessly, resting her hands on either ankle and staring him in the eye. 'So do you want to go back in the water and look for more?'

He paused. He imagined for a moment that if he answered too quickly his voice might crack and, not wanting that to happen, he shrugged first and then shook his head, clearing his throat before daring to speak. 'No,' he said eventually. 'Not just now, I think. Maybe later.'

'Good,' said the girl, stretching forward, her body moving slowly up his until he was forced to lean further and further back on the grass. 'Let me see it again,' she said, reaching into his pocket and removing the nugget before holding it up to the light. He did nothing to stop her. After a moment she looked down at his face and gave him a wide smile. 'Can I have it?' she asked quickly, her voice sharp, her words grasping for the object. Bill said nothing for a moment. He didn't want to give it to her but he also didn't want to do anything to displease her lest she move her body off his for even a moment. 'Tell you what,' she said. 'If you can find it, you can have it back.' She dropped the nugget down the front of her dress between her breasts and Bill's eyes opened wide, staring at them within her dress before looking back up at her face. 'Go on,' she said with a laugh. 'Try.' He quickly reached up and undid the strings at the front of her dress, and within a moment she had slipped out of her clothing and was helping him out of his. Immediately his mind was no longer on the piece of gold, it was elsewhere, and he made love for the first time without quite realising its cost to him. When it was over she sat up and dressed quickly, running her hand along his chest before she stood up.

'That was nice,' she said. 'But we won't speak of it back at the camp, all right?' Her voice was firm. He felt embarrassed suddenly to be lying there, so exposed before her.

'All right,' he said and within a few minutes, as if she had been a mirage all along, she disappeared. It was some time later, when he was dressed and putting his shoes back on, that he realised he never had retrieved the gold nugget from wherever she had hidden it. Embarrassed and angry with himself for his stupidity, he decided not to go back to join the others at the camp but waited instead until nightfall, when he took a small raft and made his way instead along the river, eventually landing at a shore which appeared to have a town in the distance. A town which turned out to be Julesberg, where he found himself now.

'So, Mr Cody,' said George Chrisman. 'You want to be a Pony Express rider, yes?'

'Yes,' said Bill with a sigh, unwilling to give the man the satisfaction of a long drawn-out begging speech. Chrisman seemed disappointed by this but it was obvious he wasn't going to get anything more out of the lad and he hadn't exactly been inundated with applications.

'All right,' he said abruptly. 'The job's yours if you want it. But it's hard work, mind. You sure you're up to it?'

'I'd say I am. I've worked hard all my life.'

'You'll be riding over a land of forty-five miles, between stations fifteen miles apart and you'll need to get to each one within an hour of leaving them. That's a recipe for saddle-sores if ever I heard one, so you better have the seat for it. Pay's all right though. You still up for it?'

'Still up for it.'

'Then like I say, the job's yours if you want it.' And so it was that my great-grandfather Bill Cody began his first paid employment as a rider for the United States Pony Express, and had his first experience of having to pay for love, all in the same week.

Isaac frequently told me tales about our ancestor, but the one person he almost never spoke of was my mother. She left when I was only four years old, yet I've never resented her for that. As a child I was preoccupied enough with the fact that Isaac was twenty years older than all my friends' parents without wondering why I was almost the only child in my class without a mother either. Sometimes I felt as if both my parents had died and I was being brought up by an elderly grandfather, so fitting to that role did Isaac seem. But considering how obsessive my father became about his family tree and my part in it, it's worth mentioning the roles of the two people in his life who contributed the most towards his loneliness, and his drinking, namely my mother and his father.

Annabel Reid was a Blitz child, born in London at the height of the Second World War. Her mother was a seamstress and before that had acted on the stage, although she had no great successes that I know of. Her father was an officer in the army and was home on leave when she was conceived. After her birth, when the bombing of the capital became more and more frequent, mother and daughter, and Annabel's older brother Howard, moved to the south coast to stay with cousins and they saw out the war there in relative comfort. Sadly, her father – my grandfather – was killed in the war, although my mother was not left fatherless for long, for my grandmother remarried within a year to a local butcher and never returned to London. The speed of her marriage scandalised some, but their union was apparently happy and little more was heard from them.

My mother, on the other hand, waited until she was eighteen, at which point she climbed on board a bus which took her to a train station which then took her to London. She arrived in the city just as the sixties were blooming and took a flat with another girl in Battersea, on a quiet road shaded by the nearby park. Eighteen years in the quiet of the countryside had made her ready for adventure and she threw herself into city life with the air of one who had been in solitary confinement all her life and then suddenly released. Initially she worked in a fashionable clothes shop but she found that her lifestyle demanded more money than a shop assistant was paid and since she was spending so much of her time in nightclubs anyway, she began to work in one, sleeping by day and living by night. She had – according to Isaac – a string of relationships before she met him, and ran with a cultured crowd, the artists of the day, the photographers, the pop-stars.

'She claimed she could have married a Beatle,' Isaac told me in one of our rare discussions about Annabel. 'She claimed he was chasing her for months and that she didn't go for it because she just didn't fancy him.' He shook his head in disdain. 'I never believed her on that one. Unless it was Pete Best. Knowing her luck, he'd have been the kind of Beatle she'd have hooked up with. The one who got kicked out. Said she met Princess Margaret a few times in the clubs and that they were fast and furious. I took it with a pinch of salt. Liked to make herself sound big, you see. Liked to think she was worth more than other folk. That's why it never could have worked out with us, you see. She didn't want a painter and decorator for a husband. She wanted Lord Bloody Snowdon.'

My parents met at a nightclub and although Isaac was almost thirty years older than her, she was drawn to him. He told her stories, not of Buffalo Bill Cody, but of life inside the prison where he had spent a good portion of his thirties and these were the kinds of stories that the girls of London nightlife at the time admired and responded to. Isaac kept his regular daytime existence to himself and impressed her by spending his money frivolously, keeping her in whatever jewels and gifts he could afford. Having obviously decided not to marry a Beatle, she settled for Isaac and they were married in 1969, the year of *Abbey Road*, when she moved down the road from Battersea Park to Clapham, where Isaac had his home. I was born seven months later and by 1974, when the Beatles had long since split, so did she. She had been attending a local clinic for high blood pressure and her doctor there obviously caused it to increase even further because she left Isaac shortly afterwards and emigrated with him to Canada.

It's hard for me to remember her as I was only a very small child when she left but from what I do recall, life in a small house in Clapham with a painter and decorator was never going to be enough for her. I'm not sure that Canada proved to be much better, but she was unhappy with her marriage to Isaac from the start and was not afraid to show it.

For his part, the adjustment to married life was even more of a struggle. A bachelor for fifty-one years, set in his ways, accustomed to his own company, the introduction of a restless young woman into his household was a disruption he could never have truly expected to work. They were of different generations, and Isaac expected things of his wife which she had no intentions of giving. For him, having found her husband she should have been content to stay at home and look after him. He was wrong. She would regularly disappear in the evenings and he was powerless to control her. Instead he was left with a crying baby and a bottle of whisky when I had finally drifted off to sleep. After she left him, he was never particularly bitter. He felt angry, of course. His pride was hurt, not least because the doctor who had replaced him was not much younger than he himself – perhaps he could have understood it better if she had fallen for a man her own age. But he got over her quickly and there was never any question on either of their parts of me going to Canada with her. Isaac was a mistake, she told me once, and while she never said quite the same about me, it felt like the obvious rejoinder. She was there and then she wasn't; all three of us survived.

Isaac's father, on the other hand, was not a nice man. Like his son, Sam spent a portion of his life behind bars but his crimes were more serious. Sitting in a bar in the 1920s he spotted a young man on the other side of the room eyeing up his wife. This went on for some time and my grandmother was oblivious to it as she had her back to the man, but Sam was aware of it and he waited until the young man stood up to use the bathroom, at which time he followed him inside and, holding him against the wall, cut out one of his eyes with a penknife. He probably would have cut out the other one too had the screams of the young man not alerted the people in the bar, several of whom rushed in and pulled Sam off him. He was sentenced to seven years in jail, and during the sixth he was responsible for a fight which left another man in a wheelchair. It was a further five years before he saw freedom, by which time he was in his forties and unable to adjust to living in society. Returning to life with his wife and growing son, he demonstrated his position as head of the household by regularly beating them both, but only to the point where he would not be convicted of any serious crime even if either of them had the courage to report him, which of course they never did. My father left the house as soon as he could, and shortly afterwards my grandmother died. Isaac broke off all contact with Sam, never speaking to him again during his lifetime, although he did suffer the cost of his funeral.

Unlike the relationship with my mother, which Isaac

was able to come to terms with due to his new role as single parent, I don't believe he was ever quite able to forget the violence of his youth and the legacy which his father left for him. Also a drinker, Sam passed that trait down to his son, and even the capacity for violence, which certainly existed in Isaac, albeit in a mostly dormant fashion, was a family trait which was brought on display from time to time throughout my own youth. There is violence in every man in my family as far back as I can tell and I often thought that it would end with Isaac until I eventually discovered what anger and grief can make possible in anyone. What they could make possible in me.

My great-grandfather met his great friend Homer Lee while riding for the Pony Express around the western American states of the 1860s. Lee, who went on to serve in William McKinley's cabinet in later life as secretary for agriculture, was also a rider for the Pony Express but his life to date had been a lot less colourful than his new friend's. For one thing, he had never left the state of Kansas and lived with his family on a substantial ranch fifteen miles north of Julesberg. The Lees were a wealthy land-owning family and Homer had been brought up with the kinds of privileges and luxuries which few boys at the time enjoyed. It was through some personal act of rebellion, a need to assert himself as separate from his family, that he joined the Pony Express riders in the first place, and it was seen as a curious step for a boy of such privilege, for to be employed with such an outfit required hard work and discipline, traits not often associated with his type. Mr Lee didn't challenge his son, however, and allowed him to follow the course that he felt was right for him, believing – correctly as it turned out – that in time Homer would return to the family fold.

Bill and Homer became in the habit of meeting in the evening times as my great-grandfather was returning to Julesberg after his day's work and Homer was riding home and settling down on his family's property for an hour or two with a smoke and a bottle of whisky, pilfered from Mr Lee's supplies. Homer was a tall lad of nineteen and was known in the town as something of a rascal, having made one of the servants at his house pregnant when he was only sixteen. The girl had been sent away and nothing had been heard of her since and the word was that Homer was a cold character, unfeeling towards others, and it was a rare person who had anything but disdain for him. In truth, the girl had been sent away by Homer's father and, while he had not been in love, Homer had regretted her loss and throughout his life wondered what had become of mother and child, whether the latter had even been born.

'I was out near Drewshank today,' Bill told Homer during one of their long summer evening layabouts on the grass of the Lee estate. 'Delivering to some folks up there and it turned out there'd been a murder there a few nights earlier.'

'A murder?' said Homer, sitting up and taking notice of something a little out of the ordinary.

'The whole town was up in arms over it. The man who died left a wife and twelve children.'

'Drewshank's a no-good place anyway,' said Homer quietly. 'What's the point in getting involved with the things they do?'

'I didn't have any choice,' said Bill defensively. 'That's where I was sent. Why, you been there?'

'I been near there. Heard tell of the place. They had

a sheriff once, name of Carter I think, who could put a bullet in a target from one hundred feet away. Did it as a regular treat for the town on Sunday afternoons, I heard. Everyone would come out and watch him and he loved it so he started getting more and more tricksy with his shots. One afternoon he blew the head off some five-year-old girl by accident and on account of that her father took his gun and blew Carter away while he was trying to apologise. Then that man was hung. All took place within a couple of days. I'd stay out of there if I was you. Things have a habit of turning nasty there.'

Bill frowned. 'I don't think this murder had anything to do with that,' he said after a moment. 'This had something to do with the confederates, I think.'

'Well that don't surprise me,' acknowledged Homer. 'All those towns along the Kansas–Missouri border are going crazy right now. All fighting each other. Everyone turning up dead all the time. Don't want to think what's going to happen to us when the war hits here. You ready to join the army, Bill?'

'I guess,' said Bill. 'I hope I get my chance, that's all.'

'Oh you'll get your chance, there's no doubt about that. The whole state's ready to burst into flames any minute. You and me, we'll be lucky if we live to see Christmas. Come on up the house, there's someone I want you to meet.'

The two young men walked slowly up the hill towards the Lee mansion. Bill had never been invited inside before but he had always wanted to go in. It was a large plantation-style ranch, although this was a union family, not a confederate one. They held no slaves, only free men, but Bill noticed that those men were

86

plentiful and did not look much happier just because they were getting the best part of a dollar every week and the word 'freedom' assigned to them. Homer took his wealth for granted; he had the privilege of being able to lead a dissolute and thoughtless youth, secure in the knowledge that he would never have to work for a living if he chose not to. As Bill entered the enormous white stone door of their mansion, he tried to compose himself and behave as if this world was one with which he was quite familiar. Afraid that he was staring around too much, he looked down at his feet instead and was drawn to the fact that of the two boys, Pony Express riders both, only one of them had a clean pair of boots with silver stirrups at their side.

'This way,' said Homer, leading his friend up the main stairway and through a small hallway which led to a pair of glass-tiled doors. He strode towards them confidently, a landowner in waiting. 'Come on,' he said, pausing for only a moment as he looked around and saw Bill standing nervously a few feet behind him. My great-grandfather could hear voices coming from within that room and was unsure about joining them. 'What's the matter?' he asked.

'Nothing,' said Bill, suddenly wishing he was elsewhere, his natural enthusiasm and sense of adventure deserting him for once. 'I was just . . . Do you think I should be in here?'

'You're my guest, ain't you?' asked Homer, hesitating for a moment before going back to Bill and putting an arm around his shoulder. He smiled at him, his white teeth gleaming, his skin brown and clear. Everything about him, Bill thought, testified to his easy upbringing. Not only did he have money, breeding and intelligence, the bastard was handsome too. 'Don't worry,' he added. 'I just want you to meet someone, that's all.'

He swung the doors open and stepped inside, taking Bill with him. Two men were sitting by the large, open fire, debating vigorously. A bottle of bourbon sat between them and the room was misty with cigar smoke. One of them, the man on the left, Bill recognised as Homer's father, Stanton Lee. They had never actually met but Bill had seen him from time to time wandering around the estate or riding in of an evening while he was sitting talking to Homer. The other man was a stranger to him.

'Father,' said Homer in a raised voice when it became clear that neither man was going to stop speaking and acknowledge them. 'There's someone I want to introduce you to.'

'What's that?' asked Stanton Lee, looking around irritably and squinting through the smoke. He was a fat, red man, mostly bald but what hair he had on the sides of his head he had grown long and they hung around his face like a curtain on either side. His voice had a strong Southern inflection and he looked as if standing would take some effort. Bill stood to his full height and stared right back at him.

'This is Bill Cody,' said Homer, pulling him forward. 'You've not met my father, have you Bill?' he added and my great-grandfather shook his head. He stepped forward and shook Stanton Lee's hand.

'Pleased to meet you, sir,' he said. 'I think maybe we've seen each other around and about.'

'Around and about where?' asked Stanton. 'Do we frequent the same gaming tables or is it in the local whorehouse that we run into each other of an evening?'

Bill stared at him, open mouthed, unsure what the correct response to such a question was. Stanton sucked on his cigar noisily and although he stared right back, he didn't seem to require an answer. Homer felt nothing of the awkwardness of the moment and took two glasses from the sideboard before sitting down on the sofa and indicating that Bill should join him. 'Over here,' he said, pointing at the second man, 'is a friend of my father's. The reason we came in here,' he added to the two older men, 'was because my friend Bill here has recently returned from Drewshank—'

'Lord save us,' muttered Stanton Lee, shaking his head as if even the name of the town was like a curse on them.

'Bill seemed to feel that there was trouble brewing down there. A murder of some sort the night before last. I thought maybe we should bring it to your attention, seeing as you like to be kept informed of troubles before they happen.'

'Seems to me the trouble's already happened,' said the second man in an even tone of voice 'On account of the murder having already taken place, that is. This is something of a . . . what do you call it . . . closing the barn door after the eh . . . after the . . .' He clicked his fingers several times in quick succession as he tried to remember the phrase.

'After the horse has fled,' said Homer. 'Yes, I know. I just thought we should mention it to you anyway. Senator, may I introduce Bill Cody to you. He's a Pony Express rider like me. Wants to join the army someday, he says. Wants to fight in a war.'

The man raised an eyebrow and extended a hand to Bill. Shaking it was like taking hold of the innards of a recently gutted fish. The fingers were long and waxy, as if he had died some weeks previously, and the shake was weak and effeminate. 'Only a fool wants to fight in a war,' he muttered. 'Jim Lane,' he added after a moment through his thin lips. 'Pleased to meet you, Mr Cody.'

'And you sir,' said Bill, wondering whether he could wipe his hand on the seat beside him without it appearing too obvious. 'You've been to Drewshank too then?'

'Not in some time,' said Lane. 'Although I may be there, or thereabouts, quite soon.'

'We're going to wipe those confederate bastards off the face of the earth,' said Stanton suddenly, leaning forward and pointing his finger at the two boys. 'You know what we just heard they've done now? They only went down into—'

Before he could finish his sentence, Lane had placed a hand on Stanton's arm, tapping it twice quickly to indicate that these were not matters for open discussion as yet and certainly not in front of a couple of greenbacks like Homer and Bill.

'Senator Lane represented Kansas for some years,' said Homer, to fill a quiet moment. 'He's not in the senate now but he keeps himself . . . busy, politically speaking.' Bill nodded his head quickly. He knew of Senator Lane, for he had been the Kansan senator throughout Bill's own childhood, but he had not made the connection at first. He had a reputation of fierce loyalty to the union and he was not a man who minced his words, having brought himself to the point of censure on several occasions while serving in the Capitol. Since his retirement from public office, he had returned to the state of his birth but he had not stepped away from active duties as he moved from the acceptable face of the senate to the more dangerous world of hands-on warfare.

'The senator,' continued Homer, 'leads a group of jay-hawkers down near the—'

'That is not a word which we use to describe our-selves, young man,' said Lane in a loud, brusque voice. 'And I'll thank you not to use it in my presence. We are union men, that is all. That's a good enough term for me.'

'He leads a group *of union men*,' Homer corrected himself with a slightly disrespectful tone in his voice, 'who are waging war along the state borders at the moment. The confederates are afraid of them,' he added in a proud tone of voice.

'The confederates are *not* afraid of us,' said Lane quietly, looking across at Stanton Lee, who nodded in agreement with that sentiment. 'They are too strong in their beliefs to waste time fearing their enemies. The enemy is there to attack, not to have emotional feelings towards.'

Homer nodded and looked a little disappointed. He was trying to show support for both his father and the senator but appeared to be failing on both counts. Now it was his turn to wonder whether he should make a hasty retreat. Before thinking of a way, however, the senator asked a question of him.

'What's a fellow like you doing riding around in the Pony Express anyway?' he asked Homer, ignoring Bill as if the job was just about menial enough for a fellow like him. 'Why aren't you fighting for your beliefs too? Ain't an army uniform fancy enough for you?' he asked, glancing up and down at the boy's Pony Express outfit with disdain.

'My son has very few beliefs, I'm afraid,' said Stanton Lee, affecting a tone of mock self-pity. 'He finds the hardships of riding his pony around the countryside all day just about as much as he can handle, what with having to concentrate on his drinking and womanising so much.'

'It's a worthwhile job,' protested Homer, keeping his voice civil, knowing that he would be wrong to embarrass his father in front of a man like Senator Lane. 'Somebody has to do it.'

'Well this Bill Cody fellow can do it, can't he?' said Lane. 'So why don't you come with me tonight, eh? We could do with lads like you. You're fit and healthy, ain't you?'

'This Bill Cody fellow,' echoed Homer through gritted teeth, 'is the reason why I came in here in the first place. He's the one who wants to see more action. He's the one who wants to join the war, not me. I thought you might like to meet him for that very reason.'

For the first time, Lane turned his attentions to my great-grandfather and he studied him up and down carefully. Bill stayed silent; he felt slightly irritated that his friend had failed to inform him of his intentions before offering him up to a potentially fatal new employment. However, that was balanced with his excitement about joining the jayhawkers. Even if it was a term that the senator did not like to employ, it was common currency among people of the neighbouring states and those of one mind with the jayhawkers saw them as heroes and adventurers all. The Pony Express had been fine, but this was something else. This was what he had been dreaming of: war. A chance to prove himself.

'You want to come fight with us, boy?' asked Lane and Bill nodded enthusiastically.

'Surely,' he said. 'I know all about what the jayhawk – what you union men do, I mean.'

'You're of a mind with us then?'

'I am. And I've killed before. I killed an Indian when I was a boy.'

Lane laughed bitterly and shook his head. 'Well for Christ's sake don't say it like it's a badge of honour,' he said. He paused and thought about it for a moment. 'You got family around here?' he asked. 'People who might object to me taking you away to certain death?'

'None at all,' came the reply. 'My family are all out in Iowa. Least I think they are as I haven't seen them in a couple of years now.'

'Well, very few of my boys have,' said Lane sadly before nodding his head quickly and enthusiastically. 'All right then. You want to come fight with us, you're welcome to. You're welcome, I say,' he repeated, smiling briefly for the first time and shaking Bill's hand again, an unpleasant experience. 'It will be something to have two fine lads like you fighting alongside us. We'll show them Missouri devils a thing or two, am I right?'

Homer had been grinning away like a Cheshire cat while Lane had been warming to Bill but the smile disappeared from his face now quickly. 'Two?' he asked. 'No, I think you've got it wrong, Senator. I was just bringing Bill in to introduce him to you. I thought you might have a place for him. But I'm happy where I am right now, thanks very much.'

'With the Pony Express?' asked Lane with disdain. 'When there's a war to be fought? What kind of yellow son of a bitch are you anyway?' His words were insulting but the tone he used made them sound on the right side of good humoured so that Homer would be unable to take offence.

'Seems to me it could be the making of you, boy,' said Stanton Lee, blowing huge rings of cigar smoke towards his son so that it seemed as if the matter was already settled. 'What do you say, Bill? Would you be willing to have a brother-in-arms fighting alongside you down there on the borders?'

Bill opened his mouth and looked from father to son with uncertainty. He could hardly say no, but he did not want to drag his friend into a situation which he did not want to be part of. Instead he decided to assume that the question had been rhetorical and sat back and said nothing instead. Homer Lee looked miserable. This interview had not gone at all according to plan.

'Well that's settled then,' said Senator Lane, slapping a hand down on the side of the chair and coming alive at last, as if his whole day had been only geared towards the recruitment of fresh jayhawkers. 'Your father here has kindly offered me a bed for the night but we'll be leaving at the crack of dawn for Lawrence. So you boys better get off and get some rest now. From now on you'll be taking your orders from me.'

They stood up and shook hands with the two men. Closing the door behind them, Bill grabbed his friend's arm enthusiastically but was disappointed to observe how pale Homer's face was.

'You all right?' he asked, and the older boy nodded slowly.

'That'll teach me,' he said, his voice low and unhappy. 'Try finding a way out of this now.'

'I don't want a way out of it,' said Bill, his voice betraying his excitement. 'What's wrong with you anyway? Don't you want to fight?'

'I don't have a problem with fighting,' explained Homer. 'Dying don't seem like such a good deal though.' Bill frowned, unsure how to answer his friend but he didn't receive an opportunity for the older boy walked

94

away towards his room. 'The senator's right,' he said as he disappeared out of sight. 'We'd better get some sleep if we're to go fight a war tomorrow.'

My great-grandfather went to fight in a war, a lot of which was centred around one of the oldest conflicts the world had known: the issue of slavery. At the same age that he was putting on his uniform and having sleepless nights at the thought of having his head blown off at any moment, I had never set foot outside London, was still attending school each day in my uniform, and was living in a small, two-bedroom terraced house with my ageing father, who had made a pass at my sixteen-year-old girlfriend while I had been out of the room.

It was a few weeks after Agnes had first met Isaac that I heard what had actually happened that day. We were in a coffee shop, with Adam and Justin and a girl that Adam was trying to impress, drinking cappuccinos and pretending that they were merely a symbol of the bohemian lifestyle we would shortly be living, once we left school. The girl Adam was with – I think her name was Claire – had taken umbrage at a comment Agnes had made earlier and was sulking quietly, her nose buried in her coffee cup as Adam attempted to fill the awkward moments with chatter. Eventually, the conversation turned to older men and women, and who we would be attracted to outside of our age group. Everyone named a few people but when it came to Agnes's turn, she shrugged and said she didn't go for anyone over twenty.

'No one?' asked Claire sarcastically as if she could read Agnes's mind and knew that she was lying. 'Not even . . . like, Richard Gere?'

'Not if you paid me,' said Agnes, maintaining her

composure. 'I don't like it when older guys hit on me. I'm sorry, I just don't.'

'I'm three months younger than Agnes,' I pointed out with a laugh and she gave me a cool smile in return.

'Your father hit on me, you know,' she said suddenly, out of the blue and we all stopped talking and stared at her. The smile froze on my face and I looked at her in disbelief.

'What?' I asked. 'What did you say?'

She looked away from me. 'I said your father hit on me. And he's an older guy. Way older, actually. But relax, like I said I don't go for older guys.'

'He's very much an older guy,' Adam pointed out.

'What do you mean he hit on you?' I spluttered, refusing to believe her and wondering why she was stating this so casually. 'When did he . . . what did he do?'

'That afternoon that I was around in your house,' she said, and to her credit she looked a little shamefaced now, as if she had regretted bringing up the subject in the first place. 'You went out of the room for a bit and—'

'When? When did I?'

'I don't know,' she said with a sigh. 'You probably went upstairs to fix up your little Cowboys and Indians, I can't remember. All I know is you went out for a couple of minutes and he came over to me and . . . well, he hit on me.'

'What did he do?' asked Adam, leering at her. Claire staring at her with wide eyes.

'It doesn't matter what he did. You know when someone's hitting on you, okay?'

'She's right,' said Claire, determined to be part of this. 'The same thing happened to me one time with

96

this guy who—'

'What are you talking about?' I said, my stomach churning inside as this information settled into my brain. 'Are you serious or are you kidding around? If you're kidding around, just tell me because this is . . . this is . . .'

'Jesus, William, I'm sorry I brought it up,' she said, putting her cup down dramatically on the table. 'Forget about it, all right? Maybe I made a mistake.'

'You just said you know when someone's hitting on you!' I shouted. 'How could you have made a mistake?'

'Hey, it's not her fault, whatever happened,' said Claire and all three of us shot her a *stay-out-of-it* look.

'I can look after myself, Claire,' said Agnes quickly. There was a tense silence for a minute or two as I tried to piece this together in my head. I was growing more and more angry inside, but I was also amazed because throughout all the years since my mother's departure, Isaac had never displayed any interest in other women, had never brought one home to meet me, never asked one out, had slept alone every night for twelve years. In my arrogance, I had assumed that in his sixties he had put all thoughts of romance outside of his head. The idea of him showing an interest in a woman felt strange to me. The thought that it could be my girlfriend, some- one forty-five years younger than himself, made me feel sick. I stood up.

'I'm going home,' I said.

'*Jesus*, William, don't be such a fucking drama queen,' said Justin and I shot him an angry look.

'Let him go if he wants to go,' said Agnes, always unwilling to be the one who asked me to stay. 'If you want to be a child about this, go right ahead. You're only embarrassing yourself.'

I stared at her in disbelief. 'How is this my fault?' I asked her angrily. 'You're the one who—'

'I'm the one who what? If you've done nothing, I've *definitely* done nothing. I'm the innocent party here. So just sit down and finish your coffee and let's get the hell out of here.'

'I've got something I've got to do,' I said. 'I'll see you later.' I stormed out of the coffee shop and went across the road to the bus shelter, seething inside, willing her to come out and join me. If she cared about me at all, I thought, she'd check on me to see if I was all right. She wouldn't let me go in such anger. In the distance I could see the double-decker bus which could take me home picking up passengers at the previous stop. The traffic was heavy and it would be another couple of minutes before it reached me. I was torn between a desire to go back inside and be with Agnes, and the need to go home and confront Isaac. Either way I had to be actively doing something and standing there, waiting for the bus to make its way slowly down the road, was driving me crazy. She never appeared so when it arrived, I got on.

Isaac wasn't home yet but I had already resolved in my head what I would do. I went to the shed in our back garden and found a large cardboard box and brought it upstairs and set it on the floor outside my bedroom, and then I got to work. The first thing to come down was the cowboy posters on the wall, and the large sepia photograph of Red Cloud, the leader of the Oglala Lakota, which had been staring at each other on either side of my bedroom for as long as I could remember. The tape which held them up was stiff and came away from the wall easily and I wondered how they had managed to survive this long. Taking only a moment to draw a breath of courage, I held the posters at their sides and crumpled them up into large balls, tossing them out of the room and into the centre of the cardboard box with accuracy, like basketballs into a hoop. Next I tackled the series of armies who had been chasing each other around my shelves since my childhood, never catching their prey, always hunting each other down determinedly. I took great clumps of them in my hands and carried them out of the room, throwing them away too. Members of the Fifth Cavalry, confederate soldiers, union jayhawkers all disappeared, along with the Cheyenne, the Comanche, the Arapoha, all of whom had been living in mutual harmony for the best part of sixteen years; every type and species of man which the American west had claimed as her own landed in a heap in the box, a mass grave for these little plastic warriors.

The memorabilia came next, the toy guns, the lassoes, the wooden replica of the Deadwood stagecoach – the original of which my great-grandfather would one day take on the *State of Nebraska* across the ocean from New York to London – the Indian headset with feathers and band which had been one of my most treasured possessions as a child; all of them were discarded until the box was overflowing and I had to get another. My room was being stripped bare as I took each element of my childhood and my father's obsessions and discarded them one by one. Finally I arrived at the enormous model of Fort Laramie, where three of the most important treaties between the government and the Indian people had been signed during the 1850s and 1860s, which stood on my desk. Isaac and I had built it together when I was a child and it had taken us the best part of two months to complete it. It was heavy and complicated but as we had not taken as much care as we should have, I had always been very cautious when handling it, afraid that it would fall and break if due care and attention was not taken. Out of habit, I picked it up gingerly and carried it out of the room. I stood holding it over the box for a few moments, knowing that this was it, the final act of revenge, before letting it fall to the ground, where it crashed noisily, some pieces of it falling off and breaking. I lifted my foot and let it crash down on top of it, destroying the Fort and sending pieces of it spinning around the carpet.

At last it was done and my room looked empty. I had never seen such space in it before and realised how few possessions I actually had which could truly be called my own. I brushed my hands against each other in order to clear off the dust and turned, intending to leave the room now and bring the boxes outside to where the bin men might collect them later, and jumped to see Isaac standing in the doorway, his frame melting even before my eyes as he stared inside the room in disbelief, wondering what had happened, what had made me take my memories and his history and simply throw them away. I stared at him and swallowed nervously, my anger of an hour earlier satisfied now and altered into a slight nervousness and embarrassment at what I had done. Isaac looked at me and shook his head sadly, his mouth opening and closing as he tried to find words. The thought of Agnes came into my mind now and I flinched, my hands tightening into fists, and without a word, without any explanation I walked slowly to the door and closed it in his pale and unhappy face.

I would not be a child any more.

Chapter Four

East and West

My great-grandfather went to live at Fort Lawrence, Kansas, the headquarters of the jayhawkers, that group of men who were organising sorties against the confederate bushwhackers of the Kansas–Missouri border and killing as many of those men in battle as they possibly could. It didn't take long for Bill and Homer Lee to settle into life at the barracks and their experience riding for long distances at a time as part of the Pony Express saw them join a gang of scouts and spend the majority of their time galloping across the prairie lands, where my great-grandfather always felt the most at home.

They bunked upstairs in a house run by a Mrs Theodore Adams. The lower part of the house was a small saloon and the rooms upstairs were mostly used by young jayhawkers such as them. Lawrence itself was a thriving town with several saloons, a schoolhouse, a whorehouse and a couple of grocery stores to its name, and the boys made frequent use of all except the schoolhouse during their stay there. They saw little of Jim Lane after their arrival there; once he had signed them up to his cause he had little more personal use for them and instead introduced them to Patch Bellows, the officer who dictated where the scouts should go each day. From time to time they would run into Lane in the town but on such occasions he centred his attentions on Homer, asking whether he had heard from his father recently, and more importantly whether he had written to him himself, and mostly ignored Bill, who seemed unworthy of his consideration.

'We're not seeing the fighting I expected,' complained Bill one evening, lying back in his bunk with his arms folded behind his head. 'All this scouting, there's got to be more we could be doing. I want to see some action, some adventure!'

'We could go out and get ourselves killed,' suggested Homer. 'Would that help?'

'I don't mean that,' replied Bill with a sigh. 'I just mean that all we seem to do is ride around the prairies all day long, watching them bushwhackers from a distance and reporting back to officers who don't seem to care much anyway. Why can't we go down and fight a few sometime, Homer? Show them what we're about.'

'Because there's two of us and usually twenty or thirty of them,' replied Homer. 'Why do you think, you damn fool? Do you *want* to get yourself shot to pieces, is that it? That's not going to help much when it comes to you being the great adventurer, is it?'

Bill said nothing for a time, and simply lay back and brooded instead. He knew Homer was right; there were certain jobs that had to be done and unfortunately for him, he was involved in doing one which did not fill him with excitement. He still enjoyed the freedom of the plains and the prairies but that freedom was curtailed by the detailed instructions that Patch Bellows gave them every morning of where they should go, who they should watch and what time they should return.

Meanwhile, William Quantrill, the leading confederate who was Jim Lane's sworn nemesis, was moving closer and closer towards the border with his army. After several bloody skirmishes, reinforcements had been sent from Lawrence to help out the jayhawkers closer to the river. For the time being they were holding them off, but there was trouble in store. The scent of battle was moving closer and closer towards the fort and when news came of Quantrill's sacking of Bunkport, some twenty miles to the south of Lawrence, the air at their camp became increasingly troubled.

'They took Bunkport with no more than thirty men,' shouted Patch Bellows at a fort meeting during that week. Most of the officers and soldiers, including Bill and Homer Lee, were in attendance, listening for Jim Lane's assessment of what had taken place, and what they should do next in order to secure their own safety. 'And over three hundred lived there!' he added. 'That's the kind of force we've got to be prepared for. We need to get the army to send reinforcements or we face certain death.'

'What happened at Bunkport was an anomaly,' countered Lane, and although his voice was strong and deep enough to carry above and across them, when he spoke the room tended to silence, for he was both respected and feared in equal portions. 'Bunkport was not an army town after all. Civilians lived there, not trained soldiers. They were ill-prepared for fighting. Maybe that was our fault,' he admitted, shrugging his shoulders slightly as though blame was not a currency he often traded in. 'Maybe we should have sent—'

'Civilians or not,' called out Sam Greeley, interrupting the senator. 'They were people that some of us knew. I've got a sister lives in Bunkport with her family.

Quantrill put her out of her home and burned it to the ground. Where's she to go now? Can you tell me that?'

'Sam, I sympathise with you and your family, of course I do,' replied Lane quickly, silencing the shouts with a raised hand and a firmness in his voice that suggested he wasn't going to get carried away into either sentimentality or personalities. 'But it's like I say – they were not army folk. They didn't know what to do when the enemy came calling. We will be prepared. I tell you that now, people. We will be prepared. And we will fight to the death if necessary.'

True to his word, plans were quickly put in place to defend themselves for the inevitable moment when the confederates attacked Lawrence but it became something of a contradiction to have a fort of soldiers determined to push forwards and join in the war, and then order them to remain in that fort awaiting the arrival of the enemy. Bill wasn't happy with it and was one of a group of men who petitioned Lane in private to be allowed to set forth for the border in groups. Bill's voice as a leader had grown substantially since he had joined the jayhawkers. Although he was still younger than many of the men who had been there before him, his determination and bravery had seen him earn the respect of the other men. He had stopped telling his Indian story too and relied not on his own narratives but on his deeds to forge himself a reputation. But Lane was adamant; there were plans to be made, he insisted. They would be ready for Quantrill when he came.

In late August, 1863, Bill and Homer Lee, along with four or five other men were riding slowly along the mountains near Lawrence, another quiet day of uneventful scouting coming to an end. The sun was drifting slowly down behind them and they were ready to begin their move back to the fort, but broke first for a rest and some water and to allow the horses some time to regain their strength. They lay down on the mountain top, leaning against the rocks for support, some with their eyes closed and their hats pulled down over their faces and talked for a change of things other than war and killing. One of the men had a sweetheart at the fort and he planned to ask her to marry him. His name was Angel Law and his father had been sheriff at Bunkport, the town which had recently fallen to the confederate bushwhackers. Both Law's father and mother had been killed that day, along with his sister Elsie, and he had been deeply bitter and upset for some time; his sweetheart had kept close to him during the worst moments and he felt ready to propose now, seeking some kind of return to the family life which had been stolen from him. The other men teased him gently over his romance, but envied him at the same time for his intended was a well-liked girl, and they were happy for him. Had it been any other man, lewd comments might have been made about the speed with which Angel wanted the marriage to take place, but circumstances being what they were, this was avoided.

'I think I'm going to take her away from Lawrence,' said Angel quietly, taking a sip from his water bottle as he looked off into the distance, away from where the fort lay and in a different direction to Bunkport as well; he looked towards a place he had never been before, somewhere out beyond the horizon.

'You're leaving the jayhawkers?' asked Homer Lee, surprised, for it was a rare man that ever did that. It was generally thought that there were only three ways out: the war could end, you could desert, or you could be killed. The first seemed impossible, the second unthinkable and the third was an option they didn't like to consider at all.

'Might do,' replied Angel. 'I've been speaking to Senator Lane about it. He said I could do worse than become a sheriff myself. Like my father,' he added, his voice a shade quieter. The men nodded sagely and looked at the ground in silence for a moment. 'He knows a few towns up north that are looking for men,' he continued after a respectful pause. 'Said he'd put in a good word for me. I think Candice might go for it, don't you reckon?'

'I think anyone offered a chance to get away from all this madness would be a fool not to take it,' said Homer Lee in a resigned tone.

'It's not that I'm afraid to stay,' said Angel.

'No one would think that,' interrupted Bill, who liked Angel and had befriended him from the start. He was an admirer of Candice's too – Angel's intended fiancée – but he had never expressed his feelings, knowing that her heart belonged to only one man.

'Some might say it though,' said Angel. 'And that worries me because I don't want anyone to think I'd be running from a fight.'

'There's plenty of fights up north, I dare say,' said another man chirpily. 'Lots of opportunities to get yourself shot all over this damn country. Don't think you'll be escaping them anyway.'

Angel smiled. 'It's just a thought for now anyway,' he said eventually. 'I'd have to speak to Candice first. I have to ask her to marry me first,' he added. 'But that's tonight's job.'

'Well then, we best get back to the fort,' said Bill, standing up and brushing the dirt from the seat of his pants. 'Never let it be said that Bill Cody stood in the way of true romance when he—' He broke off and looked around him nervously. Something was stirring.

'What's up, Bill?' asked Homer Lee, and Bill put a finger to his mouth quickly, urging the men to stay quiet for a moment. They all listened. No one could hear a thing.

'You don't hear that?' asked Bill eventually, looking around at them as if he was going mad. They shook their heads one by one, looking at their friend as if he had lost his mind. There was silence for a moment and Bill was about to speak again, about to say they should head for home when Angel spoke.

'I hear it,' he said and the tone of his voice made the men shiver, for they heard it as well now and they knew what was coming. They looked over the edge of the mountain and in the distance they could hear the pounding hooves of the horses and could see, gradually becoming more and more visible in the darkening evening, the blue and red insignias of the confederate bushwhackers. Had they been closer to that army, they would have seen the thin, determined face of William Quantrill at their head, flanked by Bloody Bill Anderson, the terrifying mass murderer who had led the charge at Bunkport, and Frank James, brother of Jesse, who was there as a paid mercenary, bringing his band of loyal followers with him. In all, 450 men and their horses galloped across the prairie towards Fort Lawrence that evening, determined that by the end of the night, they would be dining there.

Bill and his friends cursed their luck and rushed to their horses but from their vantage point at the top of the mountains it was a difficult and dangerous ride back down the mountain and although they all made it safely, it took time as the horses were unsure of their footing and an error could have seen them toppling over the canyons to their death on the ground below.

The fort at Lawrence was merely the central focal point of a thriving town, and when the confederates arrived there, it was closing down for the night, the wives and children already asleep in their homes, most of the men there too, the others in the saloons drinking or playing cards. They heard the sounds of the horses and when they came to their windows, the town was already being overrun by bushwhackers. Jim Lane was asleep in his bed and being awoken by his wife when Patch Bellows took to the steps of the courthouse, not twenty feet from Quantrill and called out to him. The town went quiet as they waited for the brief exchange of words.

'What do you want?' shouted Bellows, feeling naked without his gun and his jacket, unaware that he even still held a glass of whisky in his right hand. 'What are you doing here, Quantrill? We'll rouse you out of it, I warn you.'

'What's your name?' called Quantrill.

'Patch Bellows,' came the reply.

Quantrill nodded for a moment before signalling to his accomplice Bloody Bill Anderson who, without a moment's hesitation, raised his gun and shot Bellows clean through his one good eye. He fell dead to the ground and, dramatic to the last, Anderson raised his gun aloft and blew the smoke away from his face. The people stared in shock at what had happened, and horror at the thought of what might come next.

'Now,' said Quantrill, his voice clear and ringing. 'Cleanse this town.'

Within seconds, his army were shooting people at will, the townsfolk running and screaming back to their houses even as the confederates pulled them out, ripping at their limbs, shooting every man, woman and child they could see. Families were torn from their homes and the buildings set on fire.

Bill, Homer Lee and the others arrived at the height of the town's destruction to see a band of laughing teenage boys on horses shooting small children who were standing on the porches in terror. Bill circled back towards the courthouse, where he saw Patch Bellows's body lying out on the steps. The town was in flames and it became difficult for anyone to see who was union and who was confederate, the only giveaway being that the ones who lay dead on the ground tended to the former. My great-grandfather lost sight of his colleagues for a time as he broke into the mêlée and killed several confederates himself until, from a distance, he could see the man who he was sure was Quantrill himself. His picture, a daguerreotype, had been reproduced in the newspapers and on posters in the town and his was a familiar, nightmare face. He was riding his horse a little removed from the action, observing as his men plundered and killed, burned and shot. Bill reached for his reins, intending to ride towards the confederate leader and put a bullet in his head, aware that he would surely be killed himself within moments of that killing, but before he could move he was almost knocked off his horse by the force and speed of Angel Law, who had also spotted Quantrill and was making towards him with a fury unmatched by any there. Bill watched and saw Quantrill slowly turn his head, aware that something dangerous was coming his way, and Angel Law lifted his gun and aimed it squarely at the head of his father's killer. Quantrill's mouth opened in silent understanding. There was only a split second left to him and his hand was too far from his side to reach for his gun. In that moment, Bill thought he could see resignation on the face of the confederate leader and wondered how someone could be so immune to thoughts of death that he could stare it in the face and not so much as flinch. Perhaps he was aware that his time had not yet come, because before Angel Law's finger could close on the trigger, he was shot in the head by an unknown confederate. Quantrill barely watched, merely grabbing the reins of his own horse and disappearing into the smoky haze which the fires and the gunshots had created. The Fort Lawrence massacre; a confederate victory.

I was nineteen years old when I fled England. Adam and I, in need of a break from our humdrum lives, had saved our money and with no particular destination in mind, had gone to a travel agency and scanned the brochures for ideas. Our plan was to travel somewhere remote and completely alien to us; that ruled out Europe or America. I had been determined anyway not to go anywhere near the areas of the American west where so much of my fantasy childhood had been spent. Although it interested me still and there was a part of me that wanted to see the places which I had only heard about, my life had been too dominated by those stories and I needed a change. In the end we chose Japan for no other reason than it was distant and exotic and spent six weeks engaged on a crash course to bring our language skills up to beginner level. The plan was to teach English to those Japanese children who had not already been snapped up by students on their gap years and travel from place to place, perhaps eventually moving on towards Thailand, Singapore or even New

Zealand. We were in no hurry; neither of us had any meaningful employment, nor were we desirous of any, and we had little intentions at that point of going to college. We were both trying to get away, that was all.

Although my two friends and I had remained close throughout our youth, Justin decided not to join us on our travels, being more interested in a future career and college place than we were and in his own ambitions as a musician. He had been writing songs since childhood and had a decent voice too and, like half the people of our age at the time, was trying to set up a band. Neither Adam nor I had any fixed ideas about our futures. I had vague notions towards writing and liked the idea of being a journalist on a London music paper, but notions were all they were. I did nothing to achieve that ambition but it was a stock answer whenever anyone quizzed me on my plans for the future. Adam's mother had died earlier that year and he had gone through a difficult time, but he was slowly coming out of it and it had initially been his idea that we should buy a one-way ticket somewhere and see what happened. I jumped at the opportunity.

'I don't know what you think you're going to achieve over there that you can't achieve here,' Isaac commented, unhappy about our plans but unable to do anything to stop me, now that I was officially an adult. 'You should be starting to make a living rather than gallivanting around the world.' He protested a lot and placed numerous objections in my way but I took each one with equal good humour, unwilling to start a fight, hoping that we could part on the best possible terms. In the end however, despite my best intentions, it was a chilly departure. He didn't come to the airport to see me off, but insisted on carrying my rucksack to our waiting taxi, and shaking my hand rather than hugging me as I said goodbye. It would be some time before I would see him again.

We landed, exhausted but eager, in Narita, Tokyo's International Airport, twelve hours after leaving London on a hot, clammy evening in late May. Naturally, most of the signs were written in Japanese characters and I was seized with a sudden fear upon landing, the recognition that for the first time in my life I was in a foreign land with a language and alphabet I could not recognise. The sense of isolation terrified me at first. The faces of the people were unfamiliar to me, the sounds and smells of the airport separate to those of Heathrow Airport, or the tube, or the South-West train line which took me to and from my home, not far from Clapham Junction. I swallowed nervously and looked across at Adam whose face betrayed the same instant feeling of terror as my own.

'What do we do now?' I asked quietly, grateful that it was he and not I who held the guidebook; it implied that he was obliged to take charge. 'How do we get out of here?'

'We need to get into the centre of Tokyo,' he said in as confident a voice as he could muster. 'We can figure things out from there.' We had already arranged a stay for three nights in a cheap hotel in the centre of the city, having decided that it would be best if we had somewhere comfortable to stay during our first few days of relocation and adjustment. 'So we just need to find a train . . .' We stared around us with a certain feeling of impotence. The airport terminal was crowded, and the people were rushing back and forth as if their very lives depended on it. After a few moments of staring around blindly, I tapped his arm and pointed at a sign

112

which had a picture of a train drawn helpfully beside the word *densha*. It pointed towards an escalator and we stepped on board, allowing it to take us to the lower terminal where, by following the signs, we arrived at a platform and bought a ticket for the *Keisei tokkyu* service for Tokyo Station. The trip took just over an hour and I enjoyed it, knowing that this was the last time we could let responsibility slip from our shoulders for the foreseeable future.

The hot air had turned to drizzle by the time we reached the central train station and – although I would have thought it impossible – it was even more crowded than the airport terminal we had left. What seemed like millions of people charged through, shoulder to shoulder, a shifting snake of bodies carrying the Japanese people, all dressed alike in business suits, from the entrances to the trains and back again. We managed to force our way through however, our rucksacks weighing us down inconveniently, and I felt an urge to close my eyes and sleep.

'We'll get a taxi when we get out of here,' shouted Adam, looking back to check that I was still behind him. 'This is madness.'

I was pleased that he had said this, and looked forward to arriving at a hotel where I might relax away from all these people and this noise. I wondered why we hadn't chosen New York or Sydney, Milan or Paris, rather than this insane city but kept repeating in my head that I had only just arrived and that it would take time to adjust. Once out on the street, a number of *takushii* passed us by and we attempted to wave them down, but it was only from consulting our guidebook that we realised that those with the red lights on were free, while the green meant occupied, quite the opposite of what one might have expected. The Daimaru department store opposite us had music blaring from it and heavily laden shoppers with varying looks of stress or panic on their faces poured from its doors like water through a broken dam.

'Do you know where we're going?' I asked Adam, hoping for reassurance, and he nodded quickly, pulling a piece of paper from his back pocket.

'I wrote it down,' he said, showing me the name of the hotel we had booked written in both Western lettering and Japanese script. I nodded and thrust my arm out just as a red-lighted *takushii* approached us and he pulled up abruptly throwing open the door for us and we climbed inside eagerly 'Domo arigato,' said Adam immediately – *thank you* – practising one of the phrases we had both acquired from our Berlitz tapes over the previous month and a half. The taxi driver responded quickly, whatever he said taking the best part of thirty seconds to end, and we both blinked and swallowed nervously. He spun around then, a small, thin man of about thirty, with a gold medallion around his neck and a dirty white cap on his head, and reached back for the piece of paper Adam was holding, grabbing it off him, glancing at it briefly, and pulling away from the kerb. Tourists were obviously nothing new to him.

We swept along the streets of Tokyo, narrowly avoiding killing half the natives, as Adam and I gripped the edges of our seats nervously. Our driver negotiated the roads with only one hand on the steering wheel, the other stretched across the back of the passenger seat as if his wife or sweetheart was sitting there, but seemed able to drive at sixty miles an hour through narrow streets without either causing an accident or breaking into a sweat. About five minutes later we pulled up outside the Yaesu Terminal Hotel – we could have easily walked the distance had we known our way around the city – and paid our fare before stepping inside.

'*Konbanwa*,' said Adam, bowing formally at the desk, his forehead almost touching the small golden bell which was used to attract the bellboys. The action produced a look of astonishment on the face of the receptionist, who looked about twelve years old but was probably twice that. I suspected his performance was slightly over the top.

'*Konbanwa*,' she replied, not returning his bow. *Good evening*.

'*Yoyaku shimashita*,' he continued – *I have a reservation* – another stock phrase committed to memory at an earlier date.

'*Hai, shitsurei desu ga o-namae wa?*' inquired the girl, tapping away at her computer while barely looking at either of us. *Yes, what is your name, please?* Adam stared at her and smiled and I was pleased that the question had been directed towards him and not me. '*Shitsurei desu ga o-namae wa?*' she repeated, looking at him now suspiciously and he turned and looked at me in confusion, already beaten by the first piece of conversation that had come our way. I shrugged and bit my lip; I felt like laughing, the situation seemed so ridiculous. I looked back at the girl who was looking me up and down now with a frown and opened my mouth to speak, before realising I had nothing whatsoever to say and closing it again.

'Your names?' she said with a sigh, knowing that we could be there all night if she did not give in to us a little. 'What are your names?'

'Oh, our *names*,' said Adam, relieved that she could

115

speak English, his voice sounding as if he had merely misheard her the first two times. 'Adam Spears,' he said, raising a finger to indicate that that was he, 'and William Cody,' he continued, pointing over at me. The receptionist tapped away busily at her computer, making a few notes on a pad of paper, before disappearing into a back room for a few minutes without a word. We hovered from foot to foot nervously; I think we were both terrified to admit our fear that our reservation had been lost and didn't want to say it out loud in case it would be tempting fate. I noticed an old Japanese man sitting by the window staring at us. He wore a pair of glasses with lime-green lenses, which struck me as somewhat unusual. He was nodding his head quickly up and down as if agreeing with some internal conversation. Although he appeared to be looking directly at Adam and me, I felt he didn't even see us and wondered whether this was the way he passed his days now, an old man in a hotel lobby, nodding for something to do. Eventually the receptionist reappeared, and now she had a key in her hand which had a room number printed in several scripts – 124 – and she pointed down the hallway towards the elevators before turning away from us dismissively.

Assuming that our work there was done we walked away and were shortly inside the small room which would be our home for the next five nights. It was cramped and had two short, thin beds separated only by a bedside table with a lamp on it, but they looked inviting and I could hardly wait to crawl inside one of them and get some sleep. The window opened on to the street and the sounds of the people and the cars carried up noisily but I didn't mind, as such things rarely bother me. We had a small bathroom with a shower stall and

I debated whether I would take a hot shower before sleeping but decided against.

'I'm going to take one anyway,' said Adam opening his rucksack and pulling out a towel. 'I think I'm into my second wind and it might knock me out.'

'What time should we get up at?' I asked him, looking at my watch and wondering what time it was back in London.

'It doesn't matter,' he replied. 'Let's not set any alarms. Sleep as long as we sleep. We probably need it.'

I nodded in agreement and took off my runners, my T-shirt and jeans and stroked my chin casually to see whether I would need a shave when I did wake up. I brushed my teeth carefully at the sink and looked in the mirror at the dark bags forming under my eyes. 'I look like death,' I said, yawning even as I hit the end of the sentence.

'You'll be fine,' Adam replied, rooting around for his soap. 'You're just tired.'

'Yeah,' I said, stepping back into the bedroom as he disappeared inside the bathroom for his shower. I closed the door behind him and a moment later heard the water pour into the basin, and then its more muffled sound as he stepped beneath the spray. He began to sing quietly and I smiled to myself; he had a good voice but terrible taste in music. 'Right then,' I muttered to myself, closing the curtains and stepping towards the bed closest to the wall where I had placed my rucksack after coming into the room. I was about to climb into bed when my attention was taken by three small framed photographs on the wall and curiosity made me step towards them to see what they were. The photos were each about a metre away from each other, one over my bed, one over Adam's, and one between the two. On the left there was a picture of an old Japanese man and his wife in a formal pose, their hands locked together at waist height, looking for all the world as if they were the unhappiest couple in the Far East. On the right – mysteriously – was a photo of the Eiffel Tower. I couldn't quite see the relevance of it in a Tokyo hotel and almost muttered some comment to myself before I looked at the centre picture, when my tired eyes opened wide in surprise and my mouth dropped. 'I don't believe it,' I said, stepping forward and peering at the brown sepia print of a middle-aged man with an impressive moustache, standing in profile to the camera, his cheekbones well defined, the line of his jaw sharp and imposing. Beneath the photograph, but within the frame, was the name of the subject, written in English. *'Buffalo' Bill Cody*, it said in clear Times New Roman. *1846–1917*. Although I did not realise it at the time, the photograph was taken by Ellen Rose, of whom I would learn more in time. I shook my head in disbelief and reached a finger out to touch the face of my great-grandfather, stunned that he should appear before me only hours after my arrival on the other side of the world. In his hands he held a gun, and I recognised it only too well, for it had been pinned to the wall of my London living room for as long as I could remember.

I might have stared at it for hours, but the sound of the shower water being switched off in the bathroom snapped me out of my reverie and I climbed into bed immediately. I imagined that I would lie awake for some time, thinking about this coincidence, but I felt myself grow sleepy immediately, barely hearing Adam's voice as he climbed into his own saying *'Oyasumininasai.'*

'Good night,' I answered mechanically. I'll try Japanese from tomorrow, I thought as I drifted off to sleep.

My great-grandfather was nineteen years old when he married Louisa Frederici, who he had met in St Louis the previous year while stationed at the military head-quarters there. Ms Frederici was, by all accounts, a great beauty although her photographs suggest a heavy-set, troubled young woman with a lantern jaw and dark eyes. At first, Bill allowed Louisa to make the decisions in their relationship, so enamoured was he of his new bride that he set aside his own natural ambitions and desires in order to satisfy the more settled lifestyle of the married man. The war had ended in 1865 and Bill spent a short time driving a peaceful stagecoach across the prairies before agreeing with his fiancée to buy and run a small hotel in Kansas.

A state of cold war was in existence between the former combatants of the confederacy and the union but for a time my great-grandfather managed to distance himself from any trouble while he settled down to domestic life. Their hotel – the Golden Rule – kept him busy for a time, although he soon grew restless with the mundane day-to-day business of their new investment and longed to ride free across the prairies once again. Louisa, however, had other plans.

'We need to get the army to settle more people in Kansas,' she complained as she sat in her parlour, balancing their receipts against their expenditure unhappily, frowning at a broken fingernail for a moment. 'Or get Nebraska into the union so there'll be more people passing through.'

'Nebraska will be in soon enough,' he replied,

imagining what it would be like to be able to help settle a state, as his father had done before him.

'Tomorrow wouldn't be soon enough,' Louisa pointed out. 'We need to keep the hotel busy or what hope have we got for the future?'

We're doing all right, aren't we?' asked Bill, who tended to keep a firm distance between himself and the financial matters of the Golden Rule, preferring to stay out front, greeting their guests, telling romantic stories of his adventures – some real, some fictional – as those patrons gathered in the bar. 'We're paying our bills.'

'We're paying them, of course,' she replied, not look-ing across at him but tapping her pencil gently against her lips instead as she stared at the rows of figures in concentration. 'Of course we're paying them, Bill, but there's not much left over for us when they're paid. We need to make some savings.'

'What do you need savings for? Haven't you got everything you need right here?'

'For the future,' she explained carefully. 'For expan-sion.'

Bill frowned. It had not entirely been his idea to open a hotel in the first place. He had fallen for Louisa the moment they had met, mostly because she had been attracted to him and made her feelings known without any shame. At the time an inexperienced man in matters of love, the sudden notion that a female could care for him prompted unexpected feelings of romance in Bill's heart and he had proposed marriage on a whim, and she had accepted immediately. Louisa had made it a condition of their marriage, however, that they settle down to a stable existence; she had been attracted to the daring and youthful adventurer of the frontiers, but what was attractive in a fiancé was not necessarily

120

so charming in a husband. Bill had agreed to this, however, for what was marriage to him but another untried adventure. They purchased the hotel from a distance through an agent, sight unseen.

'What kind of expansion?' asked Bill suspiciously. 'Really, Louisa, you're turning into Abraham Lincoln. Always wanting to expand your empire further and further west.'

'We may not wish to continue living and working in one hotel,' said Louisa, ignoring the jibe. 'I certainly don't wish to be cooking meals for overweight cowboys for the rest of my given days even if you do. If we can make a success of the Golden Rule here, why there could be a chain of Golden Rules right across the state of Kansas. Across America,' she added, her eyes taking on a distant look as the curvy marks of dollar signs began to appear in them. Louisa Frederici Cody was ahead of her time when it came to global enterprising.

'I could go scouting for fresh locations, I suppose,' said Bill, considering the advantages of a new life riding from state to state, looking for places which might need a Golden Rule Hotel. He didn't imagine there would be too many who would, but that didn't bother him so much. At least it would get him out of town every so often.

'You'll be staying right here where I can see you, Bill Cody,' interrupted Louisa, pouring cold water on his hopes. 'You made an agreement with me when we married, don't you remember?'

'I remember just fine. But you're the one who's saying we should—'

'We'll speak to Mr Banks,' said Louisa, smiling across at him like a young mother about to pat her son's head and hand him a lollipop for good behaviour. Mr Banks was the agent who had set them up with the Golden Rule in the first place; he kept in contact with my great-grandfather and his wife, the latter more than the former. 'He'll advise us what to do.'

Bill didn't bother to protest. He was still new to wedlock and anxious to please his young wife but there was a contradiction inside him which forced him to wonder whether he had made the right decision or not. Each day he saw cowboys and soldiers passing through their town, riding together, stopping at the local saloon or at his own Golden Rule bar to drink for a few hours and share stories. He envied them their comradeship, their devil-may-care attitude and their freedom. He felt alone and bored. He had begun to suspect that stability and marriage were not things which were part of his natural destiny.

'You should speak to the army,' said Louisa, and he snapped out of his reveries and looked across at her in a daze.

'What?' he asked. 'What was that you said?'

'I *said*,' she repeated with a sigh, 'you should speak to the army. Find one of your old friends who might know a thing or two about what's happening in these parts. About the railroads for one thing. If we could get a train running through Salt Creek Valley, then the numbers of people passing through here would naturally increase. We'd have dozens of overnight guests, not to mention passing trade for the restaurant and bar. Don't you know anyone who controls the railroads?'

He was about to point out that he had been a scout and a union jayhawker before becoming a married man and not a train driver, and thus his contacts in that line were limited when the bell over the bar door rang, indicating customers. He smiled and stood up, pointing towards the bar and Louisa nodded quickly, returning to her figures. They could continue their discussion later, she believed. She was wrong.

Bill entered the bar just as two men in army uniforms came up to it. They were laughing and had an arm around each other's shoulders. Their faces were drawn and tired but there was an expression of vitality in their eyes which my great-grandfather could not help but notice.

'Good day, gentlemen,' he said affably, picking up a towel and dragging it across the bar in front of them, wiping away the dust carelessly. 'What'll it be?'

'We'll have two whiskies and then we'll have two more,' said the man on the right, slapping his hand down on the bar with a wide grin. They were both around the same age as Bill, twenty, but were stronger, with three-day beards, and they wore their hair shoulder length as opposed to their host, who had a neat, tight haircut, administered by his wife with the aid of a pair of scissors and a pudding bowl.

'Two whiskies it is then,' said Bill, placing a couple of shot-glasses before them and uncorking a bottle. 'Where are you fellows coming from?' he asked, glancing at their army uniforms enviously. His own checked shirt, braces and grey trousers seemed a poor substitute.

'Fort Riley,' came the reply of the man on the left who, Bill noticed for the first time, had only one arm. A memory came flooding back as the man continued, pointing the finger of his left arm at him. 'I know you, don't I? It's Bill Cody, right?'

'David Yountam,' said Bill with a wide grin, knowing him immediately now although their seven-year separation had, given them both a new appearance, no longer the scrambling teenage boys they had been, but rather experienced men of the world, one a soldier, one a veteran. 'What brings you here?' he asked, another shot of whisky being dispensed to both quickly.

'We've been with Custer's army,' said Yountam. 'Like old Lew Simpson, he doesn't seem to mind a soldier with only one arm. It's one better than none, he told me.'

'General Custer!' replied Bill in admiration. He had not yet met the famous general but his legend had already spread far and wide from the many brave charges he had made during the war. At twenty-three he was the youngest general in the army and President Lincoln's trusted friend and adviser. 'How on earth did you get in with him?'

'Why, the same way you got us both and Albert Rogers along on that wagon trail a few years back,' said Yountam. 'I went to see him and asked him could I join and he said yes, surely. There's nothing more these generals like than a man with mind enough to just say what he thinks. This is another soldier, by the way,' indicating his friend. 'Seth Reid, this is the bravest fellow I've ever known, Bill Cody. Killed an Indian when he was only a child, you know!'

'Pleased to meet you,' said Reid, extending a hand but Bill thought he could read in it a sense of distance, as if the stranger was happy to endure a conversation with a civilian but had heavier matters to consider, the types of thoughts which a soldier and a mere bartender could not necessarily share. Bill shook his hand but returned his attentions to his old friend.

'And what about Rogers?' he asked, recalling their cynical tent-mate of years earlier. 'Did he join you too? Is he still with Custer?'

Yountam shook his head sadly. 'Killed,' he said. 'Shot

124

during the war. Left a wife and baby too, you'd never believe it but it's true.'

'Killed,' said Bill in sorrow, shaking his head sadly, although he was rarely moved by talk of death any more, having seen so much if it in recent years.

'And you?' asked Yountam, his happy voice lowering a notch as he attempted not to sound judgemental. 'You . . . you work here then? I took you for a lifelong soldier!'

'My wife and I . . .' began Bill, feeling it necessary to explain himself but then shaking his head in defeat. 'Yes,' he admitted. 'I own this place. We run it together. Thinking of expanding though,' he added hopefully. 'Soon there'll be a chain of Golden Rules all across America,' he said, echoing his wife's words of a few minutes earlier but unable to infuse them with as much enthusiasm as she had done.

'And a free drink for me in every one, I hope?' asked Yountam.

'But of course! What else could I do for a solider such as yourself? And an old friend at that!'

'You could pour us another drink,' said Reid sharply, pushing his glass forward and turning to say something to Yountam just as Bill reached for the bottle. It was empty and he was forced to walk down to the end of the bar where he kept the unopened boxes. As he reached down for one, he looked at the two men and felt embarrassed and unhappy. He shouldn't be pouring them drinks, he thought. He should be sitting on that side of the bar with them, in uniform, happy and carefree.

'So how long have you been here, Bill?' asked Yountam on his return.

'About six months,' he replied. 'We got married in St

Louis the month before that and bought this hotel immediately.'

'And where is she then, this wife of yours?' he asked. 'Are we going to meet her or is she in hiding?'

As if on cue, Louisa entered the bar area dressed in bonnet, shawl and coat, and looked at the men with some disdain, concerned that the dirt of their uniforms would spoil the oak-trimmed surface of the bar that Mary, the girl they employed for a few hours each day, had scrubbed clean that morning. 'I'm going to the store,' she said to Bill offering them only the briefest of nods. 'We can talk later about—'

'Louisa!' said Bill, taking her by the arm and turning her to face the two men. 'Look who's arrived. This is my old friend David Yountam. And another soldier, name of Reid. You remember I told you about Yountam, don't you?'

Louisa blinked as she racked her brain for the memory. 'Yountam . . . Yountam . . .' she said, almost ready to admit defeat.

'We were on the trails together when we were boys,' he said enthusiastically, to help her remember. 'The wagon train that got burned to cinders?'

'Oh yes,' said Louisa after a moment, her voice making it clear that she hadn't the first idea what he was talking about. 'How do you do, Mr Yountam?' she asked, extending her right hand, but as he had none himself he was forced to grasp hers in his left and she took a small step backwards in obvious discomfort, her cheeks growing suddenly pink.

'Lost it in a fight with a buffalo when I was a boy,' he explained quietly and a frosty silence descended on them, Bill licking his lips and looking from one to the other with a wide, toothy smile as he hoped that

126

someone would say something. 'Before I knew your husband, that is,' said Yountam eventually, in order to break the silence. 'I must admit I never thought I'd see him settling for a quiet life like this,' he added, meaning no offence but understanding immediately by the look on Bill's face that his words had hurt. 'I meant settling *down* to a quiet life,' he corrected himself. 'He's a lucky man,' he added, but he was no actor and they could tell he was simply trying to correct a bad situation. 'Having a wife and a . . . a business to enjoy.' His words trailed off into the emptiness of the room and he looked down at his drink with a frown as his companion, Seth Reid, snorted a quick laugh, as if the world of the small-town businessman was as nothing compared to the excitement and adventure of his own.

'Right,' said Louisa after a moment, stepping away without giving either of them another glance. 'I may be a few hours,' she said, looking at her husband, the words coming through thin lips, sounding as if she blamed him entirely for whatever social awkwardness had just taken place. 'Libby Turner is ready to have her baby at any moment and I want to call on her to see how she's doing. I'll see you later then. Mr Yountam,' she said, nodding her head at him to say goodbye, unwilling to shake hands again. 'Mr . . . Reid,' she said, forcing herself to remember his name.

'Goodbye, Mrs Cody,' said Yountam and when she was gone, he looked to his old friend with an apologetic glance. 'That went well,' he said quietly.

'Don't worry about it,' said Bill, unable to look his friend in the face. 'She's . . . she's working hard to keep this place together. She's not enamoured of the army life.'

'And you?' he asked. 'Are you happy here?'

Bill looked up and their eyes met. He thought about it, wondered whether it was correct to confide so much of a personal nature in someone he had not seen in so long, let alone another man who he did not even know at all and who seemed slightly contemptuous of him. He thought about it and decided he didn't care.

'No,' he said. 'I'm miserable'.

'In that case,' said Yountam, draining his glass and standing up to walk towards the bathroom. 'You've got a couple of hours. Remember that.'

'A couple of hours?' asked Bill as his friend disappeared and then, almost to himself, 'what does that mean?'

'She said she wouldn't be back for a couple of hours,' said Seth Reid in a clear voice, looking up and addressing the bartender for the first time. His face broke into a smile, revealing dirty brown teeth that looked as if they would not continue to be part of the man's mouth for much longer. 'And we have to leave within one hour,' he added.

Bill exhaled and nodded, biting his lip as he began to understand.

Adam and I stayed in Tokyo for about two weeks before deciding to travel south-westwards towards Osaka, Kyoto and ultimately Hiroshima. We learned at an early stage that we were never going to master the language and took instead to committing to memory a series of simple phrases which could help us travel, eat and sleep with the minimum amount of fuss. After a time, some of the more common symbols and lettering became familiar to us and the initial feeling we had when we had landed at Narita Airport – as if we had suddenly been deprived of several of our senses – melted away. The people were friendly and helpful to foreigners, which was a relief, and we stretched our money so that we would be able to survive for as long a period as possible.

Before leaving Tokyo, we visited the gardens of the Imperial Palace, where it became something of a relief to meet some fellow Westerners with whom we could converse. Adam and I got along pretty well but inevitably, the constraints of being solely in each other's company and conversation twenty-four hours a day were beginning to show. There were a few tense moments but for the most part we tried to stay civil to each other. Still, we knew we could do with some new people to talk to. The gardens seemed to be filled with more Westerners than Japanese and we mingled with them as we began to explore. The palace itself was off-limits to visitors but we spent a couple of hours wandering around the plaza at Uchibori-Dori where the lawns and trees were cut with almost surgeon-like precision. It was forbidden to walk on the bridges which connected the plaza to the outer limits of the palace walls and so we stepped casually on to them, expecting at any moment a sho-gun to come running towards us, samurai sword swinging through the air, ready to decapitate us, but as nothing happened, and there was no further access granted from there, we drifted back in the direction we had come.

Not far from the plaza was an open-air bar and as it was a warm day, we sat outside and ordered a couple of draught beers which were brought out to us at our table, foaming over the sides of the *jokki dai* in which they were served. Our plan was to begin the journey towards Osaka the following morning and we were discussing it when a couple of around our age asked us whether they could join our table.

'Sure,' I said, taking my bag from the seat beside me; we were seated at a wicker table of four seats and as Adam and I were facing each other, they were able to take the seats beside us. In the garden itself there were several other empty tables so I assumed that they wanted to talk. 'How's it going?' I asked them casually, for I could tell by the girl's accent when she had spoken a moment before that they were Americans. 'Hot enough for you?'

'Too hot,' she replied, dazzling me with her smile while her boyfriend combed his blond hair away from his face with his fingers, using the other hand to signal to the waiter that they would both have what we were having, a quick snap of the fingers, pointing back and forth from Adam's drink to mine, and then two fingers raised to indicate that he wanted one for both him and the girl. Rude but effective.

'You're obviously as good on the Japanese language as we are,' I said, grinning at him and he laughed.

'We've been here two and a half months,' he replied, 'and I still can't figure out a single word. Jenny's better, aren't you?'

She shrugged but didn't disagree. 'I took a course before I left,' she said quietly. 'I tried to get him to come too but he wouldn't.'

'Where are you from?' asked Adam, sitting back slightly in his seat as the waiter brought their drinks and took the money.

'Michigan,' said the boy. 'I'm Mike Naylor by the way. This is Jenny.' We introduced ourselves and shook hands and an awkward silence hit us for a moment as we decided which way the conversation should turn from here. 'So where you guys from?' he asked eventually.

'London,' said Adam. 'We haven't been here long ourselves. A couple of weeks, that's all.'

'Just tourists?'

'Sort of. We're tourists now but we're going to travel on and we may need to stop somewhere and find some work if we start to run out of money. How about you? Two and a half months is a long time to spend here.'

'Oh we haven't been in Tokyo that long,' said Mike, taking a long drink from his beer and savouring it for a moment. His chin was covered in stubble, and he scratched at it irritably; he looked like all he really wanted was a shave and a shower. 'We only got here last week but we took a bit of a break and just relaxed for a while. We're doing the whole tourist thing this week. Hence the Imperial Palace.' He gestured towards the imposing structure hidden behind the walls in the distance. 'We want to get to the Tokyo Museum in Ueno yet and . . . where else?'

'Shinjuku,' said Jenny.

'Oh yeah, that's right, Shinjuku. The red-light district. Got to see that. They say it gives Amsterdam a run for its money, you know? It was a bit of a last-minute decision coming here at all to be honest so we have to see what we can. My parents gave us some money as a wedding present and we decided to blow it all on a three-month honeymoon.'

'I think they wanted us to spend it on furniture or something,' said Jenny with a sneer. 'Like *that* was going to happen.'

'You're on your honeymoon?' I asked, smiling at them in surprise. They nodded. 'How old are you?'

'Twenty,' they said in unison.

'Twenty,' repeated Mike on his own. 'It's young, I know, but . . .' He waved a hand in the air as if the whole thing was neither here nor there.

'I don't know anyone that age who's married,' said Adam, staring at them as if they were a pair of freaks. 'It's a good way to spend your honeymoon though.'

'We figured it would be memorable,' said Mike. 'We came up with a good plan.' They proceeded to tell us how they had spent the first two months of their married life in the southern province of Shikoku, where they had taken part in Japan's most famous pilgrimage, dedicated to the Buddhist monk Kobo Daishi. It was a thousand-kilometre trail and took in eighty-eight temples along the way.

'You walked a thousand kilometres?' I asked, amazed by the idea, and resisting the temptation to look down at their feet to see whether they were swathed in bandages.

'We walked it all right,' said Jenny, reaching over to grasp her young husband's hand in solidarity. 'From the first to the last. Some of the other pilgrims cheated, they—'

'They didn't cheat, Jenny, they just did it a different way,' said Mike in a conciliatory tone, as if the Zen aura hadn't quite left him yet. He was wearing a pendant around his neck and I wondered whether it was a symbol of the pilgrimage or something he had brought with him from home.

'OK, it's not *cheating* as such, but they didn't do what we did.'

'They were old, so many of them!' he protested.

'They still didn't do it.'

'They did it when they were younger. A lot of

Buddhist Japanese undertake the Shikoki Pilgrimage,' he explained, looking at Adam and me in turn. 'But they wait until they're retired to do it. You know, two months is a long time to be away from your home and your . . . your job or whatever,' he said, in a tone that suggested he wasn't quite sure what the word *job* actually meant and was in no hurry to find out. 'Also, I guess a lot of young people here just aren't as interested in these kinds of things. It was a strange time.'

I shook my head and felt a great urge to take a long walk with him right at that moment and hear his stories. 'What were they like?' I asked. 'The people, I mean. We haven't really got to know anyone here. It's hard when you can't speak the language.'

'That was the great thing about it,' said Jenny. 'We couldn't speak Japanese, most of the other pilgrims couldn't speak English, we were definitely the youngest by, like, about thirty-five years, but it was the best two months of my life. We really got to know these people. They became like family to us, every one. There's hardly a province in Japan where we couldn't go now and have a bed for as long as we wanted one. If one of the pilgrims themselves doesn't live there, then they've got family who do.'

'That's amazing,' I said. 'I thought I was doing something extreme packing up and coming to Japan in the first place, but that . . . what made you want to do it? Are you . . . ?' I wasn't quite sure whether it would be rude to phrase it as such but figured it was a simple question and I may as well just ask. 'Are you Buddhist, the two of you? Is that why you wanted to do it?'

'No,' said Mike laughing. 'We'd barely even heard of Buddhists except in some dumb Keanu Reeves movie a couple of years back. We just wanted to come to Japan,

133

somewhere different, and when we got here we got travelling immediately because we didn't want to stay in the Lonely Planet Tokyo and ended up in Shikoku. We heard about the pilgrimage, it was just about to start, so we said what the hell. You should try it.'

I laughed. I knew I probably would never try it but admired them for doing so at the same time. We ordered more drinks and as the sun went down crouched closer and closer to each other at the table, eager for more stories of each other's lives.

'Each one of the eighty-eight temples,' Jenny told us, 'represents one of the eighty-eight evils which the Shingon Buddhists believe beset everyone's life. Visiting each one makes the pilgrim confront a devil and exorcise it. It's the ultimate action of the Shingon Buddhist, like a Jew returning to Palestine and visiting the Wailing Wall. A Catholic receiving the Pope's blessing in St Peter's Square in Rome. To the believer these actions signify a marked point in the penitent man's life, a point which is superior to all their other actions. Completing the pilgrimage brings one a step closer to Buddha himself. They say that many people die within a year of returning from the pilgrimage as they have nothing left to achieve in life.'

'That could also have something to do with the fact that they're all so damn old,' pointed out Mike with a smile and we laughed. They were holding hands between their seats as they spoke and seemed almost unaware of their doing so. I looked at them and felt a tinge of envy; I was alone. I had Adam, of course, but effectively I was alone. There seemed slim chance of finding any romance in Japan due to my total lack of ability in the language department, and yet despite that, I already knew that I would stay in this country for some time, regardless of my travelling companion's plans. I was starting to feel at ease here and I think a part of that was due to my sense of disorientation. Nobody knew me, I knew nobody, I could collect and discard friends – acquaintances just – on a nightly basis, just like we were doing here. We were having a wonderful evening but part of that was because we knew – Adam and I, Mike and Jenny – that we would not see each other again after that night. It was a relief, in a way, to be so casual about things; we could be anything we wanted to be. And still I envied them.

'So where's the next pilgrimage to then?' asked Adam and they shrugged.

'Nowhere for now,' said Mike. 'That was the big one for us. That's what we'll remember as our honeymoon. We'll hang around Tokyo for a little bit more maybe, then we have to go home.'

'Back to Michigan?'

'Back to Michigan. College is calling us. Still, we'll have a good story for the grandchildren.' I smiled and nodded. 'You've gone quiet, William,' said Jenny after a moment. 'Are you tired?'

'No,' I said, sighing and leaning back, smiling around the table as if I could just reach over and hug them all. 'I was just thinking about London. I was thinking about my father,' I added, nodding slowly. For some reason I felt a sting of tears behind my eyes. I was surprised and embarrassed and blinked quickly to prevent an onslaught.

'What does he do?' asked Mike and I told them that he was retired.

'It's just what you said about your pilgrimage being a good story for your grandchildren. I mean I think that's a good thing, passing stories down from generation to generation. That's what Isaac, that's what my *father*, did for me.'

'William's father believes he's a cowboy,' said Adam facetiously and I shot him a look of disapproval.

'He doesn't believe he's a cowboy,' I said, a little irritated. I looked at the other two who were looking at me and waiting to see what I had to say; they had told me their stories, it was time to tell them mine and unlike Isaac, I couldn't quite find the words. 'My great-grandfather,' I began, unsure whether I could even say it without making them laugh. I really didn't want them to laugh; this far from home, having run away from everything I was tired of, I wanted them to take me seriously if I had the desire to tell them at all. 'Isaac, that's my father, well he claims that his grandfather was American. He fought in the civil war, was a scout and so on. The thing is he claims that his grandfather, my great-grandfather, was Bill Cody.'

They stared at me blankly and nodded. 'Bill Cody,' said Jenny. 'That's—'

'My name, yeah. Except I go by William.'

'Who's Bill Cody?' asked Mike. I looked at him in surprise and forced a smile. I wasn't sure if he was having me on. I looked back at Jenny who seemed equally unaware.

'Bill Cody?' I repeated. 'Buffalo Bill Cody? You've heard of him, right?'

They both frowned. 'I *think* so,' said Jenny. 'Wasn't he in that movie with Doris Day?' I stared at her now as if she was mad.

'No, no, he wasn't an actor. Well actually he *was* an actor eventually, but no, he wasn't in any movie with—'

'I don't mean *in* it,' she said, clicking her fingers as

136

she tried to bring back a memory. She looked at her husband for support. 'What was it, Mike?' she asked. 'That movie with Doris Day in it?'

'Was Rock Hudson in it?' he asked.

'No, it was that guy from *Dallas*. What's his name. Howard Keel. What was that movie? It was a musical. *Annie Get Your Gun!*' she cried then enthusiastically, pleased that she'd got it at last. 'He was in that, wasn't he? That guy Howard Keel played him!'

Both Adam and Mike looked as if they didn't have a clue what she was talking about, but I did and shook my head. 'No,' I said quietly. 'That was Wild Bill Hickok. Howard Keel played Wild Bill Hickok.'

'Not the same guy?'

'Not the same guy,' I agreed. I sat back and shook my head. 'I can't believe you don't know who he is!' I said, amazed. There was complete silence for a moment, until I asked in a quieter voice: 'You *really* don't know who he is?'

'Kind of,' admitted Mike, perhaps taking pity on me. 'I mean I think it rings a bell. Somewhere. I'll take your word for it though. You're really related to that guy?'

'Yeah, yeah,' I said, a little deflated; this was the first time I'd ever come across someone who had failed to be either impressed or scornful of the fact that I was Buffalo Bill's great-grandson. 'So they tell me.'

'So you're an American then?'

'Well, like a *sixteenth*,' I said. 'Like my left hand or something.' I surprised myself by actually feeling annoyed. In recent years I had been trying to dissociate myself from everything to do with Buffalo Bill Cody and had caused a serious rift to develop in my relationship with Isaac in order to do that. And now here were two people who seemed unimpressed by it. Maybe it didn't matter so much. But then, wasn't that what I'd been saying to Isaac for years?

'The first night we were in Tokyo,' said Jenny eventually, sensing my discomfort, 'the night we got back from the pilgrimage, we had a drink in a bar and there were twenty guys there all dressed like Elvis Presley. The whole package. Big white collars. Sequins. Sideburns. The lot. Of course they were Japanese, but other than that they were just a bunch of regular Elvises.' I stared at her and raised an eyebrow as if to say *So?* 'They all thought they were related to Elvis, you see,' she said. 'They claimed to be his sons, all conceived when he visited Japan. I mean they were nuts, you know?'

I nodded slowly. 'Right,' I said, disliking the association she was making. 'So tell me,' I said after a pause. 'Who was this Kobo Daishi guy then?'

I don't know how Mike's and Jenny's marriage turned out, but my great-grandfather and Louisa Frederici were married at the same youthful age and within a year he had hot-footed it out of the Golden Rule Hotel. He rode off with David Yountam and Seth Reid to Fort Fletcher where he came into contact for the first time with General George Custer, who was stationed there at the time, leading sorties into Indian territories as the settlements continued and the reservations began to be brokered. Custer took little regard of my great-grandfather at first but they began to travel more in each other's company after some initial scouting expeditions together proved to the general that Bill was just as brave and adventurous as he.

Bill wrote to Louisa from the fort and explained to her that he was not cut out for life as a hotelier. He missed the excitement of life on the prairies, he said, and the company of other men who were opening out the western frontiers and settling states, just as his own father had done. Deciding on cutlery for tableware, choosing between different lace patterns and organising servants to change the bed linen just wasn't what he was meant to do with his life. He was intended, he claimed, for a higher purpose.

Louisa, needless to say, was devastated. Now just twenty-one years old, she was left with a hotel to run on her own and a child on the way. Travelling alone, she came to see him at the fort and they had an emotional reunion but he was not for turning. He asked her to stay with him, offering her the life of an army wife, always on the move and in potential danger, but promising that one day soon they would build their own home on the prairies but she declined for now, perhaps distrusting his promises, and probably having every reason to do so. Instead she returned to Salt Creek Valley while he remained in Fort Fletcher. They had married in haste and would pay the price for a long time to come.

For now he continued to scout with General Custer, and learned from him too as their friendship grew stronger, but with the civil war having ended and a new war having begun – that between the United States government and the Indian tribes fighting to maintain their land – he could sense that time was drawing to a close for him there and that new challenges were approaching. It didn't take long for him to see where the new dawn for the American west was coming from and, ironically, it related to something that Louisa herself had remarked upon towards the end of their time together at the Golden Rule.

The railroads.

Chapter Five

Rome, London, Tokyo

The Kansas–Pacific railroad was the most important of all the new railway systems being built to aid mass transportation and to help settle the outer reaches of the union. Much of the work was being undertaken by the Chinese immigrant population who worked long hours in dangerous conditions for less pay than their white colleagues. When my great-grandfather left the army for a time in 1868 to return to scouting, it was as an employee of the Kansas–Pacific railroads, and he was accompanied by his old friend David Yountam. At first their work entailed mapping the land through which the tracks would eventually pass but after a time, as the work came closer towards the state line and there were increasing numbers of railroad employees to feed – almost twelve hundred in total – he turned his hand once again to buffalo hunting, earning large amounts of money for his ability to capture and kill more than his quota of fresh meat every day. Privy to the increasingly expansionist plans of the railroads, Yountam and Bill soon decided to resign their commissions in the army outright and aim instead to exploit the potential of the west's industrialisation while they still could.

'How much cash do you have now anyway?' asked

Yountam one evening as they sat in the Fresh Morning Hotel near Fort Harker, nursing hangovers from too much whisky the night before and rubbing their eyes through lack of sleep, for the hotel was a popular whorehouse and they had taken advantage of its charms. 'You've saved a lot, right?'

'About fifteen hundred dollars,' replied Bill, proud of his nest-egg. This was a substantial amount of money at the time and had been amassed due to his success as a buffalo hunter and also his thriftiness, for there was little on offer in the places he visited that could cause him to spend any of his savings. Whisky and women, necessities of life rather than frivolous entertainments, were two of the only luxuries he afforded himself at the time.

'Fifteen hundred dollars,' said Yountam with glee, wishing he still had both his arms so he could rub his hands together greedily. 'And I've got almost a thousand myself. So that makes . . .' He looked up at the ceiling and squinted, his schooling not being what it might have been.

'It makes nearly twenty-five hundred dollars, David,' said Bill with a smile. 'I suppose it can't have been easy for you learning to count on your fingers. Maybe you should use your toes as well or you'll always get stuck.'

'I was twelve years old when I lost my arm,' Yountam pointed out defensively. 'As you well know, Bill. Mathematics and I have never been good friends. But as you say, that's twenty-five hundred dollars. A lot of money if you know how to use it right.'

'I've got my share of the Golden Rule too,' added Bill, remembering the hotel he had left behind for Louisa to run almost a year earlier.

'Is that still making money for you? I thought when I

141

rescued you from that domestic hell hole that it seemed like a dead place.'

'It was,' replied Bill sadly. 'I don't own it any longer though. It's been sold to a prospector from … California, I believe.' In the time since he had left Kansas, the plans and promises he had made his young wife had fallen through. The railroads still hadn't arrived anywhere near their business, so the hotel was never full, but Louisa had found herself unable to run it without her husband anyway, particularly as her pregnancy had advanced, and had returned to her mother's home in St Louis instead, selling the hotel for twelve hundred dollars and forwarding a portion of it to Bill at the fort as a full and final payment.

'How much did you get?' asked Yountam. 'Eight hundred? A thousand.'

'One hundred and fifty,' said Bill reluctantly.

'One hundred and fifty? Where's the fairness there?'

'It's all I asked for,' said Bill, wishing he did not have to discuss the matter. 'There's a child on the way. Louisa will need all the money she can get.' In truth, it had been Louisa's decision to send her estranged husband only a fraction of the proceeds from the sale of the Golden Rule. She had written to him at that time, condemning him for leaving their enterprise and their marriage but, the times being what they were, had informed him that she would follow him whenever he gave her the word but that it was up to him to do so; she would not come if she was not invited, baby or not. So far, he had declined to reply. He felt some guilt about his actions but his brief experience of domesticity had convinced him that it was not the life he wanted.

'Well still, that's nearly twenty-seven hundred dollars,' said Yountam, managing to add the figures

142

together this time without as much difficulty. 'We're rich.'

'We're not married, David,' my great-grandfather pointed out.

'No, but we could be business partners. I've been thinking about these railroads. You don't want to go on working on them for ever, do you?'

'It's honest work. I enjoy it. I don't see why we can't go—'

Yountam leaned forward to interrupt him, careful to make sure that no one else was listening. 'These railroads . . .' he said. 'They're opening up the state. People are going to start travelling through here soon. The government are going to start settling people here. You know how it works. You've been doing this long enough.'

'Sure,' said Bill. 'I know they will but so what?'

'Kansas is mostly open territory still. We could use that money to buy a stake of land and set up a town of our own. What do you say? We buy the land, we build houses and stores. Once it's established and the rail-ways are coming through we're bound to have people coming there. And when it's ours, we can sell people the lots for them to build their businesses on. What do you say? I seen it done out in Brent Lake Falls near Missouri not so long ago. A fellow I knew there made ten thousand dollars in one year. What would you say to that kind of money?'

Bill opened his eyes wide and whistled as he thought of it. 'It's a big plan,' he admitted. 'It would take some work.'

'That's the beauty of it,' said Yountam, enthusiastic now for he had been practising this speech for some time. 'All we need to do is set up a couple of stores and

143

saloons, and maybe open a hotel of our own, then we offer the business lots free of charge to whoever wants them. We provide the buildings, they provide the businesses. Pretty soon, we've got a thriving town and we're taking all the money from the entertainment on offer.'

'That could work,' admitted Bill. 'Maybe. But I don't want to be a hotelier again. I saw enough of that at the Golden Rule. I'm not meant for jobs like that.'

'You might not be but I am,' said Yountam. 'I can't ride the prairies for ever. Don't even want to, truth be told. I'm not like you, Bill, I want to settle down. I'm not looking for adventure so much now as a place to rest my head at night. Especially now, with Clara expecting.' Clara was Yountam's wife, also recently pregnant, but to whom he was much more devoted than my great-grandfather had ever been to Louisa, though such devotion did not keep him out of the whorehouses. 'You wouldn't have to do anything you didn't want to do. Just put half the money up front, then take half the profits when they start to roll in. That's it. That's all you've got to do. What do you say? Are you in?'

Bill thought about it but it seemed like too good an opportunity to pass up. 'You'll have to show me where you're thinking of,' he said. 'I don't want to say yes for sure till I take a look at it.' Although he was far from being a pragmatist, my great-grandfather was not about to throw away all the money he had in the world on a scheme which could fail by the following week. He had too many plans for his own future to let that happen.

'I'll take you there tomorrow morning,' replied Yountam with a satisfied smile. 'Early morning. First thing. You'll see it at its best.' He had already had ideas about where they should settle their town and had done a little scouting himself in recent times before presenting the idea to Bill and the following day they rode a couple of miles north to a point where there was just vast, open spaces and climbed down to take a look around. 'What do you think?' he said, stretching his one arm out wide to indicate the emptiness of the area.

'Here?' said Bill, already regretting the fact that so much free and open space had inevitably – either by them or others – to be covered with houses and businesses. Someday, he imagined, there would be no prairie ground to travel across at all and it was people like him and Yountam who would be blamed for the loss.

'Right here. It's perfect. The railroad's going to be going along about half a mile from here so that's close enough to build a station there and for people to be able to walk into the town from it.'

'It looks good,' said Bill after a pause, worried that they were committing themselves to the project too quickly. 'You're sure the railroad's coming through here though? 'Cos if it doesn't we're in trouble and you know that.'

'It'll be here within a year,' said Yountam with conviction. 'You've seen the plans. You know where they're headed. They're aiming for Sheridan, that's the final stop on the line. And you can't get to Sheridan without going through here first, unless you want to go up all the way up to Canada, cross over to the Nebraska Territory, and down through Utah before coming in from the other side. Of course that would add another two years or so to your journey so it don't seem likely.'

'Funny,' said Bill in a dry voice, breathing in the scent of the prairie dust as if it could magically inform him as to whether a town belonged there or not.

'Six months from now you're going to see those

Chinese pouring through here laying the tracks,' continued Yountam. 'I'm telling you, Bill, this time next year the trains will be passing through and we, my friend, will be kings of all we survey. We have to be quick, that's all. Because if we don't buy it soon, then someone else is going to. You can be damn sure of that.'

Bill nodded and walked slowly around the area, imagining where the town could stand, where the saloon would be, where his own house could be erected, what job he could do when it was built. He was warm on the idea and Yountam could tell that he needed only a little more gentle prodding and the deal would be firmly struck.

'I've spoken to George Jacobs,' Yountam said, referring to the government official at Fort Marker who was nominally in charge of the settlement of a hundred-mile radius, although most of the plans were made within the centralised government by Abraham Lincoln's appointees. 'He says that we can have it all for thirteen hundred. Now that's a bargain if ever I heard of one.'

'Thirteen hundred?' said Bill, surprised. 'That's not bad. That's a good price.'

'It's a damn good price is what it is. We buy the town for that. Spend another six hundred constructing the buildings. Another three or four hundred stocking the stores and the saloon as we're going to be owning them, then let the businessmen come in and set up whatever they will. A hardware store maybe. A blacksmith's. Anything at all, don't make no difference long as it's profitable. We keep a percentage of whatever they earn, of course,' he added. 'For all the work we've put in. That'll be in the contracts.'

'You think people will agree to that kind of deal?'

'Don't see why not. They did over in Brent Lake Falls, Fellows there were near as dammit to millionaires come the following spring. But they were entitled to that money. People like them and us, we're ideas men, that's what. We deserve to be made rich.'

He stopped talking and waited for a moment, wondering whether he should make a final push but just as he was about to open his mouth to speak again, Bill stamped on the ground, looked up, spat in his hand and held it out to his friend to seal the deal. 'Partners?' he said, a wide, nervous smile crossing his face.

'Partners,' said Yountam.

My great-grandfather had a restless spirit and it's a trait that I've always admired in him. That and his unwillingness ever to admit defeat. He took each adversity as if it was no more than a minor setback and was always ready to pick himself up and begin again. He pushed further and further west across America, as if he was the very personification of the land-settling programme, and always seemed to be one step ahead of the progress of the union. Where he went, America followed. It was something I kept in mind as I continued to live in Japan, and found myself feeling more isolated and lonely as time passed. Isaac always said that the only place that Bill felt ill at ease was in familiar surroundings; it was that trait that set him apart from other men. I envied him this quality and wished that that particular gene of the Cody family had been passed down to me.

Adam grew weary of Japan after a few months and decided to move on to Australia where, he believed, life could be a lot less difficult and a lot more fun. He

147

wanted me to come with him and I was tempted by his talk of a few months making our way down the Gold Coast, learning to surf, working on our tans, meeting people who could understand what we were saying, but in the end I declined. I had not yet had my fill of this exotic country and although I felt uncomfortable and alone there, I was determined to stay until I could feel that I had somehow become a part of it. And so we separated, agreeing to meet again in London when we were next there.

Watching him as his bus drove out of Tokyo station, however, I felt an urge to run after it and climb aboard, but resisted. Although I felt incredibly alone as I made my way back to my hostel, I determined that I would make the most of whatever adventures lay ahead of me. Nevertheless, despite my determination, I felt a great weight within me for days, tension and fear blending perfectly to make both my mood and my courage flag.

I left the city myself a few days later and travelled westwards towards Kyoto, the ancient capital of Japan, which initially seemed almost as crowded and busy as Tokyo had upon my first arrival there. However it was not quite as intimidating now as my Japanese had naturally improved and I was able to read most of the street signs and make my way to a hostel without too much difficulty. I hoped to earn some money by finding employment as a teacher of English with one of the many schools which my guidebook told me were located within the city. I took a room at the Higashiyama Hostel in East Kyoto, not far from the university, hoping that someone there would be able to help me in my search for employment. It was cheap and spartan but I wasn't looking for luxuries as I spent little time there anyway, mixing my search for work with sightseeing around the city.

On my third day in Kyoto, I discovered the Korakuen School, named after the famous gardens founded by Ikeda Tsunamasa, one of the most popular tourist attractions in Western Honshu, and climbed the narrow, spiral staircase to its offices with high hopes. I remember thinking how the steps were incredibly narrow and wondering how many accidents had taken place as people ran down them. The paint was chipping away at the side and I hoped that the school had not been closed down in the year or so since my guidebook had been published. Although I had been assured by student agencies in London before I left that positions as language teachers were numerous and available to any who wanted them, I was beginning to despair of finding work and did not want to be forced to leave Kyoto, as the drain on my finances of finding another city, accommodation and employment could bring me close to the edge. However, this was not to be the case for it was at the Korakuen that I not only found a job which could keep me for my time there, but also discovered my destiny.

I tapped on the glass-fronted door and, receiving no answer, pushed it open gingerly; an ill-mannered young man frowned at me from behind a desk as I stepped inside as if I was the last person in the world he wanted to have to talk to, despite the fact that we had never met before. He wore glasses and pushed them up his nose a little as he looked me up and down with disdain. I glanced down myself, worried that a great stain had appeared on my shirt or jeans without my noticing it, but all appeared in order. Granted, I was not dressed for a formal interview, but then I was merely making

149

inquiries there, and not hoping for a full-time position with the Japanese treasury.

'*Hai*,' he barked at me. '*Nani?*' As ever, I hoped my meagre grasp of the language would suffice and I knew enough to recognise a 'hello' and 'what do you want?' without much difficulty. It was generally considered rude not to at least attempt Japanese first and so I stepped up to his desk, flashed him a benign smile, and did my best, hoping he would quickly save me by reverting to English.

'*Hai. Watashi no namae wa William Cody desu.*' *Hello. My name is William Cody.* He stared at me blankly and offered no response. I racked my brain for an appropriate follow up. '*Gakusei desu,*' I added. *I'm a teacher.*

I had hardly uttered the phrase when a stream of sentences came pouring from his mouth at rapid-fire speed. His hands gesticulated furiously in the air and his eyes narrowed until I thought he might jump up and hit me. I gestured with my hands for him to stop as I took a step backwards and used two phrases which had become extremely familiar to me, for I had used them perhaps more than any other sentences since my arrival in Japan. '*Motto yukkuri hanashite kuremasen ka, nihongo wa hanashimasen.*' *Could you speak slowly please, I don't speak Japanese well.*

This stopped him for a moment. There is probably nothing more disconcerting than someone speaking fluently in a language in order to explain that they cannot actually speak that language. The pause was a calm before the storm, however, for within a few seconds he was screaming at me again and waving towards the door, obviously ejecting me. It was a good job I had said that I was a teacher, I thought, and not a student as this was a good way for the Korakuen School to lose business. But I was unwilling to argue with him and turned to go, irritated and shaking my head at his rudeness and would have left at that moment had another employee of the school not appeared from a door beside the young man's desk. He stopped in mid-flow when he saw her and looked a little shamefaced for he appeared quite ridiculous, hovering above his seat like that and screaming at an innocent stranger. His colleague – a young woman of around twenty-three – asked him a quick question and he answered her immediately, his tone suggesting defensiveness. I couldn't understand their dialogue but whatever she said in response then was expressed aggressively towards him and he opened and shut his mouth quickly, not knowing how to respond to her.

'I'm sorry,' she said, stepping out from behind the desk and walking towards me, her hand outstretched. Her English was perfect and her accent lent each word a precise definition. 'Our receptionist is sick this week and we are having to cope with this stupid temp.' She turned and looked at him, shouting something indecipherable – he was staring at us both with a look of contempt – before turning back to me and smiling. 'I don't think he is all there,' she said conspiratorially. 'He hasn't bathed in a week and I caught him chasing butterflies earlier.' I nodded slowly, unsure whether this was a local idiom or whether she meant it literally; I couldn't help but laugh and, once I did, she gave a small giggle too and covered her hand with her mouth. Before she did I could not help but notice the even white teeth within, each one perfectly straight, and hoped she'd smile again soon. 'I'm sorry,' she said eventually. 'How can I help you?'

'You don't mind if we speak English?' I asked.

'Not at all. I like to speak English here. It's what we're here for.'

'Good,' I said. 'Because I'm afraid if we spoke Japanese you'd never understand me and I'd sure as hell never understand you. I might be only asking you for directions to the nearest train station and instead end up saying that we should get a divorce. I think I might have used the wrong words with your friend over there. Maybe I offended him.'

'Well we'll never know,' she said quickly, as if the whole incident mattered not a jot to her. 'And anyway, I think we should try to work things out first, rather than get divorced, don't you? Think of the children. They should be our first priority.'

I stared at her in surprise for a moment before laughing and shaking my head. I shrugged. I wanted desperately to think of a witty rejoinder but found myself momentarily lost for words. Luckily, she picked up my slack by speaking again. 'Would you like to come into my office to talk? I think we're being watched,' she added quietly, nodding towards the temp. I agreed and she led the way into a small room with a desk and computer and two grey filing cabinets. It was quite bare but a few potted plants dotted around gave it a pleasant feel. I sat down opposite her and she stared at me, her face the most open expression of interest and sincerity I had encountered since I had arrived in Japan. It's a clichéd thing to say but the fact is that I felt warm inside when I looked at her and I felt like we knew each other well, or would do soon. I felt there was no need for small talk as we would have so much to say to each other.

'Right,' I began after a few moments, realising it was necessary for me to say something or we would simply sit there staring at each other for hours. 'First off, my name's William Cody,' I said.

'I am Hitomi Naoyuki,' she said formally, giving a brisk nod.

'It's nice to meet you, Ms Naoyuki,' I said, slipping my tongue around the vowel sounds.

'You're an American?' she asked.

'English,' I responded, shaking my head. 'London. South London. Clapham, actually.' I wondered whether I should give her the street and the house number too but decided against. 'You probably don't know Clapham,' I said and she gave an almost imperceptible shrug which I took to be a no. That's okay,' I said. 'It's not very famous. It's just a small, eh . . . just a small . . . well I guess it's a town. There's a train station there. A junction . . . it connects . . . places.' I was making no sense and knew it. I blushed and looked away.

'I'm from Shizuoka,' she said, sensing my discomfort. 'We also have trains. Don't think you're so special, all right?' I looked up at her and her face was deadly serious but when she saw the look of dismay I had adopted, she burst into laughter and once again covered her mouth with her hands. 'I'm sorry, Mr Cody,' she said after a moment. 'You just look so serious, that's all. I'm just teasing you. Forgive me.'

I gave a quick laugh. 'Right,' I said, frowning and wondering how I could regain either my self-control or perhaps a shred of dignity.

'How can I help you anyway?' she said. 'I assume you didn't come here just to argue with my temporary receptionist.'

'No,' I admitted. That wasn't top of my list for the day. I'm . . . well I'm looking for a job, to be honest.'

'As a receptionist?' she asked and I shook my head.

'No, no,' I said quickly. 'Not as a receptionist. As a teacher. Teaching English.'

'I see,' she replied, pulling out a form from a drawer of her desk. 'You are trained, I presume?'

'Well I did a TEFL course,' I said, a white lie as I had indeed done one but it had only lasted for a weekend and I'd spent most of it reading a book at the back of the class as the teacher discussed participles and subjunctives. 'And I've done some teaching before.' Again, a small lie; I had helped a friend's brother with grinds in history and literature.

'We are always looking for qualified teachers,' said Hitomi, brushing her long dark hair away from her face with her fingers. I stared at it; I had never seen such fine hair. She sensed me staring and I blushed again, diverting my attention to the walls and a photograph on her desk of an elderly couple standing on either side of her.

'Your mother and father?' I asked, nodding at the picture. She hesitated before answering.

'Yes,' she said.

'Which is which?' I said without thinking, meant as a joke but immediately unfunny. My stomach churned in horror and she frowned and squinted at me as if she was trying to decipher my meaning before returning to her form.

'You are available on a full-time basis?' she asked.

'Not really,' I said. To be honest with you, Ms Naoyuki, I—'

'Hitomi,' she said quickly. 'Please call me Hitomi.'

'Hitomi then.'

'And you are called Bill, I suppose?'

I shook my head. 'Just William,' I said and then gave a quick laugh. 'Just William,' I repeated, winking at her like an insane man. She didn't get the reference and I sighed deeply; this was not going how it should. I smiled at her and shrugged. 'I'm sorry,' I said. 'I'm feeling a little . . . light-headed, I think, today.'

'Perhaps you are still getting used to Japan,' she offered, helping me out.

'Yes. Well I've been here four months now,' I added. 'So it shouldn't really be that. I just . . . I had a late night. Couldn't sleep very well. Things on my mind. Money troubles.' I was giving too much away and knew it but somehow I seemed incapable of stringing a sensible sentence together while she was present.

'Perhaps, Just William,' she said, leaning forward, 'you would like a glass of water? I could get the bailiff to bring you one.'

'The bailiff?'

'Sorry. I like crime movies and Court TV. They always offer to send the bailiff for water if someone seems stressed. Listen to me,' she added, looking away and talking to the wall. 'I sound like a crazy woman.'

'I'm fine,' I said, reaching up and brushing my hair away from my eyes. 'Honestly, I'm fine. Where were we anyway?'

'I was asking if you could work full-time?'

'Yes, that's right. Well I could, I suppose, but I'd rather not. I'm hoping to—'

'That's all right. We need part-time teachers too. Flexible people.'

'Oh I'm flexible all right, I agreed, nodding quickly. I'm a very flexible person.' I was going to add something about my middle name but decided against it. 'I just need a part-time job to support myself while I'm here, that's all.'

'And how long will you actually be here?' She stared

at me and I wasn't sure but I hoped that she was asking this because she wanted my answer to be the right one.

'For the foreseeable future,' I said. Hitomi smiled.

'Let me tell you what we have on offer,' she said.

Later that evening, we were in a bar in Pontocho together at a small table, a lit candle flickering between us, leaning forward towards the flame, ostensibly to hear each other better even though the acoustics were fine and we could make out every word. The formalities of the job interview out of the way, Hitomi had asked me whether I knew anyone in Kyoto and I had admitted that I didn't and, after a slightly embarrassed pause, she asked whether I would like to meet her later in the evening for a drink. I agreed immediately, and for the first time I did not allow my eagerness to embarrass myself, simply nodding and arranging a time and place. There was a new bar which had just opened, she said, that she wanted to try out. A friend of hers had been there recently and recommended it. Agreeing that I might end up somewhere north of Melbourne if I tried to locate it myself, I told her I would meet her back at her office later that evening and we would go there together.

In the meantime, I went back to my hostel and had a close shave, before taking a long, hot shower and dousing myself in deodorants. The sticky nightlife of Tokyo had always made me perspire and I imagined that the youthful areas of Kyoto would be no different. I changed in and out of T-shirts several times, like a teenager going on his first date, and by five o'clock, two hours before we were due to meet, I was dressed and ready and sitting on the edge of my bed, watching the clock tick away noisily, tapping a foot on the ground as I waited for the time to pass. Afraid of breaking into a sweat while I waited, I took off my shirt and hung it carefully on a hanger outside the wardrobe and sat, bare-chested by the window, attempting to read a book to pass the time. I could barely focus on the pages. Eventually, however, the time came to leave and I took a taxi to the Korakuen School, afraid that after all that I would make a mistake and lose out on my chance to see Hitomi again.

Although she had been in work all day, she had also found an opportunity to change and appeared in the doorway in a simple outfit, stonewashed blue jeans and a white T-shirt, which accentuated the honeyed toning of her skin. She wore a simple chain around her neck and only a small amount of make-up. She took my arm as we made our way through the streets, guiding me through the crowds expertly.

'A girlfriend of mine was here two nights ago,' she said as we spoke to each other in the candlelight. 'Over the course of the evening, fourteen different men approached her and asked her whether she was on her own. And she was with her boyfriend at the time. They waited until he went to the toilet apparently.'

'He must have had a weak bladder,' I said.

'He didn't go fourteen times, William,' she said, tapping my bare forearm with a sense of familiarity that I liked, the tip of her finger rubbing across the hairs there for a moment before she took it away; already we were establishing roles and personas for ourselves, for whatever our relationship was to become. 'What do you think? He would go to the bathroom and one man would approach her and she would dismiss him, then another and she would say

157

no, are you crazy? Then another and she would say look, here is my six-foot-tall boyfriend returning to me. How I love him, how special he makes me feel!' she added with a sigh before looking at me and poking her index finger into her mouth and making a gagging sound. 'She is a crazy romantic,' she explained. 'She talks about this man like he is the bee's whiskers and the cat's knees.'

I laughed but didn't correct her; obviously she wasn't entirely word perfect. 'I suppose she's in love with him,' I suggested, enjoying the idea of sparking off her a little, particularly in a conversation which revolved around romance;

'I suppose she is,' she admitted. 'But he's a lousy man. Lousy. He made moves on me too only a few weeks ago so . . .' She shrugged and looked away for a moment. 'And what about you, Just William Cody?' she asked. 'Where is your love? Don't you have one?'

I smiled. 'I'm all alone,' I said. 'A stranger in a strange land.'

'That can be hard. I went to New Zealand once. Have you been there?' I shook my head. 'I went there after I first learned to speak English. I wanted to try it out and it seemed like a convenient place to go. It was not good though. I was not good enough and found it difficult to make sense, especially when people spoke quickly at me.'

'To me,' I said.

'Yes, that's it. To me. Anyway, most people were not helpful. They didn't want to waste their time talking to me. Maybe that's what you're going through too.'

'You took pity on me?' I asked and she looked back at me, a small smile appearing. She paused before answering and when she did she spoke quietly.

158

'I didn't take pity on you,' she said defiantly. 'Not at all.'

'But you came out with me.'

'You agreed to come,' she pointed out and I laughed. 'Maybe we took pity on each other,' she suggested.

'Maybe we just like each other,' I said quickly, holding her gaze for a moment before turning away, knowing that after a line like that, one should change the conversation immediately, leave it hanging and turn elsewhere. 'Your family,' I said therefore. 'Do they live in Kyoto too?'

She smiled, possibly aware of what I had done. 'Yes,' she said. 'There are four of us. My parents, my brother Tajima and I. Tak is nineteen. He is to be an architect. He likes Japan. He doesn't want to leave. He says that now, but maybe in a few years he will feel differently. I do.'

'You want to leave?'

'Someday soon I think, yes. I've lived here for twenty-three years, all my life. I want to try life elsewhere. Europe maybe,' she conceded. 'More likely America. I think I would like to live in America. New York. Empire State Building,' she added. 'Madison Square Gardens.' She'd obviously been reading the travel books. We ordered two more shochus, a local drink which tasted a little like vodka but was served in highball glasses with a lemon mixture added in. It didn't taste very alcoholic but Hitomi had assured me that it packed a punch and I could already feel it beginning to loosen me up. 'Maybe some day,' she said with a smile.

'I'm part American,' I said eventually.

'You're what?' she asked, not understanding my phrasing.

'I'm part American,' I explained. 'Only a small part.'

159

'Which part?' she asked with a smile.

'A very small part,' I said. 'My great-grandfather was American. Makes me about one-sixteenth American too.'

'Really?' she said, interested now. 'Your great-grandfather . . .' She thought about it. 'That would be your grandfather's grandfather, is it?'

I shook my head. 'My father's grandfather. My father's name is Isaac. His father was Sam Cody and he was born in England, but his father was an American. From Iowa originally. Born in a log cabin in 1846, or so I'm told.'

'That's good,' said Hitomi, nodding appreciatively. 'And what did he do in America, your great-grandfather?'

'What didn't he do?' I asked, laughing. 'He lived, shall we say, a varied life. He started off as a bullwhacker – that was a kind of teamster, leading wagon trails across America—'

'Wagon trails!' she exclaimed, her eyes opening wider, a feast of western movies probably beginning to play across her imagination.

'Then he did a little prospecting for gold before joining the army. He was a union jayhawker, fought against the confederate bushwhackers and even met up with General—'

'You said he was a . . . what was it . . . bushwhacker?'

'Two different things,' I explained. 'They just sound the same. The bullwhackers were the teamsters, that's what he did. The bushwhackers were the confederate armies. He fought against them.'

'Oh,' she said, looking confused.

'It doesn't matter,' I said. 'His life was one long drama, that's all that matters.'

'But your own grandfather,' she asked. 'You said he was English.'

'Yes, that's right.'

She shrugged. 'So how did this happen, if his own father was an American?'

'It's a long story,' I said, unwilling to get caught up in it all. 'I'll tell you another time. You need to speak to Isaac. My father. He's the one who knows all the stories, the family history. He keeps it all up here.' I tapped my temple. 'I tell him he should write it down before it's too late but he doesn't want to. Doesn't have the patience, I don't think. He just likes to tell people about them. Likes an audience. Bores them with this stuff, I guess. I don't like to go on about it really.'

'But it's good, William,' she protested. 'To know who your family are, where you came from. It's important. Don't you feel that?'

I shrugged. I was making the mistake of trying to decide what she wanted me to say, rather than telling her what I actually felt, and she could sense this. 'Don't tell me if it makes you uncomfortable,' she said, a touch of irritability creeping into her voice and I shook my head quickly, reaching forward without fear and taking her hand in mine, grasping the fingers of her left hand with the fingers of my right and stroking them carefully.

'No,' I said. 'It doesn't make me uncomfortable at all. You're right, it is important in its way, but it's also something that I can't just tell you in one evening. You must understand that my great-grandfather is probably the most significant figure in my life, definitely the most significant in my father's. He's between us, you see.' I shuddered and looked into her eyes as I tried to explain and for the first time that evening I barely saw her. 'You talk about history, family history,' I continued.

161

'That's all my father talks about. It's what he is. A history book dressed as a man impersonating a father. He's spent the last twenty years telling me every story about that man's life and I've enjoyed them, believe me, I've enjoyed every one, they intrigue me, but that's all I am to him, you see. An audience. He makes himself feel important by telling me who his grandfather was and makes me feel insignificant by not caring who his son is. That's why I can't go into it all right now. It's very personal, you see. I'm here to escape that for a while. Can you understand that?'

I continued to hold her fingers and – perhaps it was the candlelight – but I thought I could see a glaze of a tear forming in her eyes. She smiled and looked away and then, stretching forward kissed me gently on the lips and pressed her hand against my cheek. I barely responded, surprised by the suddenness of her actions, and simply allowed her lips to rest on mine, pressed firmly against them for a few seconds, until a moment later when she sat back in her chair and shook her head sadly.

'I want to go to America,' she said eventually. 'You went from England to Japan, so you understand it. I want to go to America.'

I sighed and nodded; I could think of no response. I saw the waiter and indicated that we would like the bill.

Russell Rose met Bess Pearse at the circus in 1866. He was a performer and she was visiting with her parents. Russell, who was nineteen years old when they met, had been in the circus for four years by then. An orphan since the age of six, he had been brought up by a maiden aunt who beat him regularly and appeared to derive great satisfaction from the blows. At the age of fifteen, when he reached almost six feet in height and considered himself far too old for such ritualistic thrashings from a tiny, elderly lady, he packed a bag and disappeared in the middle of the night, never to return. He walked for nineteen miles eastwards until he was in the heart of England. He had no great idea where he was headed or what he would do when he got there; he just knew that adulthood was about to begin and was looking for adventure and employment, combined together.

Four days after leaving his aunt's home, he came across the Regis-Roc Company, a travelling circus in the traditional style, complete with animals, stuntmen, clowns and freak shows. He paid two pennies to watch a show – an investment in his future, he told himself – and made a mental note of the running order and the acts he believed he could be a part of. Unlike the rest of the audience, he found the clowns ridiculous and unfunny; he wanted no part of their entertainments. The animals scared him. A thin young woman with a startled, manic look in her eyes placed her head inside a lion's mouth and Russell gripped the sides of his seat in panic, expecting the jaws to close at any moment and sever her head from the rest of her body. Another climbed aboard an alligator in a huge pool which was brought into the centre of the ring and escaped unharmed from her potentially fatal swim. The audience applauded ecstatically as she emerged unscathed. The freaks were suitably freakish: traditional bearded women, a man with what appeared to be a third arm growing from his left shoulder, another with eyes in the back of his head, a claim Russell's aunt had often made about herself but for which he had no evidence.

The only act which seemed appropriate for him was the stuntmen and the position he coveted the most was that of trapeze artist. A troupe of four performers, three men and a women, kept the audience gasping with their feats high above the Big Top and as they performed without a safety net, the act was even more exciting. Russell applauded enthusiastically as they took their final bows and realised that he had found a career for himself.

The manager of the Regis-Roc, Albert Kincaid, refused him a job with the trapeze act but did offer him a position as a rigger with the circus, helping to put it together and disband it again after each show, for which he would be paid a small but reasonable amount each week, and fed into the bargain, an offer that Russell accepted with enthusiasm. If he worked out well and studied with the performers, Kincaid told him, there was no reason in time why he would not be able to face death on a daily basis also.

Bess Pearce was a servant girl, working in a house in west London, where she worked almost ninety hours a week for a pittance of a salary. Like Russell, she had no parents and had been in service since her twelfth year. Her life consisted of little but scrubbing and cleaning, bowing and scraping, but having never known anything different neither her aspirations nor her dreams allowed her any ambition for the future. With a friend, she saved a small amount of money every week for a monthly entertainment and on an autumn evening in 1866, she attended the circus and watched in fascination the various sights laid on for her entertainment. She was particularly drawn to the lithe young man, nineteen years of age now like her, in the black leotard who climbed slowly to the top of a ladder high above the arena before breathing in deeply and swelling his chest out again as he held on to the one barred swing which soon took him flying through the air from one side to the other. He swooped and dived as the crowd gasped and seemed to float forever in the air before one of his colleagues caught him by the ankles, a moment before he would have plunged to certain death, and all applauded enthusiastically, especially Bess who had never seen such a handsome fellow as this and whose bravery and skill only served to enhance her attraction. A few moments later, when he performed some complicated manoeuvre with a pretty girl wearing an identical leotard, she felt a twinge of envy and waited until the group were back on the sandy floor of the Big Top, taking their bows, before staring forcefully into the eyes of the young man, willing him to look at her. After a moment, sensing something out of the ordinary, he did look in her direction and for the first time all evening felt himself lose his sense of balance.

They married at the end of the year and Bess left her position to join the circus as a cook. They had a small section of one of the wagons to call their own and spent every night there wrapped in each other's arms, trying to keep their sounds muffled through embarrassment for their fellow wagon-mates. Bess became pregnant quickly and in late 1867, just over a year after she had first laid eyes on her young husband, gave birth in her wagon home – while Russell performed a triple-axel manoeuvre above the heads of three hundred natives of Cardiff – to a baby girl, who they christened Ellen Rose.

My great-grandfather and David Yountam bought the land upon which they planned to build their town and hired a group of men at a small cost to create all the buildings they needed. Within six weeks they had constructed two hundred houses, all solid with log, and the necessary businesses in the centre to keep the residents of the houses fed, watered and entertained. They ploughed all their money into their endeavours, reaching the point where they had spent almost all their savings and were forced to sell some of their few belongings in order to complete their ambitious plans. In near record time, however, they were back on the land and staring not at a wide open prairie but at a town, a real town that they had built themselves and that they owned. Their risk, their money, their dreams. Along with Clara Yountam, they walked through the buildings, thrilled to see the stock which had been bought in for the hotel and the saloon and speaking to the employees they had hired to run them.

'All we need now,' said Bill as they settled down on the porch of what was to be his own house with a steaming flask of coffee to share between the three of them, 'is a name. We never thought up a name for this town. Any suggestions?' All three were silent for a moment; they each had their ideas but none wanted to be the first to say it. 'How about Cody?' said Bill after a time, figuring that someone had to go first.

'How about Yountam?' said Yountam.

'I like Claraville,' said Clara with a distant look. 'I think it sounds homely.'

'How about we discount all three ideas and come up with something that refers to none of us,' said Bill, laughing at all their delusions of grandeur. The others agreed and they set to thinking again.

'We could try Harker,' said Yountam. 'We're not that far from Fort Harker after all.'

Bill shook his head. 'We want something of our own,' he said. 'Not something linked to one of the forts. How about Railtown? Once the trains come through, that'll be—'

'Railtown's not a place I'd want to live,' said Clara quickly. 'Sounds like it would always be noisy and filled with strangers. You need something that's going to want to make people stay there. When they hear the name of the town, they need to say, why I've always wanted to visit such and such a place. Something exotic.'

'Bangkok,' said Yountam cheerily. 'Australia. Paris. Tokyo.'

'Rome,' said Bill. 'I always wanted to see Rome. I've never been to Europe but if I went there, that's where I'd like to go. And anyway, that was built by two men at the start, wasn't it?'

They thought about it and no one had any objections. 'I guess it's historical,' said Yountam, nodding his head.

'And exotic,' admitted Clara.

'Then Rome it is,' said Bill as they clinked their mugs together. 'And here we are, the new Roman emperors, Bill Cody and David Yountam. All we need to do now is get the Christians in.'

'And watch out for the lions,' added Clara, whose sense of history was better than either her husband's or my great-grandfather's. It was to prove an unhappy prediction though, for while the Christians did soon approach, they did not look out for the lions and soon they were snapping at their heels, ready to bite, ready to eat them alive.

For the first few months, all was well at Rome. The settlers made their way towards the town and soon most of the houses and businesses were let. Of course, they were nearly all offered free of charge and on the percentage basis which Yountam had suggested, but the numbers of people living there were making the saloons and stores profitable, and the two partners had made sure to keep the grocery stores for themselves, a business which Clara oversaw. Everyone waited patiently for the arrival of the railroads which would bring the fresh business and travellers which each of them needed and every time they were asked, Bill and Yountam replied that they would be there soon. Any day now, any day.

It was on a chilly autumn evening, almost six months after they had christened their town that Bill was sitting once again on his porch, alone, watching as the sun went down. He was drinking a beer and wondering whether he should head down to the saloon for a night of card playing when a tall man dressed from head to foot in black strolled towards his house, looking a little lost. Bill had never seen this man before and was taken by his appearance.

'Ho there friend,' he called as the stranger came closer to him. 'What business brings you here?'

'Well now,' came the reply, as the stranger took off his hat and looked up at his inquisitor. 'This is Rome, isn't it?'

'It is.'

'Then I'm here looking for either a Yountam or a Cody. Two fellows who lay claim to this place.'

'Lay claim because they bought it fair and square,' said Bill cordially. 'Aye, and built everything you see here too. I'm Bill Cody,' he added after a moment, sensing no danger or hostility from this man, but genuine business.

'Then you're the man I'm here to see,' he said. 'May I come up to speak to you?'

168

Bill nodded and indicated the empty chair on the porch and the man came up and sat down on it, accepting the beer which my great-grandfather handed him with a nod. Neither of them spoke for a few moments and looked not at each other but out towards the town. Bill had chosen this house not because it was the largest one – although it was, fit for a family of six and not a man on his own – but because it was at the edge of the town, at a point from where he could see those approaching it, or entering it, or leaving it. He had a clear view of the central point between the hotel and the saloon and could just about make out the families as they made their way up the hill towards the church on a Sunday morning. He enjoyed being able to watch over his townsfolk and always had a word for them as they came to and from. For the first time in his life, he was enjoying domesticity, to the point where he was considering writing to Louisa again and inviting her and their daughter to join him there. He hadn't fully decided on that yet, though, for there was a young woman in town, the daughter of the local blacksmith, who was keeping him occupied most evenings and he didn't want to sacrifice that particular occupation just yet.

'You deserve some congratulations,' said the man. 'You've got a fine, thriving town here. I'm Jack Webb, by the way. Pleased to meet you,' he added, extending his hand.

'Bill Cody,' said my great-grandfather. 'And I thank you for what you say but we're still in early days here. Most of these people are still just settling in. But we're doing well. Good times will be ahead too though. Once the railroad comes.'

'Ah, the railroads,' said Jack Webb, nodding his head

sagely. 'Everyone is waiting for the railroads, are they not?'

'Makes sense, I guess,' said Bill. 'We all want more people coming through our towns. Good for business. Good for Kansas. And what's good for Kansas is good for Bill Cody.'

'True,' said Jack Webb. 'But you know I been all through this state and I've seen a few towns like this in my time. And some of them, well they survive, they thrive, they make rich men out of folk like you. Others, they go under just as quickly as they went up. And you know what the difference between them is, don't you?'

'It's like I said,' said Bill. 'The railroads.'

'The railroads,' said Jack Webb. 'You're absolutely right. They mean the difference between life –' he held a hand out flat in the air – 'and death.' He clicked his fingers and took his hand down again.

There was a silence for a moment until Bill turned in his chair to look at the man. He stared at him for a moment before asking his question. 'And you, friend,' he said. 'What business are you in anyway?' Jack Webb smiled across at him and said the words again, this time just making the slightest sounds with his lips, knowing that Bill knew already. The railroads. 'I thought as much,' said Bill. 'I been waiting for this moment. Well, me and my partner have anyway. We knew you'd come sooner or later. We've been waiting for you. Yountam said we should go searching for you but I said hold tight. He'll come. He'll come when he's ready.'

Webb laughed. 'You were right to wait,' he said. 'But I'm here now. And I'm in a position to make you an offer.'

Bill frowned. What kind of an offer?' he asked.

'An offer which a wise man would be a fool to turn

down. I'm authorised, on behalf of the Kansas–Pacific railroads, to make you an offer for a four-fifths share in this here Rome. If this offer is accepted, then you and your partner will be entitled to hold on to the remaining one-fifth share, splitting it any way you like, and take whatever profits that might entail. This offer will be good for the next seven days only. After that, if we have not heard from you, we will assume you are rejecting it. We won't ask again either. It's a one-time-only offer.'

Bill stared at him incredulously and suppressed an urge to laugh. 'One-fifth?' he said. 'That's a one-tenth share each? You've got to be kidding me.'

'If you're splitting things fifty-fifty, then yes, Mr Cody, you'd have a tenth each. As for your other question, no I'm not kidding you at all. I'm perfectly serious.' He spoke very affably; he had been trained to be non-confrontational.

'And this offer you're making,' said Bill after a moment. 'Assuming we were interested in selling, which I can tell you now we won't be, but assuming we were, well how much money would we be talking about?'

'The fact that you're asking implies that you're not disinterested, Mr Cody,' said Jack Webb. 'The Kansas–Pacific railroad can make you an offer of three hundred dollars for a four-fifths share in the town of Rome. If you accept, why, I can get the money for you first thing tomorrow morning, once we sign the contracts of course, which I have in my briefcase.'

Now Bill did laugh. 'Three hundred dollars?' he said, shaking his head as if the very idea was beyond insane. 'You've got to be playing with me. Have you any idea how much money we've put into this place?'

Jack Webb shrugged. 'Going on past experience,' he

171

said, 'I'd say somewhere around two thousand, maybe two and a half.'

'Closer to three thousand, Mr Webb. Ten times what you're offering.'

'For a four-fifths share.'

'Ten times, Mr Webb.' Neither man spoke for a minute and Bill could feel himself beginning to grow angry. He could sense that such a ridiculous offer would not be made unless they either assumed he was a fool or they had an alternate plan in hand.

'Perhaps you'd like to consult with your partner, Mr Cody,' said Webb after a reasonable amount of time had passed. 'A one-fifth share in a town like this, in a railroad town could still net you a reasonable income. You'd have your investment back in a few years, five years tops.'

'I don't need to consult with him, thank you very much,' said my great-grandfather. 'I can say no on behalf of the both of us. We don't need your three hundred dollars. So if there's something else you've got to say now, I suggest you cut right to it and end this business here and now.'

Webb nodded. 'All right, Mr Cody, I respect what you've done here so I'll be honest with you. You do understand, don't you,' he added with an apprehensive tone of caution slipping into his voice, 'that I am just an employee of the Kansas–Pacific railroad company? That I myself am not making this offer and do not stand to make any money out of it myself.'

'I understand,' said Bill with a sigh. 'Don't worry, I'm not going to shoot you in the back if I don't like what I hear.'

A small nervous laugh escaped from the man's mouth. 'The fact is, Mr Cody,' he began. 'If you do not

172

accept this offer, and accept it within seven days at that, then I will be forced to re-route the –' He paused and rephrased this last sentence. The Kansas–Pacific Railroad Company will be forced to re-route their intended line five miles east of here to a plot of land which they have an option on. They will then build their own town there under similar lease-holding arrangements to yours here and invite businessmen and families to join them there. And they will own all the town, Mr Cody, not just a four-fifths share in it.' He paused and looked a little shamefaced. 'I've seen this before,' he said quietly. 'I'd advise you to accept the offer.'

By the time he had finished this speech, Bill had seen the town of Rome, the town he and Yountam had conceived and built together, go up in smoke. He had not heard of this tack before and could hardly believe it was taking place, for the railroads were big business and in possession of the lands of fortune which he would never be able to lay claim to, despite the times that lay ahead. He knew immediately that if he did not accept the offer then Rome would burn.

'I don't need seven days, Mr Webb,' he said quietly, looking away, sure that he could see Clara Yountam in the distance walking slowly across the centre street, one arm placed protectively beneath her stomach for her baby was due any day now and she had swelled to huge proportions. 'I can give you my answer now.'

'You won't regret it, Mr Cody.'

'My answer is no, Mr Webb. It's no now, it'll be no tomorrow and it'll still be no seven days from now. So go on. Build your town. See where it gets you. I won't die. It's just another chapter, that's all.'

Jack Webb opened his mouth to protest but couldn't think of any words to say. He had been in this situation three times before. Once, the fellow had threatened to shoot him and he'd had to flee the town quickly. The second man had wept and begged him not to take his town from him. A third had recognised that he was a mere officer of the company but raged and stormed throughout the night, refusing to allow him to leave. None had ever won. But he had never seen such a cool and relaxed attitude to his announcement before. 'I'll leave you then,' he said, standing up and shaking Bill's hand. 'And . . . I am sorry, Mr Cody,' he added, a guilty strain in his voice. Bill said nothing, but continued to sit on his porch for the rest of the night, watching his town go about its business. He did not go to the saloon to play cards for he felt distinctly unlucky that dark night.

Within a month, the town of Ellray had been constructed five miles east, just as Jack Webb had implied. The tracks for the railway were being laid simultaneously with the foundations of the houses and stores and almost immediately the residents of Rome gathered their belongings together and relocated to the new town. The last to leave were the Yountams and Bill himself. They had lost all their money, were unemployed, but had two hundred houses to call their own. Before they left, they doused the main street with gunpowder and set a flame to it before walking away, unwilling to allow anyone else to come in and take their town again when their back was turned. As Rome burned, my great-grandfather moved on to his next adventure, where he would finally earn his name.

Over the coming months I saw more of Hitomi than of anyone else, and yet for a long time I never got to meet her family. We became lovers not long after that

174

evening in the bar in Pontocho and from the first our compatibility was striking. At twenty years of age my experience of sex was limited to one long-term girlfriend – the difficult Agnes – and two one-night stands, all of which I had enjoyed with the usual teenage excitement, but it was only when Hitomi and I first got together that I began to understand a little about passion. She had been with only one less partner than I; her first boyfriend had been at school with her but they had broken up only a year before, on her twenty-second birthday, while her second had been a short-lived affair with a colleague which had ended when a streak of violence was revealed in him. We loved being together and we loved making love together; that was something we would never outgrow. It was difficult for Hitomi to spend the entire night with me as her parents always expected her home but from time to time she would claim that she was spending the weekend with a friend and we would retreat to a small hotel along Shijo-Don, willing to use some of our earnings in order to be together into the morning, away from the noise and bustle of student life in the hostel. She slept with her back to me, my arms wrapped around her, a leg slung over hers so that we could hardly have felt closer to each other. Those weekends awoke a sensibility in me which I had never known before. Sometimes, waiting for her in the bar or sitting at our dinner table while she visited the bathroom, I would watch out for her and when she would appear my eyes would be glued to her every step as she came towards me; it wasn't her beauty that possessed me, but her very presence. Her voice on the phone filled me with excitement. To love and be loved in return, I knew nothing of those feelings before her. And I was foolishly jealous; I would see her joking with the barman while she collected our drinks or even conversing with a chambermaid while I searched the room for our lost key and I would feel envious that she was talking to them and not to me, even though I knew there was no reason for any insecurity on my part, for our connection was real and two-sided and nothing could have come between us then. We were as one.

After much persuasion on my part, she eventually agreed to introduce me to her family and we spent a torturous evening with Mr and Mrs Naoyuki in their Kyoto apartment. Hitomi's brother Tajimo – known as 'Tak' – was there too, and highly suspicious of me from the start. Although we would eventually become long-distance friends, only slightly wary of each other, Tak and I got off to a rough start that evening for, although he was the younger brother, he was very protective of his sister and seemed to take it personally that she had found a relationship with a foreigner rather than a Japanese man. He was only five feet six in height, giving me the advantage by half a foot, and I think this intimidated him as well.

Mr and Mrs Naoyuki, of course, were gracious and attentive to me, but I could tell that they shared their son's feelings, for they would ask me questions and give each other glances after I responded as if I was only confirming the dreadful things they already assumed about me.

'Hitomi tells us you are partly American,' said Mr Naoyuki as we ate and I raised an eyebrow in surprise.

'Well not really,' I said. 'My great-grandfather was an American, but that's about it. I'm pretty much English through and through.'

'I was in England once, you know,' he continued. 'Brighton. Do you know Brighton?'

176

'I know *of* Brighton,' I admitted. 'I've never been there though. When were you there?'

'It was many years ago,' he said gruffly as if I had offended him. 'I don't wish to discuss it.'

'Your father,' said Mrs Naoyuki, changing the subject entirely. "What does he do for a living?'

'He's retired now,' I told them, 'but he used to be a decorator.' Tak gave a contemptuous snort but when I looked at him he pretended that some of his food had gone the wrong way. I decided not to fill them in on Isaac's early life as a career criminal, nor the fact that he had spent a portion of his youth detained at Her Majesty's pleasure.

'I'm going to be an architect,' he said, his voice suggesting that I should bow down before him and praise him for his creativity.

'Congratulations,' I said.

'And your mother,' asked Mrs Naoyuki. 'She is well too?'

I thought about it, unsure what was the correct answer. I decided to simply tell the truth. 'She's fine, as far as I know,' I said. 'She lives in Canada. We don't really see each other.'

'How does she live in Canada?' asked Hitomi's father, looking at me as if I had suddenly cursed.

'They're divorced, you see,' I explained. 'She re-married and moved to Canada. Her husband's a doctor.' I hoped that was a good thing.

'It's not that uncommon,' Hitomi told her parents but they looked at me as if I was the bad seed regardless.

'So your home is broken?' asked Mr Naoyuki sadly.

'Father!' cried Hitomi.

'That's all right,' I told her, placing my hand on hers protectively. 'It's not broken,' I said, turning to look at her parents and sitting erect in my chair as I did so. 'It was never really together in the first place. My father lives in London. My mother lives in Canada. In our own ways, we communicate with each other.'

'And you're in Kyoto,' said Mr Naoyuki with a shrug before muttering something in Japanese which I could not catch. I was going to ignore it out of politeness but Tak saw to it that I didn't miss out.

'My father says that it's a strange family which lives on three continents and isn't broken,' he said and Hitomi immediately punched his arm, soliciting an angry remark from her mother. I let the comment go. Under any circumstances I would not have wanted to insult Hitomi's parents, but if they intended to be rude to me, I was even more convinced that I should hold my peace. Take the moral high ground.

The evening continued, however, much along these lines and while we were ostensibly friendly to each other, there was a reserve and hostility which I suspected was not just due to the fact that we were strangers. Leaving later, I begged Hitomi to return to the hostel with me for the night, but she grew angry with me then.

'Why do you ask me to do that?' she said in a hushed voice at the door. 'You know I can never do that without lying to my parents.'

'I just want us to be together tonight, that's all,' I said. 'Is that so wrong?'

'But why now? Why tonight?' she continued.

'I don't know!' I protested. 'Why do you think? It's not like we've never spent the night together before.'

'You want to do it now because you want my parents to see that's what we're doing,' she said in an accusatory voice. 'And Tak too. You want to tell them look, you can be rude to me and insult me and call my family

178

anything you like, but look at me now as I'm fucking your daughter.'

'That's not it,' I hissed at her, taken aback by the vehemence of her language, the way that hearing the word 'fuck' uttered from her lips upset me. 'That's what you think I'm about, is it? If it is, then you don't know me at all.'

'You know that's what you're doing, William. You want to go in there to them and say they don't own me any more? That you do? Just because you're fucking me?'

'Don't say that, Hitomi,' I said, taking her by the arm, and incredibly I thought I could feel a sting behind my own eyes now. 'Don't speak about yourself like that. Don't speak about us like that. That's not how things are with us at all. I love you, you know I do.'

'Then don't try to prove things to my parents about us,' she said. 'We are you and me. No one else. All right? You have that, William? You heard that? Don't try to prove things to my parents, all right? Someday I'm going to leave Japan and I need them to understand why I'm doing it.'

I nodded and turned on my heel and stormed off into the night. We rarely argued but when we did, Hitomi always ended it by pointing out her intention of one day leaving Japan; neither of us ever mentioned whether I would be going with her or not. However, in time that argument, like all our arguments, subsided and we returned to our previously happy state. We did not visit the Naoyukis together again – ever again, in fact – although from time to time we would meet Tak and his date for drinks in the evening. Perhaps on one of our birthdays or if he had a job interview in the city. On these occasions we began to get on quite well and gave each other a grudging respect, although there was always a sense of awkward embarrassment whenever Hitomi would leave us for a few minutes, while we attempted to find common ground to converse on.

A year passed in Japan, and then eighteen months, and I became fluent in the language and worked full time for the teaching agency. The money was good and my savings grew and I found myself so consumed by the Japanese culture, while still feeling alienated by it, an unwelcome visitor, that I began to write about my feelings there and kept a journal of my life in Kyoto and the people I met. I approached it from the point of view of the ignorant foreigner and my pieces were humorous enough to be published by a local English-language newspaper, who eventually agreed to begin a weekly series which I would write and which helped to supplement my income. In the meantime I began to take a greater interest in writing, and read a lot more, immersing myself not just in Japanese literature but also in the western books which I had largely ignored for many years. I turned twenty-two in Japan and gave up my teaching job in favour of a full-time position with the newspaper where I wrote features and editorials, a job I soon began to love and take great pride in. Hitomi was proud of me too and liked introducing me to her friends as her 'writer boyfriend'. She told them I was one day going to write a novel but I quickly told them that this was not true. I had found my calling, I thought, and it was journalism. I kept a portfolio of my work and knew that I was getting better. The fact that there were only two places I felt truly comfortable – alone in my apartment with Hitomi by my side, or sitting in front of my word processor, hunched forward, reading the words aloud as I typed them in, pausing, reading again, deleting, rewriting, scrapping parts of a sentence, paragraphs from a page, always working until I had said all I needed to say and could place my full stop. Physically, I could feel myself changing. A healthy sexual life discarded my childhood. I cut my hair and allowed a small growth of dark stubble to grow along my chin, which I sculpted meticulously every morning. I became a new man that year; I had found two things which made me happy: love and work. And then the letter came and a period of my life drew to a close.

In all the time I had been in Japan, I had been a poor communicator with Isaac. I sent him the odd postcard, a letter on his birthday and at Christmas, and on rare occasions would phone him up for a little stilted conversation, but whenever we spoke it was difficult. I knew that he believed I had betrayed him in some way. It was true that we had not laid eyes on each other in almost two years and while I was fully aware that he had no other living relative to speak to in London, it was a thought that I tried to bury at the back of my mind. I had found a form of liberation for myself in Japan; I hated to think of Clapham and Battersea and Lavender Hill and the train station and the crowds of people heading for those platforms every morning, pushing past each other, carrying Styrofoam cups of coffee as they charged into work or charged home again, their skin pale and blotchy, their eyes barely open. There was nothing there for me; I felt my days with Isaac and Buffalo Bill Cody were part of a different life and wanted no more of either of them. And I knew that I was wrong to do so but I didn't care. I tried not to think about them at all. And then he wrote to me.

It was a short letter, only half a page long, but it gave the essential details in the starkest terms. Isaac was going to die and he didn't want that to happen without seeing me one last time, without trying to make amends for whatever it was (he said) that I thought he had done to me. Could I come to visit, he asked. If not, he understood and someone would contact me when it was over.

I read the letter in shock. I had taken it from my mailbox on a Saturday morning and climbed back into bed to read it; I was still there when Hitomi let herself in at lunchtime and found me sitting there, my head in my hands, the pillows strewn around me, my eyes puffy from tears. She read the letter and asked me what I was going to do.

'What choice do I have?' I said. 'I have to go home. I want to go home,' I added to make myself sound like a better son, like a better man, even if it were not the case.

'Of course you do,' she said, but her face was pale and scared. 'Don't worry, I'll arrange it for you.'

'Come with me,' I said quickly, reaching up and taking both her hands in mine. 'Come with me, Hitomi.' I looked at her and pressed one of her hands to my bare chest, in the spot where my heart was, hoping that she would feel it beating beneath the skin and understand why it did so, and she did but she stayed silent. 'Don't make me go there on my own,' I said. 'I don't want to be without you.'

She stayed silent for a long time but eventually, she shook her head. Before speaking, she began to cry. She sat on a chair and buried her face in her hands. 'I don't want to,' she said simply, raising her hands in resignation, as if this was something that was completely beyond her control. 'I just don't want to,' she repeated.

'You don't want to?' I shouted at her, appalled. 'What does that mean? How can you just not want to?'

'I don't want to go to England,' she said. 'If I go to England, I'll die there.'

'You'll what?'

'I just don't want to go there!' she repeated. 'You have to go. I know you do. So you go. But I don't want to. I want to go to America.'

'Oh fuck America,' I shouted at her. 'Enough with the I-want-to-go-to-Americas. You never go, Hitomi! You keep saying you're going to go but you never do! You'll die in England? Well I don't know what the fuck that means but I'll tell you this, if you stay in Kyoto you'll die here, that's what. You'll end up rotting in your parents' apartment for the rest of your life and one day Tak will be the only person at your funeral. Do you understand me? Do you hear what I'm saying?' I was screaming at her and had jumped out of the bed to march up and down the room. I came down close to her face and took her head in my hands, pushing it forward so that it was buried in my chest, before pushing it down further and further. She kicked her feet out and her shoe slapped into my shin, causing me to fall to the ground, clutching it in pain. 'What the fuck did you do that for?' I asked, crying now myself. 'Please come,' I added immediately, not caring about the physical pain at all. 'I need you.'

And then, without another word, she stood up, looked in the mirror, fixed her hair calmly and left the room. I stayed on the floor for a time and when I stood up the first thing I saw on the bed was the crumpled-up letter and I sighed. *Thanks, Isaac,* I thought. Time to go home.

*   *   *

183

Waiting for other opportunities to present themselves after the destruction of his town, my great-grandfather returned to work as a bullwhacker for the railroads and quickly became known as the best buffalo hunter in the state. At the same time another hunter, Billy Comstock, was gaining equal recognition in Missouri and his champions were declaring him the master bullwhacker in America. In order to settle the question, it was decided that a competition would be held with $500, and no small amount of pride, as the prize.

Comstock was a bulky man, a few years older than Bill, and not as dedicated to his work as my great-grandfather was, preferring to idle away his time in saloons when he was not working. For this alone, Bill felt that he could beat him and a date was set when they would meet and contest each other. Word of the competition spread around the neighbouring states and crowds began to descend on Kansas on the weekend it was to take place in order to see the great acts of daring which would surely take place.

'The trick is to ride with the head of the herd,' Bill told Matt Stepson, the young lad who took care of Bill's horse Brigham for him as they prepared for the day's hunting. 'Shoot the head of the herd and keep shooting whichever animal replaces the head and you steer them in your direction. At that you have a better chance of making more kills.'

'They say Comstock kills fifteen bulls a day in Missouri,' said Matt, unsure whether his employer would be able to beat that, for Bill generally killed no more than an even dozen when working for the railroads.

'We'll have fifteen dead within the first ninety minutes, my boy,' replied Bill with a laugh. 'Believe me, this is no regular day's work today. There's more at stake. Pride, for one.'

'Well your audience is certainly ready for it,' said Matt. 'There must be two hundred people gathered on the prairie.' Bill nodded. He was pleased with the turnout, looking forward to impressing the crowds. He liked the idea of being at the centre of their attentions and putting on a show for them. Earlier in the week Comstock had protested the numbers who were planning on watching the contest, claiming that such a crowd would scare the buffaloes and they would not linger nearby, but he had been assured by the organisers that this would not be the case and that all spectators would be kept together in a plot of land of sufficient distance that they might enjoy the entertainment without their having any negative effects upon it.

'We should have charged money for attending,' Bill pointed out, the first signs of the future showman beginning to develop in him. 'We could have put that five hundred dollars to shame if we'd made these people pay to watch us.'

The contest began with Bill Cody and Billy Comstock on separate ends of the prairie. My great-grandfather was using a breech-loading .50 calibre rifle, while Comstock was armed with a Homer which was a more accurate shot but took longer to reload. The crowd cheered as they began their contest and within an hour Bill had killed thirteen buffalo to Comstock's nine. That margin widened throughout the morning and when they broke at lunchtime the scores were at thirty-eight to twenty-three in Bill's favour. The spectators all tried to speak with both contestants as the huge picnic lunch was served for their celebrity had grown over the weeks approaching the hunt. Bill was speaking with the sheriff of Sheridan, where the prairie was located, when he spotted a familiar figure walking towards him, baby in arms.

'Louisa,' he said, stepping towards her quickly and kissing her cheek. 'I never expected to see you here.'

'I'm sure you didn't,' she replied quietly. 'I saw the advertisements in St Louis and thought I should come see how my husband spends his time when he's away from his duties and responsibilities.'

'Poorly, I think,' replied Bill. 'This is a mere pastime, that's all. I'm back on the railroads, hunting buffalo to feed the crews.'

'I know all about what you're doing, Bill. Don't think that news does not come through to me from time to time. I may have misplaced my husband but I still have some friends.'

Bill shrugged. It was good to see her again although he did not want to begin an argument while he was in the middle of this contest. He took the baby out of Louisa's arms and held her beneath the arms at eye level to take a good look at her. The baby stared back at him in astonishment.

'She's a good size anyway,' he said. 'What did you call her in the end?'

'Arta,' replied Louisa. 'After my grandmother.'

'And why not after mine?' he asked. 'Aren't my family traditions as important?'

'Perhaps if you'd been there, things would have been different.'

Bill frowned and refused to be drawn on it. 'Well she's a pretty thing,' he said. 'So you're back to stay then, are you? Had enough of St Louis?'

Louisa bit her lip. She had little choice for she had grown frustrated with living with her parents as a married woman and had decided to give marriage another try. 'Until something better comes along,' she said with a slight smile, in order to show him that she really was willing to give it another go.

'Then we will have to speak later,' he said. 'For I have a contest to finish.'

And when it ended, he had sixty-nine buffaloes to Comstock's forty-six and accepted the $500 prize with magnanimity, handing it directly to his returned wife who placed it within her bag immediately.

'Congratulations to both of you,' said the sheriff, who was presenting the prize from a hastily erected platform. 'You've done yourselves proud. Billy Comstock, you killed forty-six buffalo today and that's no mean feat, no mean feat at all. Congratulations to you, sir.' The crowd applauded him politely while his own friends let out an enormous cheer to salve his wounded ego. He smiled bitterly and scuffed the ground with the toe of his boot. 'But you, Bill Cody,' continued the sheriff. 'Sixty-nine buffaloes is about the most I've ever heard of being killed by any one man in a day. It's a great achievement. I won't be able to think of you as plain old Bill Cody any more, my friend, but as Buffalo Bill. That's the name for you now!'

The crowd let out a huge roar of approval and my grandfather ascended the platform, arms raised above his head like a prizefighter, milking his every moment in the spotlight. Even as his newly christened name settled into his mind, and he determined that he would hold on to it ever after, he could see the dollar signs forming.

Chapter Six

Reacquaintance

The winter of 1868 found my great-grandfather re-aligned to the Fifth Cavalry but living a quieter life than he had in recent years; incredibly, despite all he had achieved so far, he was still only twenty-two years old at the time. He had mended his marriage somewhat and Louisa and he were reconciled and living in comfort in a small house with their baby daughter, not far from the fort where the soldiers were stationed. He had brokered an unusual deal with the military command whereby he would be called upon for certain potentially dangerous scouting missions into Indian territory but he was not committed to serving as part of the regular infantry. He enjoyed his life this way and his burgeoning celebrity was not something the army could easily set aside. The name 'Buffalo Bill' was beginning to spread through the neighbouring states and his adventures and bravery were things with which they wanted to be aligned. The Indians in some parts of the states of Kansas, Oklahoma, New Mexico and Colorado were continuing to put up strong fights in order to retain their land; there was widespread feeling for the first time that some tribes might be successful, an outcome which would have been disastrous to Andrew Johnson's administration.

To combat this, the president had placed all his faith in one general – George Armstrong Custer – to drive them out into the newly established reservations. To this end he was given responsibility for bringing the armies in from the west, destroying whatever encampments they found along the way, and doing whatever had to be done to ensure success as they began that winter's push.

George Custer was born in Ohio and had joined the army at a young age, finishing last in his class at West Point. Once graduated, however, he proved himself to be not only the bravest man in the army but also a brilliant tactician; what he had lacked in the classrooms of the military academy was more than made up for by his behaviour on the field of combat. Abraham Lincoln appointed him the army's youngest general and he became legendary almost immediately, as much for his striking appearance – long golden locks, brightly coloured uniforms which he designed himself – as for his actions. He drew men to him, men who wanted to share in his deeds and reflect some of his glories on to themselves. Over the course of five years he served under three different presidents, Lincoln, Johnson and Ulysses S. Grant, and considered himself superior in courage and leadership abilities to all but the first.

Although they had never met, President Johnson had taken a liking to Bill through the newspaper reports of his exploits. Ever since the great buffalo chase, during which my great-grandfather had earned his nickname, he had been involved in ever more exciting spectacles, usually designed to show off his skills as an entertainer, if not as a soldier. Eliza McCardle Johnson, the president's wife, had seen Bill perform at Saltoun, where he captured eighty buffalo in one day while riding bareback on a horse he had never seen until that morning. The first lady had been impressed as much by his handsome, youthful looks as by his bravery and had flirted openly with him at a dinner afterwards, causing some distress among the other people seated at their table. Afterwards, the head of the largest buffalo had been mounted and sent to her in Washington and it was said that she kept it on the wall of her dressing room, scandalous in itself. Reporting back to her husband on Bill's success, the president made it clear that he wanted to keep Buffalo Bill, as he was now regularly being called in the newspapers, as an ally and had granted him his desire to be aligned to the cavalry without actually being a part of it.

The relationship between the general and the showman was an ambivalent one from the start. Bill had long been an admirer of Custer's; indeed when he had first left the Golden Rule Hotel in St Louis with David Yountam and Seth Reid, part of the allure had been to attach his fortunes to that of the great warrior whose name at the time was only beginning to be spoken of with reverence. They were of similar age, and their careers had been equally precocious, but where Custer had made his name in the army, Bill had made his for the most part in civilian life, caring less for a uniform and a rank than he did for adventure and challenge. The general's name had become well known across the nation for his youth and successes had also proved something of a good public relations tool for the Andrew Johnson administration, which had succeeded to power upon the assassination of Abraham Lincoln in 1865. However, when they met they found that they were simply not suited to each other and found that while they rarely argued outright, there was a tension between them that neither seemed able to define or solve. Custer was known to distrust Bill, for he observed in him a lack of commitment to the union ideals – an observation which was correct – and felt that my great-grandfather was only interested in his own glory and growing fame. Of course, Bill had a similar feeling towards the general, believing that a display of precocity in such an organised field as the cavalry shouted itself out as something more than simple idealism.

However they were thrown together in Kansas in 1869 while the next move against the Cheyenne people was being planned and they had no choice but to make the most of it. They often went out on scouting expeditions together and were perfectly cordial to each other, even taking part in a mini-tournament together where Bill easily won the rounds devoted to the capture and killing of animals, but lost badly to the general when precision shooting was the goal. There was a sense at the fort that it was only a matter of time before the two men came to blows, but they were as aware of that as anyone, and knew that such an eventuality could only prove harmful to each, and so worked to maintain their steady, troubled relationship. It was during that winter however that one of their most fraught moments occurred, in front of no less a personage than the new president of the United States.

Ulysses S. Grant had begun his administration earlier that year, having easily beaten the one-term Johnson, and as a military man, he was friendly and admiring of Custer, but there were scarcely two people more different from each other. Grant had worked his way up through the ranks slowly, from private to commander-in-chief. He was also more cautious regarding plans to move the Indians off their land and into reservations, attempting to broker peaceful deals wherever possible, while Custer was more in favour of gathering huge ranks of cavalry men and simply chasing them away, killing as many as necessary.

Two weeks before Christmas that year, Bill and Louisa were at home one evening, Louisa making a new blanket for their daughter's bed while Bill smoked and brooded by the fire. Their own relationship had settled down since they had returned to each other. Louisa was determined to hold on to her marriage no matter what; Bill was less eager but had little choice. They spoke little in the evenings, having little to talk about. A knock on the door was a relief to both but a surprise also, as they rarely received visitors.

'Tom Barton,' said Bill, looking up happily as one of the young camp runners, a boy of about sixteen, poked his head through the open doorway. What brings you out to us this evening? Looking for a drink and a smoke, I'll bet.'

'No sir,' replied Tom nervously, looking towards Louisa who was narrowing her eyes at him suspiciously. As a rule she distrusted visitors, particularly those who had little other reason to be there than to deliver messages. She turned her lamp a little more in his direction to get a closer look at the lad; he was tall for his age, and handsome, but his long black hair looked as if it had not seen soap or water since the previous Christmas and she had a curious urge to drag him outside to the well and submerge him in it. 'Evening, Mrs Cody,' Tom added, nodding at her.

'Good evening, Tom,' replied Louisa, putting her work down and standing up, brushing down the front of her skirts slowly. 'You'll have a little dinner with us, won't you? It must be hungry work riding along the prairies this late at night.'

'I won't if it's all the same to you,' he said. 'I've had my dinner already. I'm just here to deliver a message to Mr Cody, ma'am.'

'What have I told you time and time again?' asked Bill with a sigh. 'Haven't I told you to call me Buffalo Bill? That's what my friends call me, you know, and if you don't want to call me by my name I'll have no reason to think you're a friend any more and I might have cause to shoot you then. What do you say, Tom? Are we friends?'

'Sure we are, Mr Cody,' said Tom, stuttering slightly in his nervousness. Although he was accustomed to being around army men who believed in their own magnificence and revelled in their myths, there was something about my great-grandfather that always worried him. 'Buffalo Bill, I mean,' he added quickly. Most people had started to call Bill by this name, particularly those who were younger than him, but he still had to insist on it from time to time.

'Well that's better,' he said, smiling with satisfaction. 'Now what's this message you're in such a hurry to hand over to me. Has the war against China been declared now?'

Tom stared at him and opened his eyes wide. 'The war against China?' he asked in amazement. 'No, they haven't announced anything of the—'

'My husband is teasing you, Tom,' said Louisa quietly, pouring a cup of tea for the boy and handing it to him, despite his earlier refusal. 'Bill thinks it's very funny to tease the young men around here, forgetting he was one of them himself once.' She pronounced her husband's name deliberately, omitting the 'Buffalo' as she always did. He did not correct her.

'The message, Tom,' said Bill gruffly, unwilling to

continue a conversation whereby his wife might end up mocking him in front of a private. 'What does it say? Who's it from?'

'From General Custer, sir,' he answered quickly, flustered by the dialogue so far. 'Says he wants to see you over at the fort tonight. Something important's about to happen, I think. There's officers running round like crazy men over there.'

'Really?' said Bill. 'And what do you suppose it's all about?'

Tom thought about it. 'Well I don't know,' he admitted. 'All I know is that everything was calm and then a runner arrived from Parkworst and all hell broke loose. We must be about to begin another push.'

'Surely not tonight,' said Louisa with a sigh. 'Why, that's just madness. It could wait until the morning, couldn't it? What's one more day?'

'It won't be another push yet,' said Bill in frustration. 'They don't just announce those things without any build up. No, it's something else.' He raised an eyebrow and sucked on his pipe thoughtfully. 'Well,' he said after a long pause. 'You've delivered your message, Tom, and I thank you for it. You can get on back home to the fort now if you're not staying for some food.'

Tom nodded but stood still for a moment. 'Aren't you coming with me, sir?' he asked.

'Where to?' he asked innocently.

'Well back to the fort. Like I said, General Custer wants to—'

'How did you find my house, Tom?' asked Bill, cutting him off before he could finish his sentence. The boy looked confused.

'How's that?'

'I asked how you found my house. You had a message

194

to deliver, you got on your horse, you rode on over here. How did you know where to find me?'

Tom looked utterly confused now and glanced across at Louisa, hoping she might save him from this conversation, but she was back at her weave now and appeared to be paying little attention to either of them, muttering quietly to herself instead at the crazy actions of the army and her own foolishness for having ever become involved in a life as troublesome as this one. 'Well, I just found you,' he replied eventually. 'I mean everyone knows where you live. It's not a secret.'

'And General Custer,' asked Bill. 'Do you think that *he* knows where I live?'

'Sure he does,' said Tom. 'I mean he must do since he—' He broke off suddenly, realising where this conversation was going. Bill raised a finger and wagged it in the air, grinning mischievously.

'If the general wants to see me,' said Bill, 'he can do what you did. He can get on his horse and ride on over here. I'm at no one's beck and call in the middle of the night, not even a man like George Armstrong Custer. You go back and tell him that. You tell him what I said, you hear me?'

The blood seemed to drain from Tom's face and he opened his mouth, trying to find the words to express how little he wanted to be entrusted with such a task. 'You don't mean that, sir,' he said. 'You don't want me to say that to the general?'

'Sure I mean it,' said Bill. 'I'm not a man to waste my words or my time. You get on back over there and tell him that I'm about ready to turn in for the night and if there's anything that won't keep till the morning then he best get on over here himself and let me know what it

195

is. End of story. What's the matter with you, boy? What do you think he'll do to you?'

'Shoot me, sir.'

Bill laughed. 'He won't shoot you,' he said. 'You're just the messenger. Go on now. Tell him what I said. But tell him he's welcome here at any time, night or day, if he wants to come and do us the honour of paying us a visit,' he added graciously.

Tom nodded sadly, still fearful of the response he would get from General Custer when he delivered this message. 'If that's what you want, Mr Cody,' he said.

'Buffalo Bill,' said Bill patiently.

'Should he come tonight?' asked Tom, turning to leave now, hoping that Bill might change his mind before he had to return to the fort. Bill shrugged.

'It's like I said,' he answered. 'Anytime he wants. If it's urgent.'

It must have been deemed urgent because an hour later Bill sighed when he heard the sound of a horse galloping towards his home and he knew immediately who was its rider. Custer wasted no time on ceremony and marched straight into the house, slamming the door behind him as he entered. 'You always ignore the orders of a ranking general, Cody?' he shouted, standing tall with his hands on his hips, the cold air outside making steam appear to rise from the general's head so that he appeared like a man possessed of a devil.

'Orders, General?' asked Bill, not standing up but looking the general directly in the eyes nevertheless. 'Tom Barton merely told me you'd like to see me, that's all. He never mentioned anything about orders. If I'd known it was an official command from a United States general, why, I would have put on my best suit and ridden right over there to see you. Even though I'm not actually in the army and therefore not responsible to you,' he added quietly.

'Don't play at word games with me, Cody. When I ask to see someone, I expect them to come running. Enlisted man or not.'

'Expectations can be cruel things,' admitted Bill. 'I once thought I was going to be able to live a nice quiet life, running my own town, making a pot of money, and having women and whisky at my beck and call. Didn't work out that way. Speaking of which, there's whisky over there if you want a glass.' He nodded in the direction of a side table, where he had laid a bottle and a fresh glass a few minutes earlier in anticipation of his visitor. Custer shook his head in frustration and poured himself a glass before offering it to Bill.

'You're a hard man to talk to, Bill Cody,' he said. 'And don't ask me to call you by that ridiculous name either,' he added, raising a hand in the air as Bill prepared to say his nickname. 'You can save that for the newspaper reporters and the boys who think you're some kind of American hero.'

'You don't think I'm a hero then, General? I who killed sixty-nine buffalo in one day. That's not heroic?'

'Heroism is for the battlefield, Cody,' he replied. 'Not the Big Top. I don't doubt you're a brave man. A fool of a man, I've thought sometimes, but there we are. Nicknames are for schoolboys, that's all. What is it with you egotists and your need for these things? There's that other fellow now, Hickok, you know him?'

'I know of him,' replied Bill. 'We haven't had the pleasure of each other's company yet.'

'I met him ten months ago over near the Ohio border,' said Custer, spitting a piece of chewing tobacco towards the fireplace and missing, the sticky mess landing on the floor instead. He ignored it. 'Damn fool of a man if you ask me. He got up on a stage and started to sing songs and dance with the girls and I don't know what else. You call that a man?'

'I don't call anyone a man until I have the mark of him and like I said, we haven't—'

'Well that damn fool, he goes around calling himself "Wild Bill". And more of an idiotic, mother's sop of a man I've never met in my life. Wild indeed! There's nothing wild about that man but his behaviour. Still,' he added after a thoughtful pause. 'I suppose you've got the manners of a buffalo.'

'I'll save you the trouble of saying that I smell like one too, on account of the fact that I know I do since I spend most of my time around them. But then rather a herd of buffalo, I think, than a cavalry of stinking, teenage soldiers.'

'I speak my mind, Bill, you know that.'

'You do, General. And I'm sure you haven't made this distance at this hour to insult me or talk philosophy. You must need me for something. You may as well just get on with it so there'll be some chance of a little sleep before whatever it is needs to begin.'

Custer nodded and drank back his whisky in one shot, reaching for the bottle again almost immediately. 'President Grant is coming to visit us,' he said. 'Bringing some newspaper men along for the ride, it seems. They're looking for interviews.' He uttered the word as if it sullied his mouth.

Bill's eyes opened wider and he sat up, more alert now than he had been all evening. The word 'publicity' was beginning to sound in his ears. 'What's that?' he asked. 'What newspaper men?'

'It's all a lot of nonsense, of course, but Grant needs to

gain a little more popularity. This first year hasn't gone well for him, you know that much. Seems he wants to have a little piece of my glory reflected on to himself. Nationally speaking. Make the American people see him as a man of action and valour.'

'*Your* glory?' asked Bill. 'If it's only your glory he's after then what are you doing here? I can't help him with that.'

'*Our* glory then,' admitted Custer. 'Damn it, Bill, what do you want me to say? We've got our reputations, you know that. For right or wrong, we've established names for ourselves and what's wrong with putting those names to some good use? The president thinks he can seem like more of a popular figure if he's seen to associate with us more.'

'If he's seen to command us more, you mean. He wants to take credit for our accomplishments.' Custer said nothing, unwilling to appear disloyal towards his commander-in-chief. Bill waited long enough to make the general feel uncomfortable before speaking again. 'Makes sense, I suppose. When's he coming then?'

'Day after tomorrow. Wants us both to greet him. Wants an enthusiastic welcome, I'm told, because the reporters will be there and they're going to be watching every word. There's been talk that the president and I don't get along and they're just hoping that something amiss happens.'

'Like you blow his head off when your shooting goes astray?'

'Bill,' cautioned the general. 'Remember who you're talking to. There's only so much I can listen to.'

Bill laughed. 'Well everyone knows you don't get along,' he said. 'That's supposed to be the news, is it?'

'Whether we do or whether we don't is neither here

nor there. I'm a military man, I'm a general, and he's my commander-in-chief. I'll do whatever he tells me to do, no questions asked. If he wanted me to blow my own head off, I'd do it. Or yours for that matter. And if he sent someone to tell me he wanted to see me in the middle of the night, I can damn sure tell you that I'd get on my horse and go see him and not tell him to come see me if he's all that interested. That's what respect is all about.'

Bill took the rebuke in good cheer but said nothing for a moment. 'And I suppose,' he said eventually, 'they're going to be watching you and me too.'

'I suppose they will.'

'And I suppose you're going to tell me that I've got to be deferential towards you the entire time. Is that it? You want to make that clear right from the start?'

Custer sat back and shook his head. 'Look, Bill,' he said. 'I don't know what it is I'm supposed to have done to you to earn your contempt but do I have to point out again that I'm a general in this army?'

'But I'm not in this army,' Bill pointed out. 'I'm a freelance operative. Always have been. I don't take orders. I take assignments. And you're wrong anyway; I'm not contemptuous of you. Not at all. I admire you if you want to know the truth.'

'Well you make sure not to show that.'

'We're different people,' he said. 'We're looking at the world in different ways. You seek order, advancement, a career path. Tell me you don't want to be sitting where Ulysses Grant is sitting now one day in the future. Can you tell me that?'

'What's wrong with ambition? You're ambitious. You try to make your name known as often as possible. I would have thought this was a perfect opportunity for you. What the hell is that goddam nickname for if not for that? Mixing with the president and the army's most celebrated general for an evening with a bunch of newspapermen hanging off your every word? I would have thought that was the kind of opportunity you would have killed for. And all I'm asking you to do is show a little understanding of the order of things. That's all I'm asking. I don't think it's too much to look for either.'

Bill stood up and threw a log on the fire. He stared into the flames and thought about it. Custer was right about one thing; he was ambitious and he did like to see his name in print as often as possible. And this was a good opportunity for some national publicity. 'All right then,' he said, turning around and stretching his arms out to indicate that he had been bested for once. 'I'll do just as you ask. For one night only I will be the perfect subordinate and follow your every command, hanging off your utterances as if they're a bunch of new commandments sent down from Moses himself. That's what you want to hear, isn't it?'

Custer smiled. 'You shouldn't make everything between us into a battle, you know,' he said. 'You never know. It might be fun.'

Bill frowned. 'Don't let your men hear you saying that,' he muttered.

The Regis-Roc Circus travelled the length and breadth of England from its inception in 1851 until its eventual closure just before the outbreak of the First World War. During that time many of the most famous circus entertainers of the time – David Rickton, the celebrated trapeze artist; Elijah and Eliza Hunter, the Siamese twins; Richmond Tappil, after Houdini the most famous escape artist of the era – performed their acts under its

201

Big Top tarpaulin, and as a child Ellen Rose managed to see and be enthralled by all of them.

Her childhood was an unusual one as her father and mother, Russell and Bess, led such curious lives. She came to appreciate her father the most when he was suspended one hundred feet above the ground, balancing on a high wire or flying through the air with the ankles of one of his colleagues gripped between his fists; on the ground they had little to say to each other. Bess was her prime educator. When she was not peeling potatoes or cooking soups for the acts, she took to the task of educating her daughter with the kind of determination which had never been shown to her in her own childhood. She was determined that the girl would grow up with more possibilities in her future than she had ever been afforded. Bess had one simple ambition: that Ellen would never have to cook for or clean up after anyone but herself.

Ellen, however, was not a captive student, finding her lessons dull and pointless. Even as a very young girl, she knew there was only one thing she wanted to do with her life and that was to follow her father up the ladder and join him as part of his trapeze company.

'By the time you're old enough to go up there, I'll be too old to catch you,' he told her, shaking his head as if he wished that things were different but there was nothing he could do about it.

'You could train me now,' she suggested. 'I'm seven years old.'

'That's too young to be flying trapezes,' he insisted. 'I'm not going to be held responsible for you falling and breaking your neck.' In truth he was torn between his own love of the act and his terror that his daughter would seek to copy him.

'Jane Shallot flew the trapezes with you in Edinburgh at Christmas,' Ellen pointed out, her precocious memory having stored up the dates and times of many of the performances and the guest artistes that her father had worked with in different cities. 'And she was only twelve.'

'Jane Shallot had been working in the circus for years,' Russell Rose replied. 'She knew the trade. Nothing was going to happen to her. She was a legend before she hit double figures.'

'I was born in the circus,' insisted Ellen. 'I've been watching you up there since before I can remember. I don't even know what you did before joining the circus.'

'Nothing,' said Russell sadly. 'If you want to know the truth of it. I did nothing. But at least that nothing was something in itself. You don't want to be born, grow up, live and die in the circus, do you? There's so much more out there. Isn't your mother educating you to better yourself?'

Ellen thought about it and her brow furrowed deeply as it always did when she was deep in concentration. Russell couldn't help but smile and felt an urge to reach out and trace the lines in her forehead, smooth them out, make her happy again. She opened her mouth but thought about what she wanted to say before uttering a word. When she did, her statement was clear and concise and she uttered each syllable with determination. 'I want to do what I want to do,' she said. 'And I don't think anyone should be able to stop me.'

Russell shook his head sadly. 'Well I'm not training you and I can tell you for sure that neither Jimmy nor Elizabeth will either.' These were his colleagues who would do whatever Russell told them when it came to his daughter. Ellen was dissatisfied with this answer and stormed off to their wagon, refusing to speak to her father for two full days. In the meantime, he recounted the conversation to his wife, Bess, who agreed with him and insisted that Ellen be allowed nowhere near a trapeze or a high wire.

'She's so angry though,' said Russell, feeling like making a conciliatory gesture. 'Isn't there some way of cheering her up?'

'She'll see sense. Just let her be.'

'I don't like fights, Bess. You know that. I'm always afraid that something will happen to me whenever I have a fight with you or Ellen and then I'll be dead and there'll be no way of taking back the things that were said. I don't like to leave a quarrel.'

'Don't worry about it,' his wife replied. 'I told you she'll snap out of it. She's a child. Children sulk. And what's she going to do, after all? Run away and join a circus?'

Russell smiled and shook his head. He had the impression that Bess had been waiting seven long years to use that line.

I left Japan within three days of receiving Isaac's letter. Although we had spoken infrequently since I had left England almost two years before, the realisation that he was about to die shook me as nothing before ever had. I liked knowing he was still there and that I could most likely count on him if I needed him. I had no choice but to return to him. However, there were things to be taken care of before I could go home. I quit my job with the newspaper, an act which upset me as I had grown to love my work there. My boss, a middle-aged man named Ryu Mori who had shown no emotion towards me whatsoever in my time there, seemed close to tears when I told him that I had to go and his reaction brought me close to embarrassing myself as well. He hugged me as I prepared to leave, an act that amazed me from one so generally self-contained. I cleared my desk and packed a portfolio of my work; even in distress I was aware that I would need to find employment back in Britain and although the prospect of work on a newspaper there did not fill me with excitement, it was important to be prepared for any eventuality.

I tried to contact Hitomi but she refused to take my calls. I was sure that she was upset about my departure and didn't want to aggravate the situation by meeting again. She had made it clear that she didn't want to come to England with me but I didn't know whether I had impressed upon her the fact that I had no choice but to go. For someone who believed so much in family, I was surprised that she could not see this.

My flight was scheduled for a Thursday morning and on the Wednesday afternoon I went to the school where we had first met to say my goodbyes. Walking up the small side stairs which led to her office, I had a sense of déjà vu, recalling those early days in Kyoto when I had known nothing of the place, the people or the language; the feeling of isolation returned to me and I wondered whether the time I had spent in Japan had been profitable or not. For some reason, I could remember very little of it other than the time I had spent with Hitomi. To me, she was Japan. She was what had kept me there more than anything else. I needed to tell her that.

I heard a sound from her office, the sound of a desk drawer being firmly closed, and paused to take a deep breath. It was important that I decide exactly what I wanted to say to her and yet an opening phrase would not come to my mind. Instead I took a step forward, assuming that when we laid eyes on each other, anything that needed to be said, would naturally appear. However, just as I was about to open the door to her office, its occupant emerged, almost bumping into me, and to my surprise it was not Hitomi at all, but her brother Tajima.

'Tak,' I said, taken aback by his presence for I had never seen him in this building before and was unprepared for a conversation with him. 'What are you doing here?' He stared at me for a moment, his thin lips narrowing even more so that they almost disappeared inside his mouth entirely, baring his teeth like a woken watchdog. He was carrying a sealed box, the kind one puts files or books in, and during the silence between us he placed it on a nearby desk, stepping away from it quickly as if it was an unexploded bomb.

'Hello William,' he said in an even tone, his perfect English enunciating every syllable as ever. 'I thought you had gone back to England.'

'I'm going tomorrow,' I answered, straining to see behind him whether his sister was in the office or not.

'She's not in there, if that's what you're hoping for,' he said, noticing the direction of my eyes. 'If it's Hitomi you want to see.'

'Of course it's Hitomi I want to see,' I said aggressively. 'What else would I be doing here? Signing up for a language course? What are you doing here anyway?' I repeated.

He shrugged. 'My sister had some work she needed to do from home,' he replied after a pause during which I felt he was trying to think of an answer that would seem plausible. 'She's not feeling too well today.'

'She's sick?'

'She's not sick, she just needs a few days off work. Mental health days, I like to call them.' I frowned and wondered whether he was suggesting that Hitomi had lost her mind. 'When you have a cold or have broken your leg or something like that, you take time off work, right?' he explained. I nodded. 'You're physically sick then, you see. But some days you get up and you just know you can't go in that day. You need some time off. There's nothing physically wrong with you, but up here . . .' He indicated what I had always thought was the empty space between his ears. 'Up here you just know you need a little time to yourself. I call that a mental health day. Everyone needs one from time to time.'

'Mental health day,' I repeated, nodding slowly and wondering whether he was just trying to fob me off. 'Right. Well I did want to speak with her, Tak, so . . .' He sighed and tapped the side of my arm.

'Look, William,' he said, 'I have a little time to spare. Why don't we get a drink together? Say goodbye in style?'

I glanced at my watch; it was ten past three. I had the rest of the day free. I had hoped to be spending it with his sister rather than him but at the same time, I felt I could hardly refuse. He might let me know how she was feeling, what she was planning to do. I agreed and after putting the box in his car we strolled to a side-street and a bar which was not as busy as some of the other after-noon bars and ordered a couple of Western-style beers for a change. My taste buds had become accustomed to the Japanese variety, however, and I pulled a face at first when I sipped it.

'I was sorry to hear about your father,' said Tak after

the preliminaries were out of the way. 'He will be all right, I hope?'

I shrugged. 'I don't know, to be honest with you,' I said. 'He didn't say much in his letter. Just that he hadn't long left and wanted to make his peace with me before he died. He's not a young man, you see. He was already quite old when I was born.'

'You haven't phoned him to find out what the matter is?'

I felt slightly bashful now. 'I didn't want to,' I explained. 'Whatever is wrong with him . . . well I didn't want to hear it over the phone. I want to see him. To tell him that I'll be there no matter what. I guess the fact that I'm flying halfway across the world will prove that in some way. We haven't always been that close, you see.'

He nodded and said nothing for a short time, as if he was trying to take this piece of information in and understand it better. I stared into the white foam popping quietly at the top of my beer and ran my finger along the edge, putting it to my mouth every so often to lick it clean. Eventually he spoke again. 'Why is that, William?' he asked me. 'Why are you not close? You told us that you grew up with just him as a parent.'

'That's right,' I said. 'I did.'

'I would think that would bring a parent and child closer together, not further apart. He was rough with you, growing up? He beat you?'

'No, no,' I said quickly, shaking my head to dissuade him of any such notion. 'No, nothing like that. That's not the kind of man he is. No it's just . . .' I thought about it; I wasn't sure myself. 'It's not that we have anything against each other exactly,' I explained, as much to myself as to him. 'There's no specific incident that

208

I hold against him. It's just that we don't seem able to communicate at all. He shows no interest in me or who I am or what I want. He doesn't see me as a person in my own right, but as some kind of extension of some ludicrous family history.'

Tak snorted. 'And what else are we than that?' he asked. 'You don't believe in ancestry?'

'I do,' I said. 'I guess it's important, but that's the only level we seem to communicate on. From as far back as I can remember, Isaac has told me stories about his grandfather. Adventure stories. Histories. I'm sure some of them are true, some are probably exaggerated as they're handed down. The point is that these stories, this ancestry, is the only thing in which he seems interested. There are no other levels between us. He hasn't any interest in who I want to be in the future, just who we all were in the past.'

'And that's why you left?'

'I left because I grew up. I needed to get away. But yes, in some way I felt that if there was distance between us, if we communicated for a year or two by letter or by phone, then we would have no other choice but to talk about things that had nothing to do with this great Buffalo Bill legend. He'd ask about me. He'd want to know something about *my* life. I thought that would happen.'

'And did it, William? Did it happen like that?'

I shook my head. 'It didn't quite work out the way I planned,' I said quietly. Tak looked around and with a quick flick of his fingers ordered a couple more beers. I placed my hand across the top of my mine and frowned. 'I should be getting on,' I said. 'I need to see Hitomi before I go.'

'Let me ask you something,' he interrupted, ignoring

what I had said and paying for the drinks as they arrived; I accepted mine with a sigh but determined that it would be my last. 'This great communication you were hoping would happen between you. Did you speak regularly on the phone since you came to Japan?'

I opened my mouth to defend myself but found there were no words to excuse my actions. 'Not often,' I admitted.

'And letters,' he continued. 'You told him about your life here in letters? You wrote about Kyoto, your job with the newspaper, Hitomi. Perhaps you made fun of the evening you spent with my family and our strange customs?'

'Tak, don't be ridiculous,' I said quickly, injured. 'Why would I do that?'

'But you wrote to him, yes? You found a new opportunity to tell him about your life here and that made things better?'

I struggled for an answer. 'It wasn't that easy,' I said, wishing I had never accepted his offer of a drink. 'You know how much pressure one comes under here. I was working, I was busy, I had Hitomi. I didn't have time for many letters. I mean I wanted to, but . . .' My words trailed off. There were no excuses. I had left home, convincing myself that my relationship with Isaac would improve if we could communicate without his storytelling pastimes getting in the way, but once gone I'd left him far behind me. Tak could see that I had realised this myself and looked a little smug as he continued with his drink, leaning over to stare at a group of office girls who had just walked in. He gave a little whistle and winked at me.

'Hubba hubba,' he said in a strange tone, as if he had picked up the phrase from an American TV show and had determined to use it. I was in no mood to play along.

'Look, Tak,' I said. 'I'm leaving tomorrow morning. I have to see Hitomi tonight. She won't take my calls. Where is she? Why won't she see me?'

'She doesn't want to go to England,' Tak said, and his tone shifted immediately back from the confidant of a moment ago to the protective brother, distant with his sister's suitors. 'She says she'll die if she goes to England.'

'Again with the dying,' I said with a groan. 'What's with that? That's just stupid.'

'She's a superstitious girl,' he explained. 'She must have read something when she was a child that said she would die if she went there. I don't know. She's always said it.'

'Well it's just stupid,' I repeated angrily. 'She could die anywhere. Any of us could. Why won't she speak to me? I . . . I demand an answer!' I added, aware how archaic and ridiculous the phrase sounded, but short of standing up and beating it out of him – something which was unlikely to take place – it was all I could think of to do.

'Hitomi feels . . .' He licked his lips and thought about it as if he wanted to be sure that he phrased this correctly. I held my breath and waited for him to continue. 'She feels that now is a time when you should be with your father. She believes she would only be in the way.'

'But I love her, Tak,' I said simply, unsure how he would take such a declaration but he seemed almost moved by it for he reached across and patted my wrist twice, his gesture of support I assumed.

'I think she loves you too, William,' he said. 'But

211

sometimes people need to separate to solve other things in their lives. You need to see your father. You need to be there for him when he dies. And Hitomi needs her own space too. There are things she needs to do.'

'Such as what?' I asked, convinced that I knew her and her needs just as well as he did.

'Such as her own things,' he said. 'You are both young,' he said with a laugh. 'You're flying to London tomorrow morning. Well you'll be there by tomorrow night, am I right?' I nodded. 'It's not like you need to be parted for ever. Just trust in the right thing happening.' I sighed. This was not the response I had hoped for. 'Your priority,' he continued, 'must be to your family. First and foremost. As Hitomi's is to hers. Believe in that, William. Trust in it. Let her go for now, and go back to London.'

I sat back and could feel the tears coming into my eyes. The future looked suddenly bleak. I had lost the girl I loved and the next few months appeared to hold nothing but loneliness, sickness and perhaps death. And London. How little I wanted to return there. There was only one thing to do in the time left to me. I signalled the waitress for more drinks. 'And keep them coming,' I told her.

When I arrived at Heathrow Airport, I could barely keep my eyes open with tiredness and even though I had just returned to London for the first time in two years, I briefly considered unravelling my sleeping bag in the corner of the terminal and trying for a few hours' sleep, until I realised that I would probably be still unrolling it when a security guard would come along and move me on. Instead I decided to take a shower in the airport facilities as I wanted to be alert and ready for when I met my father again. Isaac was seventy-four years old by now and had never been a particularly avid driver; indeed, he had sold his car some years earlier so I was planning on making my own way to Clapham. Also, I wanted to surprise him, and was beginning to grow quite excited at the prospect of seeing him again.

Incredibly, almost immediately I began to feel the same sense of cultural isolation in the airport as I had when I had first arrived at Narita. Suddenly I was no longer a stranger in a foreign land, but a native, just like everyone else. I saw other young people wandering around with backpacks, suntanned legs and faces returning from abroad, pale, fully dressed bodies clutching each other nervously as they began their own trips away and I wanted to approach them and tell them about myself. *I've been to Japan for two years*, I wanted to shout. *I had a job, a real job, a good job too. I fell in love in Japan, you know. And I'm only back because my father's ill, I could be anywhere I wanted otherwise.* I felt an amazing urge to share my adventures with someone, to tell them my stories, and started to laugh as I thought that's just what Isaac would do too. Tell a story about it. Turn it into fiction.

The shower was cool and fresh and I washed the dirt and dust of the journey off my body, turning my face up to the spray and brushing the hair back out of my eyes as I tried to readjust to this new situation. Even the shower water felt different to me, the soap the airport provided was cheap and barely raised a lather, but nevertheless I stayed there for about twenty minutes before drying off and changing my clothes. I'd worn a pair of knee-length shorts and a T-shirt for the long journey, but changed into a pair of combats now and a fresh shirt. Too late, I considered shaving my face clean for I had

213

been sporting the same level of stubble for about a year and wondered what I would look like without it but decided against it. Having washed and dressed, the last thing I wanted was to start all over. I brushed my hair and as it had grown a little long, tied it back behind my head before looking at myself in the mirror. This was the new me, I thought. Or rather the old me. The British me. *Konnichiwa, William-San*, I said loudly, insistently, eager to hear the phrase again and a young man a few feet away turned to look at me, wondering whether I was addressing him. I frowned and, with a quick nod, gathered my things and left.

There's a strange sense of the familiar, even in a place one hasn't been to in a long time, and making my way down the escalators beside the Costa Coffee and across the terminal for the walk to the tube station, I felt a strange mixture of emotions, torn between a desperate sense of horror that I was here again and a delight in being among things which I had not thought about in so long. It was only as I stared at the ticket machine, trying to remember how much I should pay for the journey, that I realised what I really wanted was to be able to share this experience with someone and wished for the hundredth time that Hitomi was there with me. I wanted to hold her hand at the wall chart for the underground system that stands beside the machine and show her the different-coloured lines and what they meant, where their destinations were. *We'll be taking the Piccadilly Line to Leicester Square*, I would have told her. *Then the Northern Line down to Clapham. The tube doesn't go to the junction but we can get a cab from Clapham Common.* She had been my guide for so long, I wanted the opportunity to be hers. To show her that I could be in charge too.

Neither train was particularly full and I stepped out of Clapham Common Station at eight o'clock in the evening. It was late summer and the sun was going down. A small team of cricketers passed me by, laughing loudly, heading for the pub, I assumed. Across on the common I could see a group of teenagers – boys and girls – finishing up their football game and gathering their things where they had used them to make goalposts. I wondered: should this be nostalgic? Is this the London I grew up in? and wasn't sure. I couldn't place my emotion, didn't know what it was expected to be, and so for want of anything better to do checked my watch and calculated the time it was in Kyoto and what my friends there would be doing now, before hailing a cab and giving him the address I had not uttered in a long time.

'Been away, have you?' he asked as we drove along, noticing my several bags and their airport tags. I didn't much want to get into conversation so looked out the window as I answered, hoping he would spot my lack of interest in the rear-view mirror and leave me alone.

'Japan,' I said. 'I've been living there for the last year and a half.'

'Japan, eh?' he said with a whistle.

The house hadn't actually changed an iota and yet somehow, it seemed smaller to my eyes, as if time had shrunk it. The paintwork was noticeably chipped, but then it always had been. The curtains on the inside seemed grimy and colourless, and yet we had always owned those curtains. They probably hadn't been washed in years. The small front garden was relatively neat but would need attention in a week or so; Isaac had often enjoyed working in the garden but had rarely done more than keep it tidy. I used to wonder what it would look like if he wasn't around to do it as I had no interest in gardening at all.

I have always kept a key ring in my pocket and throughout my time in Japan, along with the keys of my own apartment and those of the newspaper office in which I worked, I had always kept the front- and back-door keys of our Clapham house. I have no idea what use I thought I would have for them on the streets of Kyoto but I kept them nonetheless and liked to see they were there. I reached into my pocket for them as I stood at the door and was struck by how empty that key ring was now with just these two left on it. I didn't like the fact that it was so light and that this house was the only place I had private access to any more. It made me feel like a child again. I frowned and brought the smaller key to the lock before changing my mind. Having not informed Isaac of my arrival, it would probably be too much of a surprise if I just opened the door and marched in. As yet, I still did not know what was wrong with him and didn't want to shock him into sudden death. Instead, I pressed the doorbell and stepped back, waiting for more than a minute before realising that I had not heard it ring. I reached forward and pressed it again, harder this time, and could hear it sound within the house and then this was it, the point of no return. I stood tall, shook my shoulders slightly and coughed to clear my throat. My stomach churned and the bright light in the frosted glass of the door began to shade slowly as the figure of my father came towards it. He reached up and opened the door and peered outside; it was growing darker now, autumn was not far away.

When Isaac first told me the story about Buffalo Bill, General Custer and President Ulysses S. Grant, I was a little dubious. It was one of the later stories he told – I don't think I heard it until I was about thirteen and beginning to grow weary of his tales anyway – and the convergence of three such famous men seemed a little too coincidental for my liking.

'It's in the records,' Isaac insisted. 'It's a matter of historical fact. Look it up in any of the history books and you'll read about it there. The coincidence isn't that they should all be together at that point; the fact is that they *were* together because they were powerful and that in turn led to their legends. There's nothing unusual about it. Nothing coincidental.' I wasn't sure but it was a story I liked anyway for although it was fairly uneventful, it was one that displayed a lot of the characteristics of my great-grandfather which would define his later life.

The election of General Grant to the presidency had been something of a sham. His predecessor, Andrew Johnson (who had replaced the assassinated Lincoln) had been unfairly impeached in 1867 and he was later acquitted in the senate on charges of treason, bribery and other high crimes and misdemeanours, but impeachment had resulted in a reorganisation of the voting procedures in the southern states along anti-racist lines, splitting the Republican Party and securing the election of Grant over the New York governor Horatio Seymour due to the massive amount of vote boycotting which took place. Once the election had been secured there was widespread dismay at the manner in which the election had come about and despite the fact that he had secured a majority of votes, Grant became an unpopular figure almost immediately. Seymour continued to protest his loss and it was proving difficult for the new president to claim an effective mandate. To counter this, he sought throughout that first term to improve his standing among the American people and brought newspapermen with him wherever he travelled, the first president to be so observed and followed by the national media.

The respect afforded to General Custer and the growing popularity of Buffalo Bill presented President Grant with a perfect opportunity for a media story and he arranged to dine at the fort in order to be seen as the leader of his own invented trinity. Custer was the more nervous in advance of the meeting, fearing that something would go wrong and he would incur the wrath of the president, but my great-grandfather enjoyed the proceedings, looking forward to the glittering state occasion.

When the president and his entourage arrived on a late autumn evening in 1870 he slowed down his horse a mile from the fort so that the newspapermen who were riding at some distance behind could precede him. There were eight of them in total and they went on to the fort, announcing the imminent arrival of the party, and waited to make notes about the exchange of greetings between the most important men. General Custer and his wife Libbie were at the head of the party, the general wearing an outlandish military costume of his own design. (It was one of Custer's idiosyncrasies that he was, in his spare time, a clothing designer, like General Patton seventy years later, and only ever wore uniforms which he had made himself.) Bill and Louisa remained a few steps behind and were less anxious than the general for they had nothing to lose and could not be held at fault if anything untoward happened.

The president arrived with an entourage of fourteen and, like Custer, he was dressed in his military uniform, albeit one of a less garish design than that of his most famous general. The greetings were effusive and the newsmen took note of how warm the greeting was between each man. Custer then introduced his own wife to the president and she curtsied graciously, at which point Bill and Louisa stepped forward to be introduced. My great-grandfather had never met Ulysses S. Grant before, had never met any president for that matter, and for once felt slightly humbled as he was introduced. Grant greeted him affectionately and brought both men over towards the press pack who threw questions at them immediately.

'Mr President,' shouted one. 'Are you here to advise General Custer on plans for moving the Cheyenne from their territory?'

'I'm here for my dinner!' roared Grant. 'That's all. We'll be leaving politics off the menu.' No one believed that for a moment.

'General Custer!' cried another. 'When will the push begin?' Custer barely looked at his inquisitor; unlike the other two men he was no fan of newspapers and declined to answer any questions. This was a time when such people were under no pressure to speak if they did not want to.

'Mr Cody,' came another shout. 'What are your plans for—'

'That's Buffalo Bill, son!' said the president with a laugh. 'Don't you fellows have any respect? Why, this is only the bravest man south of the Mason–Dixon line. He earned that title, boys! Have the decency to use it!'

Bill smiled to himself at the endorsement and raised his hands in the air. 'I'm here to eat a meal with the president that good old General Custer invited us to.' He looked across at the general who eyed him suspiciously.

'Will there be buffalo on the menu tonight?' asked one wag.

'Yes,' said Custer curtly.

'General Custer has spent the last few days roaming the prairies looking for just the right buffalo to feed a president with,' laughed Bill, grabbing the attention of all now. 'He needed one with a hide big enough to fit the seal of this president and it took him a while to find one.' There was a silence from all quarters as everyone waited to see how Grant would react to such a jibe, but to everyone's relief he laughed heartily and threw his arm around Bill.

'I'll warrant that if you had General Custer here and Buffalo Bill out on the prairies shooting for buffalo, you'd have a good afternoon's hunting,' he said. 'What do you say, men? You on for a little one-on-one?' Bill and Custer looked at each other and said nothing. This would not have been a good idea as neither man might have recovered from defeat and, if such a match took place, one of them would be forced to. Luckily it was not to be as Grant had other things on his mind. 'Maybe someday we'll do that,' he said, to the relief of them both. 'But not anytime soon. We've got a lot more pressing business than horseplay for now. That's all for now, fellas. We'll see you inside.'

The party moved inside for the meal and throughout it my great-grandfather and the president courted each of the members of the news pack. Custer sat aloof, unable to join in, for he was a distant fellow at the best of times and could no more create his own publicity than Bill could walk away from his. He envied my great-grandfather his showman abilities. The president and Bill got on very well that night and became firm friends, something which the newspapers reported in detail afterwards. It was a bad night for General Custer, who never forgave Bill for upstaging him and would have loved the opportunity for the one-on-one hunting combat that never happened had he not been so fearful of the consequences of defeat.

From that night, their wary friendship became a deep-seated hostility and one which, at their next meeting, would flare up into their most destructive encounter.

'Yes? Can I help you?' I couldn't help but smile. Instinctively, I put a hand to my face, wondering whether I had really changed that much over the previous two years.

'Isaac,' I said, grinning at him. 'It's me. William.'

'William!' he gasped, walking forward into the twilight now and I steadied myself for what differences I might see in him. I didn't know what the nature of his illness was and what physical effects it might have had on him but felt prepared for the worst. However, that was unnecessary as he didn't look much different than the last time I'd seen him. A few more grey hairs perhaps but as always he seemed in fairly good physical condition for a man of his age. 'I didn't recognise you. I wasn't expecting you, you see. If I'd known, I would have . . . I would have . . .' He struggled to complete his sentence but was clearly unsure of what he would have done had he known, so I reached forward and we hugged awkwardly instead. 'Well come inside,' he said, looking out at the driveway to see whether I had much luggage but there were just the two small bags and my rucksack. I'd travelled light when I'd left England in the first place and had only brought home with me those things I felt I couldn't leave behind. 'Do you want a hand with those?' he asked, stepping outdoors but I waved him back inside.

'I've carried them halfway across the world,' I told him with a smile. 'Don't worry. I think I can manage them up the stairs.' I brought them in but dropped them in the hallway for the time being. The air was a little musky and I wanted to open a window – I suspected he never bothered with such niceties – but felt it would be a little rude to suddenly reappear and insist on having things my way.

'Why didn't you tell me you were coming?' he asked, looking me up and down as if I was a car he was considering buying. 'You've grown taller, haven't you?'

'I wanted to surprise you,' I said. 'And I think I've probably hit my full height, you know. I am twenty-two years old.'

'You're taller than me!'

'A little.' I stood at just over six feet in height; Isaac stood a little under. The physical difference between us, however – the body's strength in youth against its fragility in age – exaggerated our relative sizes. I had always felt big in Japan as the Japanese are generally physically smaller. Standing with a group in a bar one always felt larger and more muscular, and therefore somehow more masculine than others; I hadn't expected to feel that way back home in London and hadn't until I was standing alongside my father again. 'You're looking well,' I offered, feeling we had plenty of time to get into that one and not wishing to bring it up just yet.

'You'll have a cup of tea,' he said, ushering me into the living room where the remains of his dinner was on a table in front of his armchair; he'd been watching a soap opera. I recognised the actor on screen, a dark-haired boy in his mid-teens who'd started in that show

222

a few months before I'd left London, when I'd been a regular watcher. Seeing him there brought back a flood of my own memories from that time, evenings when I'd sat in front of the TV for hours on end, following these dramas as if my whole life depended on them. The sound of the London accents jarred me for a moment; they were more pronounced than I had heard so far but as different from the Japanese tongue as anything I could imagine. I stared at the screen and realised fully that I was back home and that nothing had changed. My stomach churned again.

'You know what?' said Isaac, coming back into the room and switching off the television, the dark-haired boy's face collapsing into a small dot at the centre of the screen which took a moment to disappear. (It was an old set.) 'This calls for a drink. I should really have a fatted calf ready, shouldn't I?'

I smiled. 'Don't go to too much trouble,' I said. 'I'm pretty tired anyway. Maybe just one drink. A nightcap. I'm still on Japanese time and need to catch up.'

'How long are you here for? Are you on your own?' he asked quickly, rooting for as much information as he could get in as short a time as possible.

'For good, I guess,' I said. 'For the foreseeable future anyway. And yes, I'm alone.'

'For good,' he echoed and his face was beaming. 'Now this'll be just like old times. This is marvellous.'

'I got your letter,' I said quickly, unsure whether the moment was appropriate yet but he vanished again almost immediately before returning with a bottle of whisky and two glasses. I shook my head.

'I'd prefer a cold beer if you've got one,' I said. 'I'm really thirsty. Or just a Coke maybe.'

'I think I have,' he said. 'Hold on.' He went back to

223

the kitchen and I looked around the room, noting the memories of my childhood in every corner and on every wall. Everything was pretty much as I had left it. Over the fireplace was the painting of Buffalo Bill Cody which had been hung there before I was even born. The books were all the same and, I presumed, had been untouched since my departure. The carpet was old, the curtains could have done with a wash, but for the most part he kept the room quite tidy. On a whim, I turned around and glanced up at the wall and was not surprised to see the Smith & Wesson gun perched on its usual hook. I smiled and shook my head.

'One cold beer,' said Isaac, handing me a bottle. 'Sit down, sit down. There's so much to catch up on. If only I'd known you were coming,' he said yet again.

'I got your letter,' I repeated. 'That's why I came.'

'That was good of you,' he said quickly. 'So how was Japan?'

I opened my mouth to speak but it was hard to find words to describe it. If this was to be a getting-reacquainted conversation, I hardly felt like I could describe the country and its people to him in a few empty sentences. A part of me didn't want to either as I was afraid that once I had spoken of it, he might never ask again. 'That's a long story,' I said. 'I'll fill you in another time. It's good to be home,' I added, wanting to say something emotional, something that might express my feelings in some way. I was afraid of the conversation about his illness and wanted to let him know that I wasn't just there on a mission of mercy.

'It's good to have you here, son,' he said. 'It's been too long.'

'I'm sorry I didn't keep more in contact.'

'Oh, you were busy, I understand that. I didn't exactly

224

write much myself. But you've got it out of your system now and that's a good thing.'

I felt a twinge of irritation suddenly; that old feeling that he didn't have a clue who I was resurfaced. 'Got what out of my system?' I asked quietly.

'The travelling. All of that. Japan. I mean I know that I couldn't live there for ever, I don't know about you. I wouldn't be able to deal with the food for one thing. I like to know what I'm eating. I've got respect for my stomach.'

I had a sudden urge to jump up, run out of the house and head straight back to Heathrow. 'Well I liked it there,' I muttered. 'We'll see about the future.'

'You know I saw those friends of yours in town a few weeks ago? What were their names again? Adam and Justin, wasn't it?'

'Yes, yes, that's right,' I said, looking up hopefully. 'Where did you see them?'

He shrugged as if he couldn't quite remember. 'Coming out of a pub probably. Where else. They said hello. Asked when you were coming back. I said I didn't know.'

'They're here then? They're in London?'

'I often see them around,' he said, reaching down for his glass. I smiled. This gave me a glimmer of hope. Things couldn't be all that bad if they were here. I hadn't heard much from Adam since he had left Japan for the Australian Gold Coast. We'd exchanged some e-mails but they'd slipped away. The last I'd heard he was on his way to South America, but that had been almost a year before. I'd sent a few cards to Justin, and he'd written once or twice, but again it was difficult to stay in touch when our lives had diverged so much. Still, I knew it would be good to see them again and debated whether I was alert enough to go drinking with them that very night before I decided it would be rude to disappear so soon after my reappearance, even though I really wanted to.

'So . . .' I said, already struggling for words, searching for that missing conversation I'd been denied all these years. 'What are you . . . what do you do now? How are you filling your days?'

'A-ha!' he cried, his face breaking into a wide grin. 'That's news for another evening too. I'm very busy at the moment, I don't mind telling you. I may need your help with a little project I have on the go.'

'Sure,' I said, shrugging my shoulders, imagining that he might want to redecorate the house perhaps. 'Whatever I can do.'

'There's lots you can do, William. Lots you can do. This will be just like the old days, father and son working alongside each other.' I was unsure which old days he was referring to; some mythical ones between us, or an idyllic one he had dreamed of perhaps, but didn't bother to question him. I yawned suddenly, the exhaustion of the previous thirty-six hours finally hitting home and felt an overwhelming urge for bed. 'Look at you,' said Isaac laughing. 'You're exhausted. I haven't seen you this tired since you were a little boy. Why don't you go on up to bed and get some sleep. You've barely touched your beer. We can talk tomorrow.'

'Well if you don't mind . . .' I said. 'I could do with a rest.'

'To bed then,' he said, and it was like we had gone back in time about fifteen years. 'I'll clean up here, don't worry. Your bed's all made up.'

I had stood up and was walking towards the door when that phrase pulled me back. I turned around and looked at him in surprise. 'My bed's all made up?' I asked. 'How come? You didn't know I was coming?'

He looked at me and for a moment I thought I could see his face redden slightly before he reached back down to the table to clear away the bottles. 'Sometimes I make it up,' he explained. 'Just to keep the room fresh. You never know who's going to drop by, do you? Visitors, I mean.' I thought about it. I supposed not but nevertheless, it struck me as a little odd. 'Go to bed, William,' he insisted. 'I mean it now.'

I nodded. I went to bed.

The note was brief and to the point and left me completely amazed.

'William –,' it began, 'forgot to mention last night – I'll be away for the next couple of days. Business trip. Sorry about this but you'll have to sort yourself out until I come back. See you Tuesday.' He hadn't bothered to sign it. I had slept very late, not waking until well after midday, the jet-lag having caught up with me at last. I still felt quite groggy as I pulled on a pair of shorts and a T-shirt and went downstairs for some breakfast but Isaac's note woke me up completely. How could he have just vanished within twenty-four hours of my reappearance? It didn't make any sense. And as for that line about a business trip? In twenty-two years, I'd never known him to have to go on any such thing. I shook my head and went back to bed for an hour, dozing now, wondering what was going on in my father's life these days that I was not privy to and whether I should have returned home sooner than this.

Once I'd grown used to the idea, I quite enjoyed the thought of having the house to myself for a couple of days. Although I'd lived alone in Kyoto, I'd almost never had any time to myself. When I wasn't working, I was with Hitomi or some of the friends I'd made through the newspaper or through her. I'd led a busy life. It was rare that I had the chance to just hang out on my own, watch television, read a book, and it felt nice. I wanted to know more about Isaac, of course, especially about his illness, but it could wait a couple of days. It had waited this long already.

I phoned Adam and arranged to meet him and Justin in our local that evening and spent a long time getting ready. I was excited about seeing them again; two years was a long time to be away from my best friends and I wondered whether they would have changed much. They were the closest I had to brothers. I decided to arrive a little late in order to make an entrance; presumably they had seen a lot of each other since Adam's return a year earlier, so I would be the guest of honour on the evening.

I scanned the pub when I arrived, looking for them. The surroundings were exactly as I had left them. The same wallpaper on the walls, the same ratty carpet. Even the music had hardly changed; I entered to the sound of Chesney Hawkes, which was blaring from a jukebox. I'd heard that song every day for about three months the previous year because Hitomi had loved it and played it relentlessly. At first, it was hard to spot my friends as the bar was quite busy but eventually I saw them seated at a side table near the fireplace, chatting to each other happily. I was immediately dismayed to see they had brought dates with them; I knew from Justin's brief letters that they had both been involved in relationships for quite a while now but nevertheless it hadn't occurred to me that they would bring them along that night, as it was my first time to see them again and I thought it would just be for us. It made me want to leave instantly. They hadn't seen me yet and I slipped into the gents quickly to take a look at myself in the mirror. I wasn't sure why exactly, but I wanted to look my best when I met them all. Our childhood days had ended, I thought. Perhaps this was the beginning of our adult relationships.

'Evening all,' I said quietly as I finally approached the table and all four of them looked up at me, Adam and Justin's faces breaking into a wide grin almost immediately. They stood up and we all burst out laughing in our excitement and bear-hugged each other, saying little for the moment, just taking in the fact that we were together again happily. They made their separate introductions to me, Adam introduced Kate who he had fallen in with while travelling and they had become a couple somewhere between Athens and Morocco apparently, now she lived with him just down the road; Justin introduced Mark, who I had met briefly before leaving London a couple of years earlier anyway but who I had barely got to know before leaving for Japan. I shook hands with these two strangers, not quite knowing what to say to them, and there was an awkward silence for a moment before Kate announced that it was her round and disappeared for a few moments before returning with a tray-load of lagers.

'It's good to see you both,' I said, looking from Adam to Justin with a cheesy grin on my face. 'I can't believe it's been so long. Too long. I'm sorry I'm such a crap writer.'

'I thought you were a journalist,' said Kate quickly, looking confused.

'I mean I'm not much of a letter writer,' I explained. We exchanged pleasantries in the group for a little while before naturally pairing off into two groups, my two friends and I involved in one conversation, Kate and Mark involved in another. As I glanced across at them I wished that Hitomi was there to join them. I didn't exactly feel like a gooseberry, considering I had just returned to the city, but nevertheless I couldn't help but notice that I was the only one of us who would be going home alone that night. The three of us had grown up together but I felt it would be a very adult thing for us to be sitting in a pub talking, while our partners chatted to each other as well. Maybe someday, I reasoned.

'After the Gold Coast, I went to Thailand,' Adam told me as we caught up. 'Did the whole student-traveller thing there. Then on to India, where an elephant nearly killed me. I didn't stay there long though and moved up to Turkey and Greece, then over to North Africa before coming home. Kate and I met along the way.'

'Cool,' I said, the only response that sprung to mind.

'What was Japan like?' asked Justin, another regular question but unlike when Isaac had asked me, I tried to give some semblance of an answer.

'The thing about it is that from the moment I got there, I felt like an outsider,' I explained. 'And that never changed. Even when you grow a little more proficient in the language and you can read the street signs and so on, you never stop thinking that you're different there, probably because physically you're different and you're trying to communicate in a foreign tongue. Everything was like a different world. But once you grow used to it, you learn to love it. I loved it anyway.'

'Will you go back?' Mark asked me, rejoining the conversation, and I shrugged.

'I'm not sure,' I said. 'My father's sick. That's why I'm here.'

'Isaac's sick?' asked Adam, looking at me in surprise. 'I didn't know that. What's wrong with him?'

I felt a bit embarrassed since I wasn't quite sure how to answer him. 'I'm not too sure, to be honest with you,' I explained. 'He wrote to me and told me . . . well he said that he wasn't well and I should come over to see him before it was too late.' I shrugged. 'So here I am,' I added.

'Jesus, sorry, William,' said Adam. 'I didn't know. I see him around a bit and he looks fine. I guess he's pretty old though.'

'Yeah, he said he saw you and Justin a couple of weeks back,' I muttered.

'Well we run into each other all the time around town. And Justin sees him in the bank almost every day, don't you?'

I turned to look at Justin who interrupted quickly. 'Not every day,' he said, looking down at the table. I stared at him in surprise.

'In the bank?' I asked. 'What's he doing in there every day?' Justin said nothing and I looked around, sure there was something going on here that I wasn't being told. 'Justin?' I said. 'What's going on?'

'I don't know,' he replied, looking at Adam as if he wanted to tell him off for divulging a confidence. 'He's in sometimes, I guess. I'm not sure what for.'

'Well what could he be in there for?' I demanded. 'He's not exactly got millions in his account, has he?'

'William, I don't know,' said Justin in a firm tone of voice, placing his hand decisively on the table to indicate that he wanted to move on. 'Tell us more about your trip, okay?'

I stared at him and scratched my head. The whole thing appeared to be growing more and more bizarre.

231

First the letter, then Isaac's mysterious disappearance, and now these frequent trips to the bank. I wished it was Tuesday already as I wanted to get to the bottom of it. I considered continuing this conversation but it was obvious that they didn't know much about it and if I pushed things, an awkwardness would only develop.

'So, William,' said Mark after the silence had grown unbearable. 'You didn't get married or anything over there, did you?'

I laughed and shook my head. 'Not quite,' I said.

'What happened to what's-her-name?' asked Adam. 'You were involved in something, weren't you?'

I nodded. 'Hitomi Naoyuki,' I said in a quiet voice and for some reason my eyes went to Kate's as I said her name. 'Yeah, we were involved. About eighteen months altogether.'

'What happened?' asked Kate. 'Is she following you back here?'

I thought about it; it wasn't something I'd considered. 'I don't think so,' I said. 'She's got some phobia about England. Thinks she'll die if she comes here.' They all stared at me blankly and I shrugged as if to say *don't ask me*. 'Anyway,' I continued, hoping to explain things a little better, 'She's got her family in Kyoto. And her job.'

'Maybe it was for the best you came here then,' said Kate in an offhand tone as another tray of drinks arrived. That hit a nerve and I shot her an irritated look.

'Why?' I asked. 'Why do you say that?'

She looked at me as if the speed of my response had surprised her. 'Well,' she said. 'I just mean that if you broke up because you had to come back and see your sick father, the relationship must have been ending anyway.'

'No,' I said, shaking my head furiously. 'That's not it. That's not it at all. We were nowhere near to breaking up. Everything was going fine. She just didn't want to come with me, that's all.'

'Okay, take it easy,' she said. 'I was only saying. I mean do you plan on going back to Japan? Is she waiting for you?'

I didn't know whether she was or wasn't but felt unwilling to let Kate know that. 'I have to play it by ear,' I said eventually. 'See what's happening with Isaac and if all is well, then yes of course I want to go back.' Although those were the words I uttered, I felt a sudden anger towards Hitomi which had not been present before. Kate was right; it had been a pretty stupid reason for us to break up and after eighteen months it was cruel of Hitomi to let me leave the country without so much as an explanation or a kiss goodbye. I clenched my fists and felt the enormity of what had happened for the first time.

'We're going on holiday ourselves soon,' said Justin after a moment. 'America. Taking a month off and travelling around some of the southern states.'

I smiled. Not another one who was going to be bringing home tales of Kansas and Missouri to haunt me with. I excused myself and went to the other side of the bar, out of sight of my friends, and asked for some change. Checking my watch I calculated quickly that it would be early morning in Kyoto and that Hitomi would be getting dressed for work. Shielding myself from the noise of the bar and the music, I fed a couple of pounds into the phone and dialled her number, waiting for the connection to be made. I let it ring until it eventually cut off but no one had answered it. What surprised me was that Hitomi's answering machine, on

233

which I had left countless messages in the past, did not pick up as it normally did after the fourth ring. I assumed she must have unplugged it for some reason but even this surprised me, as she was paranoid about missing messages and had never even so much as switched it off in all the time I had known her. Wondering whether I had dialled the wrong number in error, I tried again but with the same result. I stood by the phone for a moment, confused by her, by Isaac, by London; for the first time in years I felt as if I was not in control of my life and that there were things going on which I just couldn't see. I began to feel a little paranoid myself and had to shake myself out of it, blaming it on continuing jetlag which might take a couple of days to pass.

I paid for one more round and rejoined my friends, glancing at my watch as I sat down, hoping the evening would end soon so I could go home and be alone with my thoughts. In the meantime I put up a pretence of good humour.

When Isaac eventually returned home, he surprised me almost as much as I had him. It was four days later and I had slept fitfully during that time, anxious for him, confused by the secrets which seemed to be hovering around my head. A few nights after that evening in the pub, Justin and Mark, Adam and Kate and I went out again; having got the awkward initial meeting out of the way we were more free to enjoy ourselves and drank a lot before heading to a club for some late drinks and to dance. I had tried to phone Hitomi several times since that earlier evening but with no success and she lingered on my mind, my mood shifting between longing, confusion, a desperate sense of loss and outright anger. When I stepped inside the nightclub that evening, a single friend with two couples, I resolved to put her out of my mind and moved like a tiger from girl to girl before clicking with someone whose name I never even caught. I brought her home with me that night and we had sex, nothing more, before falling asleep on separate sides of my bed, barely aware of who the other was, neither one of us particularly caring. I was making her a cup of tea the following morning, attempting dismally to make conversation, when Isaac walked in and stared at us both with a mixture of amusement and irritation.

'Hello,' he said, extending a hand to her in a pointless gesture; both she and I knew we would most likely never see each other again once she walked out the front door. She wanted only to leave and I made no attempt to keep her there; in my head I was feeling less than the man I knew I was. In eighteen months I had never been unfaithful to Hitomi, had never wanted to be, and now that had changed. It was meaningless and had nothing to do with her, I knew that much, but nevertheless I felt guilty. The girl left, I took a shower and came back downstairs to confront my father.

'You might have phoned,' I said as we had a cup of tea together. 'I was worried. You just disappeared off. I didn't know where you'd gone.'

'Well at least it was only for a few days and not a couple of years,' he said irritably. 'Don't speak down to me, William, do you hear me?'

'I'm not speaking down to you,' I protested, feeling a little chastised. 'It's just that I arrived here and you immediately ran off without a word.'

'Did you not get my note?'

'Yes, I got your note, but it was hardly an explanation, was it?'

'I had business to take care of,' he said and for the first time it occurred to me that he was wearing a suit and tie and his hair had been recently cut. For a dying man in his mid-seventies, he looked remarkably sprightly.

'What business?' I asked in frustration. 'What are you up to anyway? Isaac, we need to talk,' I added in a more plaintive voice. 'You hardly said anything in your note, only to tell me that—'

'I told you I would be away for a couple of days,' he said, his voice raised slightly. 'What more do you—'

'Not that note,' I interrupted. 'The one you sent me in Japan. The one that brought me home in the first place.'

He frowned and looked as if he was trying to rack his brain to recall it. 'Oh yes,' he said, and I thought he looked a little shamefaced as he said it. 'That's right. I did write to you there, didn't I?'

'That's why I came home,' I continued, speaking quietly now and as I came towards my next sentence I had an urge to reach out and place my hand across his on the table. 'You said you were sick,' I explained. 'That you didn't have long to live. Tell me about it. What's happened? What's wrong with you?'

He licked his lips and seemed about to speak but changed his mind and stood up instead, bringing his cup across to the sink and rinsing it out, his back turned to me as he finally spoke. 'I'll be fine,' he said. 'Don't worry about me.'

'Don't worry about you?' I asked, amazed by his nonchalance. 'How can I not worry about you? You're dying. You're my father,' I added. 'I want to help you. What does your doctor say?'

He turned now and looked at me, his eyes squinting as he took me in. 'How old are you now, William? Twenty-two?' I nodded. 'Do you know that when your great-grandfather was twenty-two he was married, had built a town, burnt it to the ground, killed who knows how many thousands of buffaloes, hobnobbed with generals and presidents, brought a Russian—'

'Isaac,' I said firmly, interrupting him. 'I know all that. What's your point?'

'My point is, *William*,' he said, stating my name firmly, his tone implying for once that he would rather I didn't use his given name. 'My point, since you ask for it, is that he was not bumming around the world, doing nothing with his life.'

'Who wasn't?' I asked, confused.

'Your great-grandfather,' he said. Who do you think?'

I looked at him as if he was mad. 'Okay,' I said slowly. 'Now getting back to your illness—'

'William, I've come up with a plan,' he said, returning to the table and sitting down with a gleam in his eyes. 'You want to make something of your life, don't you?'

I shrugged. 'I guess,' I said non-committally. 'But I'm doing all right. I've got a career of sorts started.'

'Doing what?' he asked, as if he had never been informed of it.

'Well, the writing of course,' I said. 'Journalism. Things are going pretty well for me in Japan. I've made a lot of—'

'Oh that's not worth anything,' he said dismissively and my eyes opened a little wider in surprise, irritated by how my life and what I did with it meant so little to him. He must have sensed that feeling because he immediately sought to disabuse me of it. 'It's because

237

I care about you so much, William, that I've come up with this plan,' he said. 'I've thought of something you can do. Something we can do together. Just hear me out, that's all I ask.' I sat back in my chair and folded my arms to indicate that I was prepared to listen. A sick feeling in my stomach began to form; I knew instinctively that I was not going to like what I was about to hear. 'I'm starting a new business,' he began.

'A business,' I said in a flat tone. 'What do you mean? What kind of a business? You're seventy-four, for God's sake.'

'So what if I am? That doesn't mean I'm ready for the scrap-heap yet, you know. What do you think this country is most in need of at the moment? What do you think the people want that they just don't have?' I thought about it. A couple of vaguely political answers sprang to my mind but, knowing that none of them could possibly be anywhere close to where he was going on this, I held my tongue and waited for him to tell me. He held his hands in the air, the palms facing me, and pulled them away from each other slowly, as if to indicate a curtain opening at the theatre. 'Entertainment,' he announced with a flourish. 'That's what they're missing, William. That's what they want. Entertainment. Something to snap them out of the humdrum. Entertainment,' he repeated for the third time.

'Right,' I said, trying to take this in. 'Okay then. So your plan is . . . ?'

'To give it to them. What do you think is the greatest form of entertainment the world has ever produced? Think about it now. It's an easy one.'

I gave a low whistle and decided to humour him for the moment. The greatest form of entertainment I could think of. 'Something that can be performed in public, you mean,' I asked innocently.

'William.'

'Okay, give me a minute.' I thought about it. 'I don't know,' I admitted after a moment. 'Movies? Books? Roller-coaster rides?'

'Roller-coaster rides are very good things, William,' he said in a dry voice. 'Very good things indeed. But surprisingly, that's not what I'm thinking of. Try again.'

'I give up,' I said. 'I'm sure I'll never get it. Just tell me.'

He leaned back in his seat and a glow seemed to emit from him as he did his curtain trick again. Staring me right in the eyes he said, 'The wild west shows,' before sitting back and looking at me triumphantly.

I blinked. 'The wild west shows,' I repeated. 'What are you talking about exactly?'

He barked out a quick laugh. 'What do you mean what am I talking about? How many times have I told you about them? What's your great-grandfather most famous for, for heaven's sake?'

'Shooting buffaloes,' I said.

'*No*,' he said irritably. 'He's famous for his wild west shows. You know about them, they travelled all over the world, bringing the wonders of the west to places that had never heard of them. Cowboys, Indians, shooting matches, daredevil horse riding. Look at all the people he knew there, Wild Bill Hickok, Annie Oakley, why it was the greatest thing that ever hit the world! People talked about it for years.'

I could feel my face begin to pale slightly. 'What exactly are you getting at?' I asked him slowly.

'I'm setting up my own wild west show,' he said, banging his fist on the table with excitement. 'I've been

239

working on it for months now. I'm trying to get the financing in place to hire performers, organise lorries and tour dates. Of course, I'm too old to get bank loans but that's where you come in.'

'Me.'

'Yes, you. You're young, you're enthusiastic. You know almost as much about these things as I do. With your energy and my knowledge it'll be the greatest hit of the century. Think about it. We'll be millionaires!' I could barely believe what I was hearing and didn't know whether to laugh or cry. Isaac was getting carried away now, though, and didn't seem to be noticing my reaction. 'The greatest of them all,' he continued, 'was the Congress of Rough Riders of the World. Remember that? That was your great-grandfather's most famous show. Every form of western life was in there. Every warrior from around the world. Did you know they performed before Queen Victoria at her jubilee? He was the most famous man in the world then. That's what we'll do, William, you and me. Only ours will be so incredible it will put the Congress of Rough Riders into the shade. What do you think? It's a great idea, isn't it?'

I stared at him and tried to count to ten in my head before responding. I reached six. 'There's nothing wrong with you at all, is there?' I said quietly. 'Except for your obvious mental problems,' I added.

'What?' asked Isaac, confused by my question.

'I said,' I repeated between gritted teeth, my tone becoming louder as my sentence progressed. 'There's nothing wrong with you, is there? You're not dying at all?'

'Dying?' he said, laughing nervously. 'Well whoever said I was dying?'

'You did,' I pointed out. 'You wrote me a letter. I was

three thousand miles away, living my life, and you wrote to me and told me you were dying. You said you wanted to see me before it was too late. I came home to be with you when it happened.'

'Well,' he said, a crack appearing in his voice. 'I mean . . . I'm not a young man, William. I'm sure I don't have that long left. But I never meant to give you the impression that I—'

'You lied to me,' I said. 'You led me to believe that you were about to die and I packed up my things and left my home and the woman I love and came here, all so you could tell me some ludicrous story about the fucking wild west shows!' I was shouting now and had even raised myself off the seat a little. I hovered above it in anger, gripping the armrests in order to keep my hands away from his throat.

'That's not it,' he muttered, panicking now. 'Sit down, William. That's not what I . . . we can . . . this can be a great success. If you'd just think about it for a moment.

I didn't wait for the end of the sentence. I left the room quietly, not even slamming the door behind me, and went straight to my room. Sitting on the edge of the bed I wrapped my arms around myself, automatically rocking back and forth; the room appeared to be spinning on me. For the life of me, I could not believe what I had just heard. Looking up, I noticed something that I had not realised since my return. All the posters and memorabilia which I had taken down when I was in my teens had returned to my room. So accustomed to them was I from my childhood and youth that I had barely registered their return since I myself had come home. I stared at them and began to laugh hysterically. 'It's an obsession,' I said aloud. 'It's a fucking obsession!'

Chapter Seven

Celebrity

One of the many myths of the American west is that is was an enclosed society, a series of states gradually shifting from Indian to white control, one which excluded the outside world almost entirely until the settlements had reached their end and the reservations were in existence. While there is some truth to that, there were also times when the land outside of America entered into their activities and played a surprising part. One such entry formed the last occasion when my great-grandfather and General Custer would be in alliance.

President Grant was beginning the last year of his first term and was again attempting to endear himself to the voters by presenting himself not just as an American leader, but also as one who embraced dignitaries from around the world. When he received a message early in 1872 that the Grand Duke Alexis Alexandrovitch, the son of the Russian Czar, wished to visit the prairie lands of the mid-west in order to hunt buffalo, Grant saw the perfect opportunity for a good public relations exercise. It would also be the catalyst that would lead Bill away from the prairie lifestyle for ever.

Custer and Bill were given the task of preparing a

reception party for the Grand Duke and organising the hunting party which would take place over three days. The president made it clear in his briefing how important this exercise was and both men were intrigued by the task, being not a little overawed by the presence of such a dignitary within their ranks. It was agreed that the hunt would take place near the Red Willow, on the North Platte region of Nebraska, not far from where the Sioux tribe was located under the leadership of Spotted Tail. Buffalo roamed freely on the plains in that part of the country and the Sioux had been given permission by the government to hunt there during the winter months; it was agreed therefore that an emissary would be sent to Spotted Tail to seek permission to use the land – more out of courtesy than anything else – but also to invite the Indians to play a part in the visit, thus ensuring greater harmony between the two cultures. General Custer wanted to send a small troupe of enlisted men to speak to the Sioux, but to his surprise Bill volunteered for the job.

'What worries me is that your reputation will precede you,' he told him, mulling over the idea. 'You're well known for being part of the Republican movement which has moved a lot of their fellow tribes from their land. Don't you think they might have some measure of hostility towards you?'

'A lot of what they hear isn't true anyway,' countered Bill. 'Spotted Tail will know that. He'll be insulted if you send someone he hasn't heard of. It must be an acknowledged leader or he will take offence. Be certain of it.' Bill was referring to the dime novels which had been published over the previous year recounting the adventures of 'Buffalo Bill' on the prairies. Although they were written by a series of ghost-writers, he had sanctioned them and taken great pleasure in their success. Most of the stories were pure fiction but based, he liked to claim, on his own character, which was one of heroism and fortitude. In truth, he was attempting in his real life to become more like the character depicted in the books. Custer resented the success of these books but tried to hide his dislike; fortunately he himself remained a popular hero or a greater hostility might have arisen between them.

'Perhaps,' said the general. 'But if you end up being killed, I will let it be known that you insisted on going yourself. I won't be seen as your murderer.'

'God forbid,' said Bill with a smile, and the next morning he jumped on his horse Buckskin Joe and set off for the Sioux camp. It took him a day and a half to reach it and the closer he got, the more nervous he grew at what might lie ahead. The possibility of death and scalping was a strong one but he believed that if he could get to the chief before being spotted by any of the young men, whose aggression might overpower their sense, he would be able to make the trip a success. To this end, once he had the camp in view, he waited out of sight on a mountain top until late evening before creeping surreptitiously in.

The tent which Spotted Tail resided in was easy to spot as it was at the very heart of the camp and stood taller than any of the others. A fire burned within and Bill could make out the shadows of two men inside, talking animatedly. As he grew closer he could make out the harsh vowel sounds of the Lakota language, which he was not well versed in, and hoped that he would be able to identify himself and make himself understood by the tent's occupants before he was taken for an assassin and murdered. Standing outside the tent he gave a brief cough before raising the flap and looking inside, one hand held up in a gesture of peace. The two men – one Indian, one white – stopped talking and spun around to look at him, but neither seemed overly perturbed or afraid. Immediately Bill recognised the white man as Todd Randall, who had lived with the Lakota Sioux for many years and had acted as an interpreter between the Indians and the whites on many occasions in the past.

'Chief Spotted Tail,' said Bill in a humble voice. 'I apologise for calling on you so late at night. My name is Buffalo Bill Cody. I am sent by General Custer to speak with you.' As he spoke, Randall translated in a low voice and at the mention of his name he clapped his hands together in excitement and ushered Bill inside.

'Buffalo Bill,' he cried with excitement – his words also being translated at speed as he spoke – 'such a prestigious visitor! We have heard of you many times.'

My great-grandfather smiled a little. 'My name does seem to be attracting more and more attention,' he admitted. 'These adventure stories written about me are mostly fabricated however,' he added, recalling some of the anti-Indian activities which the dime novels had recorded.

'The stories may be made up, but they're based on your true character, are they not?' asked Spotted Tail; Bill decided to allow the question to stand as rhetorical. He looked at the older man by the light of the fire. He was probably in his mid-forties and had the darkest black hair, shoulder length, that he had ever seen. Normally it would have been tied behind his head, but now, late at night, it sat around his shoulders giving him an almost feminine appearance. His skin was dark and lined and a scar ran from beneath his left eye to the corner of his mouth.

'Again, I apologise for the lateness of my visit,' repeated Bill. 'I thought it was safest to come at night when I might approach you directly. I was unsure how strong the welcome your people might give me would be.'

'You were wise,' said Spotted Tail. 'There are many of my people here who would have had the hair from your head had they seen you. You are not as popular with them as you are with me, you know.'

'And am I popular with you?' asked Bill, prepared to play the sycophant if necessary.

'You have not harmed the Lakota Sioux as yet,' stated Spotted Tail. 'Until you make an enemy of me, you are my friend. And for you to be here now says to me that you want something from me. I'm always ready to listen to a man who wants something from me because in these days, I never know when I might need something in return.'

Bill nodded. He turned to look at Randall, considering whether he should include him in the conversation but decided that it would be rude not to. Randall was the translator and held no sway over their discussions. He turned back to Spotted Tail in order to state his business. 'A great chief is visiting us from across the waters,' he said. 'The son of the Russian Czar.'

'Visiting us?' interrupted Spotted Tail. 'Who is this us?'

'Visiting America,' said Bill. 'He comes to hunt buffalo.'

Spotted Tail let out an enormous laugh and slapped his hands down on his knees heartily. 'What kind of crazy people are these Europeans?' he asked. 'He comes across the world to hunt buffalo? He is either idle or stupid. Have they no buffalo of their own in Europe?'

Bill thought about it and realised such a thing had never occurred to him before. 'I don't know,' he admitted. 'All I know is that he's coming here because he's an avid hunter but has never been able to hunt buffalo before. He wants to try it.'

'Perhaps he has been reading your books as well?' asked Spotted Tail with a sly grin. 'Your legend is truly spreading far and wide, my friend.'

'He may tell us his reasons when he gets here,' said Bill, ignoring the question.

'And you, why are you here now? What can I do to help you?'

'General Custer and I wanted to speak with you of this visit,' continued Bill, mentioning the general's name because he knew that a message from him would be something which the chief would respect. 'We hope to bring the Grand Duke to the Red Willow. As you know, the buffalo there number in their thousands. Even a European could hardly miss one there.'

Spotted Tail sat back and breathed heavily, tapping his chin as he considered it. 'The Red Willow is where we hunt, Mr Buffalo Bill,' he pointed out. 'The Lakota Sioux. Your *government* has even said it should be so,' he added, uttering that second word as if he held it in contempt anyway.

'We're aware of this, Chief,' said Bill. 'Which is why we wanted to ask your permission to hunt there. And also to invite you to join us.' Spotted Tail looked up again, intrigued by this offer. 'General Custer proposes that we bring together thirty men from our camp and thirty of the Lakota Sioux to guide the Grand Duke on his hunting expedition. We will hunt together, eat together and, if you agree to it, the Sioux can perform their grand war dance at a feast on the third day. We will prove therefore to our European neighbours that we are people who are living in peace and harmony alongside each other.'

'You believe we are?'

'I believe we could be,' said Bill. 'There is distrust, of course. Wrong has been committed on both sides in recent years. This could be an opportunity, however, for our two peoples to learn more about each other. I believe this could be a positive step, Chief,' he added forcefully.

'I think you might be right,' agreed Spotted Tail, smiling gently, and my great-grandfather felt relieved that he had succeeded in this mission with so little effort. 'I believe I would like to involve myself in this action. And the feast you speak of, we will sit with General Custer and this Grand Duke, yes? We will share a table.'

'We will.'

Spotted Tail nodded. 'Then we will accept your offer,' he said. The bargain had been struck and without any element of discord. After agreeing to the details, Bill left the camp with as much stealth as he had approached it and returned to General Custer the following day.

In spite of what had happened, I stayed in London for almost two months. My initial fury with Isaac for the deception he had played on me had lessened when I realised that not only was his remorse genuine, but his reasons for the deceit had been rooted in love and loneliness. During a difficult conversation between us, he made it clear that he had felt that a part of him was missing without me there. We were family, he pointed out. The only family either of us had.

His business enterprise was also based on fact. He had

indeed been in contact with the bank and, incredibly (it seemed to me) they were getting close to giving him a business loan in order to set up his new wild west show. However the conditions of such a loan were based on my involvement in the enterprise; no bank was going to lend such a sum to a man in his seventies, but when an enterprising young man in his twenties was on board as well, the risk did not seem so great. The house was to be used as collateral and Isaac had some savings to invest as well. He talked me through the figures and the plans and, in theory, they were reasonably interesting. He knew enough about the way these things worked to put together a good portfolio of ideas; however his belief that there was an audience for such a venture was one with which I was not entirely in agreement.

Out of respect for him, though, and knowing how little he would have to live for if I did not agree to join him in this project, I gave the matter a lot of thought. I weighed up the pros and cons and spoke to the bank myself. I took a weekend trip to Dublin with Justin and Adam to decide for sure and we spent two days getting riotously drunk, a part of us knowing that it would be our last trip together. And then I came home and told Isaac 'no'.

His disappointment instantly turned to anger. He cursed me for an ungrateful son and stormed around the house like a demon possessed. Finally one evening, in a fit of pique, he lashed out and punched me in the face, splitting my lower lip as it crashed against my teeth so that a thin stream of blood ran down my chin and on to my shirt. Although it was a relatively minor wound, it seemed to snap something inside him and rather than become apologetic and realise how destructive once again his obsession with history and his ancestry had become, he became apoplectic with rage and demanded that I leave his home immediately. I had no choice but to agree and, packing light bags, I went to stay with Justin for a couple of days until I could organise a flight.

Throughout all those weeks, Hitomi had remained on my mind. I was torn between my love for her and my inability to destroy my father. I knew from the start I could only have one of them and it had always been so that wherever I was was the place I felt most obliged to. And so during that time I chose my father over Hitomi and when he rejected me, I felt able to return to her. We had not spoken once during our time apart. For the first two weeks she had – I assumed – been screening her calls and had never returned any of the numerous messages I had left for her. After that, the operator told me that the line had been disconnected and I assumed that in her anger with me, she had changed her number.

I wrote to her then and opened my heart in a letter in a way I had never done before. When I sat down with paper and pen, I wrote her name on the top of the page and then paused, wondering what it was I really wanted to tell her, determined that I would reveal all of myself to her and beg her to take me back. And that's what I did. It was a love letter in the old-fashioned sense. I told her the things I'd done wrong and how much I missed her. I admitted that I had been slower to tell her that I loved her than she had ever been and that I was sorry for that and yet it was true, I did love her. In a moment of either insanity or a desire to be brutally honest, I revealed that I had been unfaithful to her while in London and then took back the words, saying that no, it had not been an infidelity, not for a moment; I had merely had sex with another girl and that was all. I laid my life in her hands and, knowing that I might be back in Kyoto before she even received the letter, asked her not to call me immediately or to write, but instead to think about my words, to question how much I also meant to her, and that I would see her soon, and we would put everything right. It was the most important piece of writing I had ever done.

Arriving back in Japan a week later, I felt a great sense of relief; I truly believed now that I was coming home. I hadn't seen Isaac again before leaving London and that preyed on my mind slightly, but now my mind had shifted. I was back in Japan, which meant that I was more Hitomi's lover than Isaac's son.

A young man, a couple of years older than me and strikingly handsome, opened the door of Hitomi's apartment when I rang the bell. My heart had been pounding inside my chest a moment before and when I saw him standing there I had to steady myself immediately, the very moment convincing me that she had found someone else.

'Can I help you?' he asked in perfect English, an amused smile flickering around his lips. He was bigger than most Japanese men, easily as big as me, and strong too. He held a glass of red wine in his hands and it occurred to me that while Hitomi always enjoyed opening a bottle in the evening when we were there, I almost never joined her, preferring to take a cold beer from the fridge or a Coke. I stared at the glass in his hand as he gently swirled it and wondered foolishly whether that was all it would have taken to have held on to her; a simple glass of wine.

'Hitomi Naoyuki,' I said, trying to keep my voice level. 'Is she home?'

He frowned and shook his head. 'Perhaps you have

the wrong apartment?' he asked and I laughed, believing that he knew exactly who I was and was simply trying to get rid of me, afraid of a fight or a rival for Hitomi's affections.

'I want to speak to Hitomi,' I said firmly. 'Tell her it's William and tell her I want to speak to her. Tell her now, will you?'

He laughed and I could feel my blood begin to boil. 'I told you, William,' he said, his tone mildly insulting now. 'There is no Hitomi here. You must have the wrong apartment.'

I was ready to shove past him and storm through to the living room when a woman appeared by his side, looking at me quizzically. 'This is my wife,' the man explained and I caught a flash of his wedding ring as he put an arm around her shoulder. 'This man is looking for a Hitomi . . .' He glanced towards me. 'Narajuki?' he asked.

'Naoyuki,' I said, confused now but the woman shook her head. Speaking to her husband rather than directly to me, she reminded him that Hitomi had been the previous tenant. She had moved out a week before they had moved in, and they had moved in some five weeks earlier. The husband sighed and clicked his fingers.

'That's right,' he confirmed. 'I'm sorry, I knew the name meant something . . . I couldn't quite remember. You are a . . . friend of hers?'

I laughed slightly. Almost every time in the past that Hitomi and I had been out together and introduced to new people, they had asked me whether we were 'friends' as opposed to a couple, as if the idea of a Japanese with a Westerner, while perfectly within their limits of taste, was still slightly curious to them. 'I'm her boyfriend,' I

252

said, an edge of anger coming into my voice which he detected and disliked.

'If you are her boyfriend then you should know where she lives,' he said. 'And you clearly do not. Perhaps we should say goodnight.'

'Wait,' I said quickly, placing my hand against the door as he tried to close it. 'An address,' I said. 'You have an address for where she moved to?'

'She left no forward address,' the woman said, addressing me now with kindness and I could tell from the way that she said it that she wasn't lying. 'She was gone before we arrived. A whole week. We never met her.'

There was nothing more to be said so they simply closed the door in my face. I stood there for a moment, feeling lost and confused, before leaving the building and heading for a cheap hotel that I knew of nearby, believing that a good night's sleep would help me organise my thoughts better. It was getting late anyway; I reasoned that I could arrive at her office tomorrow and speak to her then.

However, when the morning arrived and I returned to the place where Hitomi and I had first met, the office was locked and when I looked through the glass on the door, it was obvious that there was no business in there any more as the room was entirely empty. As I walked away I noticed a sign advertising it as to let.

I stood in the middle of a busy Japanese street and felt like throwing my arms in the air. I had two choices left. The first was that I could go to her parents' home, where I doubted very much that she would be staying, and see whether they would give me her new address or telephone number, a scenario I believed was unlikely.

So I chose the second option and waited outside Tak's architectural offices one evening until I saw him come out – alone, luckily – and ran across the road to confront him, narrowly avoiding getting run over by a car as I did so. The horn sounded long and loud and one or two people looked in my direction irritably, but not Tak, who I had to run to catch up with and who I tapped on the elbow as I finally reached him. He stopped and turned, looking at me blankly for a moment before realising who I was and then his face broke into a wide smile, which surprised me a little, for he looked genuinely pleased to see me.

'William Cody,' he said, shaking his head. 'I almost didn't recognise you. You've shaved for once.' Instinctively, I stroked my cheeks and chin. 'I thought you were back home.'

'I am, Tajima,' I said with a smile, granting him his full appellation for once.

'Back home in London,' he said quickly. 'You know what I meant.'

I shrugged. 'I was,' I admitted. 'I just got back. I was waiting for you. I've been standing across there.'

'You missed me that much, eh?'

'Ha,' I said without a smile. 'Have you time for a drink?'

He glanced at his watch. 'Perhaps,' he said after a pause. 'I can't stay for long. I have a date with a young lady from Nagasaki who I have been pursuing for many months. Hubba hubba. She has the longest legs I have ever—'

'I won't keep you long,' I said quickly, not really wanting to hear the details of his latest paramour. 'Let's go to the Reu House.' This was a bar I had been in many times before which only employed pretty, blonde

American girls to wait on tables. It was a popular hang-out and not far from where we were.

'But the Reu House is where I am meeting my date,' he said. 'I don't want her to arrive and find us there together. Perhaps she would get the wrong idea about where the night is heading.'

I raised an eyebrow. 'You're taking a date to the Reu House?' I asked, amazed. 'You're the native here, Tak. That's like holding your wedding reception in a strip club. You don't take dates to the Reu House! You sit there gawking at the Noo Joisey hardbodies while she gets more and more fed up and leaves after two drinks. That's lame, man.' He looked mildly put out and I regretted having said that as, after all, I was relying on him for information. 'Look I'll just stay for one drink,' I said. 'Let's just go there. It's nearby. I promise I'll leave before she arrives.'

He nodded reluctantly and we made our way there; it was conveniently close to his apartment too and I suspected that Tak had planned it that way in case the evening went particularly well. His sense of opportunity had clearly overwhelmed his sense of romance. Once there, I wasted no time in getting to the point.

'I've been calling Hitomi,' I said. 'Her phone's been disconnected.'

'Really,' he said in a non-committal tone.

'I've been calling since I went back to London,' I continued. 'She never returns any of my messages. Then it's disconnected. I went to her apartment and she doesn't live there any more. I went to the office and it's been boarded up.'

'You've been busy,' said Tak.

'Don't give me a hard time,' I asked, shaking my head irritably. 'Where is she? What's happened to her?'

Tak laughed and leaned forward. 'You went away, William,' he said. 'You left her. You went back to England. For all she knew you were never coming back.'

'I'm back now,' I pointed out.

'You made a choice,' he said. 'And you chose England, am I right?' I said nothing for now. 'Hitomi has made choices too.'

'What kind of choices? Where is she? Has she started a new job? Is she working somewhere else?'

'I can't tell you that, William,' he said. 'She asked me not to.'

I stared at him, amazed by this. 'She what?' I asked. 'Why would she do that? It doesn't make any sense.'

'She feels – I think – that your relationship was not meant to be. She believes your heart is in England and as you know, she'll—'

'Die if she goes to England. I know. She's told me.'

'So she couldn't follow you there. She believes your choice was the right one.'

'Tak,' I said firmly. 'Just tell me where she is, will you? For God's sake, I need to talk to her.'

'I can't do that, William,' he repeated in a calm voice that annoyed the hell out of me. 'Hitomi is my sister and she gave me strict instructions on what to do if you ever contacted me. I can tell her your number if you want, but other than that. . .' He shook his head, indicating he could go no further. I knew there was no way that I could convince him and so, frustrated beyond belief, I scribbled down the phone number of the hotel where I was staying, and the number of the newspaper offices where I had worked before, telling him I could be contacted at either of those for the time being. We parted quickly after that and I went straight home, believing that he would probably have called her a moment after I left the Reu House and that she might be calling even then. I was wrong. Ultimately, I was never to receive another phone call from Hitomi while I was in Japan.

Disappointed by our lack of contact and trying to find a way to keep my mind occupied while my search went on, however, I tried to re-establish my life in Tokyo, renting a new apartment and returning to work at the newspaper. My editor was delighted to see me again; strangely, my column had proved so popular that when it had ended, they had received many letters from readers demanding its return. It was a popular newspaper with both Japanese and visiting or ex-pat Westerners alike and my articles on living in a foreign culture – an innocent abroad – had clearly kept them amused and entertained.

My articles were easy to construct. Every week I would write two thousand words on what I had done over the previous seven days. More often than not the events I depicted were either entirely fictitious or based on something I had heard had happened to another. I played the role of the slightly clumsy, unlucky-in-love Englishman; the floppy-haired ex-public schoolboy attempting to become immersed in another culture. Ironically, while my Japanese readers could laugh at my foolishness for being a stupid foreigner, the Westerners also laughed at me, believing that they – who I was attempting to lampoon – were nothing like the kind of idiot portrayed in my work. As well as the column, I wrote some other pieces for the weekend magazine and had begun writing some celebrity profiles (usually of visiting Western movie stars) before my enforced return to England.

To my surprise, the return of my column provoked

great approval and shortly afterwards the newspaper received an offer from the Associated Press for syndication in a range of newspapers across the Asia-Pacific region. Overnight, and with absolutely no extra work on my part, my salary increased six-fold and I found myself in the curious position of being comfortably off and a minor celebrity in the city.

This celebrity increased further when – to my fury – I began to receive copies of the other newspapers syndicating my work and saw that above my byline and beside my photograph was a line drawing of a cowboy figure blowing smoke away from the top of a large handgun. They had obviously picked up on the fact that my name was the same as the great western hero Buffalo Bill and, without even thinking for a moment that we could possibly be related, had run the picture to draw attention to the column. Soon, I found that I would get looks around town or in restaurants or bars as people realised that I was that William Cody, the idiot Englishman who wrote the funny stories, and point at me from afar. Happily, my celebrity was minor enough that I was rarely approached by anyone, but from time to time a drunken lout, having saved up his joke all night and believing that he was the first to come up with a phrase of such originality, would creep up beside me and shout 'Stick 'em up,' a phrase which always had the power to bring me straight back to my childhood classroom days.

I tried to enjoy my new-found fame – I wanted to enjoy my success as I had never imagined that I would have any – but it was difficult for I had never felt as lonely as I did then. My mind was on my loss twenty-four hours a day. The fact that Hitomi was out there somewhere and I could not find her left me constantly wondering what she was doing. I wanted Hitomi and believed that I had lost her, partly through Isaac's deception, and partly through my own sense of family responsibility. I became angry with myself, embittered; I drank more, I slept around. I became complacent and caused a distance to grow between my colleagues and myself as I became more convinced of my own celebrity and importance; I was twenty-three years old and despite all the good things that were happening to me, I had never been so unhappy.

And then, one evening while getting slowly drunk on my own in (ironically) the Reu House, attempting to chat up the American waitresses with little success, for they knew me only too well and one or two had already made the mistake of coming home with me, I was approached by a young Japanese woman of my own age who had been peering at me from a bar stool for about thirty minutes before making her way over.

'Excuse me,' she said. 'It's Wilbur, isn't it?'

'William,' I said, irritated that she could read the column, commit my picture to memory, but find herself unable to remember my name correctly.

William, that's right.' she said apologetically. 'You don't remember me, do you?' I squinted and tried to place her; she didn't look familiar. 'Mayu,' she said, pressing a hand to her chest lightly. 'We met once, about a year ago? At Hitomi's birthday party?'

'Oh yes,' I said quickly, recovering even though I didn't have the first clue who she was. 'Of course. Mayu. How are you?'

'Fine, fine,' she replied and we stood there and stared at each other for a moment with nothing particularly to say. 'You're back in Kyoto,' she said eventually, stating the obvious and I nodded.

'Apparently,' I said in a dry voice.

'But are you just back on business? I can't imagine you'd want to leave Hitomi on her own in a place like that for very long.' She gave a laugh and I immediately perked up and put my beer down so that I might focus on her a little better. I didn't want to make it too obvious that I was unaware of Hitomi's whereabouts, in case she got scared and didn't want to reveal any more. Fortunately, she hadn't finished speaking yet. 'All those sexy French men,' she said, laughing a little more and her face flushed slightly. 'I wouldn't be able to resist them if it was me.'

'Well, I trust her,' I said quietly, my heart beating a little faster in amazement that such a conversation was actually taking place. We're very happy after all. Have you ever been there, Mayu?' I asked.

'To Paris?' she replied and I felt like giving a little gasp of delight but held myself in. 'No, not yet. Some-day, though, I'd love to go. I've always imagined it's such a romantic city.'

'It is,' I said, despite the fact that I'd never been within a hundred miles of it. 'It's beautiful. Especially at this time of year. I'm only here to organise ship-ping the rest of Hitomi's things over there. We don't think we'll ever leave. You should come visit us, you know.'

'I'd love to,' she said, a little taken aback I think by my sudden enthusiasm and generosity. 'I'll have to start saving.'

'Well we could put you up,' I said, trying not to over-do it too much. 'Hitomi would love to see you. Just give us a call. You have our number, don't you?'

'No,' she said, looking around as her friends were standing up to leave and waving for her to join them.

'But don't worry, I can call Tak someday and get the details. He's got your number, yes?'

'Don't phone for a while,' I said, ecstatic now and anxious to be rid of her, ignoring her last question. 'We're going away on a trip for about six weeks. Perhaps after that?'

She frowned and nodded. 'Well all right,' she said. 'Give her my love, though, won't you?'

'Absolutely,' I said, standing up and giving her a kiss on both cheeks, Parisian style. She seemed shocked now by my forwardness and walked away quickly with a wave. Her friends were staring at me and I think one of them must have recognised me for he said something as she returned and she shook her head before looking back at me, confused, as if she was wondering why someone was claiming that I was the popular young newspaper columnist in Kyoto when I was actually supposed to be living in Paris. I gave her a wave and didn't look up again for a few minutes, until I was sure that she was gone.

Sayonara, Kyoto, I thought to myself.

Ellen Rose devoted the best part of a year to trying to persuade her parents to allow her to join the trapeze company of the Regis-Roc Circus. Her father, Russell Rose, tried everything he could think of to dissuade her but it was to no avail. Eventually it became clear that if he wanted anything resembling a peaceful life he had little choice but to train her.

'Think about it,' said Bessie, Russell's wife, the evening before her first lesson. 'Her insistence is probably based on the fact that we've always said no before. Maybe once she starts to learn and has to spend hours working on the routines, she'll get bored with it and give up.'

'Let's hope so,' said Russell, although he was not hopeful that that would indeed be the case. The trapeze company always used a net while training but removed it for the performances. The possibility of death made their act more exciting to the spectators and in their fourteen-year history, they had never suffered any serious accidents. It was agreed that Ellen would not be allowed to perform in front of spectators until all the members of their troupe were absolutely convinced that she was proficient in their art. Ellen was only five feet two inches tall; she weighed about a hundred pounds and in theory was perfect trapeze material. It was decided that she would partner Joseph Craven, a twenty-seven-year-old veteran of the troupe, who was only an inch taller and about twenty pounds heavier than her. Craven had been performing for eight years and was considered one of the most daring and inventive of the company; he was delighted to be given the task of training Ellen because it gave him an opportunity to spend time with her and he had long considered her to be the most beautiful woman he knew.

By now, Ellen was seventeen years old and still single. She suspected that her new tutor was enamoured of her but tried to discourage him, as she was not at all attracted to him, and found herself growing irritated by the look of excitement which came into his eyes whenever he had to twist her around by the ankles or throw her up in the air and catch her lengthways by the waist. Often, while in mid-air, she could see a faint line of perspiration forming on Craven's forehead, some tiny beads along his upper lip, and felt her body grow rigid with distaste.

'You have to be more fluid with your movements,' he would say on those occasions, almost collapsing under her as she fell. 'It's like catching a dead weight. You have to try to lose all sense of your body when you're in the air.'

'I'll try,' Ellen muttered, wishing that she could change partners, but having tried so long to join this troupe, there seemed little chance that she could simply pick and choose who to work with now that she was finally in.

Russell and Bessie often watched from the bleachers as Craven taught their daughter the routines and each worried in different ways. Russell was afraid that his daughter's idolising of him was eventually going to cause her harm, thereby making any potential accident his fault. Bessie, on the other hand, had hoped that Ellen would not stay with the circus at all but would find for herself a life outside of it. She had made her own life there and been very happy, but it was an enclosed world which she had joined from the outside. Ellen had never known anything except for it and the way things were going, she never would. This was not something she wished for her daughter and actively prayed that she would grow bored with the whole thing.

In the meantime, Craven continued to teach Ellen and continued to lust after her as she dreamed of only one thing: making it up the ladder of the Big Top for that evening when she would give her debut performance as a trapeze artist. She was convinced that she could become a star.

The Grand Duke Alexis Alexandrovitch arrived with a large entourage a few weeks after my great-grandfather had spoken to Chief Spotted Tail and arranged that both their people would work together to present an image of harmony to their illustrious visitor. He had travelled from Paris to New York and spent several weeks there, meeting with the governor and several members of Ulysses S. Grant's cabinet before heading southwards to a dinner engagement with the president. However, it was the appointment with the famous Buffalo Bill Cody which was most exciting to him and when he arrived at Red Willow, he greeted him effusively. General Custer was a little irritated by this since he, as ranking officer, headed the official greeting party for the Duke, but he tried not to allow his feelings to be too obviously displayed.

'I have never seen land like this,' the Duke told Custer through an interpreter. 'Today, we have ridden for hours across prairies that are more open and free than anything we have at home.'

'Don't worry, Duke,' said Custer quickly. 'We hope to change all that soon. The government plans to create great cities across these lands. America can be an even greater country a hundred years from now with the work we are putting in place.' The Duke looked aghast, Custer having misinterpreted his comments about the land as being negative ones.

'But that would be a disaster,' he said, looking around as if it might all be swallowed up within minutes. 'You cannot destroy such beauty, surely?'

Custer looked a little flustered but tried to carry on as best as he could. 'We'll be making it better,' he explained. 'In the name of progress there are always sacrifices which need to be made, don't you agree? Is your father, the Czar, not doing similar things in Russia?'

The Grand Duke snorted, his expression implying that he was merely a fortunate relative and not one given to inclusion in the plans of his mother country. 'The Czar would never want to destroy lands like this,' he said. 'Even if we had such places, which we do not. It would be unforgivable. It's lucky we came here when we did. Perhaps there would be no hunting in a few years' time?'

Custer laughed and looked a little awkward, turning now to my great-grandfather for some assistance. 'We plan on bringing more people to these areas,' explained Bill, touching the Duke lightly on the elbow. 'So that they can experience what we have come to know as one of our great natural resources. You have heard, no doubt, of how we are building great railroads across the country?'

The Duke smiled and paused for a moment, wishing to frame his response without giving offence. 'I know that there are thousands of immigrants building your railroads. They come from very far away to this America in order to make you great, isn't that so? From China, Japan, Tokyo. Tens of thousands of people climbing on board boats to bring themselves here for a better life and they end up building your railroads. The ones that don't die either getting here or building them, that is. This is a clever country, I'll give you that.'

Bill smiled but Custer could feel his anger beginning to surface. This was not a good start to three days of diplomacy. The Grand Duke, a heavy-set man with a prominent jawline and dark eyes, stared at him, silently daring him to respond to this deliberately provocative conversation, but Bill changed the subject to one concerning his reasons for being there. 'Do you do much hunting in Russia, Duke?' he asked politely, receiving a gruff shake of the head as a response.

'The hunting there is nothing like what you have here,' he replied. 'From what I am told you have thousands of buffalo roaming free to hunt whenever you want.

Where I come from, such animals would be killed and eaten immediately.'

'We do have strict guidelines,' pointed out General Custer. 'It's not as if anyone can simply come along and kill as many of the beasts as they want. This land, for instance, is reserved for hunting by the Lakota Sioux, one of the tribes common to this part of America. They have always—'

As Custer began a potted biography of the Lakota Sioux for their guest, Bill remembered that their Chief, Spotted Tail, was standing a few feet away with the leading members of his tribe and had not, as yet, been invited into the conversation. Motioning him to approach he interrupted the general and introduced him to the Grand Duke.

'Spotted Tail has graciously allowed us to hunt with the Sioux on the Red Willow land over the next couple of days,' Bill explained. 'It is a great privilege for us to hunt with such brave warriors,' he added, a true diplomat who didn't particularly believe what he was saying, but was enjoying irritating Custer with his homely good humour. The Grand Duke stared at Spotted Tail in surprise, for he had never met a member of an Indian tribe before. The chief was dressed in his full formal attire and presented a colourful, if slightly threatening, appearance. The two men shook hands awkwardly and the group retired to the tents for refreshments and rest. The night was drawing in and a feast was planned for the evening with an early finish so that the hunt might begin properly the next morning.

Despite his enthusiasm for the hunt, the Grand Duke slept late the next day and looked a little the worse for wear when he eventually joined his three hosts at the head of the hunt. He had stayed awake too long the night before and drunk too much wine and now his head was pounding with the hangover it had produced. Spotted Tail stared at him defiantly for they had come dangerously close to trouble when the Russian had spent more than an hour flirting with the chief's oldest daughter, a sideshow which by coincidence had kept his eyes away from the fact that my great-grandfather was busy seducing his youngest.

Although the Grand Duke was an experienced huntsman he had no experience with animals of the size of prairie buffaloes and Bill could tell that he felt a little intimidated to be riding alongside himself, Custer and Spotted Tail, any of whom could have felled half a dozen animals with little more than an angry look. Because of this, and thinking that it might give him more confidence, he had invited their guest to ride on his own horse, Buckskin Joe, whose own fame was growing alongside that of his master.

'When I was in New York,' the Duke told Bill as they ambled slowly along the prairies, taking in the sight of the roaming buffaloes before beginning the kill, 'I went to see *The Killer on the Prairies* at one of their theatres. You have seen it, I presume?'

Bill laughed. 'I haven't, as yet,' he replied. 'Although I have read reports that it's a popular entertainment.'

'It's only the finest piece of theatre I have ever had the joy of watching,' replied the Duke. *The Killer on the Prairies* was the first adaptation of the Buffalo Bill dime novels to be performed on the stage and had been the hit of the season on Broadway. The well-known actor Ned Buntline had written the script and was playing the part of Bill himself in a melodramatic adventure which concerned the kidnapping by the Cheyenne of a young girl, the daughter of one of Bill's friends, and my great-grandfather's attempts to bring her back before she could be violated. It was playing to packed houses in New York and it was rumoured that another production would soon be going on the road and travelling across the country.

'As it happens, I've never been to New York,' said Bill contemplatively. 'Perhaps I should go. But I've always felt that the big-city life may not be what I am destined for.'

'With a fame as wide as yours, my friend, I would imagine you could go anywhere and be given a hero's welcome. When I saw that play, the audience applauded so wildly at the end that had you been there you may well have been torn limb from limb.'

'Well if that's the response I can expect, then perhaps it's best that I stay away.'

'I exaggerate, of course,' said the Duke quickly. 'But it's not everyone who has the bravery to perform such deeds. That was one of the reasons I wanted to come here, you know. I've read all the stories about you. I've followed your career with great interest. I wanted to hunt with the great Buffalo Bill Cody. Money offers us some advantages in life and I wanted to use mine for these things.'

'Then you're wasting your money,' replied Bill with a laugh, although he was revelling in the compliments. 'Those stories . . . they're mostly fiction. They choose events that have taken place and spin them into some grand adventure story. Really, they're only based on very limited information. This play, for example. None of that story ever happened. Although I did spend three weeks chasing a Cheyenne from town to town across Ohio last year for he had killed a man, a friend of mine, but there was no girl involved.'

'And what did you do when you caught up with him?' asked the Grand Duke.

'I killed him, of course,' came the reply. 'What would you have me do? Hand him in to the authorities? An eye for an eye, Duke. That's my motto. Perhaps not as heroic as the novelists would have you believe, or the playwrights, but there we are. The truth is not always as exciting as the reality.'

Custer chose this moment to slow down and pick up the pace with the two men. 'Should we begin?' he asked. 'There's a fine herd of buffalo just over this hill. Ripe for the plucking, I would say.' He called to the group to stop and the three men, along with Chief Spotted Tail, rode a little forward to survey their prey. 'As the guest of honour,' Custer began, clearing his throat and speaking in a loud voice so that all could hear him, 'you have the privilege of taking the first shots.' He had addressed the Grand Duke, whose face betrayed a slight twitch when these words were uttered. He looked around nervously.

'I do?' he asked. 'Do we not hunt together?'

'Traditionally, the guest of honour rides first into the pack and only when he has killed his first buffalo do the rest of the party join in,' said Custer. He was torn now between his obligation as host and his enjoyment of the Grand Duke's discomfort.

'Grand Duke,' said Bill quickly, reaching into the side bags of his horse, an unfamiliar beast to him since he had lent his regular steed to the other man. 'I brought something for you to aid you in your first buffalo hunt. Something which has brought me luck in the past.' From the saddle bag he removed the Smith & Wesson gun which his father had owned before him and had given to him as a gift after he had saved his life; the same gun which Bill would one day leave to his own Sam, who would pass it on to his son Isaac, who would place it on a hook on his living-room wall and forbid me to ever touch it without his permission. 'This was my father's gun,' he explained, handing it across to the Grand Duke Alexis, who examined it carefully. Bill had spent a portion of the previous evening cleaning and shining it and it looked as good as it ever had, the elegant carvings glistening in the noonday sun. 'It shoots well and true,' he continued. If you would like to use it today, then you are welcome to.'

The Grand Duke accepted the gun gratefully, checked that it was fully loaded and, aware that everyone was watching him, he gave a loud shout and dug his stirrups into the side of Buckskin Joe, who reared up and charged down the hill towards the buffalo below. Within moments, the Grand Duke was circling the herd and discharging his gun at will.

'He is no hunter,' said Spotted Tail, who sat on his horse between Custer and Bill. 'How many times has he shot already?'

'He better shoot one soon,' muttered Custer in reply. 'Or we're all in trouble.'

Fully reloaded now, and without once looking up at his hosts, the Grand Duke circled the herd once again and began to shoot. Bill counted the bullets in his head with each discharge of the gun and when he was sure it was empty again and that nothing had been killed he kicked his own horse in the side quickly.

'Don't follow me,' he said to the other two men as he began to ride off. It will only make things worse.'

Bill gave a loud shout as he galloped down towards the buffaloes. The Grand Duke looked terrified as they approached a particularly tame-looking animal.

'Shoot,' said Bill in a firm voice. 'Shoot now.'

The Grand Duke lifted the Smith & Wesson and pointed it directly at the head of the beast and fired. The animal's legs crumpled beneath him and he fell to the ground. A huge sense of relief was felt by all and immediately Custer, Spotted Tail and their various entourages charged down the hill, causing the herd to stampede, charging away from the men as fast as they could. The adrenalin rushed through Bill's veins for it was the sound of the hooves racing across the prairies that excited him like no other sound and, forgetting about his charge, he galloped forward and gave chase, keeping one eye on Custer at all times, aware that they would be challenging each other in an unspoken contest throughout the day.

Later that night, exhausted but happy with the day's outcome, Bill found himself alone with the Grand Duke Alexis Alexandrovitch, both men now happily drunk and pleased with their day's activities. The Duke had become a better killer once the first animal had been killed and had finally acquitted himself well, killing almost two dozen buffalo.

'I think I owe you a debt of gratitude, my friend,' said the Grand Duke. 'You came to my assistance today when I needed it.'

'It was an unfamiliar horse to you,' said my great-grandfather kindly. 'And Buckskin Joe is not accustomed to anyone's else's behind but my own. You were a worthy hunter.'

'True, but you helped me anyway when I could have embarrassed myself. All I am saying is thank you.' Bill accepted the words of gratitude with a polite nod and said no more on the subject.

'I've been thinking,' he said after a lengthy pause.

'About what you were telling me earlier. *The Killer on the Prairies*? The stage show?'

'Ah yes,' said the Grand Duke. 'You wish to go see it now, do you? Bask in the applause which is meant for you?'

'Not quite,' said Bill, an idea forming in his mind which would be the genesis of the next stage in his life, the end of his careless youth and the beginning of his life in show business. 'You said this man Buntline was good at playing me in this show, yes? He was a good actor?'

'He was very good,' said the Grand Duke. 'I believe he is well known anyway. The audience seemed to appreciate him. As I told you, the theatre is full every night.'

'Then he must be making an awful lot of money,' said Bill. 'I have heard of this fellow before, all right. I've never met him. But it seems to me he's becoming very rich playing a part which he invents for himself every night on a stage. I begin to think that it's time I took advantage of my celebrity a little and made a little money for myself.'

The Grand Duke nodded and thought about it. 'So what do you suggest?' he asked. 'You want the theatre to pay you some of their proceeds?'

'No, not that,' replied Bill. 'I just think I might know someone better qualified to play Buffalo Bill than Ned Buntline. Someone a little more familiar with the character.'

'Really? And who would that be then?' asked the son of the Czar, still a little slow on the uptake. 'Another actor?'

Bill turned to him and smiled. 'Of sorts,' he replied.

Chapter Eight

Scouts of the Plains

Over two million people live in the French capital, and I was there to find just one. I had left Tokyo soon after my conversation with Mayu in the bar where she had told me where Hitomi was now living. Of course, I didn't know where exactly she lived in Paris but decided to figure that one out when I got there. Once I knew that Paris was where I should be, I wanted desperately to be there immediately but was forced to put my enthusiasm on hold as I sorted out my affairs in Japan. Although I had only been back a short amount of time, my life had already re-established itself and I couldn't just leave without some notice. The reappearance of my column in the newspaper had proved popular to readers and I proposed to my editor that I should continue my travel column for them but would relocate it from east to west. I had never been to France before, I pointed out, and the experiences of a naïf there might prove almost as interesting to his readers as the cultural isolation of a Westerner in Japan. After some persuading, it was agreed that I should begin work on the new column after my arrival but that if it did not prove popular it could be pulled at a moment's notice.

Jetlag hit me upon my arrival in Paris. Knowing that it would, I had arranged a few days' accommodation at a hotel and took a taxi there directly from Charles de Gaulle, where I spent the next thirty-six hours catching up on my sleep and bringing my body clock back to Western time. My immediate priorities were three-fold. First, to find a place to live as I did not want to spend money on the hotel any longer than was strictly necessary. Second, to find employment. Only then, I believed, would I be ready to begin my pursuit of Hitomi, my great search. For the time being it was enough knowing that we were in the same city, breathing the same fresh air, and that at any moment we could unwittingly run into each other on the street, or in a bar or café, on the Metro perhaps. It made the city seem exciting. A panic attack hit me one evening as I realised that I had done all of this on the basis of one brief conversation with a girl I barely knew, who had merely remarked that this was the last city she had heard of Hitomi being in. Naturally she could have moved anywhere since then. She could have returned to Japan the day I had left it; we could have been ten steps away from each other between departures and arrivals at Narita and we would never have known. But I had to put such thoughts out of my head for they were fruitless. She was there, I knew it. I could feel it. I could feel *her*. And I would find her.

I took a one-bedroom apartment on the third floor of a building near the university. Since I would be in Paris for the foreseeable future, I decided to go for something nearer the top end of my price range. I reasoned with myself that my first article for the newspaper would bring in some return. It would be about my search for accommodation but naturally I would make the search seem a lot more comical and adventurous than it actually was.

My apartment was one of two on the third floor of the house and I quickly made friends with the couple across the hall. Luc Davide and his wife Annette were a few years older than me and we met on my second night there when I was invited to join in a birthday party taking place across the hall. Luc knocked on my door and introduced himself and I was pleased to meet him for he seemed friendly and open and as yet I knew no one in the city.

'Happy birthday,' I said to Annette when Luc introduced me to her, for she was wearing a badge on her lapel that said *Bon anniversaire*.

'It's Luc's birthday too,' she said with a laugh, rejecting my outstretched hand for a hearty kiss instead. 'We were born only two days apart in the same year so we're holding the birthday party on the day in between to compromise. I was twenty-nine yesterday, he'll be twenty-nine tomorrow.'

'Then happy birthday to you both,' I said, already feeling warmed by the welcome they were showing me; although we had barely exchanged greetings I felt pleased that they would be living across the hall from Hitomi and I. (At the time, that was how I assumed things would be).

'We only got married six months ago,' Annette, a New Yorker, explained to me later that evening when the party was over and the three of us were having a last drink before going to bed. 'We've been together for about five years now but it never seemed right until then. Not that things seem very different, but there we are.' I had volunteered to help them clean the apartment once their guests had gone and to my surprise they had cheerfully taken me up on it. And I liked helping out; I was twenty-four then and it occurred to me that I had very few friends. Of course there was Adam and Justin in London but we rarely saw each other and when we did, as had occurred during my recent trip home, they were usually busy with their respective partners. And there were my Japanese friends, of course, who I had left far behind me, possibly never to see again. And then there was Hitomi. I felt we had clicked immediately, the three of us, and looked forward to their friendship.

'Did you meet in Paris?' I asked them, imagining that the city of romance had brought them together.

'We met in Cannes,' said Luc. 'I was covering the festival and Annette works for a film production company here. We met at a party on the Croisette.'

'You're a journalist then?' I asked him. 'Me too.'

'Luc *was* a journalist,' said Annette proudly. 'Now he's a theatre director. He's been quite successful. His last two plays were booked solid for more than a year each.'

I looked at him appreciatively but he seemed a little embarrassed as his wife prodded him to tell me more about his productions. 'We did *Cabaret* a couple of years ago, at the Racine. It was fun. I liked that play. It started as an open-air production for three weeks at La Défense and then we moved indoors. After that I did a play by an unknown playwright here which was a hit. It was a good play, I think. It's closing soon though, so I have to start work on something else.'

'He's found a wonderful play by a nineteenth-century French writer,' said Annette. 'No one's ever heard of it but it went down a storm in the city back then. What's it called, Luc?'

'*L'Assassinat Nécessaire*,' he said. '*The Necessary Murder*,' he added, translating for me.

'That's it. No one seems to know whatever happened to the author. It's a lost gem.'

'So what about you, William,' asked Luc, always keen to shift the attention away from himself. 'What are you doing in Paris?'

Within minutes I found myself explaining my situation to them with total candour. I said that I had been living in Japan for a couple of years and had met the woman I was destined to be with there but had been conned into leaving the country by my father, a man obsessed with his ancestry. By the time I had returned she was gone, convinced that I had betrayed her.

'Why didn't you take her to England with you?' asked Annette, and I noticed how her natural New York accent, still noticeable despite the length of time she had been away from that city, had been mingled with the delicate sounds of the French in an attractive way.

'She wouldn't go to England,' I explained. 'She's always said that she'd die if she went to England.'

'You mean *literally* die?'

I nodded. 'So she says. I don't understand it either. It's some superstition she has. Anyway, I thought my father was dying so I had no choice but to go home. When I got there it turned out that he was perfectly fine. He just wanted me to come home. I gave up my entire life in Japan just because he conned me out of it.'

'He must love you very much,' said Luc quietly and I stared at him as the room seemed to suddenly spin. That was not a remark I had expected; it was certainly not something I had ever balanced Isaac's behaviour with after I had left England. I couldn't think of anything to say to him and wanted suddenly to return to my apartment to brood on this.

'William Cody,' said Annette suddenly, interrupting my reverie. 'You know, in America we have this kind of folk hero. Fought in the War of Independence, Buffalo Bill Cody, maybe you've heard of him? Same name,' she added with a laugh.

'It was the Civil War,' I corrected her. 'And yes, I've heard of him all right. I get that a lot.'

My great-grandfather travelled by rail from Missouri to New York City. As he did not know how long he might be gone for, he sent Louisa, along with their two daughters Arta and Orra, back to St Louis to stay with her parents, and this time she did so with little comment. Louisa had already grown far from the woman she had been before her marriage. The experience with the Golden Rule Hotel had convinced her that she took her marriage vows a lot more seriously than Bill ever had; however, she could see no future for either herself or her children if she sought a separation from her husband and so had decided instead simply to do his bidding without question. She would be with him when he needed her, and separate when he was away.

Out of sight, however, was very much out of mind for Bill who looked forward to the excitement of New York City with great anticipation. His friend Texas Jack Omohundro accompanied him on the trip and, as he was an unmarried man, their conversation ran to the escapades they could find in the city upon their arrival. Word had spread through the train that the famous Buffalo Bill Cody was on board and from time to time an excitable young lady would pass through their carriage, casting them furtive glances before dissolving into giggles and running away again.

'See that?' said Bill, proud of the fact that his celebrity could entice women towards him without any encouragement on his part. 'That's what we've got waiting for us on the other side, my friend. They say that New York is overrun with beautiful and eligible young women.'

Texas Jack, at twenty-four years of age three years younger than Bill, rubbed his hands together gleefully. He had been thrilled to be invited on this trip, not to mention a little surprised, for although he had always looked up to my great-grandfather and tried to befriend him, he had never thought they were close enough for him to be selected in this way. Bill, however, had asked him along as he recognised the hero worship in the boy's eyes and enjoyed the feeling of respect and admiration that came towards him in waves whenever people like Texas Jack were around. Although Bill himself was oblivious to it, many people had noticed how Texas Jack had adopted some of my great-grandfather's mannerisms and had abandoned some of his older friends from the moment that Bill had shown him some attention. 'We'll make ourselves familiar with as many of those ladies as possible,' he replied, barely able to contain his enthusiasm, determined to make Bill realise that he was every bit the ladies' man that he was. 'But what of our engagements? Will we have free time to do what we want?'

'Good God, boy, you're with Buffalo Bill Cody! You can do whatever the hell you please! Believe me, we've been invited for dinner in every house in the state but it's up to us who we reject and who we honour with our company. We'll have time to make as much sport as we wish, don't worry about that.'

This satisfied Texas Jack for the time being and he settled back to enjoy the passing landscape. He had never been east before either, having been brought up in Texas and served in the cavalry in St Louis. His father had been killed in battle when he was a child and he had grown up with eight older sisters and a mother for company. Because of this he had spent as much time around the fort as possible as a child and had joined up at the earliest possible opportunity, starved as he was for the company of other men. Like Bill, he sought adventure and excitement and had envisioned a life of scouting on the prairies in the future, hoping that when his time came to die, it would be on the battlefield like his father, a bullet or a knife piercing the uniform which he wore with pride. All such plans were made, however, before he first caught sight of the world outside of the south. The New York trip would change Texas Jack's life for ever.

They had arranged to meet Ned Buntline that evening at the Bowery Theatre and after settling in at their hotel and changing, they set off. Buntline had written the play which was showing there at that time, entitled *The King of Border Men*, which was based on a fictional episode in my great-grandfather's life. He had also been the first person to play the role of Buffalo Bill on stage, but when the success of the production forced the cast to perform several matinée performances a week, as well as their regular nightly ones, he stepped away from the footlights and hired a younger, fitter man to play the part instead. Introducing themselves to one of the ushers at the front doors of the theatre, they were quickly taken into a private room while Buntline was sent for. When he arrived, he could barely contain his excitement.

'Mr Cody,' he roared, marching in with his hand already extended. As Bill gripped it, however, he must have changed his mind as instead of shaking it, he pulled my great-grandfather to him and administered a bear hug instead. 'It's a joy to meet you,' he proclaimed in a loud voice. 'An absolute joy. I repeat, sir: a joy and an honour!'

'Please,' said Bill, slightly overwhelmed by the greeting. 'You must call me Buffalo Bill.'

'Then I'm Ned.'

'Well Ned, allow me to introduce to you my friend and colleague, Texas Jack Omohundro.'

Buntline turned to look at the other man, blinking in surprise for he had not expected another visitor, nor had he quite noticed him when he had first entered the room, so intent had he been on greeting his honoured guest. 'Texas Jack,' he said, smiling and offering a more sedate handshake. 'It's a pleasure and a privilege to meet you too. Any friend of . . . eh . . .' He seemed to lose track of the sentiment as he sized him up and down.

'Likewise, Mr Buntline,' said Texas Jack, barely noticing the slight.

'And where did you get your name from, might I ask? In some adventure, I'll bet. Am I right? Am I?'

Texas Jack looked to Bill for support but none was forthcoming. It seemed obvious enough. 'I'm from Texas,' he said. 'Born and bred there.'

'Ah,' said Buntline, a little deflated by the mundane answer. 'Well that can't be helped. Never mind. Anyway, it's wonderful to have you both here. How was your journey? Excellent, excellent,' he continued, not waiting for an answer. Bill could feel a smile coming to his lips. He had already formed a liking for this slightly overweight, red-faced, middle-aged man and was enjoying watching his flustered performance. 'The play is due to begin shortly,' he said after a moment, checking his watch. 'Perhaps I should show you both to your seats and afterwards we can talk. There are some very important matters I want to discuss with you, Mr Cody.'

'Buffalo Bill.'

'Yes indeed. Some very important matters I want to discuss with you, Buffalo Bill,' he corrected himself. 'How could I forget? Your name is on my mind almost every moment of the day after all. Not that I have any sort of unhealthy obsession; you understand, although my wife says I have. No, it's nothing unhealthy, sir, I promise you. I'm merely an admirer. A devotee. A follower, an afficianado, an enthusiast.'

'Mr Buntline, you look a little overwrought,' said Texas Jack, squinting at his host, whose face appeared to be growing more and more peach with every passing moment. 'Would you like me to get you a glass of water, maybe?'

'Water?' yelled Buntline, staring at him as if he was quite mad, his voice rising as quickly as his temperature. 'Water, you say? No time for water, my friend. It's two minutes to showtime and I've got one of my leading actors who up until five minutes ago was marching around backstage barely sober. How's he going to remember his lines, that's what I want to know? My own fault I suppose for allowing him out after the matinée without a minder. Still, a man can't keep another man under his eyes every moment of the day, can he, gentlemen? You want to talk about unhealthy? That's unhealthy, gentlemen! Oh my stars, would you look at

the time! I better show you to your seats.' He opened
the door and ushered them both out and into the main
auditorium where almost three hundred people were
settling down to enjoy the play. There was a buzz of
whispered conversation and half the eyes were directed
towards the stage, despite the fact that the curtain was
still drawn. A few empty seats had been reserved in the
third row and Buntline pushed Bill and Texas Jack into
them quickly. 'Just sit there and enjoy it,' he said. 'I'll see
you both afterwards. We'll talk then.' And with that, he
ran towards the side of the stage and disappeared into
the wings.

'There's a fellow who needs a drink to settle his
nerves,' said Texas Jack, laughing as they recovered their
composure. 'What a fool, eh?'

'A fool who's been making an awful lot of money out
of my name this last year,' muttered Bill in response.
'All these dime novels he's been writing, him and that
Prentiss Ingraham fellow. They must be making a small
fortune for themselves. And now this stage show. Look
around you, Jack. There's an awful lot of people here
have paid good money to see this blasted thing. Where
do you suppose all that money's going, eh? Not into my
pocket, I can tell you.'

'And that's what you want to speak to this Buntline
fellow about, is it?' asked Jack.

'It will most likely come up,' he replied diplomatically,
before shushing his companion as the lights dimmed
and the play began.

The stage had been designed to resemble a prairie,
with tumbleweeds and cactus plants situated at different
points along the set. The story involved the kidnapping
of Bill's sister by a group of renegade Cheyenne. Bill and
his army set off in chase and got themselves involved

in various scrapes before recapturing the woman and killing all the Indians in a dramatic finale. When J. B. Studley, the actor who had taken over from Buntline in the title role first appeared on stage the audience gave a cheer and, clearly not a method actor, Studley walked to the front of the stage and gave a ceremonial bow to all, milking the applause until he was sure that it had ended. Only then did he consent to return to character.

'He doesn't look a thing like you,' whispered Texas Jack to Bill. 'Why, he's an old man! He must be thirty-five if he's a day!'

'Aye, and a drunkard. Look at the way he staggers across the stage,' replied Bill, turning around to frown at an elderly lady who had kicked the back of his chair in order to silence him. 'Apologies, madam,' he added loudly.

In total the play lasted little more than an hour and it was clear from the reception which the audience gave it that it was a hit. Certainly, the action sequences had been exciting and the mass slaughter of the Indians at the end had proved enormously popular with the audience. Loud and rapturous applause greeted the cast as they took their bows at the end and some scattered cries of *Author! Author!* prompted Ned Buntline to appear on stage, an act which returned all to their seats and to silence.

'Ladies and gentlemen,' he said in a distinct voice, his words much better pronounced than they had been when they were in the room together earlier. His face also looked a little less engorged since Studley had managed to get through the entire performance without either throwing up or falling on his face. 'Ladies and gentlemen,' he repeated, 'you're very kind and I want to thank you for the reception you have given us all here tonight. But may I tell you that you've chosen an auspicious evening to attend *The King of Border Men*, for the man for whom this play is named, Buffalo Bill Cody himself, is actually present in this theatre and, I hope, has enjoyed the production as much as you all have.' There was a sharp intake of breath from the audience as everyone looked around and at their neighbours to see whether they could spot the celebrity in their midst. Bill swallowed nervously and sank down in his chair; for once, his love of the spotlight was deserting him.

'Let's have a look at 'im then!' came a roar from the balcony and the audience cheered their approval of this idea, a few others calling out similar requests. Buntline silenced them all again with his hands and looked towards the third row, where Bill and Texas Jack were seated.

'That's exactly what I propose to do,' he cried, gesturing to my great-grandfather to join him on stage. 'Buffalo Bill, come on up here and let these good people show their appreciation to you.'

There was loud anticipatory applause and, prodded by his friend, Bill eventually stood up nervously and shuffled up the steps towards Ned Buntline.

'Oh heavens,' cried the woman in the seat behind. 'To think I shushed him during the play! I shushed Buffalo Bill. He'll shoot me afterwards! He'll take me out and shoot me!'

More applause greeted him as he stood on the stage and Buntline placed an arm around his shoulders to silence the crowd. Bill was staring at the ground reluctantly, holding his hat in his hands, afraid to look out at his fans. 'Buffalo Bill,' said Buntline casually, as if this was the most normal thing in the world. 'You'll say a few words to these good people, won't you?'

Bill finally looked up now and as he did so some of the spotlights were switched on, catching him unawares. Momentarily blinded, he shielded his eyes with his hand and tried to speak through a dry voice. 'Thank you,' he muttered quietly and the whole audience broke into a series of *What-did-he-say*s? His speech beginning and ending with those two words, he retreated through the curtains into the safety of the backstage area, where he found himself sitting on a wagon wheel, gasping for air, the perspiration pouring down his forehead as the applause continued outside.

'That was wonderful,' said Buntline, when he appeared again, pulling Bill to his feet. 'What a showman you are! They loved you.'

'I'm sorry I couldn't say more,' explained Bill apologetically. 'I've never been much of a one for public speaking.'

'Nonsense, you're a natural,' came the reply, brushing away Bill's mutterings to the contrary. 'I've seen actors and I've seen showmen and I've seen the way different men can and can't interact with an audience and I'm telling you now, Buffalo Bill Cody, you're a natural. You may have said nothing but they loved you anyway. Didn't you see the look on their faces when they realised that it really was you standing up there? I'm telling you now, I'm going to make an actor of you if it's the last thing I do.'

'You're what?' asked Bill loudly. 'You've got to be—'

'Listen to me,' said Buntline firmly. 'Studley comes in here every day dead drunk. He's ruining the part. Oh sure, it gets a good reception but that's because it's a great play. I wrote it, for heaven's sake! Of course it's

286

great! Imagine what it would be like with a man like you in the lead.'

'But Ned,' protested Bill, laughing at the very idea. 'I've never acted in my life. You saw me out there. I could barely get two words out. In fact I *only* got two words out.'

'But such words! Such words!'

'Ned—'

'No protests, my friend. Who else can play Buffalo Bill like Buffalo Bill? Do you want your name and reputation sullied by Studley and his like? Do you want to be remembered through that idiot's performance? Do you want to make a lot of money?' he added after a pause, leaning forward and smiling gently. Bill looked at him and thought about it.

'How much money exactly?' he asked.

I began my search for Hitomi in an obvious place: I looked her up in the phone book. She wasn't listed although there was an 'S. Naoyuki' living in the *quatrième arrondissement* who I called, just in case the initial had been written incorrectly. The voice on the other end of the line however belonged to an old Japanese man who shouted down the phone in an inexplicable rage when I began speaking.

Luc introduced me to a friend of his, Pierre Guillet, who was one of the commissioning editors on a weekly news magazine in the city. I submitted my portfolio to him and he appeared to enjoy the Tokyo columns I had written and, spurred on by their success in a dozen different newspapers around that region, employed me to write for his magazine too. The combination of that job and my continuing publication in the east gave me a sufficient income for my needs and I found that the life of a Parisian writer was not a bad one at all. I lived the stereotype for a while, eating at sidewalk cafés, strolling along the Champs Élysées with a copy of Sartre in my inside pocket. I even tried to take up smoking as I thought the look would be conducive to my new position in life, but failed abysmally.

In the meantime I visited the few Japanese-French societies in the city, hoping to meet Hitomi but without success. The people who gathered in these places tended to be awkward social types who had arrived in France without knowing what they were doing there and were simply clinging to people with a similar background for fear of being washed away in the Seine.

'You should put an ad in the paper,' Annette advised me as we sat drinking coffee in my apartment one evening, waiting for Luc to return with dinner. 'Take a full-page ad in *Le Monde* some day. It'll cost you a fortune but she's bound to see it.'

'She's never been much of a newspaper buyer,' I said, shaking my head sadly. 'I don't think she'd see it.'

'Somebody who knows her might.'

'I don't know . . .' I muttered, unconvinced.

'You want me to set you up with a friend of mine instead?'

I laughed and shook my head. 'No,' I said firmly. 'No, I don't want you to set me up with a friend of yours! I'm not cheating on her just because I can't find her. I'm not just looking to get laid here.'

'William, how can you cheat on someone who you're not even seeing?'

'We *are* seeing each other,' I protested. 'We're just not *seeing* each other, that's all.'

'Right,' said Annette. Luc arrived with food at that moment. He set straight to work on the vegetables, barely acknowledging our presence, and didn't even bother to take the cigarette out of his mouth as he chopped the food up. 'William wants me to set him up with a friend of mine,' said Annette mischievously. 'I thought maybe Claudia, what do you think?'

'I don't want anything of the sort,' I said quickly as Luc looked at me with some amusement. 'She's just trying to wind me up.'

'Never go on a blind date,' he counselled. 'They spell disaster. You're not that desperate anyway, are you?'

Well yes,' I admitted. 'I bloody am. But I'm still not doing it. Hitomi has got to be in the city somewhere and I'll find her.'

'But I want to double date,' protested Annette in a childlike whine, as if I had spoiled her fun on purpose.

'Sorry,' I said.

'Listen to me, William,' said Luc, coming around to my side of the table and sitting down beside me, stubbing his cigarette out now in an empty cup. 'Don't you think you're becoming a little . . . obsessive about this? You don't even know for sure that this girl is in Paris.'

'I don't even want to think about that,' I said, shaking my head furiously for that thought had been occurring to me increasingly in recent times. 'She has to be here. Mayu said she was here.'

'You know,' he continued, ignoring me. 'When I was in university I took a summer away and went to Athens at one point to see the Parthenon. When I got there, I bought a guidebook and found out how to get there and I went to see it and spent a couple of days in that area, soaking up the atmosphere. Then I took the bus back where I had come from. Stupid, eh?'

I stared at him blankly and then looked across at Annette, who was squinting her eyes as if she wasn't quite sure what he was getting at either.

'I don't follow you,' I said.

'William, there's a lot more to Athens than the Parthenon. I went there because I wanted to see it, I'd always wanted to see it. So I saw it and left. I didn't do anything else. If you said to me have I been to Athens, I'd say sure and you'd say how did you like it and what could I say to you? I don't know, I never saw Athens. I missed it because I was only interested in one thing.'

'Right,' I said. 'You're saying I should stop obsessing about Hitomi and get a life basically.'

'You have it now,' he said, smiling and resuming his cooking. There was silence for a few minutes as I thought about this.

'That was a bit convoluted, Luc, wasn't it?' asked Annette after a while and he shrugged and muttered something inaudible.

'Do you think I'm obsessed?' I asked in a quiet voice, looking across at Annette. For a moment, she seemed reluctant to answer.

'I don't know,' she said eventually. 'Obsession's kind of a creepy word. It suggests stalkers and the like and I know that's not who you are. You just love the girl, I guess. I mean you are a *bit* stalker-like, but I don't think there's much you can do about that. We all have our faults.'

'I do love her,' I agreed. 'She's the only girl I've ever said "I love you" to, you know.'

'Rubbish,' said Luc. 'We all say it when we need to. You must have done.'

I shook my head. 'I never have. I swear it,' I said. 'I've made a point of it. She's the only one. They're the three greatest words in the English language. I never wanted to waste them.'

'No they're not,' said Annette. 'They're not the three greatest words in the English language at all. You're kidding yourself.'

I stared at her. 'Sure they are,' I said, surprised by her lack of romance. 'Tell me three better.'

She squinted her eyes and looked away. Luc and I watched her, waiting for an answer. After a moment she smirked and turned back to us triumphantly. 'Robert Downey Jr,' she said and I burst out laughing, even as her husband sighed in frustration.

'You're right,' I said. 'How could I have been so stupid.'

Luc was making crazy signs at the side of his head and pointing at Annette. 'She's mad,' he said, smiling despite himself. 'You want to talk obsessions? You want to talk stalkers? Well *he's* her one obsession. You want to see her little face when one of his movies comes on the TV. She'd leave me for him, I swear it.'

'Damn right I would,' said Annette.

I shrugged. 'Well I probably can't compete with that,' I said. 'But the point is that I love Hitomi. So there. And I just want to make things right. I don't want to seem obsessed. It's obsessions that have got me into this mess in the first place.' She looked at me and waited for me to explain. 'I've told you about my father,' I said, for since our first discussion about American heroes I had revealed to Annette the history of my family and told her some of the stories about my great-grandfather. 'About Isaac. His obsession with family history, his need to have a celebrated ancestor who actually *did* something with his life has just coloured every moment of his own life, not to mention mine.'

291

'Well if my grandfather was Wild Bill Hickok, I'd probably be excited about it too.'

'It's Buffalo Bill, for Christ's sake,' I said irritably. 'Jesus.'

'All right, keep your wig on,' she said, laughing.

'Well people always say Wild Bill Hickok. Why can't they just remember it was Buffalo Bill? Hickok had nothing on my great-grandfather. He was just a drunk, he couldn't shoot straight, he was . . . he was *impotent*, you know,' I added, spluttering out the words. 'My great-grandfather was the first true scout of the plains. He practically invented the west. Before he came along it was just a place with a lot of land problems. He gave it a mythology, he created its history. Isn't that something to remember his name for?' I could feel my face grow red as my diatribe continued and by the end of it, I knew that Luc and Annette were staring at me with tight smiles on their faces.

'Is that what this Isaac is like?' asked Luc after a pause and I laughed, realising just how much like him I had sounded.

'Worse,' I said. 'He's infinitely worse. I don't even care that much. These are his stories, not mine.'

'You must be a lot alike,' said Annette and I looked at her inquisitively. 'Think about it,' she continued. 'You talk about these things all the time too. You've told us lots of stories about your great-grandfather and you've only known us a few weeks. You like to talk about him.'

'Well you seemed interested,' I said defensively.

'We are,' she replied quickly. 'Believe me, if you were boring us we'd have told you to stop it a long time ago. But they're interesting stories. I like to hear them. But it's you who's telling them, not your father. We don't even know your father. So you must be like him in some way if you feel the need to tell them.'

I frowned. I had never thought of it that way. I had told all the stories to Adam and Justin too, not to mention Hitomi and Tak, on many occasions throughout my life, but I had always presented them as things that Isaac had told me and not as my own. Perhaps by telling them in my own voice I was carrying on Isaac's tradition; the idea chilled me.

'And these columns you write,' said Annette, continuing with her amateur psychology now. 'You write about things that have happened to you but a lot of them haven't. They're things you've heard have happened to other people. All those Japanese columns you showed me. You couldn't have had that many things happen to you.'

'No, of course I didn't,' I said. 'But with something like that you just create a persona and let the stories come through it. It's not factual journalism. There's more licence in it than that.'

'And yet you still sign these columns as William Cody.'

'Well that's my name!'

'Which you use as a character in your columns. That's all he is, right? A character? He's not actually a real person.'

I shrugged my shoulders. 'I guess . . .' I said in a slow drawl, unwilling to agree, knowing where it might lead.

'Well how is that different from this self-perpetuating myth you talk about Buffalo Bill creating that you seem so critical about? You say he invented his own character to mythologise the west and make money from it. Isn't that what you're doing too?'

'Yes, but on a much smaller scale,' I protested.

'Well then,' she said with a flourish, sitting back in her chair with a smile as if she had just conclusively proved her point. 'Maybe then you just have to start thinking a little bigger, my friend. It's like Luc said. There's a lot more in Athens than just the Parthenon. I'm going to set you up with someone.'

'No,' I said firmly.

'Oh be nice.'

'No!' I repeated. I'm going to find Hitomi. That's what I'm going to do. She's here somewhere, I know it. I just have to think, that's all. I feel that if I just think about it, I'll figure it out. I'll find her. I know I will. We're meant to be together, you see.'

Luc and Annette exchanged a look which in a second changed from concern about me to a shrugging acceptance that if that was what I believed, then perhaps it was true.

Ellen Rose proved a more successful circus performer than her father Russell could ever have predicted. Her skill on the tightrope, across which she could practically perform ballet routines, not to mention her talents on the trapeze itself, drew such inhalations of appreciation from audiences that Russell and Bessie were forced to shake their heads and acknowledge that their daughter was a natural.

'I can't believe we waited so long to see what she could do,' said a breathless James Regis, the co-owner of the circus as he sat smoking his pipe late one evening with Russell. 'We should have guessed that with you for a father she'd have no difficulties up there. Should have had her up there years ago. How old is she now anyway? Nineteen? Twenty?'

'Seventeen,' corrected Russell. 'And how were we to know? Bessie and I always kept her away from the act because we were afraid she'd do herself an injury. I still can't say I'm that happy about it.'

'You haven't seen my box office receipts then,' replied James Regis greedily. 'I'm thinking of putting her name higher up the billing. She's becoming famous, you know.'

'Fame'll be no good to her if the celebrity goes to her head. Believe me, James, when you're on the tightropes fifty feet above ground, you have to keep your feet firmly on the ground.' Regis chuckled at what he perceived to be a joke but was quickly reprimanded. 'You know what I mean,' Russell said quickly. I'm not trying to be funny. If she thinks she's more of a star than she is, if she loses concentration for even a moment and thinks about the applause of the audience rather than the rope beneath her feet, she'll tumble. I promise you, she'll tumble. Maybe we should start to use a net,' he suggested in a quieter voice. Regis almost choked on his pipe smoke and turned on his friend quickly.

'Not a chance, Russell,' he said. 'Not a hope in hell. The Regis-Roc Trapeze Company is famous for *not* using a net. That's part of the entertainment, the excitement. How long has the troupe been performing now?'

'Eighteen years,' he replied.

'Eighteen years,' repeated Regis firmly. 'And in all that time, how many accidents have there been? Well?' he asked, sensing Russell's unwillingness to reply. 'Come on then. How many have there been?'

'None,' admitted Russell. 'But that's no reason to be complacent. I just don't want all this attention to make the girl think she's something she isn't. I don't want her to lose her head up there some evening.'

'Don't worry,' said Regis. 'She's a smart girl. She'll be fine.'

Russell wasn't so sure, but while his worries were directed towards his daughter's well-being on the tightropes and trapezes, her mind was elsewhere entirely. For although she was gaining a reputation as a talented performer and her name and picture had appeared on the bill for the first time, the lure of celebrity had captivated Ellen in a different way.

The undoubted star of the Regis-Roc Circus was a young man named Howard Losey. He had begun his career with a different circus but James Regis had lured him to his own after a substantial salary offer. Losey, twenty-five years old and by far the most athletic man in the company, had thick blond hair and the bluest eyes that Ellen had ever seen. He was a lion tamer and in charge of six of the loudest and fiercest lions in England. Without appearing to give it a second thought, Losey would march those beasts around the circus, bringing them as close to the spectators as he dared, allowing some to stray while at all times managing to keep them under his control. Those who came near him while he was working could detect a low whistle which he emitted and they swore that this was some land of subtle signal to the lions which kept them under his control. He performed stunts with them, placing his head in their jaws, lying on the sand while they trampled all over him, grappling with them in wrestling contests. By rights, this should have been an act which Ellen Rose would be unable to watch as she feared lions more than any other creature, but from the day Howard had joined their company, Ellen Rose had been besotted with him. She sat in the bleachers whenever he prepared new tricks or was simply working with his charges. She would find excuses to pass by his trailer when he was feeding the animals and often sat in the audience after her trapeze act to watch as he entertained the audience with his own stunts. When he began to romance the knife thrower's assistant, a girl closer to his own age than Ellen, she found herself devastated for the first time by love.

But whatever Ellen was feeling for him, there was another who was feeling similar emotions towards her. Russell Rose thought his daughter's greatest danger lay fifty feet above the sand of the circus floor; in reality it was only a few wagons away.

A week later, the following letter, forwarded from the Tokyo newspaper office, arrived.

Dear William,

I haven't heard from you since you left and I'm worried about you. Things weren't right there and I know you think it's my fault but you shouldn't have run away like that. All right, maybe I said I was sicker than I actually am but let's face it, son, I'm seventy-six years old now and won't be around for that much longer anyway and if you can't see your way to spending a little time with me while I'm still here, well then I just don't know what.

The bank say they won't lend me the money to start the wild west show without a partner and guarantor. I'm sending you the forms here. You don't have to have any part of this thing if you don't want to but I'm asking you to do this one thing for me, that's all. But if you think about it and want to make a life and some money for yourself well then maybe you'll reconsider and come back and help

297

me run it. I'm telling you son this thing's gonna be huge and make no mistake about that. I've spoken to some talent agencies and they've lined me up some people who could perform. Of course I'd have to audition them first as they say but that's something you can help me with too because you've got to have a good eye for those things, am I right? I don't know if we should get someone dressing up as your great-grandfather – that could be the icing on the cake or maybe it would be disrespectful. What do you think? You know the first time old Bill set up his show, he had to get sponsors too, ~~although of course they~~

Anyway, write and let me know how you are. I miss you, William. Maybe I don't show it like I should but there we are. I need these papers signed soon, son. I'm not getting any younger, you know.

Yours faithfully,

Isaac Cody

I felt guilty when I read it because in my anger against my father I had neglected to tell him that I had left Japan for France. The original postmark indicated that he had sent the letter five weeks earlier so he was probably already cursing me for not having had the decency to reply. I read the letter several times, noting how he had changed his mind about telling me one of his Buffalo Bill stories at the end, scoring it through but not rewriting the letter, as if he wanted to let me know it was still there but he was saving one for me. Then the forced humour of the last line, followed by the ceremonial sign off. I didn't know what to make of it. Signing his surname – how many other Isaacs did he think I knew? I decided to write back immediately. Although he had handwritten his, I chose to write mine on my word processor and I wrote quickly, not changing a word after I had finished it.

Dear Isaac, [I wrote]

Sorry for the delay in replying to your letter. I've moved from Japan to France. I met a girl there and we've been seeing each other for a while now. I would have told you about her while I was back in London but there never seemed to be the right time for it. Anyway, she's moved here so I've followed her. Still writing the columns. Got more now. Working hard.

I'm sending the forms back to you. I'm sorry but I can't sign them. For a start the numbers on them – I just can't be responsible for loans of that much money. I'm sorry but like I told you, I'm just not interested in setting up a wild west show. I don't know for sure but I just don't feel there's a market for those things now, maybe a hundred years ago, but not now. I know this is your dream and I know how much it means to you but Isaac I'm sorry – I just can't be a part of it.

I don't want there to be hard feelings between us. I was angry when I left London but in fairness you dragged me halfway around the world on a lie. Okay, you're right, I should visit more often but it's not easy getting the time and now that I'm in France maybe I'll be able to get across to see you more often. If I'm welcome. Let me know.

My new address and number's on top. I've got a nice place to live. Made some friends. I'm pretty happy, all told. Sorry I can't help you more but anyway it's too big an enterprise for a man your age. You've got to take it easier.

Speak soon,
William

I re-read it after I had printed it out and thought I'd said pretty much the things I wanted to say, although I wasn't sure about the last paragraph. It seemed a little patronising but I couldn't think of a better way to say it. And then I posted it.

When it was announced that the famous Buffalo Bill Cody was going to portray himself in a new play which would open in Chicago in September 1872, the applications for tickets came close to breaking box office records. The play, which was to be called *Scouts of the Plains*, was presented as another dramatic work by Ned Buntline and was initially advertised in the major cities of the north. Buntline hoped that the prospect of the play would generate enough excitement that people would come from states all across the union to Chicago in order to see it. As ever, he convinced Bill of the sense of this plan through promising him a great deal of money.

Bill was put on the payroll at a price of five hundred dollars a week – a huge sum at the time which would guarantee his status as a wealthy man – and one of the conditions which he made of his employment was that Texas Jack Omohundro would also be given a part in the production. Buntline agreed to cast him, regardless of any talent or audition, and it was decided that he would also play himself on stage.

As the group made their way to Chicago a couple of weeks before the opening night, Bill grew increasingly concerned about whether or not he would be able to perform in front of hundreds of spectators every night. 'I know you say I'm a natural actor,' he told Buntline, 'but don't you think it would make sense to begin rehearsals as soon as possible? My lack of experience is bound to show through otherwise.'

'Soon, soon,' replied Buntline quickly, for he had yet to show any of his actors a copy of the proposed script and while everyone was beginning to worry about learning their lines, Bill and Texas Jack were growing even more anxious, as they were novices in this world. 'When we get to Chicago I have to strike the deal with Jeb Nixon about the theatre and once that's sorted, we'll head straight into rehearsals.'

Buntline, always pushing things as close to the wire as possible, had advertised the play and taken bookings without yet confirming with Nixon, the manager of the theatre, that they would be able to put their show on there. While Bill was aware of this and fretted about it constantly, one thing he did not know was that Buntline had yet to write the script for the play, which explained why he had been reluctant to show it to any of his cast. He had a vague idea in his mind of what the story would contain but other than that, he had not set pen to paper yet.

Once settled in Chicago, however, Buntline and Bill arranged a meeting with Nixon and they were shown into a shabby office in a splendid theatre where, as ever, my great-grandfather was treated as a great celebrity. 'What are the cavalry doing without you, Mr Cody?' he asked as he poured them each a shot of whisky. 'Who's keeping those damn Indians in line down there?'

'Officially, I am not a member of any cavalry, Mr Nixon,' explained Bill quietly. 'And no one has the responsibility of keeping anyone "in line", as you put it. The army and the Indian leaders are attempting to reach peaceful settlements on the land and the various issues of ownership regarding it. And please feel free to call me Buffalo Bill,' he added, always keen to keep the legend alive.

'If I had my way I'd shoot the whole blasted lot of them,' countered Nixon, who had apparently been hitting the bottle before their arrival. 'The stories that come back to us in the civilised states about scalpings and the like . . .' He shuddered. 'Well it makes my skin crawl, I can tell you that.'

'I've seen just as much civilisation at a Lakota Sioux camp as I have at any military fort, I can assure you of that, Mr Nixon. Oftentimes more. Certainly a good deal more than I see in cities like this where rudeness appears to be the order of the day.'

Nixon eyed him carefully, his tendency to argue threatening to get the better of him, although he was aware that it would be a brave man who picked a fight with Buffalo Bill. 'Well that's as may be,' he said, brushing the conversation aside. 'All I know is that I have a theatre to fill and haven't been paid a penny yet. And ain't this show of yours due to begin next Monday night?'

'It is indeed, sir,' said Buntline in a hearty tone. 'And as today is only Wednesday, I believe we can take a little time to get to know the Windy City before daring to tread its boards.'

Nixon grunted. He had little time for pretentious actors and even less for writers, most of whom had never treated him with anything even approaching respect. His nightmare situation was when the writer was also the producer and director of the show, as Buntline was.

Triple trouble, he felt. 'Here's the fees anyway,' he said, laying out a sheet of figures before the two men. 'All up front of course,' he added casually.

Buntline glanced at the sheet and laughed, as if the idea of payment was an insult to a civilised man. 'These are a little on the high side, I would have thought,' he said.

'They're standard,' replied Nixon with a sigh.

'Well you do realise we'll have to wait and judge the success of the play before we pay you.'

'Money up front,' insisted Nixon. 'I'm not getting stung if the whole thing's a disaster.'

'As if that could even be a possibility, with the team you see before you. No, what I propose is that we pay you two weeks up front in order to rent your theatre and, assuming we're all happy with the arrangements at the end of that time and the seats are filled each night, we will rent from you on a monthly basis from then on.'

Nixon narrowed his eyes and thought about it. Looking away from Buntline for a moment, he stared at my great-grandfather and, appreciating that it was an actor he was addressing and not an army officer, his level of respect diminished slightly. 'Is this the first time you've acted?' he asked. Bill nodded. 'And how do you think you'll be at it, if you don't mind me asking that is?' he added politely.

'I hope I'll be good,' said Bill. 'We haven't had much rehearsal time yet,' he said, making a dig at Buntline who shifted uncomfortably in the seat. 'Truth be told, Ned here has been a little precious with his writing. None of us has seen a word of it.'

Nixon looked at Buntline in amazement. 'You haven't shown them the script yet?' he asked.

'Soon. Today,' said Buntline, looking at Bill as if he wished that he had kept his mouth shut. 'We've been busy securing actors, you see. We'll begin rehearsals tonight.'

'You're supposed to be opening on Monday! And you haven't shown your actors their scripts? Let me have a look at one now. See what the learning's like.'

Buntline opened and closed his mouth like a goldfish and decided he had better be honest. 'Truth be told,' he said after a lengthy pause. 'I haven't actually written the script yet.'

'You what?' cried Nixon and Bill in unison.

'I've got a title,' said Buntline, as if this would suffice. 'It's not as if I've been idle. It will be called *Scouts of the—*'

'We know what the title is, you damn fool,' shouted Nixon. 'It's plastered on billboards all over the northern union! How do you expect to put on a show on Monday night when today's Wednesday and you haven't even written a script?'

Bill was saying nothing; simply sitting there, looking horror struck. His stomach started to churn slowly; he wished he was back on Buckskin Joe, riding across the Kansan plains, the wind blowing in his hair, freedom ahead.

'We'll settle for the theatre,' explained Buntline in a cool tone, as if he was addressing a child. 'Then this afternoon I will write the play. We will begin rehearsals this evening and by Monday I guarantee you that my entire cast will be word perfect.'

Nixon barked a laugh. 'For your sake they better be,' he said, opening up his receipt book and starting to write in it. 'Two weeks, you say? Three hundred dollars to you, Mr Buntline.'

Buntline handed over the money and stood up to go, all the time aware of Bill's eyes piercing into him, although he managed to avoid having to look at his friend. They left the building and Buntline waited for the onslaught. Fortunately for him, none was forthcoming as my great-grandfather was pale with worry that rather than achieve a new level of fame the following week, he would end up destroying his reputation instead, making a mockery of himself in front of hundreds of strangers in an unfamiliar, cosmopolitan city. He felt sick inside. They returned to their hotel without saying a word and when they got there, Buntline retired to his room to write the play while Bill sought solace in the bar with Texas Jack.

Within two hours, Buntline reappeared, his face tomato red once again with his exertions and the play was ready. He hired a couple of clerks to make copies and immediately handed two to his lead actors who retired to their rooms to learn their lines, a task to which they proved wholly unsuited. While reading aloud from the scripts, Texas Jack displayed a natural talent for drama but Bill appeared hopelessly lost. Over the next few days, as the entire company rehearsed on the stage, there seemed little chance that he would be ready to perform by the Monday night. Prompters were set up at stages left and right and in the orchestra pit below and it was agreed that some of the extras would, if necessary, pass him by on the stage and whisper the lines to him. Rather than simply becoming increasingly nervous, Bill began to face the ordeal of Monday evening with a growing hysteria, believing that he had made the worst decision of his life and that he would regret the day he had ever allowed the Grand Duke Alexis to make him consider a career in the footlights. Ego had got the better of him and the great scout Buffalo Bill believed that the Chicago theatre would, quite unexpectedly, prove his downfall.

As with the night the two men had watched the drunken J. B. Studley career across the stage in New York City, the theatre in Chicago was packed to capacity at the *Scouts of the Plains* opening night. Members of the local establishment, congressmen, and a senator attended, along with the son of President Ulysses S. Grant, who happened to be passing through Chicago with the ageing actress Marjorie Blackwood, still a great beauty, who drew a round of applause of her own when she entered the theatre (last, naturally), and many representatives of the press.

The play got off to a rousing start. Texas Jack had worked as hard as he ever had over the previous few days and had managed to learn almost all his lines. Those which were still a mystery to him were more than made up for by his presence on stage. Texas Jack possessed a strong deep voice which carried across the auditorium. Watching from the rear of the theatre, Ned Buntline regretted the fact that it was Bill and not Texas Jack who was the true star, if not the talent, of this company.

Ten minutes later. Bill made his entrance and received rapturous applause. He had already decided that he would not follow Studley's approach and acknowledge the clapping but would instead launch straight into his performance, a move which proved to be a clever one as the dialogue he had crammed into his head as he paced backstage managed to trip off his tongue quite effortlessly. As they reached the second act, however, it was clear that he was losing control. The whispers of the prompters were becoming more and more apparent to

306

the first few rows of the audience, who were beginning to deliver a low hiss whenever he missed a cue, and the extras seemed to be on stage all the time, whispering in his ear. When Texas Jack remarked in one piece of dialogue that it felt strange for the two of them to be left alone on the prairie like this, it seemed curious to the audience that a bewigged Indian chief and the young girl who played Bill's wife, were standing on either side of him, whispering in his ear. Realising how foolish he was beginning to look, Bill decided to take the action into his own hands. He waited for Texas Jack to finish his next piece of dialogue and then stamped on the stage, surprising everyone as he launched into a loud shout.

'You know what this reminds me of, Texas Jack?' he cried and his colleague stared at him blankly, sure that this wasn't part of the script.

'No . . .' he replied with uncertainty.

'This reminds of me of the day that you and I were travelling to Ohio to meet with General Custer about his plans for the resettlement of eastern Wyoming and you got bitten by a snake. Do you remember it?'

Texas Jack remembered no such incident, for he had never been part of any such thing, but the event in question had in fact taken place, only with a different man. Striding forth to the front of the stage, Bill proceeded to deliver a monologue for the best part of ten minutes, telling a story of adventure and near death which captivated the audience, causing the ladies to hide behind their fans as both men came close to a scalping, and the men to shout raucously whenever he made a saucy joke. Throwing the action of the play out the window. Bill ended his speech and waited until the next character appeared on stage before recounting

307

another incident of adventure which had befallen him during his time on the prairies until the play became little more than an audience with Buffalo Bill Cody. The crowd, however, loved it, applauding each tale with more and more vigour, even as my great-grandfather proceeded to exaggerate and invent stories of his own fortitude as he went along. This was the Buffalo Bill they wanted to believe in. This was the man who would keep them safe and hand them the west on a platter. They hung on to his every word and Bill could feel the power his presence generated. He was a true showman, he realised, the inventor of fictions, a mythologiser of the wild west. Having always believed that he was born to be a scout and a cavalry officer, Buffalo Bill had suddenly found his true calling. He would never let the audience go for the rest of his life.

When he had grown tired of telling stories he invited all the cast back on stage and a set-to was enacted, one which had fortunately been rehearsed in advance. Naturally, all the Indians were killed and the cowboys victorious, although the fighting and deaths were mostly slapstick and delivered with humour. At the end, the entire cast received the rapturous applause in delight but eventually Buffalo Bill shuffled them all into the wings so he could make the final bows himself.

Seeing Ned Buntline standing at the back of the theatre, smiling and shaking his head happily, he winked at him. *Author! Author!* came the cry once again from the auditorium and as Buntline made to take a step forward, Bill raised a hand in the air and the playwright stopped in his tracks, noticing the look of rebuke on his colleague's face.

'You're looking at him, ladies and gentlemen,'

shouted Bill from the stage, basking in the glory. 'You're looking at the author! Buffalo Bill Cody!'

The stageshow eventually travelled from Chicago to St Louis – where Bill was once again briefly re-united with his wife Louisa – and was intermittently performed for months at a time in Cincinnati, Boston, New York and Philadelphia over the next few years. During that time the text of the play had been altered substantially so that it would include more of Bill's off-the-cuff reminiscences, which would generally be prompted into speech by Texas Jack, although the show always ended in their trademark slapstick war. Bill and Buntline made a fortune from the show, and in the early days divided the profits evenly after they had paid for the theatres and actors. After a year or two, however, Bill replaced his mentor as producer of *Scouts of the Plains* and took over the task of renting theatres, hiring actors and organising publicity himself, at which point he began to take most of the proceeds for his own pocket. Buntline had little choice but to accept this arrangement; as the original writer and producer of the show he still received a percentage of the takings, and he was only too well aware that without Bill there would be no show.

During his time producing the show, Bill made only one disastrous call, hiring his old friend Wild Bill Hickok, whose fame was almost equal to his own, to portray himself in the show. Hickok, however, was a drunk and as his name would imply was prone to unexpected behaviour. While on stage he frequently fired blank cartridges close to the legs of the extras, those hired actors who were playing cowboys or Indians in the closing comic fight, and after injuring several of them through burns, was dismissed from

309

the production. However, since his presence had been advertised Bill made the error of judgement of hiring another actor to play the part. When Hickok showed up unexpectedly in the audience one evening, he was astounded to see a slightly overweight fellow passing himself off as himself and stormed the stage, beating several shades of straw out of the poor individual and had to be carried from the theatre. From then on the character of Wild Bill Hickok was no longer featured in *Scouts of the Plains.*

Another turning point was reached in June 1876. While Bill performed his oral histories on stage – stories which, due to lack of action on his part, had taken a decidedly fictional turn – events in the south were taking a darker turn. As more and more ranches sprang up, run by recent settlers, President Grant ordered the Lakota Sioux to leave their land once and for all and organise into special Indian reservations. When they refused to do so, the Great Sioux War broke out, which would indirectly lead to the end of the Plains Indians. This war culminated in the battle of Little Big Horn, where several different tribes fought for their lives against the white armies. In a gesture of solidarity, the Cheyenne, led by Lame White Man, the Oglala, under Crazy Horse, and the Hunkpapa Lakota, under their Chief Gall, combined their forces and one of the bloodiest battles of the time took place. Custer himself led his forces into action against the Indians, his last stand bringing almost a thousand men on both sides on to the plains, and as each and every one of the white soldiers were killed, Custer fought on until a hail of bullets took him too. In terms of victory, it was the Indians' greatest success, but the scale of the slaughter and the loss of the army's most popular general, led to a massive insurgence by President Grant and very soon the Indian culture existed only in an apartheid.

My great-grandfather was informed of Custer's death during an intermission of *Scouts of the Plains* in Philadelphia and when he learned of the numbers dead he felt a fury which had never been known to him before. His own blood boiled for the soldiers' spilled blood and stepping back on stage it was all he could do to keep his anger at bay. Although their relationship had at times been difficult, fraught with the antagonism of their separate ambitions, Buffalo Bill Cody always considered General George Armstrong Custer a friend. His loss hurt him, all the more because he had not been there to fight at his side as he perhaps should have been. Instead, he had been on stage, telling, stories, making jokes, playing at Cowboys and Indians.

The second act that evening was shorter than usual; the actors could tell that Bill was not on form for telling stories. When the final climactic battle scene began, it was played out with the usual measure of comedy and action between the participants; only as Bill stepped into the fray to perform what was often a simple choreographed routine, he saw not a stage full of actors, not a performance or a comedy, but a battlefield. He could hear the sounds of rifles being loaded, bullets being shot, tomahawks whizzing through the air and being wrenched from the spinal columns of his fallen comrades. The pounding of the hooves menaced his ears. He could smell the adrenalin of the horses and the fear of the men and at the final moment of the battle, where traditionally Bill would be centre stage, a knife suspended above the head of a made-up Indian, the final freeze frame of the play before the lights went down, he could not see the actor below him but thought only of Sitting Bull, the Indian leader who had masterminded the defeats at Little Big Horn and who he held responsible for the death of Custer. Reaching down he pulled the hair of the actor upwards as he ever did but rather than holding his position and waiting for the applause, on this night he allowed his knife to sail through the air, its unexpected whistle causing the man to close his eyes in terror as the sharp blade sliced through his forelock, leaving my great-grandfather with a fistful of dark, greased hair in his hands and a shaking, terrified actor kneeling before him. He raised his hand in the air, showing the 'scalp' to the audience who stared back at him in horror, aware that this was not the way the play normally ended. They had never seen such a look in Bill's eyes before, the look of victory, of revenge, of blood. The theatre was silent as Bill breathed heavily and closed his eyes. The lights dimmed and the audience waited, unsure what to do next.

This was how he would avenge Custer, he thought. For the first time he realised the power of his own fictions and his self-creation.

I grew more and more disconsolate with my failure to track down Hitomi. After two months in Paris I gradually began to accept that either Mayu had made a mistake when she had said that Hitomi had moved there, or that she had simply passed through and had gone on somewhere else. I phoned her brother Tak several times but he was as unhelpful as always, refusing to give me any details whatsoever. Her parents were of even less use. My work was going well and my new employers were pleased with me; I was enjoying the city and, except for the lack of romance, was enjoying my life too. Annette and Luc had continued to suggest that I allow them to set me up with someone but I had resisted, not wanting to admit to myself that my relationship with Hitomi was over and that I should move on.

Eventually, one Friday evening Annette came rushing into my apartment while I was cooking dinner, threw her arms around my waist as I tasted the spaghetti and nuzzled her mouth against my neck affectionately. It was a warm evening and I had taken my shirt off to allow the breeze from the open window to wash against my skin which had grown more tanned during the summer, and the feeling of her arms wrapped around me, her fingers pressed against my stomach, excited me despite myself and I couldn't help but feel a little uncomfortable as she moved her hands to my sides and tickled me quickly.

'Quit it,' I said, turning around and tapping her on the nose with the tip of the wooden spoon I was using to stir the sauce.

'Get dressed, gorgeous,' she said happily. 'We're going out for the night.'

'I'm tired,' I said, groaning slightly and she slapped my side playfully.

'William, it's Friday night,' she said. 'And we're going out. So get showered, get shaved and get dressed. I want you looking your best and that takes time.'

'It's just the three of us though, right?' I said, lowering the flame on the cooker. 'Just you, me and Luc?'

'You, me and Luc will be there, yes,' she said ambiguously. 'We'll just get a couple of beers, that's all. Sit around and talk.' I frowned at her and started to lean back, forgetting that the cooker was hot and I felt a quick burning sensation on my skin as the two touched. I jumped forward and cursed. 'Careful,' she said. 'We don't want any obvious blemishes.'

'What's going on, Annette?' I said. 'You're not setting me up with someone, are you?'

'As if I would,' she said. 'You've made your feelings on that topic quite clear.'

I paused for a moment and squinted at her. 'You are, aren't you?'

'You're going to love her, William,' said Annette with a laugh. 'Believe me. I've told her all about you. She—'

'No,' I said quickly, turning away from her. 'No no no. I've said no to this already.'

'Oh but William, you've—'

'Annette, I don't want to be set up with someone. I've told you that.'

'I know, I know, you're in loooove. But Jesus, William, you need to meet someone! There's only so much sitting around moping you can do before you go blind, you know what I'm saying? Just trust me on this one. This girl is gorgeous. And available.'

I sighed. Although I had already determined not to go along with any such scheme, the combination of sexual playfulness which Annette had displayed towards me together with my sudden desire not to sit around the apartment all night melted my resolve. Why not, I thought. Maybe it would be all right. It was just a drink. I didn't have to let anything happen that I didn't want to happen. And if something did, well then that would be my choice too. It was a win-win situation.

'This once,' I said, wagging a finger at her. 'This once, all right? I'll go along with it this once and after that, never again.'

'You'll never need to again after tonight,' she said with a wink, heading for the door. 'Now get ready. Luc's getting dressed as we speak. We leave in thirty minutes.'

Annette had chosen a bar which I had never been to before by the banks of the Seine. It was relatively busy but not overcrowded and we were able to secure a table outside on the veranda, overlooking the water. The sun was still high and warm and the sound of the water combined with the low murmur of chatter both around us and in the passing boats below made the evening seem very pleasant and relaxing. I had opted for casual clothes, wearing a new pair of blue jeans with scruffy trainers, and a white cotton shirt, two buttons open. I wore my sunglasses and my hair slicked back from the shower. I could feel the cold beer travelling through my system and it felt refreshing.

'So why tonight?' I asked them after a time. 'Why did you set me up with someone for tonight?

'Well we're not just here for you, you know,' said Luc. 'Our world doesn't *entirely* revolve around you. We're celebrating. Annette got a new job today.'

'You did?' I said happily. 'That's great. Doing what?'

'It's with the same company,' she said bashfully but clearly happy to talk about it. 'But I'm going to be line producing a new movie. It's a big step up for me.'

'That's fantastic,' I said. 'Congratulations. Jesus, could you win an Oscar or something?'

'They're called Césars,' said Luc quickly.

'I'm not going to win anything,' she replied, laughing. 'But it's exciting. I thought I wasn't going to catch a break there for a while. Thought I might have to go back to acting.'

'I didn't know you were an actress,' I said, intrigued by this side of her character which she had never as yet mentioned.

'It was a long time ago,' she said, shrugging it off. 'I mean you know my dad's a producer, don't you?'

315

'Yeah,' I said, nodding. 'You mentioned that.'

'He's a big-shot Hollywood producer,' said Luc, holding his hands wide apart as if suggesting the size of the fish that got away. 'And he hates me. He told Annette that he thought I was too French. I mean what can that possibly mean, too French? I mean I *am* French, I'll give him that much.'

'He doesn't hate you,' said Annette, tapping his hand lightly. 'He's just not good with new people, that's all. Anyway,' she continued, turning towards me, 'when I was four years old, my dad used to take me to the studio with him sometimes and I used to really love it there. I loved all the cameras and the trailers and the way there were always hundreds of people running around like headless chickens everywhere you looked. I mean I wanted to be there more than any other place at the time. I hated it when I had to start school because it meant I couldn't go to the studio any more.' She paused and thought about this for a moment before going on. 'So I'm in the studio one day and I'm running round my father's office when he brings this woman in to see me. She's one of these big-time TV producers and he introduces me to her and she doesn't just say hello to me or shake my hand, she starts asking me loads of questions, wants to know what I want to be when I grow up, whether I can do any tricks or not. You know. She just keeps on drilling me and drilling me for more information. Then eventually she turns to my dad and she says *She's perfect, Louis! Just perfect!* And they hug each other and go out of the office again without so much as saying goodbye to me and I'm left standing there all of four years old and I'm like hello? but there's no one there any more to hear me. Then later on that evening my parents called me downstairs to speak to them and they tell me

316

that something very exciting had happened, that a TV producer is starting a new show, some thirty-minute sit-com, and she wants me to be in it. Isn't that exciting? they kept saying. Isn't that so fucking exciting? And I think it kind of is really so I take the part and before I know it I'm like this superstar kid, the show is number one in the ratings, everyone wants a piece of me and it's bye bye to any kind of sane childhood that I might have had. You're not gonna believe it, but I was a huge star once. I mean I was massive.'

I stared at her, wide-eyed, and from her to Luc, who was nursing his beer and smiling to himself.

'You're kidding,' I said. She shook her head. 'Well what was the programme then?' I asked. 'Would I know it?'

'It was a sit-com, pretty standard family fare. Called *The Family Way*. The family in the show were called "Way", hence the name. Funny, eh? I was Annie Way.'

'You were Annie Way?' I shouted at her hysterically. 'I know that show. You were Annie Way? God, of course you are! I can see it in you now. I always thought there was something familiar about you. Jesus!'

'You know the show then?' Luc said. 'We never got it here. I never saw any of it.'

'Know it?' I said, doubling up with excitement and laughter. 'I used to watch it religiously every week for about six years. It was one of the biggest shows on television. It was like a phenomenon. So why aren't you still doing it then?'

'Because I hated acting,' she replied. 'It was okay for the first year or two. I mean, I revelled in all the attention when the show first started and was climbing the ratings. I even got nominated for an Emmy, you know? Got beaten by Katharine fucking Hepburn, if you can believe that. But after a few years of it, I just

317

wanted to go to school and have some friends. I mean the only people I talked to were writers and producers and directors and actors and shit. I wanted to meet some kids. But I had a contract and my dad wouldn't let me break it or he was going to sue me or something, so I was stuck in that crummy show till I was twelve. And once it folded, I was pretty much in demand, but I refused to do any more work. My dad was like having heart failure about it because I was making more money than he was and I was in a position where I could have basically had a licence to print my own money, but I just didn't want to do it so I dropped out of TV altogether. Best decision I ever made. My dad refused to speak to me for ages though. But Jesus, I was only twelve years old. I deserved a life.' She paused for a minute to let all of this sink in. 'So there you go,' she said. 'My deep, dark secret. I was a child superstar.'

I shook my head and sighed. 'That's amazing,' I said. 'You think you know someone.'

'Hey, we only met a couple of months ago,' said Annette. 'I've still got some secrets from you, you know. I haven't given you *all* the goods yet. What time is it now anyway?'

'Nine o'clock,' I said, glancing at my watch.

'Excellent. She should be here any minute.'

'She better be nice,' I said quickly, my stomach starting to tighten slightly with nerves. It had been a long time since I'd been on a date, and I'd never been on a blind one in my life.

'I think you'll like her,' said Luc and he was biting his lip to stop himself from laughing. He glanced across at his wife who shushed him immediately.

'Well who is she anyway?' I asked. 'Where did you meet her? What does she do?'

318

'I don't really know,' said Annette. 'I only met her for the first time last night.'

'You only just met her?' I said, amazed. 'I thought you said she was a friend of yours?'

'I never said that,' she replied innocently. 'Did I ever say she was a friend of mine, Luc?'

'No,' he agreed. 'You never said that.'

'Jesus,' I said, sitting back in frustration. 'She could be a serial killer, for God's sake! You're setting me up on a date with someone you don't even know. She's going to take me back to her place, promising an uncomplicated night of passion and debauchery, tie me to the bedpost and cut my kidneys out!'

'Oh you should be so lucky. And stop dramatising everything anyway! We don't *know* her, so what?' said Annette, her face breaking into a wide smile and her eyes were focused on someone standing behind me who had just come through the doors to the veranda. I didn't turn around yet but caught the look on Luc's face as he sat up straight and gave whoever she was a split second up-down look of satisfaction. His left eyebrow raised a little in approval. 'You made it,' said Annette and there was an unmistakable note of triumph in her voice. 'William, your date's arrived.' I stood up and turned around at the same time. She was a little shorter than me and quite petite; her slim body was wrapped in a red-print summer dress which accentuated her curves. The kind of girl who men look at when she walks through a bar. I took her in at an instant and I thought my legs were going to give way as I reached a hand back to steady myself against the chair. She wiped a tear away from her eyes as I said the only word that sprang to mind. Her name.

'Hitomi.'

Chapter Nine

Reunions

My great-grandfather finished performing in *Scouts of the Plains* shortly after learning of the death of General Custer at the battle of Little Big Horn. The dramatic performances continued, as they formed the substantial part of Bill's income, but advertisements were taken out in local newspapers to inform people that he himself would not be taking part in the entertainments for several weeks. Although bookings did not diminish, as more and more people still wanted to see the show, Bill insisted that ticket prices be halved for all shows in which he did not perform. Clearly he did not want it to seem that the plays could be just as popular without him in them as with.

Genuinely upset by his old friend's death, Bill spent the next couple of days in the saloons, getting drunk and sleeping with as many of the young actresses as he could. Louisa and his relationship had so broken down that although they ostensibly lived together, they could go weeks at a time without ever laying eyes on each other, Bill preferring to spend most of his time in the town and living out of a hotel near the theatre. After a few days he decided to travel towards Fort Laramie, where General Merritt was stationed, in order to find out whether he could play a part in the Sioux War which had just been declared. He brought few possessions with him but packed one special item in his case which would cause some amazement when eventually produced. He also invited Ned Buntline to join him as he wanted a literary record of whatever might take place over the following weeks.

'I won't be expected to take part in any fighting myself, will I?' asked Buntline as their train pulled into the station nearest Laramie. 'I'm not a man of action particularly, as you know. More of a man of letters, me.'

'You'll be right beside me all the way, my friend,' explained Bill cheerfully. 'However if we're in the middle of a skirmish with a band of murdering Cheyenne charging around us, ready to take the scalps from our heads, and you choose not to take your pistol from your belt, then that's entirely up to you. I won't make you do anything you don't want to do.' This was not the answer Buntline had hoped for and he longed to return to his peaceful theatre where those who were murdered and scalped could always stand up again to take their final curtain call when the applause began.

Fort Laramie was the last great fort before the Rockies and it was there that a decade earlier the treaty had been signed with three separate branches of the Lakota Indians – the Miniconjou, the Oglala and the Brulé – whereby that tribe would not spread further across the country than what is now most of Nebraska and the two Dakotas. This giant reservation was agreed to by the Sioux leaders in return for their rights to hunt buffalo exclusively across the land but it was an agreement which had caused ten years of trouble for all. The government gradually sought to enclose the tribes tighter and tighter within that space and the Indians had never fully appreciated the significance of their sudden apartheid until it was too late.

General Wesley Merritt had taken over command of the Fifth Cavalry after the departure of General Carr and was delighted to see Bill arrive as they were old friends and the latter's celebrity added a certain glamour to their cause, in which Merritt also enjoyed basking.

'You don't mind if old Ned Buntline travels with us, do you General?' asked Bill. 'He's the writer in the company, you see, and I like to keep a record of what happens.'

'Will you be writing a play about the Sioux Wars, Mr Buntline?' asked the general anxiously. 'If so, you will portray me with honesty, I presume?'

Buntline smiled. He had learned not to say much to others while Bill was present, his employer not liking to feel either upstaged or excluded from the conversation. He listened attentively as the general and the scout discussed their plans but having no head for military manoeuvres his attention wandered somewhat and he was only brought back to the conversation by the sound of Bill's hand unexpectedly slamming down hard on the general's oak-lined desk.

'By God, I will avenge him,' roared Bill. 'I tell you now, Custer and I, we didn't always see eye to eye but I respected him, by God, as he did me and killing him . . . well that's taken this war one step too far.'

'There's no question it's ignited the hostility of the whole country against the Indians,' admitted Merritt. 'People were getting lethargic about it. This war's being going on for so long but without it actually being declared one as such. Now we can call it what it is. And we can go after those murdering savages and pick them off one by one, as they did with Custer and his army.'

'But the plan, General. What step do we take from here?'

The various armies stationed across the Platte region were preparing at that time to surround the reservation states and force battles with the tribes. It was a plan of intended genocide, but a dangerous one nonetheless as the Indians had proved fearsome enemies in recent times. They had also begun a guerrilla campaign whereby they were destroying the telegraph lines and the railway tracks of the Union Pacific Railroad in an attempt to slow down both communications and the chain of supplies to the soldiers.

'The tribes are linking up,' Merritt told Bill. 'I heard this evening that eight hundred Cheyenne are preparing to leave Red Cloud to join Sitting Bull in Big Horn country.'

'Sitting Bull,' said Bill through gritted teeth, spitting his chewing tobacco on the ground of Merritt's office in disgust at the name of the tribal leader responsible for the massacre which had claimed his friend's life.

'If they join together, they will be a stronger force than we have ever seen before,' said Merritt. 'If Sitting Bull's forces can defeat Custer, imagine what double their capacity can do. I heard from President Grant just before you got here. He wants the Fifth Cavalry to intercept the Cheyenne before they can reach Sitting Bull.'

'Can we not go straight to Big Horn?' asked Bill in frustration. 'Finish the job that Custer started?'

Merritt shook his head. 'Orders, I'm afraid. The Sixth and Eighth will be heading in that direction but will be relying on us to stop the Cheyenne. You'll ride with me?' he asked hopefully.

'I shall ride at the front by your side, General,' replied

Bill, swelling himself up to his full height. 'By God, the Cheyenne will quake when they see the two of us riding together to pick them off. Aye, and our own men will be inspired by it too.'

Merritt nodded his head, pleased by the other man's enthusiasm. He had worried that the amount of time my great-grandfather had spent on the stage in recent years might have weakened his passion for real warfare over the make-believe; there was no question that he was a little more portly than he had been in his younger days when he had been a buffalo hunter or scout for the army, but it was the good life of the theatre impresario which was giving him his extra padding. Although a celebrity, it was clear that he still had the heart for a fight, which was just as well as one would be given him.

'Right you are then, Buffalo Bill,' Merritt said, standing up to shake his hand, honouring my great-grandfather by addressing him by his stage name. 'Be ready at dawn then, for that's when we ride.'

Ned Buntline could feel his heart sinking within his chest. Death, he believed, was close at hand.

Although it seemed slightly old-fashioned, Hitomi and I embraced the idea of spending the night before our wedding in separate places and so I went across the hall to Luc, while Annette stayed in with Hitomi in our apartment. We probably wouldn't have bothered with such rigid formalities had Annette not insisted.

'It's bad luck otherwise,' she said, laying down the law. 'And anyway, since I'm the one responsible for getting you two back together, you owe me one. So do as I say or the wedding's off.' We did as she said. We had opted for a small register office wedding since neither

324

of us had family who would be attending. Annette was the matron of honour, Luc was my best man and we invited a couple of friends from the magazine and from Hitomi's office at the university to join us for dinner later in the evening. We planned it small and intimate, exactly the way we wanted it.

'You know,' I said that evening as I packed a bag full of the things I would need for the next day. Curiously, even though I was only going across the hall for one night, I seemed to need to take an entire rucksack of belongings. 'This is the first night we'll have been apart since we got back together.'

Hitomi smiled and nodded. Her hair was pulled back from her forehead and tied in a ponytail with just a rubber band. She was wearing sweatpants and a T-shirt and no make-up and looked entirely stressed out with pre-wedding nerves. She looked gorgeous. People remember different things from their wedding day, but the snapshot that stays in my mind is of that evening before the wedding, in our bedroom, packing my bag, and Hitomi looking as if she was going to collapse with worry any moment.

'Relax,' I said, coming up behind her and placing my hands on her shoulders, kneading them carefully between my hands in a familiar movement, trying to ease out the knots which were forming there. I leaned forward and kissed her neck lightly; her skin was warm and she leaned her head back towards me. 'You're not having second thoughts, are you?' I asked, only half joking.

'Of course not,' she said, shaking her head. 'I'm just tense, that's all. You don't get married every day of the week, you know.'

'True.'

'I'll be fine once it's all over. And I miss my family, you know? I wish they were here.'

I nodded but said nothing. I knew a little about how she felt. It had been just over a year since Annette had traced Hitomi to the Japanese language department at the Sorbonne; incredibly, in my anxiety to find her it had been one of the most obvious places that I had not thought of. Our reunion that night in a bar by the Seine had been emotional and upsetting at the same time. Luc and Annette had left us to get reacquainted almost immediately and we had sat there till the small hours of the morning, rediscovering each other.

Hitomi had left Japan almost immediately after I had gone to London, believing somehow that our relationship was simply not meant to be. She loved me as much as I loved her but was under pressure from her parents and from Tajima to break up with me. Although they were far from an ultra-traditionalist family, they still wanted their daughter to marry a Japanese man. In time, I grew to realise that this was not due to any particular racial motives, but entirely because they did not want to lose Hitomi to the world. And if she was to marry a man from another country, she might live in his country and not theirs. Ironically, our married life was to be spent in only two countries, and neither of them were to be the countries of either of our births.

She hadn't received my messages in Japan, and my letters had not been forwarded to her. I grew angry at the thought of Tak opening my letters and reading the sentiments of love which I had sent to her, probably mocking me for them, distributing them among his friends as signs of my stupidity, but that anger was lessened by the fact that once we saw each other again, even after such a break, Hitomi and I recognised our own faces in the other and knew that we had been designed for each other. And, as I pointed out to her that evening, we had never been apart for a single night since.

Annette enjoyed several months of smug self-satisfaction over our reunion and when we eventually decided to marry, she was overjoyed. However, even that was a small emotion compared to my own. We invited our families to Paris for the wedding but they declined graciously, sending gifts and congratulatory cards instead. It was probably for the best. Isaac sent a letter and we kept in touch frequently by phone and I agreed to visit him shortly afterwards.

The year between reuniting with Hitomi and marrying her had brought a series of good things to our lives. Hitomi, who was lecturing at the university now, was promoted to assistant-professor level and her classes had expanded as more and more students, particularly business students, wanted to learn Japanese. She enjoyed her life there and had made a lot of friends, who I saw from time to time, but in general we liked to keep our professional lives mostly to ourselves in order to keep some sense of the personal and private.

My work was now appearing in magazines and newspapers around the world and I had become quite well known for a journalist. From time to time I appeared on French television, either as a commentator on some magazine show or as an arts reviewer. I presented a one-off travel show aimed at budget holidays and was in such demand for television programmes that I sometimes noticed people giving me second glances in restaurants or bars, recognising me from my public persona. Although I pretended this was something that I did not want at all, privately I quite enjoyed the feeling of my small loss of anonymity and particularly enjoyed being recognised if I had friends with me. For a short time, ego took over, but Hitomi kept me in check.

I undertook a commission to write a book, collecting various articles of mine over the years and writing some new ones and the advances on this, combined with my income from my other work, meant that Hitomi and I became reasonably affluent for a couple in their late twenties. Although we could have easily afforded a mortgage on a house in the city, we continued to rent our apartment, as our social life with Luc and Annette was important to us and not easily sacrificed.

The wedding day passed quite peacefully and with little drama. We exchanged our vows in a simple ceremony, we kissed, and then we enjoyed a raucous evening with all our closest friends in a restaurant in the city. At the end of the night, we took a boat trip down the Seine before checking into the most expensive and luxurious hotel in Paris for two nights, a wedding present from our neighbours. We had agreed to postpone the honeymoon for a couple of months, until the summer vacation came, and had not yet decided on a location. For my part, I couldn't have been more surprised when Hitomi came to me with her idea.

It was about three weeks after the wedding and we were settling comfortably into married life. Things did not seem so different from when we had been simply living together but the rings on our fingers did, I feel, add some dimension of adult behaviour to our romance. We were grown-ups now. A married couple. We shared a bank account and divided up tasks dependent on our temperaments; Hitomi handled the bills and most of the household repairs. The kitchen was mine and interfered with on pain of divorce. I washed, she ironed.

I never made the bed, she never cleaned the bathroom. We knew what we were doing and we were happy.

Our apartment in Paris had a huge central window which, when opened, gave the room an airy and fresh feel which we both enjoyed, but it also had a wide ledge and I often liked to sit there on warm evenings with a bottle of beer and a book as I waited for Hitomi to come home. On this particular evening, there was something of a heatwave going on and I sat there wearing just a pair of white shorts and a baseball cap to screen the sun from my eyes. I remember I was reading *The Sailor Who Fell From Grace With The Sea* and had reached the part where Noboru has been discovered spying on his mother as she makes love with Ryuki Tsukazaki, when Hitomi came in and collapsed on the sofa, exhausted from her day and the heat.

'You want a beer?' I asked her as a greeting, waving my own in the air as I did so.

'Please,' she said. 'I wish we had a swimming pool.'

'When we're very, very rich,' I replied, walking towards the kitchen, my bare feet padding lightly on the expensive wooden floor which Hitomi had installed after she'd pulled up all my carpets shortly after moving in. It felt quite cool beneath my feet and as I handed her the cold beer I reached down to kiss her but she pushed me away with a giggle.

'You stink, baby,' she said; she often called me 'baby' in a curious, Japanese way. As if she had heard people say it in movies and wanted to emulate them. 'Go back to your window ledge.'

I smiled and retreated as she had suggested. She was probably right. I'd been working from home all day and hadn't bothered to shower. Sitting for hours in a hot apartment had done nothing for my personal hygiene.

I returned to my beer and my book; we had long ago established that being in the same room together did not mean that we were obliged to be constantly speaking to each other. In fact I think we both quite enjoyed the fact that we could cohabit and do different things without feeling the need to be always chattering away.

'I've made a decision,' she said eventually and I looked across at her, leaving the book open on my knees.

'About what?'

'About our honeymoon,' she said. 'I decided today.'

'Right,' I replied, a little surprised, for I had started to think it was one of those things which was going to be put off indefinitely until we would finally take a holiday somewhere and call it a honeymoon, despite the fact that we might have been married a couple of years by then.

'It's bad luck not to,' she said. 'And we should do it anyway. We haven't had a—' She corrected herself. 'In fact, we've never had a holiday together. Other than the odd weekend away.'

'We went to Cannes last year,' I said, for we had blagged our way into a trip there with Annette and Luc.

'We need a honeymoon,' she said determinedly. 'And I think we should combine it with a family reunion.'

My heart soared and I put the book away, spinning around on the ledge to face her. We hadn't really discussed it much, but I was very keen to return to Japan for a holiday as I missed the country enormously and didn't even mind that it would mean spending a couple of weeks with Mr and Mrs Naoyuki and the mail-stealing son. 'That's a great idea,' I said. 'Actually I really wanted to go back there soon myself. Not to live, but for a break.'

'Yes, I thought so,' said Hitomi, smiling happily. 'It seems like the right time to do it. It's been put off long enough through my silliness. But let's do it now, in the next couple of weeks so it really is a honeymoon.'

I thought about it; the university term would be over in a week and I was on top of my work and could afford a break. There was nothing really stopping us. 'Okay,' I said. 'You better call your parents though and see if they can put us up. Or should we stay in a hotel? Or would they be offended if we did that?'

Hitomi looked at me and frowned. 'My parents,' she said, a little confused. 'Why do we need to tell them?'

I blinked and shrugged my shoulders, as if it was obvious. 'You meant Japan, didn't you?' I said after a pause. 'That's where you want to go, right?'

'Oh dear no,' she said, a quick shudder running through her. 'No, I meant London. I meant we should go to visit your father.'

'Isaac,' I said, amazed. 'Are you serious?'

'Sure. Why not?'

I scratched my neck and could feel the heat of the sun already hitting in. 'But you'll die if you go to England,' I said.

'Yes,' she said quietly, nodding. 'I know, I know what I've always said. But maybe I was crazy. I'm not going to die if I go there. It's a stupid superstition on my part.'

I frowned. I was surprised for she had always been determined on this point in the past. And now that she was saying that it didn't matter it started to occur to me that maybe it wasn't such a good idea after all, that maybe we shouldn't tempt fate. 'Perhaps we should think about this,' I said. 'I mean it's not like we have to rush into—'

'Honestly, William,' she said, coming over and taking

331

my face in her hands, reaching forward to kiss my lips lightly. 'I'm telling you, it was just a stupid superstition, that's all. I've replaced it with another.'

'Which is?'

'That it will be bad luck if we do not take a honeymoon soon. So what do you think? Should we go?'

I thought about it and exhaled loudly. 'I guess so,' I said eventually, unconvinced. 'I'll phone Isaac.'

Joseph Craven didn't particularly like Ellen Rose. In fact, he despised everything about her except her beauty. Her natural abilities on the trapeze and tight-rope irritated him as she had already become, at the age of only eighteen, the most naturally talented performer he had seen or worked with, while he had to practise constantly in order not to kill himself while he was up there. Even after ten years of performing, he never felt that one hundred per cent confidence which those who are born to the craft feel; instead he was just good at learning it. Ellen's effect on the audience was also obvious; she had them in the palm of her hand. Her celebrity was growing within the circus world and her arrival in the Big Top always preceded a rapturous and sustained round of applause, in which she revelled. Her worst moments came when the show was over and the people had gone home and there was no one left to watch or applaud her any more. She came alive in front of an audience.

'She's a different girl out there, you know,' Russell Rose remarked to his wife Bessie one evening as they prepared for bed. 'She's shy outside the show, you know. She's not very sure of herself. But the minute she goes out there and starts performing, it's like she turns into a whole different person.'

'She likes the limelight, that's for sure,' said Bessie, who disapproved of her daughter's activities. 'It's attention seeking, nothing more.'

'I'm not so sure. She doesn't seek that kind of attention when she's not out there. When she's not in character. I'm telling you, Bessie, she puts on that outfit and steps into the Big Top, climbs the ladder and she's exactly where she's meant to be. There's no question about that. It's like she creates her own character.'

Bessie knew this was the case also but didn't like to agree with him. She still wished that her daughter would leave the circus and find her own life outside of it but that was appearing less and less likely as time went on. In the meantime, Joseph Craven, ten years her senior, continued to lust after the young girl as she had once lusted after Howard Losey and eventually decided that the time had come to be paid back for all the training he had given her.

It was after a show one evening and, unusually, they were alone in a trailer together. Ellen was drinking a cup of tea; she was tired that night because it was a Wednesday, when there was always a matinée and evening performance, and she sat rubbing her legs as Joseph Craven drank from a bottle of beer.

'Sore?' he asked through gritted teeth, watching as her fingers dragged themselves along the pale, porcelain skin. His tongue ran along his chapped lips greedily as she answered.

'I hate Wednesdays,' she said. 'I always feel tired after them.'

'Here, let me,' he said, stepping off his seat and kneeling on the ground before her, taking her hands away from her legs and replacing them lightly with his own. She jumped back a little in her seat but didn't get up; she was unsure how to take his gesture and grew irritated as he rubbed her legs. 'How's that feel?' he asked, looking up at her. 'Any better?'

'Much,' she said quickly, trying unsuccessfully to brush him away. 'I might go straight to bed though. I'm tired.'

'Not till I'm finished, you don't,' he said, forcing her back in the seat with just enough power to keep her there but not so much that she could feel threatened. 'You're all tense,' he said. 'You let me do my magic now and you'll be fine.' His hands caressed her legs and she decided within her head that she would allow this liberty to continue for another minute or two before standing up suddenly and going back to her own trailer. Before she could do this, however, she felt his hands working further and further up her legs, higher than they had any right to go, and closing in to meet each other as they moved along.

'Joseph!' she said, jumping up now and knocking him back as she did so. 'What do you think you're doing?'

'Oh come on Ellen,' he replied, standing up and wiping a line of perspiration away from his forehead. He moved towards her and put his arms around her as she struggled to free herself. 'Stop it now, girl,' he said. 'Don't I deserve any reward for all my training of you?'

'Get off, Joseph,' she said firmly and, determined not to let the situation get out of hand, acted promptly, raising her knee sharply so that he crumpled to the ground in pain. 'I'm sorry to have done that,' she said quickly, brushing herself off, 'but there can be nothing like that between us, Joseph.'

He sat up, humiliated, but he was not the sort to try and force her further and so attempted to recover his dignity and, potentially, save his job. I'm sorry about that, Ellen,' he said quickly through gritted teeth. 'Just the drink getting the better of me, I suppose.'

'Well see that it doesn't again,' she said. 'I wouldn't like to have to speak to my father about you.'

'No, no,' said Joseph quickly, an image of the hulking Russell Rose coming into his mind. 'No need for that. I made a mistake, that's all. It won't happen again.'

Ellen stared at him, unsure whether she believed him or not, unsure whether this was a situation which was indeed over. Eventually, she determined that it was, for she simply gave him a curt nod and left the trailer quickly. She wouldn't tell anyone what had happened, she decided, but if he tried it on again then she would speak to her father. In the meantime, she would not speak to him of it again and instead try to put the incident out of her mind and concentrate on her audience and performance instead.

Joseph Craven was an unpleasant character, however, and although a coward, was not the type of man who took rejection easily. Even as she prepared for bed that same evening a plan was forming in his head. If he could not have her, then he would deprive her of the thing which she valued the most in life. Her days as a trapeze artist would be numbered.

There was a lot of staring going on. I couldn't take my eyes off Isaac, who had aged terribly since I had last seen him. He was seventy-eight years old now and his whole body seemed to have shrunk in on itself. His face was lean and perhaps because he had shaved before we got there, his cheeks were inflamed and rough looking. When he shook my hand, his long fingers felt bony within my grasp. Despite myself, I thought: this is my

335

father, my genetics. This is what I will look like one day.

And Isaac could not help but stare at Hitomi. I could tell that her unfamiliar Japanese features were a source of curiosity to him. He watched her as she spoke, barely registering the words, but just watching her face instead. And Hitomi, probably feeling a little nervous by being in London for the first time, kept glancing across at me, holding on to my hand for fear that I would run away suddenly and leave her alone with this ghost of a man, her new father-in-law.

'You better call me Isaac,' he said at one point. 'Everyone else does. Even him,' he added, nodding across at me. 'Almost never calls me Dad.'

'You always told me to call you Isaac,' I pointed out. 'So what do you expect?'

'Gets very touchy too when you criticise him,' he said in a whispered voice, as if I couldn't hear him, already beginning a complicity with my wife against me which might give them a bond. 'But then you probably know that about him already.'

Hitomi smiled, wanting to remain pleasant and friendly with him, but unwilling to appear conspiratorial against me at the same time. I poured tea for all of us but we barely touched it, catching up instead on our news. I described the wedding day to Isaac and he seemed pleased with our happiness. He insisted on telling me over and over again how lucky I was to have found such a 'catch' as Hitomi, complimenting her on her beauty constantly. She knew he was just being chivalrous and polite but I appreciated his making the effort all the same. Afterwards he insisted on giving her a tour of the house – which took all of five minutes – and he showed her my old bedroom, where we were to sleep.

Getting ready for bed late that night, Hitomi sat on my old single bed and looked around in amazement. 'This is so interesting to me,' she said. 'Seeing the room where you grew up. All these things . . .' she muttered, getting up to take a look at the various possessions I had built up over the years. Although I had ripped my posters off the walls and thrown away much of my western memorabilia after my worst fight with Isaac, somehow he had managed to save those things which I had not fully destroyed. In my absence, he had returned the room to its former glory as a shrine to the west. I could tell that the room had been recently cleaned and aired but wished I was elsewhere nonetheless. For one thing, the bed was too small for both of us; it would be fine for a night or two but as we were supposed to be staying in London for a week, I figured that after a few days, neither of us would be able to get any sleep. Given the choice, we would have stayed in a hotel but Isaac had insisted we stay with him and we thought it would be rude to decline his offer.

'This is supposed to be our honeymoon,' I said. 'And look. We're sleeping in the same single bed that I slept in until I was eighteen years old.'

'I just hope he's changed the sheets then,' said Hitomi with a smile. 'Maybe we can fulfil some of your teenage fantasies while we're here.'

'Not likely,' I said. 'The walls are very thin. I think this is going to freak me out too much.'

'These pictures,' she said, walking around, looking at each of the posters and photographs in turn. 'You put these up?'

'When I was a kid, yes,' I said. 'Isaac got them for me. That's a replica of one of the posters from a play which my great-grandfather put on in Chicago in 1875.

Apparently he was performing in that play when he heard about Custer's last stand and practically scalped some poor actor on stage.'

Hitomi grimaced and pointed to another one, a sepia photograph of Buffalo Bill sitting outside a theatre with another man, a cigarette clenched tight between closed teeth, his long white hair flowing towards his collar. 'And this one,' she asked. 'When is this from?'

'A year or so before that, I think,' I said. 'That's Texas Jack Omohundro on the left. My great-grandfather brought him with him from Missouri to Chicago and they both got hired as actors to play themselves. This was before Bill took over the productions himself. And this one here,' I said, showing her the biggest, most colourful poster of all which was framed on the wall facing my bed. 'This is an original print of a poster used when he was travelling across Europe with the Congress of Rough Riders of the World.'

'The wild west show,' said Hitomi, nodding.

'Not really. The wild west show was more of a Cowboys and Indians set-up. The congress took warriors from a bunch of different countries, America, Japan, Russia, Britain and so on, and set them up in traditional costumes to act out battles. It was more international than the wild west show. It still had all the elements of that though, he just added a lot more to it.'

'It's interesting,' Hitomi muttered and I couldn't help but laugh.

'You think?' I said, sceptical.

'Well to have such a famous ancestor,' she said. 'It's interesting because it's strange. It is true, isn't it?'

I thought about it. 'Yes,' I said. 'As far as I can tell it is. I've never done much research, I have to admit. It's all gone on what Isaac's told me and I've told you most

338

of those stories. But it seems to fit. You know, the meeting with my great-grandmother, there's photographs of them together. And she did get pregnant just after she met him, so it makes sense. And you know, when he was younger, I could see something of Buffalo Bill in Isaac. Something about the way he smoked a cigarette. It reminded me of these pictures.'

Hitomi nodded. 'It's no wonder your father's so obsessed,' she said.

'I don't see how you figure that,' I said, slightly irked. 'He's my great-grandfather and *I'm* not obsessed. Why should he be?'

'You've made a life for yourself, William,' she said quietly. 'You've got a successful career. You've travelled. You've got a wife. When did your father ever have any of those things? I mean he didn't meet your mother till he was, what—'

'Fifty-one,' I said.

'Family life only hit him at the end then. You said yourself he's never been outside London. He spent time in prison, didn't make anything of his life really. His wife left him early. It seems the only things he's ever had in life have been one important ancestor and one descendant, you. One of whom is dead and the other who doesn't care less.'

'I do care,' I protested. 'Christ, Hitomi, he is my father.'

'I meant you don't care about your ancestry, William. He does. Maybe he's obsessed with it because it's all he has. He's never been able to see any future for himself.'

'You don't know him,' I said, sitting down on the bed now and looking up at her. I could feel a sting behind my eyes and wasn't sure why. I wanted her to stop talking about this but at the same time I felt I needed to go on. 'You don't know what it was like,' I said. 'It's all we've ever had between us. Can you imagine what that was like? It's all we had to talk about.'

'My father was not different,' she said. 'He tells stories of his ancestry all the time. He's proud of where he comes from.'

'I took down every one of these posters,' I said, ignoring her comment. 'Years ago I ripped them all down and thought they'd gone in the bin. Then I get back here one time and they're all back on the walls. It's not my bedroom at all, never has been. It's just part of his museum. And I'm the unpaid curator of one of the rooms, that's all.' I leaned forward and willed myself not to cry but couldn't help it somehow. The combination of seeing Isaac so frail and old with being back in my boyhood room was overwhelming me.

'You want a relationship with him, that's all,' she said, sitting down beside me and placing my head on her shoulders. 'He's never offered you one based on the two of you alone and that's all you wanted.'

'He wanted my help,' I said. 'That was why I came back here a couple of years ago. You know that. He lied to bring me here. We nearly lost each other because of him. Just so he could set up another one of these stupid wild west shows. How much is that about the two of us?'

'He wanted you to do it with him,' she said. 'That was all. He wanted you to work together.'

I sighed and dried my face. 'I can't stay here,' I said. 'Maybe you were wrong. Maybe it isn't you who dies if you come to England. Maybe it's me.'

She took my face in her hands and stared at me. Her eyes pierced through me. 'He's not dead yet,' she said in a clear voice. 'Take your chance while it's there or you'll regret it for ever. Listen to me, William, because I'm right.'

We went to bed and made love as quietly as we could. It seemed strange to have a woman in my boyhood bed and as we fell asleep afterwards I felt a strange fear of discovery when I heard the door of Isaac's room open and his footsteps going down the stairs to the kitchen. I listened but after he had switched on the light and closed the door I couldn't hear him any more and within a few minutes, while I was deciding whether I should take this opportunity to go down and talk to him on my own or not, I fell asleep.

Just over five hundred men comprised the group that General Merritt and Buffalo Bill Cody brought from Fort Laramie across the plains to intercept the Cheyenne warriors. Bill, Buntline and Merritt often rode far ahead of the group, scouting for information along the way. They were agreed that if they could reach War Bonnet Valley before the Indians, they would make camp there and await their arrival in order to ambush them, as this was the trail to the north that the Cheyenne would necessarily have to take to reach Sitting Bull's land. It took about a day and a half to reach the creek and once there, Bill and Buntline went down alone to investigate whether they had been too slow or not.

'They've not been here yet,' said Bill after they had descended into the valley and allowed their horses to rest and drink from the stream nearby. 'This land hasn't been travelled over in a week or more.'

'Then this is where we will take them?'

Bill looked around at the valley surrounding them. It opened up on either side into a vast prairie area where there was nothing in sight for miles but open land.

War Bonnet Valley itself was not a narrow valley – two hundred horses could have passed through it side by side – but it did have the advantage of being the one place between the Cheyenne home and the Sioux reservation where an effective trap could be set.

'Looks like it,' said Bill. 'But we've little time to plan. They may not have been here yet but if they left when they were supposed to, then they can't be too far away.'

They made their way back to the top of the Rockies where, at some distance, Merritt had set up camp. He had assumed that what Bill had discovered down there would be the case and did not want to be so close to the peaks of the mountains that the Cheyenne might discover them in advance.

'Do you think they know we'll be waiting for them?' asked Bill and the general shrugged his shoulders slightly.

'It's hard to tell,' he said. 'But I suspect not. Their intelligence gathering is primitive compared to ours. But they might assume that we know they're on their way. Whether they realise this is where we will be cutting them off is hard to tell. We'll just have to wait. But they'll be here soon, there's no question about that and a heavy battle lies ahead of us,' he added sadly. Unlike some of the other generals in the army – unlike Bill himself – Merritt did not find these events exciting or adventurous. He felt a close connection to the boys under his command and had lost too many of them in recent years to be seduced by the romanticism of war. If it was not for the fact that Bill's plays turned the soldiers into heroic and historical figures, he probably would have despised the younger man for his part in creating glamour out of warfare.

At this point, Bill excused himself from the company

and, taking his rucksack from his saddlebag, disappeared out of sight for a time. Merritt and Buntline watched him go and wondered what he was doing but they did not have to question it for long for shortly afterwards he re-emerged into the crowd of resting soldiers. The general turned around as the young men – mostly aged between sixteen and twenty-one – gave a rousing cheer as their hero appeared in their midst and as he made his way through their ranks and back towards the general, Merritt gasped in amazement at the sight he saw before him. Buntline's mouth dropped open in surprise and he didn't know whether to feel pride or embarrassment at his employer's actions. For although he had started the day in regulation, fairly nondescript scouting uniform, he appeared now in a uniform of his own design which was as exotic as it was grandiose. Modelled after the uniforms worn by Mexican vaqueros, Bill's black-velvet costume was embroidered along the arms with gold and silver sequins and snow-white lace. A scarlet sash crossed his chest from right shoulder to left hip and his patent-black leather boots were as shiny as ever worn by a soldier before or since. Like all his uniforms, it was one that Bill had designed himself and Buntline recognised it immediately, not as a military uniform, but as a stage costume. In fact, it was one of three identical costumes worn by Bill nightly at the Elysium Theatre during the third act of *Scouts of the Plains*, the same play he had been performing in the night he had heard of General Custer's death.

'Good God man, what are you wearing?' asked Merritt, unsure whether he should be shocked, amused or admiring of the fashion extravaganza walking towards him. Bill nodded to acknowledge the question but declined to reply, wanting the effect of the costume to sink in with people without his having to explain it. He threw Buntline a quick, harsh look, as if he was aware that at any point the other man might mention the stage origins of this uniform and wanted to make sure that he didn't. He knew that the eyes of all the soldiers were on him admiringly and wondered whether he should turn and take his bow, perhaps passing the time with them by telling them one of his stories of earlier adventures, wondering whether he was standing in an appropriate place where the lighting would be quite right for all to see him, when Merritt shouted out to the soldiers to quieten down and as they fell silent under his orders, he nodded for Bill to join him at the peak of the mountain, looking down into the valley below.

Bill squinted as he leaned over and followed the general's pointed finger until he saw what had grabbed Merritt's attention. Two men, white men, riding alone towards the valley from the opposite side, as if aiming to meet eight hundred Cheyenne on their own.

'Good God,' said Bill, amazed to see them there, an unexpected sight. 'What on earth—?'

'Couriers,' said Merritt quickly. 'They must be headed back towards Fort Laramie to deliver a message to us, there's no other explanation. They'll be going through the valley and turning to the left across the Platte, the way we arrived.'

'We should go down then,' said Bill. 'Cut them off. They'd never hear us call from here.'

'Too late,' said Merritt, looking in the opposite direction. 'They're here.'

Both men turned and saw in the distance the sight of the Cheyenne gradually coming into focus. At the speed they and the couriers were going, it would be a good twenty minutes before either reached the centre of War Bonnet Valley, but when they did, Merritt estimated they would meet at the very heart of it. They returned quickly to their troops and sortied them into position, keeping them clear from the edges of the mountain, not wanting the Cheyenne to know they were present until they were already safely locked into the heart of the creek. It would be eight hundred men against five hundred, but the soldiers had the element of surprise on their hands, not to mention better firepower, and taking this into account, it became a more even contest.

Buntline held back into the group as Merritt and Bill took the lead; he planned on retreating to the rear once the charge started, perhaps even watching from this mountain top and making his notes from there. After all, he reasoned to himself, he was not a solider but a playwright and an actor. He could not be accused of cowardice for not taking part in a battle for which he had never joined up. By the time the action began, everyone would be too busy attempting to stay alive to worry about him anyway. It was a good plan, he reasoned, and he turned his horse.

'The couriers are going to enter stage right at the same time the Cheyenne come in from stage left,' said Bill as he watched the progress of the two groups from the mountain. Merritt glanced at him quickly, disliking the terminology, and felt a sudden rush of irritation.

'This is a real battle,' he said quickly. 'You do know that, Bill, don't you?'

Bill snorted. 'We'll have our revenge here, General. Wait and see.' They watched as the couriers and the Indians did indeed enter the creek simultaneously and each paused for a second before continuing on their way. Neither group had any choice. The Cheyenne had little to fear from two men ambling towards them, even if their appearance did suggest the possibility of others. The couriers on the other hand could hardly defend themselves from eight hundred tribal warriors; their only hope was to carry on and hope that they would be allowed to pass, which was not inconceivable.

Merritt waited until the two groups were almost on top of each other before giving the order and the entire Fifth Cavalry began their charge down the mountains towards the creek below. The Indians looked up in surprise and their leader, Yellow Hand, quickly tried to sortie his group into order so that they might defend themselves. The two couriers stared around in surprise, unsure who to fear more – the scrambling and shouting Indians before them, or the hundreds of soldiers appearing as if by magic from the mountain tops.

Within minutes the battle had begun and soldiers and Indians fought against each other. Vision became impaired by the amount of gun smoke in the air and the soldiers struck out in terror at whoever was around them as the bullets and arrows whizzed past their ears, missing some, pinning others. The horses all reared up and their sounds became part of the battle itself as some threw their riders and others fell after being shot themselves. Merritt, a brave and well-decorated general, cut a sweep before him until his ear was blown off by a bullet.

My great-grandfather, however, circled the groups, killing no one and miraculously avoiding being killed as he sought out the prize he wanted the most. He saw him eventually, Yellow Hair, the great Cheyenne chief who was leading these warriors now to Sitting Bull, and Bill dug his spurs into Buckskin Joe as he made his way towards him. Yellow Hair saw him coming towards him and turned to ride away but Bill drove him towards the left-hand side of the valley beneath the rocks. As he approached him, he spotted Buntline on the mountain top, watching the action from a distance of safety, and shot a bullet in his direction so that his attention would be fully focused on him over the next few minutes. Almost collapsing from shock as the bullet narrowly missed him, Buntline did indeed fix his gaze on the familiar and outlandish stage costume of Buffalo Bill Cody as he shot the horse of Yellow Hair from under him and beast and rider fell to the ground in a heavy heap.

Bill jumped from his horse and the two men circled each other for a moment, both grinning with the determination of their violence.

'I know you,' growled Yellow Hair, sizing his opponent up and down as they circled, their arms held out slightly from their bodies as they waited for each other to reach for a gun.

'And I you,' shouted Bill back quickly. 'And this is the day you die, my friend.'

For Buntline, the seconds seemed like hours as he waited for either man to shoot, but for the two warriors they could have stood like that all day because they each revelled in the power of their moment. Two great men, two famous names, and one about to kill the other.

They reached for their guns at the same moment and incredibly, despite their proximity, both men seemed to fumble. Yellow Hair's shot whizzed past Bill's left ear, missing him completely, at the same moment as my great-grandfather's own bullet, aimed square at the heart of the Cheyenne warrior, entered his shoulder instead, throwing the Indian back against the rocks, his gun fallen to the ground, his eyes filling with terror as his nemesis walked towards him determinedly, no pause now as Bill pinned him to the rocks behind him, pulled his own knife from around his waist, and pressed it into the forehead of his opponent, just below the hairline, dragging it across and around the back of the head, slicing through the skullcap as he finished his job and the Indian fell to the ground dead, a bloody heap by his feet.

Bill stepped back a few feet, covered in blood and slime now, and looked up to the mountain top where Buntline, his audience of one, stood watching, the reporter's stomach rotating within itself as he started to retch. Bending over to throw up, he caught Bill's last line, shouted up towards him from the ground below and never forgot it again, the line being the one he heard whenever he woke in the night with that ghoulish scene replaying before him.

'Buntline!' cried Buffalo Bill the showman, the actor, the stage performer re-enacting his stage moment from a few weeks earlier, only this time holding the bloody hairpiece and top-skull of Yellow Hair in his hands as he shouted: 'The first scalp for Custer!'

Chapter Ten

The New American Way

When Hitomi and I returned to Paris, I began to make more of an effort to stay in contact with Isaac. Our visit there had upset me somewhat, for despite all his continuing talk about entering show business it was clear that he was ailing. I tried not to think about it but I knew that I might receive a phone call some night telling me that he was gone. Although I dreaded such an eventuality I still couldn't bring myself to relocate to London like he wanted, which felt nothing like home to me any more. I would have liked to return to Japan, but Hitomi was opposed to that.

'I feel about Japan the way you feel about London,' she explained to me. 'I've spent all my life there. I don't want to be there any more. You were just a visitor, that's all. I could live in London quicker than I could live in Kyoto again.'

'Well we're not going to be living there,' I said firmly. Paris had proved a successful city for us. We enjoyed our jobs, had made a lot of friends there and we were happy. However, after almost two years living there we began to wonder whether it was time we moved on. We were heading into our late twenties now and had agreed that we would put off starting a family until we had both turned thirty; this gave us a little time to see some more of the world and enjoy our youth. My travel book had been published and proved reasonably successful. The money I had earned had helped boost our savings, and although we didn't expect to make any further royalties from it, a couple of publishers had bought the translation rights, which helped us even more.

In early summer of 1997, Hitomi phoned me one afternoon at the newspaper offices and asked me to meet her after work for a drink. We arranged a place and I sat there for almost an hour waiting for her, growing frustrated by her tardiness, and frowned when she eventually arrived, slightly flustered, and immediately ordered a cold beer.

'Sorry I'm late,' she said, putting her bags down and reaching across to kiss me. I grunted. I was in a bad mood. Internal politics at the newspaper were beginning to irritate me. The editor had begun to suggest that I was no longer a naïf in Paris and so my columns were becoming a little redundant. In recent times I had begun to spread my wings anyway and was interviewing celebrities for profile pieces but the syndication of the travel column netted me a substantial amount and I hadn't wanted to let it go, even though I knew he was right.

'That's okay,' I said sarcastically. 'It's not like I couldn't have stayed in the office for another hour and got some work done if I'd known.'

'Don't be like that,' she snapped back. 'I said I'm sorry. I got delayed.'

I shrugged. We rarely had an argument but on some occasions, such as this one, I felt an overwhelming urge to start one. I had sometimes felt that our relationship was too happy and that it would be healthier if there were some points of conflict between us. Hitomi thought

I was mad whenever I suggested this and refused to play along but nevertheless, at times I longed for a little drama. Our neighbours, Annette and Luc, fought like cats and dogs and yet remained about the most secure couple I had ever known. We could hear them throwing plates at each other sometimes, or screaming for hours on end at each other using obscene French words which always made me smile, before a silence would descend and we would know that they had found some way to make up with each other.

Our beers arrived and we sat there silently for a time. I looked across the plaza where we were seated and watched as a tall young woman in a short dress and dark glasses strolled across towards the fountain while a father and son seated outside a restaurant on the opposite side watched her every movement in silence.

'What's wrong with you?' asked Hitomi after a while. 'What are you angry about?'

'Nothing,' I said. 'It's just been a long day, that's all. Dupré wants to cancel the travel column for one thing. Wants me to concentrate on the interviews and profiles.'

'Well you enjoy them more, don't you?' she asked.

'I guess,' I muttered, not much wanting to discuss it. 'I don't know. I'm a bit fed up, that's all.'

'Maybe you need a change,' she said and I glanced across at her, aware that there was something more in her voice than just making conversation. She was trying hard not to burst into a wide grin and I narrowed my eyes to stare at her.

'What's up?' I asked. 'What's going on?'

'I've been offered a job,' she said. 'A new job.'

'In Paris?'

'In America.'

351

I opened my eyes wide and exhaled heavily, unsure what to think of this potential move. 'America,' I said. 'What is it? How did it come about?'

'I applied for it, of course,' she said. 'How do you think? It's part of an exchange programme between Japanese professors. It would only be for one year but what an opportunity!'

I nodded. Although even at this early stage of information, I knew I quite liked the idea, I didn't want to appear too enthusiastic too soon and decided to play irritated instead. 'You applied for a job in America and you never bothered to tell me?' I said. 'Thanks for that. That says a lot about us.'

'I never expected to get it,' she said. 'Honestly, William, I sent in the application on a whim. Leila had applied and she was expected to get it but then she had to drop out of course.' Leila was a colleague of Hitomi's who I had met several times and liked; she was one step more senior than my wife but had recently become pregnant and this was presumably why she had declined any offer made to her. 'With her not going, I was next in line,' she continued. 'I just heard today. It really is a terrific opportunity for me. For us.'

I nodded and sighed. 'You said. And what about me?' I asked. 'Am I supposed to just down tools and come along too?'

'To do what?' she asked, unfamiliar with the idiom. 'To down tools? What do you mean?'

'Am I supposed to just quit my job?' I asked in a more aggressive voice. 'Is that what you want me to do?'

'William, it's only for a year. You've managed to bounce between countries before and find a newspaper willing to take you on. You did all right here, didn't you? And in Japan?'

I shrugged, unwilling to concede the point. 'That was different,' I said. 'This is Paris. We're talking about America here. The competition will be stronger. Everyone wants to be Woodward and Bernstein over there. I'll be a small fish in a big pond. It'll be harder for me to find work.'

'But you said you wanted to travel more,' she protested. 'You said so only last week. You said that we should try to—'

'I know what I said,' I interrupted, unsure why I was putting up such an opposition to this plan. 'Jesus, don't tell me what I said, okay?' Neither of us spoke for a moment and I could see that Hitomi was becoming upset. 'All right,' I said eventually in a calmer voice, trying to reconcile us without backing down. 'Tell me more about it at least. Where is it anyway?'

'It would start in September in New York University,' she said in a quiet voice. 'Then after Christmas we would be in the University of Colorado for nine months. We could leave again in August if we didn't like it.'

I nodded. It was tempting. 'I might have more luck in Colorado than I would in New York,' I said. 'Although, does anything actually happen in Colorado? Isn't it all just oil rigs and Stetsons?'

'Of course things happen there,' she said irritably. 'Don't be so parochial. I mean it is an entire state after all, people live there. Anyway, you could write another book if you wanted to. Do more television work. Something like that.'

'Let's think about it,' I said. 'How soon do they need to know?'

'This week,' she replied. 'By Thursday in fact or they offer it to someone else.'

'Thursday! That's a bit quick, isn't it?'

353

'They need to know,' she said with a shrug. 'They have to make plans for the semesters.'

'Then there's Isaac . . .' I muttered, not entirely sure what I even meant by this.

'What about him?' she asked. 'What, do you want to bring him with us?'

'No, of course not,' I said irritably. 'Don't be ridiculous. I just mean he's not getting any younger, that's all. He doesn't have much time left, right? Maybe I shouldn't just troop off to the other side of the world when he might need me.'

Hitomi sat back in her chair and now it was her turn to look angry. She shook her head and looked away, speaking to me through gritted teeth, refusing to even look at me. 'Don't do that,' she said quickly. 'Don't use him as an excuse please. This is my life and my career that I want to follow. You've seen your father only a couple of times in the last few years. Don't pretend you're the dutiful son now just to spite me.'

That stung and I felt myself grow even more angry with her. 'That's not fair,' I said. 'I may not see him much but that doesn't mean I don't . . . that I don't . . .' I couldn't even get the words out and she saw her opportunity to jump in.

'Don't tell me you love him,' she said. 'You can't even be in the same country as him, for heaven's sake, let alone the same room. You're the one who always tells me that you have no relationship with him, that he isn't interested in you, that he just wants you to be some sort of reincarnation of a mythical figure.'

'He's not mythical!' I shouted. 'A myth is something that—'

'I don't care,' she said, leaning forward so our argument would not be heard by all around us. 'And don't

354

correct my grammar, all right? We've been in Paris for two years now and you've only visited him once and even that was a disaster so don't say no to this opportunity because of him. If you don't want to go, then that's fine. Just say so. And tell me why. But don't make this Isaac's fault. Don't give yourself another reason to be angry with him.'

'And if I do say no?' I asked, unsure whether I should ask such a potentially dangerous question or not. (I'd watched enough courtroom dramas to know that you should never ask a question that you don't already know the answer to.) 'What then? What will you do?'

She thought about it. I knew what I expected her to say, because she was angry with me and would want to assert herself. However, as always she surprised me. 'If you say no, I'll decline the offer,' she said. 'If you think I could live without you, you're crazy. Because I couldn't. So I'd say no, all right? Is that what you want to hear?'

I felt a rush of love for her and reached across the table to take her hand, which she whipped away from me in fury. One thing I never fully appreciated about Hitomi was her ability to tell the truth, regardless of the implications for herself. Anyone else in that situation would have said that she would have gone anyway, even if that were not so, and waited to see what my reaction would have been. But even in anger she said she wouldn't go without me.

'I'm sorry,' I said. 'I'm being stupid. Of course it's a good opportunity. Of course you should go. We should go.'

She perked up and smiled faintly. There was a tear in the corner of her eye which she was blinking back but she failed and it suddenly cascaded down her cheek in a quick dart. She wiped it away with the back of her hand, annoyed with herself showing emotion now. 'So I can tell them yes?' she asked. 'I'll tell them we're going?'

I sighed and nodded. 'Tell them yes,' I said. 'But in a year's time, if we don't like it there, we can come back here, yes?'

'Absolutely,' she said. She looked delighted as we continued to talk about our plans for the rest of the evening, and even though I was sure that I was right in agreeing to go, there was something nagging at the back of my mind which didn't augur well. Unlike when I had first gone to Japan from London, or when I had left Tokyo for Paris in search of Hitomi, I was not convinced that we were doing the right thing. Somewhere I felt that this was not going to be as good a move as the others had been. I had little choice but to dismiss these thoughts as ridiculous and soon entered into her enthusiastic planning.

We spent the winter in New York, staying in an apartment on East 16th Street, near Union Square. The university rented it to us at a cheap price. It was convenient for Hitomi's work but I didn't like it much. It was quite small for one thing and I couldn't sleep with the sounds of cars and sirens going off relentlessly below. It was much smaller than our Parisian apartment had been and I found myself going a little stir crazy with the lack of space. We had placed most of our belongings in storage for our year away but had planned on shipping some of them to Colorado after Christmas, since we would be there for the best part of a year. Although I didn't tell my wife, I spent most of our twelve weeks in the Big Apple, counting down the days in my head until we could leave the big city behind and head westwards.

Hitomi, on the other hand, took to New York like a fish to water. She made friends quickly at the university; the teacher-exchange programme had apparently seen the department where she was working sending one of their most unpopular members across the world to the Sorbonne and her new colleagues had welcomed her with open arms. I was at something of a loss, however, for I was effectively unemployable due to the short-term status of my stay in the city. I found myself spending a lot of time in the cinemas and riding the subways. I saw every exhibition, painting and artefact in the Guggenheim, the Museum of Modern Art and the Whitney. I was seeing less and less of Hitomi as her work took up most of her time and began to feel homesick for Paris. I phoned Annette and Luc from time to time and the sound of their voices always made we want to return there. I began to realise that that was my true home, more than London, more than Japan and definitely more than New York. Despite the fact that I had been a near constant traveller my whole adult life, for the first time I felt displaced.

Although twelve weeks can pass quickly when one is settled, those twelve went by slowly for me, and as Christmas approached I found myself in a hotel bar near Central Park at three in the afternoon on Fifth Avenue and 88th Street with nothing to do. I was feeling lonely and depressed; over the previous three days I'd seen Hitomi for a total of one hour, having been asleep on two consecutive nights when she'd returned home. We seemed to be communicating through notes left by the side of the bed. We hadn't made love in a week and I could feel her enthusiasm for her new friends and challenges momentarily taking her away from me. It was stupid, but I was jealous. I'd spent an hour or so that afternoon in the International Center of Photography on 94th Street where there was an exhibition of Japanese photography from the war which I had read a good review of and which I'd wanted to see. There'd been some sort of accident that morning, however, and the main exhibition room upstairs was closed; instead I spent some time looking at the photographs on display in the ground-floor room and even considered buying some prints from the small shop in the lobby but decided against it and was walking back down Fifth Avenue considering a stroll through Central Park on my right when I saw the hotel and decided to step in out of the cold. It had started snowing and the air was as frosty as anything I had ever felt. I could feel my ears and cheeks begin to burn with the cold and resolved to buy a hat with earflaps later on, even though I hate hats.

I saw the bar on the left-hand side as I entered the hotel and stepped inside. It was quite small and most of the tables were empty. I chose a booth at the end by the window and took my coat off, rubbing my hands together quickly to bring the blood back. The bartender – over six feet tall and perfectly sculpted, obviously either a struggling actor, model or hyphenate – came over with a bowl of cashew nuts and I ordered a beer, which he brought presently in a tall, unusual glass which I liked drinking from. I felt an unnatural urge to steal it.

I was about to reach for the inside pocket of my coat to retrieve the book I was reading at the time when I noticed a woman enter the bar. It wasn't her beauty that made me notice her – although she was extremely attractive – but the fact that she wore a pair of the blackest glasses I had ever seen and a scarlet coat. Looking like a heroine out of an old Joan Crawford movie, or maybe Audrey Hepburn in *Breakfast at Tiffany's*, she walked straight to the bar and muttered something quickly to the bartender before taking the booth a few seats down from me and pulling out a cigarette. I glanced at her as she took her glasses off and when she caught me staring she gave me a bug-eyed look of irritation and I turned away quickly. What looked like an Irish coffee arrived for her and she paid immediately, which suggested that she wasn't going to be there very long. No tab.

I started to read my book but something about the woman had captured my attention and I found myself unable to concentrate. When I dared to look back again, some ten minutes later, I noticed that she was reading too and to my surprise, she was reading *The Sailor Who Fell From Grace With The Sea*, the same novel I had been reading on the evening in Paris when Hitomi had decided that we should go to London to visit Isaac. I thought about this coincidence and felt an urge to speak to the woman, as if it had been pre-ordained that I should. She was engrossed in the novel now and didn't notice as I stole furtive looks in her direction but the jacket of the book – which was dominated by the large brown spying eye of a Japanese boy – seemed to be winking at me and before I could talk myself out of it, I stood up and walked towards her table, leaving my drink behind me to prove I wasn't going to bother her for long, and waited there for a moment, wishing I had decided on my opening gambit earlier, before she looked up at me casually.

'Yes?' she said in a dry voice. 'Can I help you?'

'I'm sorry to bother you,' I said. 'I was just . . . sitting over there,' I muttered, indicating the other seat. 'I noticed what you were reading and felt like I should speak to you. I read it myself recently. I liked it very much.'

She thought about this for a moment, obviously deciding whether she should dismiss me out of hand or humour me a little. 'I read it when I was a girl,' she said eventually. 'I wanted to read it again.' There was an awkward silence as we tried to decide what was the best thing for us to do now. Happily, she solved it. Her sudden friendliness surprised me; she had sized me up in a moment and decided I wasn't a threat. (I wasn't sure whether to take this as a compliment or an insult.) 'Would you like to join me?' she asked, nodding towards the seat opposite her. 'Mr . . . ?'

'Cody,' I said. 'William Cody.'

She frowned, as if considering this name. 'Buffalo Bill, right?' she asked as I retrieved my drink, sat down and, unwilling to go into the details, laughed.

'Coincidence,' I said. 'I get that a lot.'

'Do you know who I am?' she asked suddenly, which surprised me. I shook my head and she seemed surprised. 'You don't? You're not just saying that?'

I laughed nervously. I'm sorry,' I said, staring at her face, wondering whether she was a movie star perhaps, or a chat-show host. 'Should I?'

She shook her head quickly as if she didn't know why she had asked the question in the first place and shrugged her shoulders. 'Of course not,' she replied. 'Why should you indeed? We've only just met.'

There was a pause and I waited for her to tell me, but no name was forthcoming. 'So who are you then?' I asked her finally. 'Or am I supposed to guess?'

'No, you don't have to guess,' she said. 'My name is Eleanor Nightingale.'

'Pleased to meet you,' I said, reaching across to shake

360

her hand. She was a little older than me, perhaps in her early thirties, and very beautiful. She kept her head turned away from the bar and the other couples so that only I could really see her. Her name meant nothing to me. 'I only came over because I thought it was a coincidence, you see,' I explained. 'I lived in Japan for a couple of years, you see.'

'Really?' she said. 'I've never been there. I'd love to go. What part did you live in?'

'Kyoto. But I travelled a bit as well. I spent some time in the south of the country, around Nagasaki. And I started off in Tokyo, of course. But mostly Kyoto.'

'I was in Singapore about six months ago,' she said. 'But that's the closest I've ever been to Japan. Is your wife Japanese?'

I was a little taken aback by the question but she smiled sweetly and nodded towards my hand which was holding my glass as I drank from it; the gleam of the thin golden wedding band caught my eye. To my surprise, I found myself regretting the fact that she had seen it. 'Yes,' I said after only the slightest pause. 'Yes, we met in Kyoto. She was born there. Are you married?'

'Not any more,' she said, looking away and exhaling quickly. 'Not since yesterday. You obviously don't read the tabloids.'

'I'm sorry,' I said, feeling it was the appropriate re-mark, and referring to the divorce and not the comment about my reading habits, which confused me.

'Don't be sorry,' she said quickly, in a tone which made me think that her next two words would not be the truth. 'I'm not. So where's your wife, Mr Buffalo Bill? What are you doing sitting in a hotel bar at three o'clock in the afternoon?'

I laughed. 'She's working, I guess,' I said. 'She's a

language professor at New York University. We're just here on an exchange programme, only for another two weeks actually. Then we're going to Colorado for nine months before going home.'

'To Japan?'

'Paris, actually. We live in Paris.'

'World traveller,' she said appreciatively. 'Quite the jet-setter.'

I laughed and could feel myself blushing. 'Not really,' I said. 'Paris is home, I think. It's just that Hitomi got this opportunity to come here for a year, to the States I mean, and it seemed too good a chance to pass up.'

'Hitomi's your wife?' I nodded. 'And what do you do then? Are you a language professor too? Is that how you met?'

'I'm a writer,' I said. 'A journalist anyway. I've written a couple of travel books, that's all.'

'Anything I might have heard of?' I gave her their names. 'Sorry,' she said.

'Don't worry,' I said. 'They weren't exactly bestsellers, but I do okay.'

She nodded. 'You know,' she said after a moment, tapping the top of her book with her finger. 'He killed himself when he was only forty-five. Completed what he thought was his best work, his life's work, and then committed *seppuku*.' She was referring to the book's author.

'Yes, I've seen his grave,' I said, lying for some reason, for not only had I never seen his grave, but I didn't even know where he was buried. He could have been cremated or buried at sea for all I knew. I dreaded her asking me further questions about it but fortunately, she didn't seem interested in those details.

'It's a strange thing to do, isn't it?' she said. 'Most people who kill themselves do it because they feel like they've failed at something. That they've got nothing to feel proud of themselves for. Mishima did it for the opposite reason. He did it because he knew he'd succeeded. He'd written his books, he'd said what he wanted to say. And there was nothing left to live for. What do you think of that, Mr Cody?'

I was unsure. She was staring directly at me and I felt that my answer was important in some way. 'I think it's a stupid thing to do,' I said. 'He was young, he had a lot to write about yet. A lot to say. I couldn't do that. Maybe he should have just stopped writing books and started living instead.'

'But then you just write travel books,' she pointed out. 'It's hardly the same thing, is it?'

'No, I suppose not,' I said. I felt unsettled, even slightly insulted, but drawn to her nonetheless. From the day that Hitomi and I had met I had never questioned my devotion to her. I had loved her from the start and, although during our separation I had slept with other women, I had never considered myself unfaithful for such events had been merely physical actions, not mental, not emotional. Perhaps that's an easy get-out for me, but it's how I felt. For when we were together, I had never been unfaithful and never planned on being. But then I had never found myself as drawn to any woman in the way Hitomi drew me; and although we had just met, I knew that I was desperately attracted to Eleanor Nightingale.

'I wish my husband had killed himself,' she said. 'It would have been easier for all of us. He's quite well known, you see. Very rich. Likes to think of himself as a philanthropist but he's just an attention-seeking, publicity-hungry bastard, that's all. We divorced yesterday and he's not been kind to me.'

'I'm sorry to hear that,' I said.

'Don't be too sorry,' she said with a laugh. 'It's not like he's left me destitute or anything. I mean I've got more money than I'll ever know what to do with. It's just the way he treated me that makes me . . . makes me . . .' Her lip curled slightly and her fist clenched. She stubbed out her cigarette in the ashtray and she stared at me fiercely, reaching across and taking my hand. 'Do you know why he left me?' she asked. I shook my head. She thought for a moment, deciding whether to tell me or not. 'He left me because our sex life was unsatisfactory.'

'Really,' I said, surprised by her candour and unsure how to deal with it. 'That's a shame.'

'Isn't it though,' she muttered in a cold voice. 'We were married for two years and he tells me I never satisfied him. That's a shame too, isn't it?' I blinked; I didn't know what the correct answer was, nor how to answer truthfully.

'Maybe you're better off without him,' I tried.

She laughed. 'I loved him more than I loved my own life,' she said, smiling. 'Why am I telling you this? I don't even know you. There were things he wanted me to do,' she continued immediately, ignoring her own question. 'Things I wouldn't do. I told him why. I have things in my past that make me . . . stop cold, Mr Buffalo Bill. Do you know what that's like? Do you? To stop cold?'

I shrugged and thought better of it, shaking my head instead. 'No,' I said simply. 'No I don't.'

'I told him what those things were, you see. I opened my heart to him like I have never opened my heart to a man before and because of that, he left me. Well then.

364

He's a lovely man, clearly. He thinks he's this great universal character, a unique and beautiful fucking snowflake. He's nothing like that really. He's a cold man. He has ice in his veins. I think he must have been dreadfully hurt as a boy to treat people like he treats them. He's also a very stupid man.'

'Sounds like you're better off without him then,' I said, employing cliché to atone for my inability to help her. I couldn't stop staring at her, despite what she was telling me. The pink flush in her cheeks aroused me. I wanted to take her hand and tell her that it would all be okay in the end.

'Yes but I love him. So how stupid is that. And that was several months ago,' she said. 'He's barely spoken to me since, except through lawyers. He's left me feeling like only half a woman. He's left me feeling . . . filthy,' she said, the word coming from deep within her, her tone descending octaves as she spat it out. 'I hate him. He's an emotional retard. I'll never love anyone like him again.' Silence descended on us for several minutes. She lit another cigarette and drew on it heavily; I could almost hear the nicotine entering her lungs. 'How old are you, Mr Buffalo Bill?' she asked eventually, and I told her: twenty-eight. 'And when did you say you're leaving New York?'

'About two weeks,' I said, swallowing nervously. 'Less than, in fact.'

She nodded. 'All right,' she said in a steady voice. 'I have a room upstairs. Do you want to fuck me?' The line came out of her mouth awkwardly, but she held her slightly embarrassed gaze to mine after she had said it. She meant what she had said, I knew. And she meant it the way she had said it. It was a clear offer. No conversation, no flirting, just a simple offer. 'Yes or no,' she said bluntly as she waited for my answer. 'I don't much care either way. Just give me a straight answer.'

'Yes,' I said.

Nate Salsbury sat waiting for my great-grandfather in the bar of the Marchfield Hotel, near Central Park in New York City, tapping his fingers restlessly against the tablecloth. He had barely slept the night before and couldn't resist yawning, even as the waiter approached him and asked him whether he would like a drink while he was waiting. He asked for a beer, hoping that it would keep him lively. Although he had met with Bill on a number of occasions already, he knew that this was the day when they would decide once and for all whether the wild west show would come into operation. The outcome of this meeting was far more important for Nate than it was for my great-grandfather; at this time, early in 1882, the melodramas in which Bill appeared were continuing to be the most popular entertainments in the city. He had no specific need to dissociate himself from them and begin a new venture, particularly one which would involve a substantial amount of money on his part with no guarantee of success. Nate had fewer options. He had blown his inheritance, such as it had been, on frivolity and had little to show for it. He did however have a good idea but needed a partner. Buffalo Bill, he believed, was the right man for such a role.

When Bill finally arrived, almost thirty minutes late, there was a spontaneous burst of applause from the other diners as he entered the room. He acknowledged them cheerfully and shouted that they would be welcome at *Another Scalp for Custer*, his latest play, any night of the week and twice on Wednesdays.

'Sorry I'm late,' he said, shaking Nate's hand briskly

366

as he quickly ordered a meal from the waitress without so much as looking at the menu. 'You should have ordered already.'

'That's all right,' replied Nate, just happy that he had shown up at all. 'I wanted to wait until you got here.'

'I'm ravenous,' said Bill. 'Been stoked up with Mary Jameson overnight. You know her?' He gave Nate a lecherous wink, suspecting that such talk would embarrass the younger man, who was prone to bouts of piety and self-denial.

'The actress,' said Nate with uncertainty.

'The very same. Louisa's been here for the last month and it's been damn hard to get away from her. Anyway, she went back to St Louis yesterday for a week's holiday and I saw my opportunity.'

Nate laughed nervously. 'Speaking of opportunities . . .' he began, but Bill cut him off with an angry shake of the head.

'Oh don't start that nonsense,' he said. 'Let's at least wait until we have a bit of a food inside us before we talk business. That won't kill you, will it? I've built up quite the appetite over the last twenty-four hours, let me tell you. What about you anyway? Haven't you got a girl somewhere? A young man like you ought to have a girl. What's the matter with you anyway?'

'There is nothing the matter with me,' said Nate in a slightly offended tone. 'I prefer not to discuss matters of a personal nature, that's all. I thought we were here to discuss business.'

'All right, damn you,' said Bill cheerfully. 'Go on then. If you can't speak civil for five minutes then let's have it. What have you got for me?'

Nate sat back and cleared his throat. He had prepared this speech carefully over the previous twenty-four hours while his prospective partner had been whoring around and wanted to make sure that it came out right. 'The wild west show as I envision it,' he began, 'would contain a number of different elements, all of which represent an aspect of life on the frontiers, a world which our audience has read about but has never actually seen.'

'They can see it every night at the theatre,' said Bill. 'Why, my plays are packed every night of the week and you must have seen the number of imitators we've inspired. They're everywhere. Not as successful, mind you.'

'Yes, they can see it on the stage,' agreed Nate. 'But those performances last for just an hour and take place in a confined space. What we can do is bring them to a wider audience, literally. And those things which you simulate on the stage, why we can perform them for real.' Bill nodded. They had discussed the basics of the shows before and agreed to them; the question came down to whether there was an audience for such a thing or not. 'The important thing is,' continued Nate, 'to ensure that everything is as real as possible. So we have cowboys, sheriffs, members of Indian tribes, buffaloes, horses, all sorts of animals. We make sure that each plays the role they do in the west and perform in big arenas where thousands can come to see it.'

'And who plays the roles?' asked Bill. 'Are you looking for actors to play them?'

Nate shook his head. 'For the cowboys, no,' he said. We can find real cowboys who want to earn some money and pay them to entertain. Why, you and Texas Jack Omohundro made a good bash of becoming actors, didn't you, and these men wouldn't even have to be acting. They just have to do what they do anyway.

Of course, they have to be good riders and quick draws. Otherwise they're of no use to us.'

'And the Indians,' asked Bill, already anticipating the answer. 'Who should play them?'

'That's where we need the actors. If we need, say, thirty Indians, we hire more cowboys and perhaps some actors, paint and feather them like the Cheyenne savages, and the crowd will lap it up. Those who are actors can be trained to shoot. You could take charge of that, if you wanted.'

Bill pressed his beard close to his chin and thought about it. He sighed heavily, lost in concentration as he decided what decision was the correct one, while Nate Salsbury waited nervously for an answer. 'It's a good plan,' he said eventually, allowing the other man to sigh in relief. 'But there's one flaw.'

'Which is?'

'The nature of the drama. When I first came to New York and started performing on the stage, the whole point of the thing was that it was to be a dramatic production. Nobody expected it to be real. The audience sat quietly, we came on in the spotlights ,and pretended they weren't there, held imaginary fights and after I'd killed half the people in the company, the curtains came down and everyone got up again to take their curtain calls.'

'Well of course,' said Nate, unsure what my great-grandfather was getting at. 'What else would they expect from a play?'

'Yes, but this isn't a play that you're suggesting, is it?' asked Bill. 'You're talking about a more real entertainment than that. A circus of sorts. You want to show what the west is actually like, naturally in a dramatic context, but outside of a theatre. When you

369

take it off the stage you owe the audience a little more validity.'

Nate nodded. 'All right,' he said. 'But I don't understand. What are you getting at?'

'I think we should hire real Indians to be part of this thing. I think we should approach a tribe of Indians, go to the leader and offer them money to come in on it.'

Nate laughed. This had been his original intention but he had dismissed it as impossible. 'They'd never agree to it,' he said. 'The wars are still going on. You can't walk into a conflict like that and just ask a tribe to give it up and join a circus like this. They'd never agree to it,' he repeated

'Of course they would,' said Bill. 'You think the wars are continuing? You're wrong, my friend. They're over to all intents and purposes. Sure, there might be some skirmishes still breaking out here and there and the Indians may be refusing to move off their land into reservations, but they stand no chance of winning. They're outnumbered a hundred to one. It's just a matter of wills at this stage. Everyone's standing their ground. Sooner or later they'll do what they're told and a few years from then they'll just integrate into our own society. It's inevitable. The majority will always win. I guarantee you that if we were to find the right Indian, if we can advertise that the right Indian is part of this thing, then we can make it the most successful show ever seen anywhere.'

'And who would that be?' asked Nate. 'It would have to be someone famous.'

'Who's the star of the show?' asked Bill quietly, smiling to himself, aware of what the answer had to be.

'Well you are,' he replied. 'It's got to be Buffalo Bill's Wild West Show, after all. It's the name that brings in the crowds.'

'Why?'

Nate raised an eyebrow quizzically. 'Why what?' he asked.

'Why does my name bring in the crowds? What's special about it?'

'Because it's famous,' came the answer. 'You're famous. You're a celebrity.'

'That's it, don't you see?' said Bill. 'We need an Indian of the same calibre. Someone who is detested as much as I am loved but whose name is as well known. Someone inextricably linked to me.' He paused for dramatic effect. 'Any suggestions?' he asked.

Nate laughed. 'The only one I can think of who matches your description is Sitting Bull,' he said. 'The people hate him for his part in the death of General Custer and you've represented him in your plays. But obviously you'd never think of casting him?'

'Wouldn't I?'

Nate Salsbury stared at my great-grandfather as if he was mad. 'You've got to be kidding me,' he said. 'He'd never agree to it for a start. And anyway I thought you detested him?'

Bill's eyes opened wide as the food finally arrived and he lifted his knife and fork to begin, but not before pointing the tip of the former at his companion carefully. 'Don't ever underestimate what a man will do for money,' he said. 'Or for a little extra publicity. Principles, war, ideology . . . these things mean nothing any more. Celebrity . . . now that's where the future lies, my friend. Buffalo Bill and Sitting Bull together in the Wild West Show. What do you think, Nate? Do you think people would pay money to see that?'

Nate smiled. He took this as a yes.

It was midsummer's night and the Regis-Roc Circus was preparing for its largest annual show. Every year on that evening they brought all their entertainers together for an extravaganza. This year it was being held in Cornwall and, despite the fact that ticket prices were increased by twenty per cent on the night, they had sold out the Big Top within hours. The Rose trapeze group had prepared one of its more difficult routines, during which Ellen Rose would perform a double somersault in mid-air before being caught by her ankles by Joseph Craven as he flew past on the trapeze before she fell. They had practised it over and over again with the aid of a net and it always went perfectly. Although there were the usual nerves before the performance, there was a general feeling that it would be a success.

Joseph Craven sat in his dressing room, rubbing liniment on his hands as he always did before a show and looked at his face in the mirror. He was growing older. His skin had grown a little sallow and his eyes appeared to be sunken into the back of his head, although that might have been partly due to the harshness of the Broadway-style arc of golden bulbs which surrounded his dressing-table mirror. He scraped his dark hair back from his forehead with a little oil but tonight he could see the scalp beneath it for it was thinning rapidly. He cursed and looked away, not wanting to see his reflection any more. As he did so, he caught sight of a couple of the young men who worked in the circus sitting outside on the grass in the sunshine, smoking cigarettes. He recognised one of them as David Bay, the teenage son of the chief lion tamer, who helped assemble and disassemble the circus as it moved from town to town. With him was another one of the construction lads, whose name he couldn't recall, but Craven watched them enviously as they lay back, chatting casually. David took his shirt off in the sunshine and stretched back with his palms flat on the grass, his eyes closing as he faced up to the sun, and Craven could see the muscular definition of his physique, strong from a combination of hard work and youth. The other boy made some comment and David sat up straight, collapsing in easy laughter, reaching out to grab the ankle of a passing girl who kicked back at him playfully. He squinted at her, his golden curls catching the light and he merely shrugged and laughed, as if it was all such an easy game. Craven shook his head and looked back in the mirror without meaning to and caught sight of the thin, ageing man in a leotard and white make-up who stared back at him and barely recognised himself. His heart sank and he sighed heavily, switching out the lights and nodding slowly as he determined on his plans for the night.

The audience was noisy as the trapeze group entered the Big Top; they had already been entertained by the lions, the clowns, a troupe of fire-eaters, and a man who threw knives at his wife for a living while she spun around in circles on a board to which she was attached. Danger had been in the air all night but no trouble had resulted. The audience wanted more of the same and the trapeze artists were there to give it to them.

'As you can see, ladies and gentlemen,' announced the ringmaster as the troupe ascended the ladders to their positions at the top of the tent. 'The Regis-Roc trapeze artists use no net during their performances. Theirs is an act of the purest bravery and danger! For this reason we must ask you to remain perfectly silent during their routine as even the slightest noise can disturb the concentration leading to calamity . . . *and certain death*!' he roared with increasing volume and melodrama. Some of the children in the audience snickered but in general the noise began to subside as the troupe began their act, although they could rarely hear anything from below, so intent were they on remaining focused on what they were doing.

Joseph Craven watched the beautiful Ellen Rose as she danced across the tightrope from one side of the Big Top to the other, receiving hearty applause from the audience which she acknowledged with a regal wave of her hand. Craven could feel his lips begin to go dry as he wondered whether he dared continue with his plans, and how much trouble he would find himself in because of them. He put those thoughts out of his mind for a few moments as he jumped aboard the trapeze and performed some manoeuvres with other members of the troupe but eventually the grand finale arrived. The initial theatrics began and he waited, poised on a small step, holding on to the trapeze with one hand as he gripped a pole with the other, waiting for the moment when he knew he should sail forth to catch Ellen Rose, the girl who had been teasing him for months, the girl who had rejected his advances, preferring to mingle with the young men of the circus rather than with him. He felt his bile rise inside his chest and watched as she slipped forward to begin her final movement and then as she soared across before letting go in order to perform the double somersault, he began the countdown in his head. From the moment she left her platform he was to count 'one . . . two . . . three' and then jump forward. He watched, waiting for the cue.

'One . . .' he thought in his head instinctively. 'Two . . . three . . .' And at that moment, when he should have released himself from the platform and sailed forward to scoop her out of mid-air and allow them both to swing upside down over the heads of the gasping audience below he did the unthinkable. He counted to four.

When, a second too late, his hands reached out to grasp the familiar ankles of Ellen Rose, they were gone and he found himself clutching at air instead. The crowd screamed as Ellen fell.

And so, lost and feeling alone in New York, I cheated on Hitomi for the only time during our marriage. Leaving the hotel later that afternoon, the scent of a virtual stranger still lingering around my body, her taste in my mouth, the memory of her fingers still pressing against my skin, I tried to feel guilty and yet somehow I failed. There had been no emotion there, no love, just fucking, that was all, and although it was wrong, I could not muster the guilt. I went straight home, however, and took a long, hot shower, washing her touch and feel away from my skin, sure that Hitomi would recognise another woman on me the moment she laid eyes on me, but she did not and I never confessed my sin. Somehow, not confessing it feels worse to me now than having done it in the first place.

I was not sorry to leave New York, therefore, and determined that our longer stay in Colorado would be a better one. Hitomi did not like the university there as much as she had the one in the Big Apple, but I found the state to be strangely liberating. Despite the sprawl of the urban centres, there were places in Colorado which were peaceful and filled with nature, and we took walks there on weekends, holding hands as we scaled mountains together or cycled across prairie ranges. The distance which had come between us in New York did not exist there and we grew close again without having to state that in words.

We lived in a university apartment in Denver and I was lucky to get a job quickly on *The Denver Examiner*, writing editorial columns on international affairs. I began to collect and edit my interviews and profiles over the years and planned on presenting them to a French publisher (where they had originally been published and where I had gained some degree of celebrity) for a possible collection. We were tied to the state from January to August but soon agreed that we would stay for at least a year and decide then where we should go next.

A couple of weeks after arriving there, I was lounging around our living room on a Sunday morning, reading the newspaper, when Hitomi suggested a drive. 'Where to?' I asked, glancing outside at the weather. It was a warm, heavy day and I did not much care for the idea of travelling too far.

'It's a surprise,' she said, winking flirtatiously at me as she settled a Denver Broncos baseball cap on her head. 'Trust me.'

I agreed to do so and shortly afterwards we were driving out of Denver and towards the town of Golden, where I had not been before. I leaned one arm out the window of the passenger seat as Hitomi drove and drank from a bottle of water. I could feel the sun burning on to my neck and turned my collar up to protect it.

We reached Lookout Mountain about an hour later

and as we drove towards it, I realised where Hitomi was taking me and felt a sharp stab of pain in my chest. Of course I had known how close we were to it and naturally I had planned on visiting at some point, but either the opportunity had not yet presented itself or I was simply afraid to go there, I'm not sure which. Either way, Hitomi had taken the matter into her own hands and we said very little as we parked the car on the road at the bottom of the mountain and slowly started to climb.

My great-grandfather is buried near the top of Lookout Mountain in a tomb which was blasted from the rocks. Approaching it, I felt an extraordinary sense of tension, combined with a desire to see Isaac, and when we finally reached it and I looked down at the letters and dates carved ornately into the stone, it seemed as if my entire life had been leading towards this mountain.

'You don't mind?' asked Hitomi, releasing my hand now in order to wrap an arm around my waist, linking us together. 'I would have said earlier where we were going but—'

'I don't mind,' I reassured her, interrupting quickly. 'I had to come here at some point.' I nodded and wanted to say more but felt myself getting lost in my thoughts, memories of childhood events and Isaac's stories returning to haunt me.

'How does it feel?' she asked finally, looking around at the incredible scenery surrounding us, to which I was quite immune.

'It feels like I should have brought Isaac here,' I said. 'He'll never make it, you know. He's too old now. Strange, though, to base your life around your relationship to someone and never come to visit them, if that's what this is.' I knelt down and placed my hand on the dusty earth and a chill ran through me. 'I know every event of this man's life,' I said, looking up at my wife. 'Or think I do anyway. I know what Isaac told me. Who knows how much of it is true and how much of it is false?'

'Does it matter?'

'Probably not,' I said. 'But it still feels odd to see your own name on a tombstone. It's like something out of *A Christmas Carol*.'

'It's not your name,' she said quickly, for Hitomi no longer liked to speak of the possibility of our deaths. 'It's his.'

'We share it,' I muttered.

'It's his,' she insisted. There was a long silence between us which was only broken when she suggested taking a photograph of me here, that we might send it to my father as a souvenir.

'I don't think so,' I said, shaking my head. 'That doesn't seem right somehow.'

'But he'll want to know,' she said, surprised by my reluctance.

'Well I'll write to him. Or phone him. I'll let him know we were here. But I don't want any photographs. We don't need that. Lookout Mountain,' I said, shaking my head as I turned around to look at the canyons below. 'Do you think it's fate that's brought us here?'

'No, I think it was my job,' she said in a matter-of-fact tone and I couldn't help but give a quick laugh.

'I don't know,' I said. 'It just seems that being here was meant to be. That I should always have come here at some point. Try to bury my obsessions along with Isaac's. Does that make sense?' I asked, not waiting for an answer before adding, 'Something's going to happen here, I think. I can feel it'

'You're just feeling strange being up here at last,' she replied, taking me by the arm and leading me back down the mountain. 'Being so close to him. It's an odd moment. There's no fate bringing us here.'

At the time I nodded in agreement for Hitomi, having managed to arrive in and depart from England without dying, had now become a big believer that we made our own fates and destinies, but inside I wasn't so sure. I liked Colorado – not nearly as much as I liked Japan or Paris – but I liked it nonetheless. And yet despite that, I couldn't wipe away my nagging fear of the place. Somehow I felt that I, William Cody, should be living as far away from Lookout Mountain as possible.

Tatanka Iyotake, the Sioux leader better known as Sitting Bull, waited patiently in his tent for Buffalo Bill to appear. He was dressed in ornate Indian costuming, the type of lavish outfit which he had only worn once or twice in his life so far. His face had been decorated by a professional make-up artist. A sparkling clean white head-dress sat atop his dark hair, stretching to the ground behind him; he wore a series of necklaces and a brightly coloured sash. Attached to his side was a tomahawk with a blunt blade. Staring at himself in the mirror, he barely recognised the warrior of old; all he could see now was a clown.

Sitting Bull had spent a couple of years in a federal jail in Dakota but upon his release in 1883 was approached by Buffalo Bill to join his new wild west show. The Hunkpapa leader had been initially sceptical of the offer, despite the financial rewards it would give him – not to mention the freedom of movement such a position could offer him and his people, who otherwise would be forced to stay within their reservations – but had agreed to meet with his old enemy to discuss the plan.

'You surprise me, asking for my help,' he said as the two men sat alone in Sitting Bull's reservation, having agreed to keep this meeting between themselves. 'It was not so long ago that you would have killed me if you could.'

'That was during the war,' said my great-grandfather nonchalantly. 'Times are different now.'

'Certainly they are,' replied Sitting Bull. 'You can travel where you want. We are kept within this reservation after having spent centuries roaming where we wished.' Bill shrugged and looked away. He had determined on his way to the meeting that he would not become involved in a political discussion. They had both fought for their beliefs during the plains wars and had both lost people they had loved. There seemed little point in raking over old ground. 'Your General Custer,' continued the Sioux leader after a suitable pause. 'You blamed me for his death, am I right?'

'You killed him,' acknowledged Bill. 'Or your people did anyway. At Little Big Horn.'

'He was trying to kill us. He was the worst killer I ever knew.'

'He was a friend of mine,' said Bill. 'I only did—'

'What interests me, you see,' said Sitting Bull quietly, raising a hand to silence the other man, 'is how passionate you once were about destroying the Sioux and how you now want to involve us in your productions. I have read about the stage shows you have performed. At the climax you end up scalping me, is this true?'

'It's a play,' said Bill, unwilling to back down. 'That's

380

all it is. It's entertainment for the masses. It's not supposed to be a history lesson.'

'Just as well. Still, I find it hard to believe that you can set those differences aside now. I don't trust you, Mr Cody,' he added, unwilling to flatter my great-grandfather by addressing him by his nickname.

'Sitting Bull,' said Bill, leaning forward with a sigh. 'I'm not trying to pretend that there have not been differences between us in the past. Of course there have. But I'm not an army officer now. Actually, I never really was. I'm an entertainer. I'm a showman. That's all. There's an opportunity for everyone to get something from all the trouble of the past. You, me, your people, mine.'

'When you say get something, you mean profit, yes?'

'Yes,' replied Bill without a trace of apology in his voice. 'And what's wrong with making a little profit? My God, it's the nineteenth century! What would you have us do? Settle down and raise families in the same place forever while you and your people are left to rot here? Or go out and see the world and make our fortunes while we're at it. Make no mistake, my friend. I'm not just offering you a job and money. I'm offering you your freedom.'

Sitting Bull sat back and smiled, shaking his head sadly. Eventually he spoke. 'It's a strange world,' he said, 'when a self-confessed showman has the right to offer freedom to an entire race of people. Is that what your war was fought for?'

Bill smiled. 'It's the American way,' he said.

Persuading Sitting Bull had not been too difficult as the Sioux leader was wise enough to recognise a way out of his predicament when he saw it; persuading the government to allow him to join, however, was another matter. The secretary of the interior initially refused to let the Sioux leave their reservation, stating that the Indians had been placed in reservations in order to lead civilised and ordered lives. The concept of a tribe touring the country with actors and army veterans performing theatrics struck him as humiliating and potentially dangerous for the people of those states. It took some time, but through discussions with various generals and commissioners, my great-grandfather finally managed to persuade the government that allowing Sitting Bull and a representative group of his people to tour with him, would ease relations between the two cultures, showing the former enemy as a man now and not a terrifying presence in the newspapers.

And as he sat there waiting, Sitting Bull found it slightly ironic that his first performance with the wild west show should be in Buffalo, New York, the name-sake town of the man who had brought him to this point.

'Are you ready, Chief?' asked Nate Salsbury, poking his head into the tent without announcing his presence first, a sign of disrespect which angered Sitting Bull. He considered remonstrating with his new co-employer but decided against it, standing up with a sigh and leaving the tent in order to mount his horse. Eight members of his family and four other members of the Lakota Sioux were awaiting him and he found himself barely able to look them in the eye as he took the lead in their parade and headed for the vast arena where the show was taking place.

Already it was two hours into the performance and the crowd were having an ecstatic time. They had started reasonably quietly with a series of horse riders performing stunts as they rode at high speed around the arena. The crowd gasped at their bravery, but this was a mere *hors d'oeuvre* for what was to come for shortly afterwards those actors playing the roles of Pony Express riders entered the fray – a job which Bill himself had done at a youthful age – and the riders began a sustained attack on what was intended to represent the Deadwood Mail Coach. Using blank bullets and choreographed fighting they managed to replicate the danger of such rides without anyone getting hurt and the increasingly bloodthirsty crowd loved it.

It was after this that the first Indians had appeared in the arena and Bill had observed from the sidelines how the crowd managed to release some of their tensions by booing and hissing at the two Indians engaged in a race – one on horseback and one on foot. Unknown to them, the Indian on horseback was a young man named Dennis Royce, a white man who had been made up to represent a tribal member, but who still lost the race by a neck to Lightning Speed, the acknowledged fastest Indian in America.

A display of marksmanship followed and the crowd roared their approval as their idol, Buffalo Bill Cody, took top honours against all comers. He even invited members of the audience to challenge him but none could match his eagle eye shots and clever stunts. He received his applause rapturously and reluctantly left their sights as Sitting Bull and his family entered the arena. The crowd went silent when he appeared for this had been the moment they had been waiting for. The Sioux leader's name had been infamous for many years by now, yet very few white men had ever seen him. Although there were perhaps a thousand spectators and only a dozen Indians there was a palpable air of tension and fear as he appeared before them. It had been agreed that neither Sitting Bull nor any of his relatives would perform stunts or any theatrical acts. Instead, they would merely trot around the arena slowly so that all could get an opportunity to see him.

'Take a look, ladies and gentlemen, boys and girls,' cried Bill into his megaphone, reading out the speech that he had written earlier. 'Sit back and stare in awe at the sight of the infamous Sioux leader. Chief Sitting Bull and his family, as they wander among you. Fear not, however, for the vanquished leader has been set free from his reservation purely for the purposes of entertaining you, the good people of Buffalo.' The crowd cheered when he mentioned the city name and by breaking their initial silence they found the courage to turn their attention to the Indians, shouting and screaming at them as they made their way around. Sitting Bull sat stoically on his horse, trying to remain focused on the route ahead of him as their hisses entered his mind, but some of his younger followers were not so calm and found themselves shaking their tomahawks at their tormentors, an action which merely led to a higher cacophony of abuse. 'Sitting Bull was the slayer of General George Armstrong Custer at the battle of Little Big Horn,' continued Bill, happy now to use his late friend's name if it improved the dramatic atmosphere, even though that sentence had not been strictly speaking accurate, 'but now he is tamed and unable to kill any more. Behold the vanquished brave!'

The crowd were torn between cheering for Bill and hissing at the Indians and, shortly afterwards when he had left the arena and returned to his tent, weaker for the experience, Sitting Bull received my great-grandfather sadly, reprimanding him for the things he had said within.

'You take the name of your dead friend lightly,' he said, the sound of the crowd still ringing in his ear. 'What kind of man are you anyway?'

'The kind who's making a living, Chief,' said Bill. 'And don't lecture me when you're making money out of this too. If you can auction off your dignity to the highest bidder, then don't criticise me for making a few dollars out of George Armstrong Custer.'

There was little he could say to this; he despised Bill but despised himself even more. The Indians had lost, it was as simple as that. Sitting Bull had no choices left. He could either resign himself to his fate in the reservations or make some money which he could distribute to his people as he wished. It was a small victory over his white tormentors; it lessened them both, but it was business, it was the way the country was turning. It was, as Bill had pointed out earlier, the new American way.

Chapter Eleven

A Perfect Stranger

Despite the initial tensions of their relationship, Sitting Bull and Buffalo Bill Cody eventually became closely allied to each other. As the wild west show toured across America, centring on the country's most important and industrialised cities – New York, Boston, Chicago – they both made their respective fortunes. My great-grandfather was not a thrifty man, however, and although he always managed to keep one step ahead of debt, he spent his income foolishly and quickly on unwise investments. His early career with both the Golden Rule Hotel and the town of Rome had proved how fickle he could be with his ideas and how easily his wealth could slip through his fingers. Even when he died in 1917, he had let several fortunes slip away and was far from a rich man. Sitting Bull, on the other hand, had a very different attitude to money. Although he had no personal interest or need for the stuff, he enjoyed earning it and as they toured the country would often undertake speaking engagements or personal appearances with various groups. The money he earned from this, combined with his income from the shows themselves, he distributed among the poor of the cities he visited. Whenever he saw begging children along the streets – children who generally stared at him with a mixture of terror and admiration – he would stop and pass out to them whatever dollars happened to be in his pocket. The leading lights behind the wild west shows were not the most financially gifted men of all time.

In 1885, a problem emerged when Gary 'Granite' Grayson, perhaps the most famous marksman at the time, and a member of Buffalo Bill's travelling troupe of performers, was himself the victim of a shooting. It was common knowledge that Grayson was conducting an affair with Paints Faces, one of the Indian women who performed in the show, but he was also considered a lech by most of the other women, many of whom had already spurned his advances. Paints Faces, however, had fallen in love with Grayson, whose reputation earned him third billing on the show cards after my great-grandfather and Sitting Bull, and when she became pregnant she hoped that he would marry her. He refused, however, and was challenged by Walks Across Streams, an ageing Indian who acted in the role of protector towards the girl. Despite Grayson's skill, he was not a brave man and while he excelled at shooting targets which could not shoot back, he had never been involved in a shoot-out with another man. Walks Across Streams recognised the younger man's insecurities and played on them, staring him out before the contest in order to achieve a psychological advantage and indeed, when the call came to shoot, Grayson's finger had barely pressed on his trigger before he fell to the ground dead.

Bill and Sitting Bull covered up the affair, for if it had become public knowledge that an Indian set free from a reservation in order to entertain the public had killed a white man, the repercussions for all could have been severe. Grayson's fame, however, made the story into quite a scandal which lent extra publicity to the show while leaving them one marksman short of a shooting gallery. My great-grandfather auditioned various people for the role but none were quite good enough; they each had a certain level of skill and proficiency which exceeded that of the average man, but that was not enough. The person to play the role had to be able to perform tricks and stunts and win the audience over on to his side.

In the end it was Sitting Bull who located a replacement. Early the previous year, while travelling through Minnesota with the show, the Sioux chief had watched a display of marksmanship given by a married couple, whose skills were quite exceptional. The husband in the team was a man named Frank Butler and he also acted as manager for their act, which had become quite popular across the state. Afterwards, they had been anxious to meet the famous Indian chief and the three had dined together privately, where Sitting Bull had complimented them on their skills.

'I'm just an amateur compared to her,' said Frank Butler, cocking his head in the direction of his wife, who laughed and blushed as her husband reached across to take her hand for a moment. 'Thought I was the best man in the county at shooting till I met her.'

'That's not true, Chief Sitting Bull,' replied Mrs Butler. 'Frank's taught me a lot since we've met. I was green before that.' She was a petite young woman of twenty-two, only five feet tall in height, with long, curly dark hair and a porcelain complexion. Her conversation was sparkling and witty and she was obviously devoted to her husband, qualities that Sitting Bull found intoxicating. He had lost a daughter himself only a year before and, while his grief and mourning had been private, it had caused him a great deal of pain. Although he had only just met Mrs Butler, he found himself attracted to her in a paternal way.

'If that is so, he taught you well,' replied the chief. 'Although you have a natural talent. I can see that in the way you shoot.'

She acknowledged the compliment with a graceful nod of the head. 'It's kind of you to say,' she said quietly. The conversation continued throughout the night and, while comparing tour dates afterwards, they realised they would often be not far from each other over the following couple of months and agreed to meet again. In the meantime, Sitting Bull and Mrs Butler began a friendly correspondence which continued whenever they were apart.

'What about the husband?' asked my great-grand-father when Sitting Bull proposed replacing 'Granite' Grayson with Mrs Butler. 'It's a crazy thing to have a woman marksman. She can't be anywhere near as talented as some of the men.'

'She could out-shoot you,' replied Sitting Bull in a calm voice. Bill had suggested that he himself take over from Grayson as he believed that no one was a match for him when it came to shooting and, although he was indeed a fine shot, the chief was only too well aware that pride was playing a part in that decision.

'Outshoot me?' he laughed derisively. 'I think not, my friend.'

'Invite her here then. Let her shoot with you. If you win, you win. If you lose, she gets the job. The husband is her business manager. He knows he's not as good as her. He'd be happy to see her in the limelight. They seem very well suited to each other.'

Bill shrugged and gave in. 'All right then, chief,' he said, laughing. 'If that's what you want, I guess you don't ask that much of me. You tell this Mrs Butler gal to get over here and we'll try her out, see what stuff she's made of. What's her first name anyway?'

'Annie,' replied Sitting Bull. 'In private she's known as Annie Butler, but her stage name is Oakley. That's what she shoots under.'

'Annie Oakley,' said Bill, nodding as he made a mental note of her name. 'Well get her over here and we'll see what she's made of.'

Annie Oakley – or Little Miss Sure Shot, as Sitting Bull had affectionately christened her – arrived the following lunchtime and most of the performers of the wild west show came out to see the shoot-out between their employer and this tiny woman who had arrived with a rifle under whose weight she looked like she might collapse at any time. No one gave her much chance of victory and treated the contest like an entertaining way to pass an hour, but the contestants took it seriously and paid little attention to their spectators as they fought, respectively, for their pride and employment.

Various targets were used, from stationary marksmen's targets to birds in the sky, and just over an hour after they had begun, a winner was declared. Of the twenty-five targets which they had aimed at, Bill had scored twenty-two, an exceptional score in anyone's book. Annie Oakley, however, had not missed a single one. Her perfect twenty-five had produced solid applause and respect in the audience and Bill, knowing he had but one chance to save his dignity, joined in that applause and congratulated her for all to hear.

'That's the finest display of marksmanship I've ever

seen,' he told her. 'Where did you learn to shoot like that anyway?'

Annie blushed and was stuck for an answer; she found Bill's reputation and fame slightly overwhelming and was embarrassed for having beaten him.

'Natural talent, Mr Cody, natural talent,' said Frank Butler, shaking his hand and hugging his wife. 'So what do you say? You want us to come work for you.'

'I think I'd be a fool to say no,' conceded Bill, realising that advertising an expert marksman was one thing but it was an even better publicity tool when that marksman happened to be a beautiful young woman. 'Can you start right away?'

'Absolutely.'

And so the deal was struck. Before much time had passed, Annie Oakley became probably the best-known marksman in America and joined Bill and Sitting Bull at the top of the billing. The relationship between the three was generally good, although my great-grandfather did find himself a little jealous sometimes at the skill of the younger woman which was, as her husband had suggested, a natural talent and something with which he himself could barely compete. He was also attracted to her which caused some tension for them, as Annie and Frank were a happy and solid couple. Louisa had long since left Bill and settled in Missouri; although they remained legally married, they almost never saw each other now and she devoted herself to bringing up their children who knew little of their father except what they saw in the newspapers or read about in the novels. Companionship was not difficult for Bill to find and he made himself free and easy with the women of the towns and cities that the wild west show visited; his celebrity always assured him the nightly affections of the local girls. Annie was different though, a beautiful young woman who he could not have. He never made any advances towards her either, recognising that he would be rebuffed, and although she was aware of his feelings, she never spoke of them with him. The shows and the touring continued; but now there was always a slight tension in the air which had not existed in the past.

Russell Rose knew that he was getting old. It was only a matter of time before he would have to retire from the trapeze-artist troupe which bore his name. Already, Bessie, his wife, was dropping hints that he should leave the tightrope-walking to younger men and simply manage and train the artists from now on. He was just putting off the inevitable, she told him. It was time to admit that the days of his being a showman and an entertainer were at an end.

'We don't have too many savings though,' he pointed out to Bessie over dinner one evening in their wagon. 'What will we live on?'

'You can still earn, Russell,' she said. 'You can still work, just like I do. Just not up high, that's all. Believe me, if you fall and kill yourself you'll be earning even less.' She bit her lip quickly, wishing she could take back the words; she couldn't believe she had said them but they were out before she realised what she was saying. 'You know what I mean,' she added quietly.

'There's no guarantee we'll be kept on though,' said Russell. 'We could be fired the minute I come down from the tightropes. Then what would we do? We have a lot of life left in us yet. We need to be able to survive. And then there's Ellen to think of.'

Bessie nodded and pressed a finger to his lips to

silence him just as their daughter entered the room. She had discarded her crutches recently but still walked with a pronounced limp and was prone to bending forward slightly as she walked, something which her doctor advised against as it only made her back problems worse.

'But it makes it feel better when I lean forward,' she pointed out irritably.

'For now it does,' he said. 'But those pains will pass if you reaccustom yourself to standing up straight. Otherwise there will be more pain like that further down the line.'

Ever since the accident, the Rose family had been struggling with tension. When Ellen had fallen from the trapeze to the ground below, there seemed little chance that she could possibly be alive. Russell had descended the ladder by shinning down the side of it, convinced that his daughter, his only child, was dead, terrified as he made his way to her side. He could barely hear the screams of the crowd or the people inexplicably charging from their seats and making for the exits, as if Ellen's fall would be followed by the Big Top tumbling about their ears. She lay quite calmly on the dusty ground, her body slightly contorted, her eyes and lips closed. Russell's first thought as he saw her there was that she was dead, but that she appeared to be simply sleeping. In fact, that was closer to the truth than he could have possibly imagined. Incredibly, her fall had not killed her, had not even paralysed her. She had damaged her spine of course and it was that injury which still caused her great pain. And she had broken both her legs, but the breaks had been clean and when she was treated and they were placed in plaster for a couple of months, the doctors announced that she would indeed be able to walk again, albeit without as much comfort or flexibility as she was used to. Of course she would never perform in the Big Top again; the fall had destroyed the one career she had ever dreamed of.

At first, Joseph Craven was blamed for mistiming the leap from the platform which led to his failure to catch Ellen, but when it became clear that her injuries, while serious, were not life threatening, many people began to apologise to him for making him a scapegoat. However, some months later, while making unwanted advances at the youngest daughter of the bearded lady, he had threatened to hurt her if she did not give in. *Just look what happened to Ellen Rose*, he hissed at her as he gripped her wrists and forced her lips to his. *Do you want something like that to happen to you?* The girl, who was unafraid of Craven, reported what he had said and the police were called in. Eventually he broke down and admitted what he had done and was arrested and jailed for attempted murder. His conviction, however, was of little comfort to Ellen Rose.

'I'm going for a walk,' she muttered as she walked past her parents that evening, aware of how they often stopped speaking when she appeared. 'I need my exercise.'

'Don't go far, dear,' said Bessie in a cheerful voice. 'You need your rest, remember. Early start tomorrow.'

Ellen grunted a response but disappeared into the night. The cold wind whipped into her eyes and she blamed it for the tears that sprung up there. Walking slowly along the road, wrapping her cardigan around her body as she felt her legs' pain begin to ease with the exercise, she wondered for the hundredth time why she had been the victim of such a crime. She hated seeing the circus performers now, for they reminded her of what she could never do again. The sound of the applause which rang through from the Big Top to the kitchen area where she worked with her mother made her skin crawl. She wanted her position back. Although she remained a beautiful young girl, she believed that her disability would mean that no man would fall in love with her. She would spend all her time in the circus now, peeling potatoes, boiling carrots, roasting beef. Before long she believed she would smell of animal fat and her skin and hair would be constantly greasy.

It was late now and her heart sank at the thought of the following day. The circus was moving to London for a very special performance and everyone was excited about it for it would be the most important and prestigious show of their lives. She dreaded it and wished it was over. Indeed, at times like this she wished her legs were strong enough that she could climb the ladder one last time to the top of the Big Top, so that she could grab the trapeze bar tightly with her hands and leap from her platform across the arena, letting go as she swung. It had been a miracle that the fall hadn't killed her. She wanted nothing more than for fate to have one more shot at her.

Although we never returned to Lookout Mountain together, Hitomi and I continued to live in Denver. This was a decision we had arrived at carefully for of the three most important places in our lives together – Kyoto, London and Paris – we never really felt at home in Colorado or developed a life there. Japan and London had been separate homes for both of us, where we felt comfortable and at ease with each other; and even though I had in theory been a visitor to Kyoto, it had become a second home for me and I always loved living there. And Paris was our home together. It was where we were married and were happy. The friends we made as a couple were there. However, in the end it was once again work commitments which kept us in Denver. The university offered Hitomi another year's teaching and increased her salary; although she had every intention of returning to Europe eventually, she decided that another full year of associate professorship would be a wise entry on her curriculum vitae.

For my part, I had reached another milestone in my life. Three weeks short of my twenty-ninth birthday, my writing career turned in an unexpected direction. To date I had published two books – my travel series and my Parisian interviews – and the latter had also been published by an American publishing house with medium success. What small amount of publicity I garnered, combined with my continuing work on *The Denver Examiner* brought me to the attention of a glossy New York magazine, the commissioning editor of which invited me to write a piece on Bill Clinton's growing troubles throughout the summer of 1998. The piece I wrote was a serious deconstruction of the media's continuing fascination with the president's sex life, the character they created for him through their writing, and to that end had a title which I had not intended to be merely humorous. However, on publication I saw that the editor had changed my title – *Let Sleeping Dogs Lie* – to the rather more puerile *The Oral Office*. Furious, I phoned the editor and argued with him for lowering the tone of the piece.

'Look, Bill,' he said and I could hear him chomping on his cigar on the other end of the line. 'The thing is—'

'First off, it's William,' I interrupted. 'Not Bill – William.'

'William then. Your piece was great. Honest it was. But it just needed a little more . . . I don't know . . . p'zazz.'

'P'zazz?'

'You got it.'

'Don't you think *The Oral Office* is just a cheap gag? Doesn't it undermine what the article is about?'

'I'll tell you what the article is about, *William*,' he said, stressing the name now. 'It's about you having a dig at every crackpot reporter out there who's getting off on the idea that they might have a little Monica of their own somewhere ready to go down on them too. Let me tell you, your piece is a lot more objective and pro-Clinton than I personally would have liked. But we're getting very good reaction from the White House.'

I allowed myself a small glimmer of ego and satisfaction at that. I liked the fact that – pro or con – the White House suddenly had a position on me. Nevertheless, I felt it important that I should stick to my guns. 'I just think you should have told me before you changed the title,' I said, determined not to lose track of this point. 'It is fairly pro-Clinton but at least the title balances that somewhat.'

'It does, does it?' asked the editor. 'Explain that to me. It's a no-meaning title.'

I sighed. *'Let Sleeping Dogs Lie,'* I said. 'First off, Clinton was sleeping with her, right?'

'Wrong. He never had sex with that woman . . . Miss Lewinsky. Not ever,' he cackled, his voice growing a little more hoarse as he perfected the Arkansan lilt which combined sanctimonious outrage at being accused of dishonesty with the obvious schoolboy pleasure

397

of getting laid. 'And he never asked anyone to lie for him. In fact, what he's got to do right now is go back to working for the—'

'Yes, very good,' I said, amused despite myself at the accuracy of the impersonation. 'Okay, maybe he didn't sleep with her as such but you get the idea. *Dogs*. Well she's no oil painting, is she?'

'Jesus, William, have you seen the picture we ran of you beside the story? You're no Tom Cruise yourself, buddy.'

'And finally,' I said in a firm voice, ignoring the dig. 'All he's done since this all started is lie about it. *Let Sleeping Dogs Lie*. Now which part of that didn't you get? *The Oral Office*!' I added, disgusted. 'Jesus.'

There was a silence for a moment as the penny – the cent – finally dropped and he exhaled with a sigh. 'Oh now I get it,' he said. '*Let Sleeping* . . . I get it now. You're right. It is better.'

'Thank you,' I replied, feeling exonerated.

'Yeah, but the fact is it didn't work until you explained it to me. You know how many people read this magazine every month? That's a hell of a lot of phone calls for you to make. First lesson in this business, my friend. Keep it simple. Don't try to be so fucking smart all the time and maybe you'll get wherever it is you want to go, you know what I mean?'

Unfortunately, I had no answer to that. I did know what he meant. However, the result of their title change was – as he had suggested – that I was seen as a friendly journalist during a difficult time and, quite out of the blue, I was invited by the White House press office to interview the president.

'You're kidding,' said Hitomi as I told her over dinner about the conversation I had had that afternoon with a

Washington official. 'The president of the United States wants you to interview him?'

'I know,' I said, laughing at the absurdity of it. 'That's what I said too. But the fact is they think I can do a nice piece on the guy. Explain his side of the story. They said he's a human being too and no one in the press is willing to take that on board. Everyone just wants to demonise him. Turn him into some sex-mad humping adolescent.'

'They're using you,' she said, twirling some pasta around her fork. 'They want you to do a PR piece for them. That's what it is.'

'I told them that's not how it would be,' I said, eager for her blessing as I knew I wanted to do it. 'They asked would I send them the questions in advance and I said not a chance and the woman just laughed and said *Off the record – you'd be a fucking moron if you did. Grill him all you want. He'll love it. He's a match for anyone.*'

'She said that?' Hitomi was staring at me, amazed, and I nodded. 'So what did you say back?'

'What could I say? I've been handed an opportunity to interview the president of the United States. Of course I said yes. You know my great-grandfather met a couple of presidents in his time. Andrew Johnson. Ulysses S. Grant. I think he met Grover Cleveland too, but that was during those four years between presidencies.'

'You're not Buffalo Bill, William,' replied Hitomi haughtily and I stared at her, suddenly irritated by her lack of enthusiasm for what was a once-in-a-lifetime chance.

'Fuck's sake,' I said. 'What's that supposed to mean?'

'It doesn't mean anything. You're the one who mentioned your great-grandfather. I thought we were talking about you and Bill Clinton.'

'We are,' I said. 'I was only saying, that's all. Come on, Hitomi. We get a couple of days in Washington. See the sights. The Lincoln Memorial. The Smithsonian. And I get to sit down and have a chin-wag with Bill Cody in the Oral Office.' She put down her fork with a bang on the table and stared at me in frustration. 'I'm kidding,' I said, biting my lip to stop myself from laughing. 'The *Oval* Office.'

'You didn't even hear what you said, did you?' she asked and I shrugged as if to say *huh*? 'Bill *Clinton*,' she shouted. 'The president's name is Bill *Clinton*, not Bill *Cody*. You said Bill Cody.'

'Oh for God's sake,' I said, frustrated with myself for my error. 'If I did, that's only because we were just talking about him. It was a slip of the tongue, that's all. I know the president's name is Cody. Clinton!' I roared, caught out again. 'Clinton, Clinton, Clinton!'

We said nothing for a few moments and eventually, Hitomi picked up both our empty plates and carried them across to the sink, dropping them in noisily with the cutlery and turning on the tap for a moment for a quick splash of water to rinse away the sauce before it stuck. Turning around then she went directly to the sofa and sat down with her arms wrapped around herself, which surprised me for Hitomi was always meticulous about cleanliness and in all the years we had been together I could not remember an occasion when she had been able to rest before immediately washing the dishes. I said nothing for some time but finally opened a window, for it was warm in our apartment and I thought some fresh air would help alleviate the sudden tension in the room. I went to the fridge and got a can of beer, pouring it into two glasses instinctively, as was our long-held tradition, and handing one to my wife as I sat in the armchair.

'No thanks,' she said, shaking her head in the direction of the glass of lager. 'You have it.'

Her sudden refusal to even drink with me pissed me off and I turned on her. 'What the hell's the matter with you tonight?' I asked her. 'I come back here with only about the most exciting piece of news I've ever given you and you just see all the negative sides to it. Now you won't even have a drink with me. What have I done?'

'Nothing,' she said, burying her face in her hands and I could see by the movement of her shoulders that she was crying. 'I just want a Coke, that's all,' she said between sobs. 'Can't I just have a Coke if I want one?'

Surprised and worried, I went over to the sofa and sat beside her, my arm around her shoulder. 'Hitomi, what's the matter?' I asked her, for she was not a woman prone to sudden displays of extreme emotion. 'Why are you crying?'

She took her head out of her hands and I stared at her, her mouth a little crooked by the sorrowful way she was looking at me. Her tears had made her mascara run and by trying to brush them away she had drawn two thin lines of black across her cheek, like an Indian warrior. I could see tiny puddles of tears waiting to drop from her lower eyelids and her chin wobbled slightly. 'God, you look bloody awful,' I said in a cheerful voice and it achieved the proper effect, for she quickly laughed and rubbed the tears away even as they fell.

'I'm sorry,' she said. 'I don't know what's wrong with me. Well I do, but—'

'Then tell me,' I said, pulling her closer to me. 'You've been uptight for days. Is it work? Is something wrong there? Remember we don't have to stay anywhere we—'

'No, it's not that,' she said. There was a silence for a moment but I allowed it to continue, knowing her well enough to realise that she would tell me in her own time what was upsetting her. 'I don't suppose you'd believe me,' she suggested, 'if I said I was worrying that Bill Clinton might turn out to be a bad influence on you?'

Now it was my turn to laugh. 'Yeah, that's it,' I acknowledged. 'Some guy from south London comes to America and gets shown the fast life by the president of the United States. Me and Bill are going to go off for a wild weekend of hookers and gambling in the Nevada desert. Actually, that sounds quite fun, now that I say it.'

'Ha,' she said dryly.

'The answer to your question is no,' I said after a moment. 'I wouldn't believe it if you said that.'

She shrugged. 'Would you believe it if I said I'm just prone right now to sudden and inexplicable bursts of temper? That I may turn into Crazyhitomi for the next nine months or so? Or the next seven anyway?'

I laughed and thought about it. It took a moment for her phrase to settle in my mind. In fact, as I recall it now I remember I was about to ask her something about whether she really wanted that Coke or not when I realised what she meant. I took my arm from around her shoulders and placed both hands on her elbows, looking directly into her face even as it seemed to swim around me slightly. I found that I couldn't actually speak. She smiled and reached across to stroke my cheek. I placed a hand on her stomach as she touched me too and, for me, those few seconds stand as the point in my marriage when the two of us – the three of us – were as connected as we could ever possibly be.

We were one unit. We were a family. I can feel her hand there still, ghostly.

The wild west show continued to tour America through the mid- to late-1880s with varying degrees of success. In general, massive profits were made whenever they travelled to the cosmopolitan cities which were furthest away from the experience of the west itself; Detroit, Illinois and Staten Island were among their most successful shows throughout 1885 and 1886, although cities such as New Orleans and Louisiana proved less popular. The climax of the American shows came with a one month sell-out show in Madison Square Gardens, where once again my great-grandfather found himself the toast of the New York set, a role in which he revelled for celebrity suited him.

In late 1886, Bill and Nate Salsbury were discussing their plans for the following year and found that they had little interest in continually returning to the same cities over and over and agreed that they should spread their wings a little. Having conquered America, it was time to conquer the world.

'We should begin in England,' said Nate. 'It's the natural starting point. From there, if we prove successful, we can move on to the continent. France, Italy, maybe even Russia.'

'The English may not wish to be reminded of American victories,' suggested Bill, wary of any remaining ill-feeling from the colonial wars. 'They might send the army to drive us out even as we arrive.'

'Nonsense. That's all ancient history. And anyway, this isn't politics we're bringing them, it's entertainment. We're showmen, Bill, you know that. They'll lap it up.'

Bill wasn't so sure but after consulting Sitting Bull, Frank Butler, Annie Oakley and other important members of the wild west show, they agreed that they would contact a publicist in London to discover whether there was indeed a market for their particular brand of entertainment. Within weeks, arrangements had been made for a show at Earls Court in London and it was agreed that the entire wild west party would depart for England at the end of March. In the meantime, Bill set about putting together the most elaborate display of western paraphernalia and characters that he could. Although they traditionally used Indians from the Lakota Sioux tribe – those who fell directly under the leadership of Sitting Bull – he wanted to bring members of different tribes to England in order to illustrate the complexity of the Indian culture in America and the various segregations which existed within it.

To this effect, he initially hired Indians from the Kiowa and Ogalallas tribes and was once again given permission by the secretary of the interior to take these men and women from their reservation in order to represent their people around the world. There was great competition among the members of the tribes to select those who would be liberated into Bill's employment but in general he selected his players on a physical basis, choosing the fiercest-looking men and the most beautiful women. The Kiowa were a southern Plains people who had been incarcerated into reservations after a fierce Texan war in the 1870s, while the Ogalallas were a Lakota people who had been present for General Custer's last stand at Little Big Horn. To their number, Bill added some of the Cheyenne and the Pawnees, a tribe who had lost much of their land during the Gold Rush. Some of their more illustrious leaders were also signed up for the show's first foreign tour. In addition to the some two hundred tribal members and cowboys or actors, arrangements were made to transport various animals, including bears, racing horses, bucking broncos and buffaloes, across the ocean, not to mention marksmen, wagons, and even the celebrated Deadwood Stagecoach which played a big role in one of the set pieces of the show. The only disappointment to Bill was the decision by Sitting Bull not to visit England. He was superstitious about the ocean crossing, believing that any Indian who set sail would find their body disintegrating from their bones within three days; this was also a blow to Annie Oakley, Sitting Bull's greatest friend and adopted daughter. However, he was quickly replaced with Ogilasa, better known as Red Shirt, who was Sitting Bull's choice as representative Sioux leader in his absence.

Crowds descended on the harbours of New York on the morning they set sail for England and cheered them on as they left America. My great-grandfather stood on a raised platform on the deck, waving his hat in the air majestically as he acknowledged the applause and appreciation of the people. Only when they were out of sight did he step down and turn to face in the opposite direction, out towards the horizon, where England and the unknown lay. To a massed gathering of his friends and employees he declared it to be the most important transatlantic voyage since the *Nina*, the *Pinta* and the *Santa Maria* had set sail from Spain at the end of the fifteenth century to discover the new world in the first place; now he, Buffalo Bill Cody, was returning to their ancestral heritage to show the world what they had achieved in the four centuries since then.

The voyage was a traumatic one for these unseasoned

sailors and more than one of them spent a portion of the trip bent over the side of the ship, staring down at the water below as they grew more and more sick. Annie Oakley took to her bed and insisted on writing her last will and testament, convinced that death was only a matter of hours away. The Sioux Indians became nearly hysterical in their belief that Sitting Bull had been correct and they were in fact going to die. Even my great-grandfather, the famous Buffalo Bill, was unable to hold a civil conversation for the first three days, so sick was he and convinced that the decision to leave the solid land of America for the unknown world of England had been the worst of his life.

However, eventually they became used to the unsteady nature of the sea and were able to return to their previous good health and even clean themselves up, ready for their next adventure as the coastline of England came into view through the clouds on a bright April morning.

My great-grandfather enjoyed the attention which he received in London. Every day the newspapers carried news of where he was visiting and who he had met, while the wild west show prepared for its opening performance at Earls Court. He travelled through the city by hansom cab and pedestrians would often notice him and cheer as he was driven past, when he would take off his hat and wave it affectionately at the public, acknowledging his applause. He stayed at the Metropole Hotel and became known as a substantial tipper, resulting in the best service from the bellboys and waiters who worked there. The rest of the wild west show stayed in far less extravagant surroundings but as Nate Salsbury was mostly responsible for putting the show together, Bill saw little of his colleagues during his first two weeks in the capital.

Three days before the opening of the show, Bill was invited by Adrian Parker, who was organising much of the publicity for their own show, to an open-air production of *A Midsummer Night's Dream*. The performance they attended was a special one for it was advertised in the newspaper in advance that Buffalo Bill Cody, along with the Prince and Princess of Wales, would be the guests of honour on the evening. Bill dressed in his finest western uniform for the event – again, a uniform designed by himself and not standard issue of any American army – and was brought to his seat in the royal box a few minutes before the play began. There were about twenty people already seated in the box, mostly guests of the royal party and a few retainers, and Bill was immediately introduced to Prince Edward and Princess Alexandra, who greeted him warmly and invited him to sit in the reserved seat to the prince's left to watch the show.

'This is an unexpected honour for me,' Bill remarked in order to ingratiate himself with the stern-looking couple whose conversational skills at first proved to be somewhat lacking. 'Where I grew up in Iowa, I little expected to find myself seated in such a place one day. A log cabin is a humble enough place for one's beginnings.'

'We hear great things of the show you have brought to London,' remarked the prince, showing little interest in information about his companion's upbringing and appearing to barely understand what a log cabin even was. 'We will be attending, of course, on the opening evening.' Bill inclined his head to acknowledge the compliment. 'We trust there will not be a great deal of anti-Empire flag waving, however,' he added, a trace of a smile flickering around his lips as he enunciated each word carefully. 'Calls for the colonials to invade the mother country, for example?'

'I assure you that our aim is simply to provide an entertaining evening of performances, demonstrating the different cultures and activities of the west. We've proved very popular in America.'

'So we have heard,' said the prince, turning back towards the stage where the curtain was beginning to rise for the play. Bill sat back in his seat, unsure whether the offhand manner which was being displayed towards him was typical of royalty's response to lay people, or whether his nationality was what was giving offence.

'Oh I wouldn't worry about him,' remarked a rather corpulent man during the interval, who had been seated to Bill's left in the royal box throughout the first half of the play. They had agreed to go to the bar together and my great-grandfather had mentioned that the Prince of Wales had seemed less than friendly. 'The fact that he invited you to sit with him at all means that he's interested in you. You're supposed to take that as a given. Don't expect politeness into the bargain. That's not at all part of his make-up.'

Bill nodded. 'I don't much care, to be honest with you,' he said. 'I've met greater men than him in my time. I just don't want to say anything myself which might be construed as rudeness or ingratitude. I like to think I'm a man of some manners, particularly in another's country.'

The larger man finished his drink quickly and ordered another, 'You'll join me?' he asked, ordering two more without waiting for an answer, more of a demand than a question.

'So what's your position, then?' asked Bill, unsure who his drinking companion was anyway. 'Are you part of the prince's retinue? Is every word I say being taken down to be used in evidence against me?'

'Not at all,' said the man. 'You think I'd be one of his flunkies? Not likely, my friend. But he likes to have me along every so often for a little colour, I think. The princess is good friends with my wife, Constance. You met her inside, did you not?' Bill nodded and made some gratuitous compliment about her beauty, which the other man took with an amused smile. 'Quite,' he said. 'Anyway, I'm a playwright, myself. Have a couple of shows running in the West End at the moment actually. So when something new opens I get invited along. Somehow they seem to think my opinion of their plays is important to them while their opinion of mine is the only thing important to me. Assuming their opinions are the correct ones, of course.'

'I'm sure you have as little control over their opinions as my audience does over mine.'

'My dear sir, I give them their opinions.'

Bill smiled. 'Perhaps I should attend one of your plays while I'm here,' he said. 'Which one would you recommend?'

Mr Wilde, for that was his companion's name, shrugged as if deciding between them was a pointless exercise. 'Any of them is worth the price of a ticket, of course, but tell them at the box that I sent you and they'll give you a good seat. Anything would be better than this claptrap, that's for sure.'

'You don't like Shakespeare?' asked Bill. 'Surely that's a heresy for a playwright?'

'I do like him, of course. But this production is hardly the most riveting of evenings, now is it? Titania is talking into her breasts for one thing. Ample as they are. She seems to keep addressing them as if she's afraid they might run away into the wings at some point. And I'm sure I could see Puck asleep at one point. I wouldn't mind joining him if that was the case.'

Bill laughed, not quite sure what Mr Wilde meant. He never quite looked at him while he spoke but scanned the bar instead, occasionally raising a couple of fingers to wave to an acquaintance across the room. 'Look, there's Carstairs, *The Times*'s drama critic,' he remarked after a moment. 'He looks like he's having almost as good a time as we are. That's good news anyway. There's nothing I enjoy more than someone else's bad reviews. Gets the morning off to a good start. Along with the tea and pastries, that is,' he added quietly.

'Ain't you got a solidarity among playwrights then?' asked Bill, smiling quietly for he found his companion amusing and cantankerous at the same time.

'Not at all,' he said. 'We scan the obituaries every morning checking to see whether one of our adversaries has died. Finally gives us a chance to say something nice about each other. The dead can't compete, you see. But you should know about the nature of rivalry, Mr Cody. Yours is the not the only wild west show touring at the moment, is it?'

Bill nodded. 'That's true,' he said, a trace of bitterness creeping into his voice. 'We've had one or two imitators in recent times. Our show remains the best though. And we're the only one who's touring the world, that says something about us, I think.'

'You're not afraid of leaving America in the hands of your competition then?'

'None of our competitors have a name like mine in their lead,' said Bill proudly, his body puffing up in self-congratulation. We also have Sitting Bull, Red Shirt, Annie Oakley—'

'Oh I've heard of her,' said Wilde. 'Little Miss Sure Shot they call her, is that right?'

'Some do.'

'They say she's the finest shot in the world. I'd like to see her shooting. I'm something of an aficionado of that myself.'

'You must come along and see her then,' said Bill. 'I'll leave your name on the box too. How's that for double dealing?'

Mr Wilde smiled and at that moment the bell rang to indicate that they had only a few minutes to return to their seats for the second half of the performance. A striking young man in a tight tuxedo approached them, strutting towards them with one hand in his pocket and eyeing Bill up and down suspiciously. Wilde got a slightly pained look on his face as the man tapped him on the arm and spoke to him without acknowledging my great-grandfather.

'Time to go back in, Oscar,' he said. 'The old bastard will be looking for you.'

'Heaven forefend,' replied Wilde sarcastically. 'You've met Mr Cody, haven't you, Bosie? Mr Cody, this is Lord Alfred Douglas, a particular friend of mine.'

'Pleased to meet you, Lord Alfred,' said Bill, stretching out his hand to shake that of the young man, who offered his reluctantly and even then barely pressed on the fingers of the other as his lip snarled slightly.

'You're Buffalo Bill, aren't you?' asked Lord Alfred. 'That's what they call you?'

'It is, to my honour,' replied Bill. 'On account of the thousands of buffalo I've killed over the years.'

'How lovely for you,' came the reply with barely

411

concealed distaste. 'That must give you a taste for dinner. Or do you eat the meat raw off the bone in the colonies?' Wilde checked his watch and looked as if he wanted to separate the two men.

'Bosie's right, I'm afraid, Mr Cody,' he said. 'We really should return to the prince. Perhaps we can continue our discussion later? Maybe I will attend your show with their royal highnesses next week anyway. Would that be acceptable? And you could introduce me to your Annie Oakley.'

'Oscar loves a straight shot,' said Bosie, leading the way back to the royal box. 'And how about you, Mr Buffalo Bill,' he asked as they went inside, uttering the name with slight contempt. 'What land of shot do you prefer?'

'Bourbon, mostly,' said Bill, reaching into his inner pocket for the small flask he often brought with him. 'Care for a taste?'

Bosie raised an eyebrow with a shudder and shook his head, saying nothing more to Bill as he took his seat. The lights went down and my great-grandfather sighed as he looked around him. With the exception of Mr Wilde, they were a cold lot. He would shake that out of them if nothing else, he thought. Wait till they get a load of my show, he thought to himself, wondering whether anyone would notice if he took ten minutes' sleep during the next act. That would ruffle them out of their stuffed shirts.

The royal party enjoyed the wild west show so much that Bill and his colleagues were invited to perform for Queen Victoria on the occasion of her jubilee the following month, June of 1887. Although she had been in mourning for her late husband for the best part of thirty years, the queen had agreed to step out in public for a celebration of her fifty years on the throne and a gala performance was to be staged in her honour. When the invitation came for their own troupe to perform, it was agreed that a scaled-down version would be appropriate as many different performers from various parts of the empire would also want to have their moment in the spotlight. However, since the evening when the Prince and Princess of Wales had attended the show and delighted in it, the queen had specifically requested that the wonders of the wild west be presented to her too and it was with great pride that my great-grandfather designed a special performance of the robbing of the Deadwood stagecoach for the evening in question, along with a display of marksmanship from himself and the increasingly popular Annie Oakley.

Hundreds of people were working at the arena that day and Bill's troupe were but a small part of it and he felt it slightly strange not to be the centre of attention for once. Some of the other performers did, however, take the time to visit him and shake his hand for his visit to London had been heavily reported by the newspapers and the acts of valour which he had invented for some of his stage shows back in America were increasingly being passed off as actual historical facts.

Special tents had been erected behind the arena where the performers could eat and Bill made his way towards one of these as he waited for his call. He was dressed in his regulation showman outfit and had paid particular attention to his hair and beard as he wanted to appear as handsome as possible for this, perhaps his greatest ever show. The tent was empty, save for a few members of an acrobatic troupe who were eating noisily in one corner. They stared at him as he walked inside, resplendent in his uniform, for they knew exactly who he was, the most famous performer at these jubilee celebrations. On any other occasion he would have invited himself to join them and regaled them with stories about his life and adventures but for some reason that evening he did not and instead wandered to the top of the tent, where a young girl was clearing away food from a buffet.

'Excuse me,' he said, approaching her and she jumped, startled, for she had been paying no attention to anyone around her and had not even noticed him entering the tent. She stared at him in surprise, for his outfit was unlike any she had ever seen before, and placed a hand to her heart to indicate her surprise, or perhaps her sudden attraction.

'I'm sorry,' she said, giving a spontaneous laugh. 'You startled me. I didn't see you come in.'

My great-grandfather looked at her for a moment, struck by her beauty, and then laughed himself. She had said no more than a dozen words to him but the lack of affectation in them, the honest surprise, was something fresh to him, her youthful voice endearing. He had the impression she didn't laugh much for within a moment she had turned it into a cough and was looking at him in a more serious, professional way.

'I do apologise,' she said. 'Can I help you at all?'

'I was hoping for a little snack,' he said. 'But if you're clearing everything away, I can always—'

'No, no, that's fine,' she said, interrupting him. 'We're still open. I can fix you something. What would you like? I could make you a sandwich perhaps?'

'Sounds perfect,' said Bill, extending his hand across the counter. 'Bill Cody,' he said. 'I'm putting a show on here for the queen's jubilee. Visions of the wild west of America, that sort of thing.'

The girl nodded her head slowly and smiled, shaking his hand but pausing before saying anything else. 'I know exactly who you are, Mr Cody,' she said finally. 'Why you're the man everyone's waiting to see. Look at them over there,' she added, nodding across at the troupe of performers at the other side of the tent who were watching the conversation between the two intently. Bill turned to look at them and frowned at their intrusiveness. 'They can't take their eyes off you.'

'It's probably you they can't take their eyes off,' said Bill gallantly and there was that sudden burst of laughter from the girl again.

'I doubt it,' she said. 'I know them too well. My name's Ellen Rose,' she added, and Bill nodded to acknowledge it.

'Very pleased to meet you, Ellen Rose,' he said. 'And what makes you think that a bunch of honest men like them wouldn't want to stare over at you?'

'For a start, one of them's my father, one of them thinks he's above me, one of them's too shy to speak to me, and one of them isn't interested in ladies at all. And even if any of them was, there's not too many people these days would show a lot of interest in a crippled girl, now is there?' Bill raised an eyebrow in surprise, not knowing exactly what she meant, but as she turned to walk towards the kitchen area he saw her reach for a stick and followed her slow, heavy walk with sadness. 'Come with me, if you like, Mr Cody,' she called back to him. 'I'll make you your sandwich out of the way of their prying eyes.'

Bill stood up and followed her back, sitting now at a tall stool beside a table as she began to fix his snack. 'What happened to your leg then?' he asked, determined not to pretend that she had not said what she had said. He watched her as her face betrayed a slight tic; he suspected people were rarely this quick and honest with her.

'I used to be a trapeze artist,' she explained. 'I grew up wanting to be one. I had an accident this one evening and fell. I was lucky I wasn't killed, to be honest with you. I suppose I have to be grateful for that.' Bill nodded and said nothing for a moment. A silence hung between them which Ellen Rose eventually cut. 'I say I fell,' she muttered. 'Actually, I was dropped. A man who had a thing for me got his nose out of joint when I wouldn't go with him. He was supposed to catch me. He let me fall instead. Not fair.'

Bill said nothing but felt his jaw clench in an unexpected anger against this unknown man who had hurt this girl he had never met until a moment before. He considered offering expressions of sympathy but decided against it. 'What happened to him?' he asked. 'The man who let you fall. He's not out there, is he?' He nodded towards the tent area and the group of men he had seen when entering. Ellen shook her head.

'No, he's long gone,' she said. 'Nothing dramatic. He admitted what he'd done and was jailed for it. That's all. He's in jail and I work in the kitchens. Not sure which of us got the better deal out of it though,' she added with a half smile as she took a long knife and cut the sandwich in half, put it on a plate and handed it across. 'Now Mr Buffalo Bill,' she said with a smile. 'Eat up.'

'Thank you,' he said. He reached out to take the plate from her and as he did so his hand touched hers and for a moment they allowed their fingers to rest there. He smiled at her. She had long dark hair and pale skin. A slight blush had crept unknowingly into her cheeks and he got the sense from her that she was looking for a release, praying for someone to save her from this life. After a few moments, flustered, she took her hand back and turned away, lost for things to say. What she wanted to do was walk around to this cowboy and kiss him. Instead, she said something she could never have imagined herself saying in a million years to a fiancé, let alone a perfect stranger. But then that was exactly what he was – a perfect stranger.

'I'll be here tonight,' she said quietly, barely aware of how she was finding either the courage or the language for the words. 'After the show. Around midnight. I'll be here then.'

Bill reached down and took a bite from his sandwich and nodded. He said nothing for now but knew that he would be there at midnight also.

Ellen Rose had never been with a man and even as she stole along the back of the trailers towards the tent where she had met my great-grandfather only hours earlier, she felt a wave of nausea rushing through her stomach with the tension of her intended actions. Although she was terrified at what might be to come, and amazed at her own intentions, she resolved not to stop walking, for if she stopped for even a moment to consider her actions, she ran the risk of changing her mind and returning to her tent and then what would become of her?

Through all of Isaac's stories, he has never been fully able to explain to me the reason why Ellen Rose and Buffalo Bill Cody were so immediately attracted to each other. My theory is that Ellen, my great-grandmother, saw in Bill a way out of the Regis-Roc Circus. He was an extravagant, famous man from the other side of the world; she was a crippled girl, albeit a beautiful one.

For Bill's part, he had long since separated from his wife, Louisa Frederici, although the legalities of that relationship remained intact. In the intervening years he had made a habit of seducing the majority of the girls who came through the wild west show, not to mention the thousands who came to see him as he travelled around America and who were happy to sacrifice either their honour or simply the night to a man with such a reputation as his. My theory is an unromantic one: she was using him, and he was just doing what he always did. Isaac, on the other hand, told it differently.

His take on that night is that Ellen Rose and Bill Cody met as arranged in the kitchen area of the tents. It was dark but Ellen lit a candle as she waited, somewhat irritably, for her paramour to appear. She glanced at her watch. There were still two minutes to go before midnight but she feared that he would not arrive. She could feel her heart beating heavily inside her chest and her left leg ached slightly, as it always did in moments of tension. The slightest thought could have seen her hurry from her waiting post and back to her safe bed, but she refused to allow herself to give in to these ideas and sat patiently, biting her lip as she nervously gripped the table before her. She could feel a warmth inside her and knew that now, at last, at the age of twenty-four, she wanted to be with a man. And what was wrong with that, she reasoned.

'Miss Rose,' said Bill as he appeared from the shadows, just as midnight struck. 'True to your word, I see.'

She sighed and nodded, as if she had given up any pretence of being there for any innocent reason. 'I was determined to come,' she said quietly, glancing around to make sure that no one could hear or see them.

'Don't worry,' he said. 'I did a quick scout around

before I came in here. Everyone's in their beds. It was a long day, after all.'

'Yes,' said Ellen. 'I saw you, you know. With the queen.' The wild west show had performed their regular routine before Queen Victoria earlier in the day and afterwards, in quite a break with her normal procedures, the queen asked for its founder to be presented to her. 'What did she say to you anyway? She looked quite enamoured.'

'She said that she had never seen such a display of courage before and that, despite our turbulent histories, she would raise a toast to America that evening at dinner.'

'And you. What did you say to her?'

'I was told not to say anything unless she asked a direct question,' he replied, stepping behind Ellen and lifting her hair out of the way so that he might kiss her gently on the neck. 'And she never did so I simply smiled and bowed. That was it. That was all the uses she had for me.'

Ellen sighed as she felt the warm breath of her intended lover whispering around her bare shoulder. As he kissed her towards her shoulder, the front of his teeth skimmed her skin gently and she felt an urge to press her body back against that mouth, so that he might bite into her and enter as deeply into her person as he could possibly do. She shut her eyes and spun around as if being carried along by the air, their lips met and he raised her on to the table, standing between her legs, edging them apart slightly despite her natural inclination to modesty.

'If he was still here,' said Bill, stepping back for a moment and looking at the young girl directly in the eyes, even as he lowered her blouse to reveal her breasts by candlelight, pale, trembling. 'I'd kill him for what he did to you.' He reached a hand down and hooked it under the knee of the damaged leg and buried his face in her bosom for a time as she closed her eyes again and leaned backwards, clearing her mind of all worry as she allowed him to do with her what he would, never interfering, never speaking, never asking for anything. When they made love, all she could see was the hero, the adventurer, the great American Buffalo Bill Cody, who was in love with her and would take her away to a fantasy life. She could never love or be loved by anyone quite like this man.

At least, that's the way Isaac tells it.

Chapter Twelve

Last Days

The Clinton piece made me a lot of friends in the New York media world. And the magazine offered me a regular interviewing position, along similar lines as the one I had held in Paris. I was happy to take it for until then I was feeling at something of a loss in Denver as Hitomi concentrated on her career and this gave me a chance to work towards my own ambitions again.

After much discussion, we agreed that we would continue to live in Denver until the end of the academic year, before moving back to New York so that I could pursue this opportunity. Hitomi wrote to the university which had employed her on our last trip there and although there were no positions currently available, they promised to keep her in mind should something come up. In the meantime, she wrote to several others and appeared confident that a job would come her way at some point once we got there.

Shane was born in early spring, the first Cody in four generations to be born in America. Hitomi was not in labour for long – only a couple of hours – and seemed surprised, even a little disappointed, that childbirth on this occasion had not been as painful as she had been led to believe it would be. Our son was perfectly healthy and his face, a mixture of our east–west genes, captivated me with its smooth skin and tiny arched eyebrows, reminiscent of the Naoyuki line, and the piercing blue eyes and snub nose of the Codys. They were released from hospital after a couple of days and we settled down to our initial couple of weeks of nervous parenting in our Denver apartment.

I phoned Isaac from home on the evening that Shane was born and told him the news.

'Where are you calling from?' he asked me.

'I'm back home.'

'Well what are you doing there if your wife's just had a baby?'

'She needed to sleep,' I replied defensively. 'As do I. We've been there all day.'

He grunted, as if this was a weak excuse but carried on anyway. 'So I'm a grandfather at last,' he said. 'Makes me feel old.'

'Isaac, you are old. You're almost eighty.'

'Yes, but I never felt it before. Have you got a name for him yet?'

'Yes,' I replied quickly. 'We had names ready for a boy and a girl in advance. We wanted to know what his name was from the moment he was born and not just call him "baby" or something. So we're calling him Shane.'

'Shane?' asked Isaac, and I could tell from the tone of his voice that he was disappointed. 'Why do you want to call him that? What sort of a name is Shane?'

'His name, that's what sort. It's a name we both like.'

'I thought you'd call him Sam. Tradition, you know.'

I shook my head and stayed silent for a moment. It was true that Isaac had been named after his great-grandfather, and that he in turn had named me for

422

mine. I had considered this and even discussed it with Hitomi; following the tradition would have meant calling the child Sam but, although we both quite liked the name, we believed that by calling him that we would be deliberately allying him to the western side of his personality. He was going to be born an American, of mixed-race parents, and it was unlikely that he would ever live in Japan – at least while he was a child. That being the case, we wanted to choose a name which had no definitive family history on either side. Hence Shane.

'We're going with Shane,' I repeated, hoping he would let the matter drop and he did then, even though I could tell that he was annoyed with me.

'Well I suppose you'll be bringing him over on a visit,' he said. 'Let him see where his father grew up.'

'Soon,' I said. 'We better wait a few months at least before bringing him on a plane. Why don't you come here in the meantime?' I suggested, knowing that he would greet this idea without any seriousness.

'No thanks,' he said, proving me right. 'I'm too old to go travelling around the world. Do you want to kill me or what?' I gave a small laugh, which seemed required, but was disturbed by his voice as he spoke. It seemed weaker and more subdued than I remembered it. Whenever I thought of visiting now, I felt slightly nervous that I would find my father a shadow of his former self. My guilt at leaving him alone in London continued although I did nothing to salve it. I was aware that he had few years left in him but had put the thought out of my mind for the most part.

'Have you been to see your great-grandfather recently?' he asked me after a pause and I shook my head, despite the fact that he couldn't actually see me.

'Not recently,' I said. He was of course referring to Lookout Mountain, where Buffalo Bill was buried and where I had been only once in my time in Denver. 'Maybe soon.'

'You should go and tell him the news,' he said and I wasn't sure if he was joking or not.

'You realise he's dead of course,' I said, attempting to be humorous but, as ever, he took me up the wrong way.

'Don't get smart with me, boy. Just because he's dead doesn't mean you can't treat him with a little respect, all right? You go to his grave and tell him about his great-great-grandson. That's the least you can do. It's important to keep the link between the generations.'

I was tired and didn't want to argue so agreed to do so. 'All right, Isaac,' I agreed, even though I knew the chances of me returning to Lookout Mountain at any point in the near future were slim. 'I'll go there soon. You want me to send you some photos?'

'No,' he said bluntly. 'You don't take photos of graves. That's disrespectful too.'

'I meant of Shane,' I said irritably. 'Do you want me to send you some photos of your grandson?'

'Oh,' he replied, a little chastened. 'Yes, that would be good. Do that. And tell Hitomi I said hello.' I nodded. Typical Isaac; don't send your love, just send a greeting.

'I'll speak to you soon,' I said. 'Take care of yourself.'

He laughed, as if the idea was outrageous, and without another word hung up the phone.

And now, ladies and gentlemen, here's the crux of it: it is the business of storytelling which always lay at the heart of my relationship with my father. He was always

424

less concerned with building a bond between us than he was with finding a common ground whereby our dialogue might continue. His subject matter was his grandfather and that has been my subject too as I have recounted our relationship and my own story. I spent a large portion of my adult life so far away from my home because I felt there was nothing left for me there; I discovered a new home in Hitomi and, subsequently, in my son. However, just as Bill wrote stories and plays about himself and created his own self-perpetuating myth, and just as Isaac carried those stories down and urged me to write about them, so the lines between what happened and what we wanted to happen blur and even I don't know where the truth ends and the fictions begin. But all stories must have a climax; in Isaac's stories of Buffalo Bill, that came with the sexual encounter between my great-grandfather and great-grandmother, Ellen Rose. In Isaac's own story, it's probably the moment of my birth and his abandonment by my mother, when he took over my teaching and training and moulded me in a certain image. And for me, it came in 1999, when, at the age of twenty-nine, my first life ended and I was forced to begin a new one.

It was a warm Saturday evening and Shane, who was then five months old, was unsettled. He was teething and his temper was getting the better of him. I'd been out for most of the afternoon, editing an article at the newspaper office, and when I got back home, Hitomi was looking a little stressed from her day. 'He hasn't stopped crying,' she said, dragging the back of her hand against her forehead, which was perspiring slightly. 'He went to sleep for a couple of hours in the afternoon but other than that, he's just been at it all day.'

I picked up the baby and held him aloft, peering into his bright blue eyes for a moment and stuck my tongue out at him. Pleased to see me back again and surprised by my sudden gesture, he stopped crying and stared at me as if I was mad. I bared my teeth at him now and growled and he cried again but when I held him close to my chest, so that he could feel my heart beating against his cheek, he quietened down and sucked on his thumb happily. I grinned at Hitomi but instantly saw that she was not in the mood for parental one-upmanship. 'It's just his teeth,' I said. 'He's bound to be like this.'

'We're out of the gel,' she said with a sigh. 'I finished it earlier. I better go out and get him some more.' The gel she was referring to was the foul-smelling mucus which we rubbed on his gums to alleviate some of the pain of teething. It was ice cold and usually did the trick but he seemed to be going through tubes of it at a ridiculous rate. I was beginning to worry that he was addicted to the stuff.

'It's all right,' I said. 'I'll get it. You stay in and relax.'

'No, William, I need a break,' she said, shaking her head. 'I need some peace.'

'Why don't I go for the gel and take him for a walk with me,' I suggested. 'It's pretty cool out so he'll be fine. The air might even send him off to sleep in the meantime. I'll put him in his pram, walk to the drug-store, and take the long way back. It'll take us about an hour. You can have a nap or a bath or whatever.'

Hitomi sighed and pressed her hand back against her shoulder. 'Would you?' she asked plaintively, and she was almost crying with happiness at the prospect of an hour's peace and quiet which she could devote entirely to herself.

'Of course,' I said, laughing. 'Look at him anyway.

He's happy right now. I'm clearly his favourite parent, by far. You run a bath. I'll stay out for as long as possible.'

'Stay out all night,' she said with a smile. 'Don't come back till the morning if you don't want to. Maybe the pair of you could hit a strip club or something. Favourite parent indeed!'

'He doesn't like them,' I replied, gathering up my keys. 'Thinks they're exploitative.' Shane's pram was sitting in the corner of the living room and I placed him inside it gingerly and put his dummy back in his mouth. The prospect of movement was keeping him quiet for now and he put up no objections when I strapped him in carefully. Walking up behind my wife, I placed my hands on her shoulders and kneaded them between my fingers, achieving just the level of pressure which I knew relaxed her and which might deliver her from the knots which lay beneath. 'You want anything while I'm out?' I asked her quietly, raising her hair at the back and kissing her gently.

'I'm fine,' she said, turning around and hugging me. 'I might want something when you come back though.'

I smiled. 'Take a bath then,' I said. 'You stink.'

'Charming.'

'I love you, you know that?' The words were out of my mouth before I knew why; I did love her, of course, I just had no idea why I chose to tell her at that moment. She looked a little surprised but pleased by my spontaneity.

'What's not to love?' she said, her final words to me, and I gave her a wink and wheeled Shane out of the apartment.

The wild west show stayed in London after Queen Victoria's jubilee celebration for another six weeks and then travelled around Britain playing in Manchester, Liverpool, Cardiff and Edinburgh. Crowds gathered along Princes Street when Buffalo Bill arrived and paraded through the city with Annie Oakley and the other members of his troupe. A reception was held for him afterwards in Edinburgh Castle where he was toasted by the Prince of Wales once again. As they travelled the country, the format began to change. Buffalo Bill's previous trips around the world had convinced him that there was more to his entertainments than simply the western aspect, although that continued to dominate the show. Now, however, he introduced performers from Russia and Mexico, Europe and the Far East, each dressed in their native costumes, each demonstrating to the audience their own particular skills and fighting abilities. Many of these talents were invented by Bill himself and not all of the foreign performers were actually of the nationality they pretended to be. To demonstrate the new multinational aspect of the show, it was re-christened 'The Congress of Rough Riders of the World' and played to packed audiences. Bill himself was planning on one more week in London before returning to the States and set off for there alone after the festivities in Edinburgh had ended.

Ellen Rose had not seen much of my great-grandfather since their one-night liaison after the jubilee show. She had woken the next morning with a great feeling of joy, for she had fallen in love the night before and believed that that love was reciprocated; she was wrong. Unfortunately for her, ever since Bill's separation from his wife Louisa, and probably for quite some time before that, he was accustomed to having relationships with the girls who followed his every move and had fallen in love with the myth he had created for himself along the way. He had worked hard to turn William Cody into Buffalo Bill and enjoyed the entertainments his self-created fantasy offered him. As he passed through London again, she made another attempt to see him, sending him a letter at his hotel and he arranged to meet her in the bar of the hotel later that evening.

'Miss Rose,' he said when he arrived, thirty minutes late. His eyes flickered over her in recognition; he was sure he could remember who Ellen Rose was but was unconvinced whether he might be mixing her up with a young girl he had met in Manchester a month or so previously. 'I'm sorry I'm late. Had a bit of business to tie up with a friend of mine.' The business he spoke of involved Marguerite Devlin, the wife of a local businessman who had made herself available to my great-grandfather after watching him performing at a benefit programme the night before.

'I was late myself, Bill,' said my great-grandmother, lying deliberately for she did not want it to seem as if she was too needy. In a curious reversal of roles, she stood up and waited for him to sit down, which he did, and she smiled nervously then as she took her seat again, holding her purse between her hands as security. In truth she had arrived a full twenty minutes before their scheduled meeting time, meaning that she had been sitting there alone for almost an hour. The eyes of some of the waiters had glanced over her several times, as they wondered what a young woman was doing sitting alone in a hotel bar in the early evening. The manager had been about to approach her when Bill arrived, thus saving her an embarrassing interview.

'I'm glad you wrote to me,' said Bill casually. 'Still with the circus then, are you?'

'Yes,' she said, looking at the ground in misery. Bill

was scanning the menu, considering tea and a sandwich, barely glancing at his companion. Several people strolled past and stared at him, for his face had become familiar in recent times through the newspapers. Ellen had prepared a lot of what she wanted to say but found herself unable to find the words now. After a few moments silence he looked across at her irritably.

'Well,' he said, struggling himself. 'I'll be glad to get home to America. I can tell you that. I think this present tour has exhausted me more than any other. And I'm not the young man I used to be.' This was true; by now, Bill was over forty years of age and although still in good condition he could feel the desire inside to begin to slow down a little. His health was beginning to deteriorate and he had already begun to suffer from heart problems. He found that, despite his still frequent amorous adventures, he needed an hour's rest during the afternoon and rarely sat through an entire performance of the show, preferring to appear only when he was specifically needed. By contrast, Ellen Rose was in her mid-twenties.

'You're going home?' she asked, surprised, her heart sinking at the news.

'I am indeed.'

'Soon?' Her voice shuddered slightly as she said the single word, stuttering the 's' in her anxiety.

'Two days from now. Our boat sails to New York City, which I'm not looking forward to, I admit. I am a great adventurer, my dear, but truth be told I'm no sailor. The trip over was bad enough. But now that I know how treacherous a transatlantic crossing can be I'm looking forward to it even less. Let's have some tea. What do you say?' Ellen Rose nodded her head and as the waiter approached, Bill ordered the beverages and a sandwich

430

for himself, inviting his companion to join him but she declined. 'If you don't mind me saying so,' he said, after the waiter had departed, 'you're looking a little peaky yourself. Sure you haven't been on a boat lately?'

Ellen smiled. 'Not recently,' she said. 'Although I quite like them. I'd love to go to America someday.'

'It's a great country,' replied Bill, not even noticing her gentle hint. 'If you ever do, you've got to go down south towards Kansas and Missouri. That's where I grew up, you know. Didn't stay there long though. Before I hit my teens I was out looking for trouble. Found plenty of it too. Killed my first Indian when I was only eight.'

'Oh my,' exclaimed Ellen in surprise, although she had seen at first hand the level of violent action that Bill's entourage involved themselves in while they were performing.

'It wasn't a safe place back then,' he said, nodding sagely as their refreshments arrived and he poured the tea. 'Of course it's all different now. The wars are over. The land disputes are coming to an end. The old west is dying away, I think. And it's a shame.'

'But you're keeping it alive, aren't you?' she asked. 'With your performances I mean. People won't forget it as long as you're doing that.'

'I'll die too, one day,' he replied. 'Times move on. These shows I do . . . well they'll still be popular during my lifetime but when I'm gone and everyone I've known – Sitting Bull, Bill Hickok, Annie Oakley – we'll just be part of history, that's all. We're barely keeping it alive as it is.'

There was a silence for a time as Ellen thought about this and Bill indulged himself in a moment of self-pity. Eventually she broke it in a quiet voice. 'You'll still be performing in America though, won't you?'

'Sure I will.'

'Take me with you,' she said quickly, wanting the words to be out before she could think about them and pull them back. Bill seemed almost unaware of what she had said for a moment and only snapped back into the conversation when he began to wonder whether he had heard her correctly or not.

'What's that?' he asked. 'What did you say?'

'Take me with you,' she repeated, opening her hands in a plaintive gesture and sighing, as if her entire future rested on this moment of hope. 'Take me to America.'

Bill was unsure what to say at first and relied on humour to get him through. 'What in hell do you want to go to America for?' he asked, laughing slightly despite a certain tension inside him. 'The west is no place for a lady.'

'You just told me I should go there,' she protested.

'On a holiday maybe,' he said. 'Someday. With your husband. But not on your own.'

'I don't have a husband,' she pointed out.

'Well damn it girl, you will have one day. And when you do, you've got to make him take you there. Look me up when you come and I'll show you around. You haven't seen hospitality until you've seen the way they treat friends of Buffalo Bill Cody.'

Ellen Rose sighed and looked out the window. She knew that he understood what she had meant but was ignoring it, not wishing to acknowledge her request. Under other circumstances, she would have accepted her rejection and let it go at that but there was more to consider now than just herself and she had little choice but to continue. 'Bill,' she said, swallowing hard but looking him in the eye nonetheless. 'What happened between us a couple of months back—'

432

'What happened between us was just what happened between us, nothing more,' he snapped back quickly, not particularly wishing to pursue this uncomfortable topic. 'Let's not make more of it than all it was.'

'But how can you say that? We . . . we . . .'

'We didn't do anything that either of us didn't want to do, that's all. There's no point pretending otherwise.'

'That's not what I thought,' she said, biting her lip to prevent tears from coming. Bill leaned forward and took her wrist firmly, enough for her to wince but without actually hurting her.

'Ellen,' he said. 'We'd only met a couple of hours previous. You didn't think there was a romance going on, now did you?'

'I thought . . . You told me—'

'I didn't tell you anything so don't pretend I did,' he snapped, squinting his eyes at her as she looked like she might suddenly cry. His tone softened. He wished to be away from this conversation as soon as possible and in order for that to happen, he had to set himself free of her immediately. However, he didn't particularly want to hurt her at the same time. 'Look,' he said. 'I'm sorry if you thought more of you and me than it was, but we both had a good time, let's just leave it at that.'

'If you take me to America, I'll make you happy,' she said, blushing as she heard the words emerge. She hated him for putting her through this but he had given her no choice.

'I'm not taking you anywhere,' he replied in a firm voice. 'If you think you're coming back to America with me, you're crazy.'

'I'm pregnant,' she said and now he drew his breath in surprise. He stared at her as if she really was insane, pressing himself further back in his chair as if she had some sort of communicable disease. Stroking his beard, he shook his head in sorrow.

'And you want me to believe that I'm the father.'

'You're the only man I've ever been with,' she said.

'A likely story.'

'And a true one. I swear it, Bill. You're the father of this baby. What would you have me do?'

He blinked and looked away. She looked very young sitting there before him. She was, indeed, almost twenty years his junior. He was not a hard-hearted man, my great-grandfather, but he had no room at the same time for unnecessary attachments. He had avoided them this long and was not about to get saddled with a woman and child at this stage of his life.

'I'm already married,' he said finally.

'You could divorce her,' said Ellen. 'You never see her anyway, the papers say so. She lives in a different state to you.'

'I can't divorce her,' he said, meaning it too. 'I won't do that.'

'I can't be here on my own. With this baby. How will we survive?'

Bill laughed. 'You've survived this long,' he said. 'You've got family, don't you? They'll look after you.'

Ellen shook her head and brushed the tears away as they rushed down her cheeks. 'You'd do that?' she asked. 'You'd just leave me.'

'You're sure it's my child?' he asked half-heartedly, even though he had entirely believed her when she had said as much. She didn't even need to respond. 'I'll settle some money on you,' he said. 'You and your baby can live here. Spend it wisely and you won't want for anything. Maybe I'll send you a little something from time to time. That's all I can do. I'm sorry.'

Ellen Rose nodded and picked up her purse. There was something in his tone that made her aware that he was not likely to change his mind. She stood up with dignity and smoothed her skirts, her hand brushing against her stomach and resting there for a moment; Bill watched her hand as she hesitated, somehow shielding the baby's unborn eyes from its father and then, without another word to her lover, she slipped out of the hotel bar and made her way home.

Night time. The streets surrounding our ground-floor apartment in Denver are quiet. We live outside the centre of town. It's a relatively peaceful suburban area. We've rented it for a reasonable price and intend to stay here until we leave Colorado. There's a second bedroom which we'll use for Shane should we still be here after a year or so. Before that if Hitomi lets me. (I think he should be in his own room sooner rather than later.) I often take him for a walk late at night if he's restless; even if he isn't it's a custom I enjoy. I get a certain proud thrill from walking along with my son in his pram. I like it when strangers pass by and glance from him to me in a quick moment, checking for resemblances, looking at the face of the man who has fathered the boy. My usual route takes me across Delarue Street towards Kemley Park which is always quiet save for the dog-walkers and we can safely amble through it at any time before dark. Tonight, like most nights, I stop at a park bench under a light and, as Shane snores in his pram in front of me, pull my book out from my inside pocket and take half an hour's peaceful reading time. It's by Philip Roth. It's a good book. Ten o'clock. Later than I realise. Two joggers run past, two young men. Strong, fit. Handsome. Together, I think. How's

Justin these days, I wonder? Haven't heard from him in a while. And Adam. He's getting married soon. Like to be back home for the wedding. That'd be good. Old friends. There's a song, my mind scrambles to remember the lyric. Good for Isaac to see his grandson too. And vice versa. He's getting old. I want to call him. I want to see him. Why can't I make the time? Now a dog-walker. A young woman. Pretty. I glance at her legs. Taut calves. She spots me looking and frowns. Sees Shane. Relents. Smiles a little. I shrug, embarrassed. She gives a little laugh and walks on. Won't speak to me. She's friendly but not stupid. Ratty-looking terrier with her. I snarl at it. It yaps back. Shane blinks back to consciousness and stares at me, confused. What are we doing here? he wants to know. I shrug again but he doesn't understand that. I show him the cover of the book. I put it back in my pocket. Stand up. The three of us – Shane, Philip Roth and I – start for home. I think of Hitomi, lying in her bath. Bubbles surrounding her. She'll have her hair pinned up with a snappy comb, I think. I'll sneak in, try and let her hair down and she'll scream at me. Whenever we shower together, she keeps her hair clear from the spray. No matter what's happening she's always alert enough to make sure it doesn't get wet. I smile. Foibles. I love her. I cheated on her once, I think. Maybe I'll tell her one day. What's the point? I didn't cheat on her. All I did was sleep with someone else. Not even that. I fucked some other woman, that was all. It doesn't matter. Enough. Check the time. Ten-fifteen. She'll be watching out for us. I've stayed out too late. I'm tired. Work in the morning. Sometimes I want to stop strangers in the street and say Guess what? I've interviewed Bill Clinton. I've had two books published. My great-grandfather is Buffalo Bill Cody. They'd call the cops. Shane gives a muffled shout, then returns to sleep. Shane's great. I feel a rush of love for him. I think I may cry for a moment. I love Shane; I want more words to express that but I can't find them. They're a mystery to me, those words. Get a grip. Why should I get a grip? Nothing wrong with loving your son. I'll communicate with him, I think. We'll talk about other things than family history. We'll talk about football games, and books, and films. When he's old enough to be embarrassed by me I'll dance the funky chicken in front of all his friends and he'll slap his hands over his eyes and shout *Dad get out of here you old fool* and I'll grumble that I never spoke to my father like that even though I did and worse. And he'll have some troubles maybe, especially if we live in London, because he's half and half. America's a good place for him maybe. Or Japan. Or Paris. I don't know. I can't make these kinds of decisions, that's Hitomi's job, although I know one thing – I'm tired of moving around. I want a little peace and quiet. Want a home. No more of this nomadic lifestyle. I'm a family man now. Speaking of which. Home. Light on in the bathroom. I can see that from here. Still in the bath maybe. More likely out and has just left it on. She's got some stupid idea that leaving it on clears the mirrors quicker when they're all steamed up. I don't know. I'd like to have those heat pads behind mirrors that stop them steaming up at all. Maybe when I'm rich and famous. Car coming. We wait at the side of the road. It's coming too slow and Shane's fidgety. We could have made it if we'd gone originally but it's too late now. Come on, for God's sake, I'm getting cold. I want to get inside. I want a beer. I want to cuddle up next to Hitomi on the couch because she'll smell like peaches from those bath salts she uses. She'll be wearing her thick white woollen dressing gown and her legs and feet will be bare beneath it. She'll have let her hair down. Call me crazy but it's a look that always does something to me. I'll sing quietly to her in her ear if we're nuzzling up together and Shane is asleep in his cot. Fiddling with my key on the outside lock. When I find it I see that the outside door is already open. Surprising. Once you go through it closes automatically and locks. I walk in and it closes behind me. Doesn't lock. I peer at it. The lock's broken. Wasn't like that when I went out, I think. Maybe it was. Didn't notice. Must remember to leave a note for the caretaker. Although she'll probably notice herself anyway. Keys back in pocket. Why did I do that? Need them for my own door. I walk through the next set and down the corridor. The lights come on around me one at a time. Shane is still asleep. And then what's this? Not my door? Is my door. Open. Lock's broken. Jimmied open. I swallow. I don't understand. My mind's a beat behind me. Why would Hitomi have the door like this? Heart sinks. Shane's in the hall. I stumble inside. Legs giving way because I'm fucking terrified of what's on the inside. Bare legs, bare feet, just like I imagined. White woollen robe. Smell of peaches. But she's lying on the floor. First thing I think is why is all the furniture pushed around? All I can see of her is her feet. What's she doing? Who's pushing past me? Leather jacket. Strong smell. Bad smell. What was that? Who was he? I'm lost. It's not my apartment at all, is it? I see her now. She's lying flat. Her hair's down all right. Half her head is dark black and scarlet. She's been hurt. Hitomi, I cry. I fall on my knees. I fall on my fucking knees beside her and I can't touch her because I'm afraid with all this blood. Her eyes blink. Blink again. Her mouth opens. Teeth bloody too. She says my name. I shake my head.

What's happened here, I ask her? What have you done? Hitomi, I shout. Get up. Get up, for God's sake. You're fine. There's nothing wrong with you. Get up. William . . . William . . . My hands reach down now to help her. The blood is warm and I gag. I don't know what to do. I'm crying suddenly. And a man's standing beside me, shouting loudly. I know him. He's my neighbour. He's a nice guy. I borrowed some masking tape off him the other day and it's sitting on my bureau. I can give it back to him now, I think. He's shouting something and I'm saying she's fine she's fine she's fine there's nothing wrong here she'll be fine and more people are running in. Hitomi, I cry. I can hear Shane outside. Can't hear anyone else now, somehow. Just him. Just me. Her eyes move again in terror and settle on mine. They lock in. I can feel them locking in as now is the time for her to say goodbye. She's looking at me. She's scared. I remember kissing her. I can taste her kiss now. The pupils still stare at me but she's gone. I know she's gone.

Later, London was dark and cold and the streets were lit by Christmas trees and festive lights. I'd made a mistake coming to Oxford Street on a Thursday evening in mid-December. Shane was wrapped up warm and had fallen asleep in his buggy but I was finding it difficult to negotiate my way through the shoppers. Middle-aged women in heavy coats and matching scarves and gloves looked at me irritably as I made my way along, from time to time banging against their Selfridges shopping bags; frustrated men stared around in despair at the doors of the department stores, too exhausted to step inside, too unimaginative to find presents for their wives. Everywhere was noise; the taxi cabs blew their horns incessantly while the traffic barely moved.

A construction crew had chosen this time of the year to begin work on a stretch of pavement on one side of the street. A crowd of people stood at their hoardings, trying to step on to the road and to the other end of the pavement, but what seemed to be an enormous lake of rainwater stood in their way. I stopped momentarily, pulling myself up and gripping the handles of the buggy tightly; I could feel a burning perspiration work its way along my forehead as I clenched my teeth. A teenage boy crashed into me as I stood there. He turned to stare at me in annoyance as he passed; his head had been focused directly on the ground below. He had earphones connected to his pockets and as he looked at me through his dark, hooded eyes, he wore a look of bored contempt. I growled and bared my teeth at him like a woken dog, daring him to challenge me. *Little fucker*, I mouthed and he squinted, considering the comment, before continuing on his way with a shrug.

More than anything else I wanted a drink. I wanted to find a pub somewhere, sit in a dark corner, order upwards of eighteen pints, and drink them all. I wanted to be carried out of the place sometime towards midnight shouting nonsense. I wanted to throw up in a gutter over Vauxhall Bridge and bury myself in towards the railings, closing my eyes, begging for sleep to come. I wanted to be drunk, that was all. But I couldn't do any of those things because I had Shane with me and he'd wake up soon and want feeding. I had to finish my shopping and get home.

I'd left Denver a few weeks after Hitomi's death. The man who had killed her – a thirty-two-year-old unemployed man named Denis Fitzgerald – had been arrested by police the following day after his fingerprints were found all over our apartment. He had a criminal past and a file on record. He was too stupid to wear gloves. He'd never killed anyone before although he had a history of burglary and theft and, although I never came face to face with him, I was told that he did not appear to be unduly fazed by what he had done. He had seen me leave the apartment that night with Shane and, believing the place to be empty, had broken in without much difficulty. By that time, Hitomi was in the bedroom undressing; she heard nothing as she already had the taps on the bath running. When she stepped out of the room, they surprised each other. She had turned and run towards the door and, probably without thinking, he had made a grab for her, pulled her to the ground and, in order to stop her screaming, had lifted the phone from the side table and crashed it down above her right ear, smashing into her temple, silencing her, leaving just a thin gasp of air exhaling from her mouth for the next half hour until I arrived home and held her while that too became lost to her.

I had made friends there, of course, but they were no use to me. I buried myself in Shane in order to give myself something to do; I had little choice on that matter. And then I decided to leave America and return home to London, believing that my old house, Isaac's house, was the right place for me to be. Naturally he welcomed me home with open arms. Although he had barely known my wife, he was genuinely upset by her death. Indeed the passion of his sorrow angered me for some reason, for I wanted to be the only one going through that pain. I couldn't accept that someone else would want it too.

Although the Denver police had offered to contact the Naoyuki family and tell them of the tragedy, I felt that was something I should do myself. It was the hardest

441

phone call I ever had to make and can remember little of it. I phoned Tak, my brother-in-law, and told him what had happened. He wept bitterly on the phone while I remained composed. He didn't blame me – yet – and said that he would tell his parents. When the phone rang the following morning in the hotel room I had taken with Shane I assumed it was the police and picked it up, making only a grunting sound to indicate that I was listening.

'Is that William Cody?' said an unfamiliar voice at the other end, but by the inflections I recognised the Japanese accent. In an instant I knew that deep male voice could only be Hitomi's father.

'Mr Naoyuki,' I said, a stab of pain hitting my chest, a feeling of guilt, as if all of this was my fault. I wondered how he had got my number. A flash photo of the first and only evening I had ever spent in their home came into my mind; I was just a kid then, I thought to myself. I didn't know what to say to him now and there was a long pause as he waited for me to answer his question. 'Yes,' I replied finally. 'This is William Cody.'

'Mr Cody, you have of course begun to make the necessary arrangements,' he said in an emotionless and formal voice.

'Arrangements . . .' I muttered. 'I don't . . . I mean what do you mean exactly?'

'Tajima has informed us what has happened,' he said with a sigh. 'There are arrangements to be made.'

'Of course,' I said.

'We would like Hitomi's ashes to be sent to her family here. In Kyoto.'

Again, a rush of pain ran through me. Her ashes. It was beyond final. Of course I knew that she wanted to be cremated but the thought of actually going through

442

with it seemed barbaric to me. And yet underneath I could see no reason why not to accede to his wishes. Already I knew that I had no desire to keep them with me. If I had thought of it at all, I probably would have wanted to scatter them somewhere peaceful. And although I was upset and angry and felt like lashing out at someone – and Mr Naoyuki being the one I was talking to, he seemed a perfect candidate – I knew instantly that the peaceful place I was looking for was her own home. Japan. Although he could not see me, I nodded slowly and closed my eyes.

'That's fine,' I said. 'I'll speak to the hospital. I'll arrange for that to happen.'

'You should never have taken her to America,' he said and I could detect in his voice a feeling that he did not want to engage in conversation with me but could not stop himself. 'You know how she felt about America. She knew she would die there.'

I shook my head. 'That's not true,' I said quickly. 'That was England. She said she'd—' I couldn't say the word. 'It was England she said that about. Not America. And anyway, that was just—'

'I don't wish to speak to you about that,' he interrupted, a crack coming into his voice, a sudden flicker of emotion. 'My grandson, however. You will need to make arrangements for him too.'

'Your grandson is my son,' I said quickly through gritted teeth, anger forcing my hands into fists. 'Do you hear me? Shane will be with me always. Do you understand me?'

A long pause ensued. I wondered whether he had just been hoping against hope that I would for some reason capitulate and hand my son over to relative strangers, and less than perfect ones at that. I already knew that if

I had one thing to live for, it was him. I knew what was important to me. 'Please ask the hospital authorities to contact me directly after your arrangements are made,' he said finally. 'We won't speak again, Mr Cody.'

'Fine with me, buddy,' – (a word I never use, so why?) – I said bitterly, hanging up the phone.

In June 1888, Ellen Rose gave birth to a boy, who she named Sam. She never saw my great-grandfather again after their meeting in the hotel when she had told him that she was pregnant; however they communicated sporadically for, despite his faults, he was true to his obligations and would send her money from time to time, although he never asked for news of the boy or made any suggestion that he would like to meet him.

Despite her parents' protestations, Ellen left the Regis-Roc Circus when Sam was just over a year old and moved to London where she found work in the box office of a theatre. She was fortunate enough to find a kind employer who had no objection to her bringing Sam with her to work in the evenings and he spent his infant years crawling around the ticket stall, and divided his childhood between the classroom and the theatre itself where he became a regular fixture and unpaid hand.

Isaac never told me many stories of Ellen Rose from the time she had separated herself from my great-grandfather; curiously his interest seemed particular to Bill Cody and not to those with whom he came in contact, even if they were part of his own lineage. Ellen was Isaac's own grandmother but he did not remember her for she died quite young, when he himself was only a child. Sam, my grandfather, became a soldier and survived the trenches of northern France, returning to

England where he was killed in a motor accident shortly after the outbreak of the Second World War. As for the tales of my grandfather, there are few for once again Isaac was reticent on the subject. These are the points where his stories end, for his characters begin to die. These were the ones he did not like to talk about. He was at home riding across the prairies of his imagination, or travelling the world with his Congress of Rough Riders, but as his heroes and ancestors grew old and proved they were mortal after all, his enthusiasm would wane. Always, however, he finished with the last stories of Buffalo Bill. Naturally, Isaac's historical world could only ever end one way – with a death.

As my thirtieth birthday approached, I found myself sunk into despair. Shane and I were living with Isaac, who was dying even before my eyes. His sight had faded a lot and he had difficulty hearing the television if it wasn't pitched up to its highest possible level. He seemed to be losing his alertness as well; I caught him looking at me sometimes with a strange look in his eyes, as if he was not entirely sure who I was. Shane seemed to scare him somewhat, although the child always wanted to sit with him. I was grieving, deeply grieving, and yet found myself cooking and cleaning and keeping house for my father, for if I did not do it, who would? Sometimes, I wanted to talk to him about Hitomi, about how much I missed her, about how senseless her death had been and how angry and lost it made me, but such conversations would have been pointless. I knew that he had already forgotten her and could never have conceived of the tornado blowing inside my mind. I felt absolutely alone and despaired for my own future.

And then, in the deepest moment of my unhappiness,

a simple offer proved a lifeline. While I had been in Denver, Adam and Kate had married, and they had made a point of inviting me to their house, which was not far away, ever since my return to London. I had gone for dinner once but found their happiness – not to mention their obvious attempts not to appear too happy lest it would upset me – too much for me and had collapsed at their dinner table, weeping hysterically, furiously grabbing at the corners of their table for support, and yet unable to allow them to comfort me. At home that night I had wanted only to join Hitomi and found myself standing by the mirror in my bedroom, a kitchen knife in my hands, staring deeply into my own eyes to see my own pain, holding the knife to different parts of my body, willing my hands to force it in, knowing all the time that I had not the guts to do such a thing, and instead dragged its blade across my face, sighing with happy pain as I cut myself, not deeply enough for any true damage, but surface scars nevertheless. I scratched it down time and again until my cheeks were a bloody roadmap of sadness, pure lost despair, before sitting on my bed in sorrow, wondering how and when this terrible feeling would pass me by. That night was a difficult night and I prayed for some release.

The release came in the form of my friends. Kate offered to take Shane two evenings a week if I would agree to go out with Adam and Justin and get – in her words – rat-arsed. Her offer made me laugh when she made it but I accepted, not really thinking that it would help but glad to get out of the house for a night and away from the responsibility of looking after my son. If I didn't have to keep worrying about him, I thought, I could at least concentrate on making myself even more miserable.

At first, I could tell that Adam and Justin felt uncomfortable with me. They wanted to help me, to comfort me, but did not know how to do it. We had known each other all our lives and were now grown men of thirty years old, with experience and maturity behind us and suddenly we were reverting to our youths once again and spending a lot of time together getting drunk. And somehow over the course of several months they managed to bring me back to some form of consciousness. Although I often lashed out at them, saying dreadful things, insulting them openly, they sat there and allowed me to abuse them until I had no choice but to believe they were truly my friends, truly cared for me and would not allow me to disappear. And when I accepted that, I knew that I was not alone after all. What they showed me was not that I had them in my life, but that I had Shane. And even Isaac. And I was loved.

'You don't have to do this any more, you know,' I told them eventually one evening as we sat in a local pub. 'You don't have to keep spending so much time with me. You have lives, you know.'

'We're not going through this again,' said Justin immediately, sensing that I was trying to get rid of them. I shook my head and patted him on the shoulder.

'That's not what I mean,' I said. 'You need to get back to your lives. We should make it one regular evening a week, not two.' They both looked at me, unsure how to respond, waiting for me to say more. I could tell that they wanted that too, that as much as they had nursed me back to health, the rest of our lives could not continue like this. 'I mean it,' I said. 'I'm not going to pretend things are perfect. Of course they're not. I'm not going to say that I don't think of Hitomi every

447

hour of the day, because I do, but the awful darkness is slipping away.'

'You do seem more . . . together,' said Adam cautiously.

'Because I am,' I said, desperate to reassure them. 'You've both helped me so much. And so have Kate and Mark allowing you both off the leashes so often to be with me. It does mean a lot to me you know. I don't know what the right words are to express it.' I sighed and breathed heavily, staring at my beer mat for a moment, twirling it between my fingers. 'You're my friends,' I said finally, a simple statement perhaps but I meant it. 'But you're not my son and he's the one I should be with, you know? He doesn't understand any of this but he's going to one day. I mean he's talking now a little and I need to be with him more than I am. For God's sake, he thinks Kate is his mother and she's not, his mother's dead and I need him to realise that. I mean it's not that I'm not grateful to her—'

'It's okay, I understand what you mean,' said Adam quickly, biting his lip and I could see his eyes were a little glazed because the lines that were coming out of my mouth were indeed the old me, or at least a slightly battered version of the same.

'Isaac's dying,' I said with a shrug. 'You both know that. He doesn't have much time left and I should spend more time with him now too. I want to just feel like I understand him before he goes. I don't want to feel that I never said things to him that I should have. You see that's how I feel about Hitomi. There's things that—' My voice cracked and I caught myself in time, stopping the sentence, knowing that I had promised myself that I would not allow every conversation to lead inexorably towards her. I breathed and pulled myself together before looking up at my two friends gratefully. 'One night a week from now on, all right?' I said. 'We'll get drunk, catch up, go home and wake up with hangovers. How does that sound?'

They smiled. I wanted to hug them but the table was in my way. Maybe I didn't need to. Sometimes people know how important they are to you and you don't have to keep showing it to them like that. I went home that night and felt as unhappy and miserable as before, but there was a difference now; I knew my life had meaning and worth and there were people in it who added to it. And they didn't want to lose me either. And that mattered. It matters now.

As for Buffalo Bill Cody, the twentieth century was not kind to him, except after he had died. He returned to America and continued to tour with the Congress of Rough Riders until he was invited by the government to be part of the plans to settle Wyoming. This brought him back to the events of his youth and he took a great pride in helping design the towns and cities which would make up the basis of the state; one of the towns, Cody, was ultimately named for him. When Nate Salsbury, his long-time partner in the wild west shows, died, he took the opportunity to invest a greater portion of their earnings in a mining company in Arizona, which soon went disastrously wrong. Within a couple of years, he had lost every penny he had ever earned, the shows had gone bust and he returned to Denver, Colorado as he reached his seventieth birthday, refusing to be broken by his bad luck. The wild west shows ended when interest in the west floundered among the American people. It would be many years later before that interest would be rekindled in nostalgia and movie reels, but there could be no denying that he was as responsible as anyone for the myths which developed over the ensuing hundred years. Myths which somehow developed into history lessons, creating an ideology and a story which was more fiction than anything else. Throughout his life he had earned and lost fortunes, the fact that his old age found him penniless was neither a surprise nor a concern to him.

As the shows began their inevitable decline, my great-grandfather poured more and more of his savings into them. Finally, he was a bankrupt and lived off nothing but his reputation. Divorced now from Louisa, he tried to become involved in the fledgling movie industry but without success. The early pioneers of short films in California were all young men attempting a new form of entertainment and had little interest in an ageing mythologiser whose time had been and gone. What little resources he had left he poured into trying to set up his own new movie company but he received no financial backing and had little choice but to retire to Denver, where he died in 1917, alone and penniless. He never did see his son, the child he had fathered with Ellen Rose, nor did he live one extra year to discover that he was a grandfather through that same child. The newspapers show that he was widely mourned upon his death but few of the articles knew how to differentiate between the life he had led and the one he had portrayed for himself on stage and in books, for the lines between the two intersected too often.

My great-grandfather was a self-invented figure. He swept from adventure to adventure, unable to ever settle down to a normal stable life, creating the character of Buffalo Bill Cody at an early age and constantly reinventing it in order to appeal to a changing nation. He was an entertainer and a showman to the last. In life he had expressed a desire to be buried on Cedar Mountain in Wyoming, but in death Louisa and his surviving children saw to it that his final resting place was Lookout Mountain in Colorado, a more peaceful setting.

Isaac died at home, in the autumn, just over a year after Hitomi. Although his last few months had found him slipping between full consciousness and near senility, the last week of his life passed by relatively peacefully. He woke one morning and had extreme difficulty breathing; a trip to the hospital saw him placed on a ventilator for a time but his doctor confirmed to me that he had only a few days left at most. He could stay in the hospital, hooked up to machines, or he could return home with a single ventilator which would keep him comfortable until the end came naturally; the choice was mine; I was told. I shook my head and gave the options to my father.

'Home,' he said, with a solid wink.

Adam and Kate offered to take care of Shane for a few days so that I could look after Isaac and I gave him to them gratefully. I was almost thirty-one years old now and I couldn't remember when I had last felt so much like a child as I did while nursing him through his final hours. In the end there was only a day and a half between his leaving the hospital and his death, but I tried to make the most of those hours, knowing that I was being given a chance here that I never had with Hitomi. He lay in bed on his last night talking to me, and I sat there in the lamplight, watching the machine clicking away, noticing how his eyelids would droop from time to time as he lurched towards sleep, even though he wanted to talk to me yet.

'You know what I want?' he said around eleven o'clock that night. I was tired myself and hoped that he would not ask for something outlandish. Something which could potentially kill him there and then.

'What's that?' I asked cautiously.

'I want a glass of whisky,' he said firmly. 'Straight up. No ice, no water. A good glass of Scotch. How about it? Will you join me?' The effort of saying six full sentences exhausted him for a moment and that last offer came out more as a wheeze than anything else, but I understood him nonetheless and nodded with a smile.

'Sure, I'll join you,' I said. 'I suppose you expect me to go down and get it for you too, do you?'

'Well if you wouldn't mind,' he said, a slight smile flickering across his lips. I fetched the bottle and two glasses and helped prop him up a little in the bed by fixing a couple of extra pillows behind his back.

'Here,' I said, offering him his glass. 'Just take it easy, all right? Don't rush it.'

He ignored my advice and took a good gulp of Scotch before turning slowly to look at me and winking. 'So what do you think of me now?' he asked then, somewhat unexpectedly. 'I don't suppose you ever thought you'd see me reduced to this.'

I didn't know how to respond to what he had said and so just smiled in a fairly non-committal fashion. 'You're fine,' I said lamely.

'I'm dying, William,' he said. 'You know it. I know it. Doesn't matter.'

I could feel a sting behind my eyes and looked away from him. I remembered when I was a child and he

452

had seemed so big, so much more enormous than me or any of my friends, and I wondered how he had been reduced to the shell he was now.

'Tell me something,' I said after a lengthy pause. 'The wild west show. If I had agreed to sign the papers, would you have really done it?'

He sighed dramatically, a long exhalation of long-suppressed irritation with me, and his voice became clear now. 'Of course I would have,' he said. 'It was my dream. My only dream.'

'Yes, but would you have actually seen it through? Made it profitable?'

He laughed. 'Probably wouldn't have made any money if that's what you mean,' he said. 'Not the point though. I would have done it. What else have I done with my life?'

'Lots,' I said, even though I knew that I would have been hard pressed to say what.

'Nothing,' he confirmed. 'Maybe it just skipped a few generations. My grandfather had it, my father and I didn't do much with our lives. It's up to you, isn't it. You're making something of yours.'

'I don't see what,' I grunted.

'You know what, I'm dying, William. This isn't about you right now.' There was a reprimand. And of course he was right. 'The thing about you,' he continued after a moment, 'is that you've always blamed me for not being close to you.'

'I haven't,' I began, not wishing to get into a fight now but he silenced me with a wave of his hands.

'Just hear me out,' he said. 'I haven't got much breath so don't let me waste it. You think I haven't been close to you, that all I've done is tell you stories all your life. Well maybe that's so, but that's where I saw our connection should be. Did you ever wonder why I told you stories about Buffalo Bill?'

'Because you're obsessed with him,' I said. *Because you wish you were him*, I thought.

'Don't be ridiculous. I told you them because they're family stories. They didn't all tell you about who your great-grandfather was. If you'd listened to them a little closer you would have seen that some of them told you who *I* was, some of them told you who you could be. It wasn't all about the history and it wasn't about showing off. I was trying to get close to you the only way I knew how.'

'It's fine,' I said, shaking my head. I could feel myself gearing up to challenge him on what he had said but knew inside that there could never really be a less appropriate time for me to do so.

'It's not fine,' he barked, sitting forward suddenly and pointing a bony finger at me. 'You're a father yourself now. You shouldn't sit in judgement of me so much. You don't know, that's all.'

'I don't judge you, Isaac,' I said quickly. 'Honestly, I—'

'You do, you do, Jesus but you do,' he said with a sigh. 'It doesn't matter though. I'm past caring. I know what I tried to do. Maybe I succeeded, maybe I failed. Who knows. Maybe someday, though, you'll find yourself telling those stories to someone else, to Shane maybe, and maybe then you'll see that my life wasn't totally in vain. That there was a reason for some of it.' A silence descended for a few minutes and finally I reached across and took the empty glass from his hands. He seemed to have fallen asleep but as my hands touched his, he woke quickly and gripping on to my wrist tightly he pulled me close and stared at me directly in the eyes. 'And one last thing,' he snarled. 'Stop calling me Isaac, all right? I'm your father. Show a little fucking respect.'

I stared back at him, part of me terrified, another part of me wanting to hug him, but he relaxed me by lying back into the pillows, releasing my hand and patting it gently. 'You're not a bad son, Bill,' he said. 'Maybe I should have started calling you that a long time ago. Maybe you've earned it after all.'

I stood up and walked to the door, watching him for a few minutes to make sure that he really was asleep before closing the door quietly and walking downstairs. I switched on the lamp in the living room and, placing the whisky bottle and glasses on the table, I filled mine again and put it on the table. Before sitting down, I walked across to the wall and took my great-grandfather's Smith & Wesson handgun down and brought it back to the armchair where I sat down, examining it carefully. It was the most polished thing in the house, my father's prize possession. I wanted to reach across for my glass but found that I couldn't. Instead I held on to the gun with both hands, tighter and tighter, my knuckles turning white as I gripped it, refusing to let it go, wanting it to be with me for just a few minutes longer.

My father had left strict instructions in his will that he was to be cremated and for the second time in a couple of years I attended such a funeral. Unlike the first time, however, I did not feel as devastated at Isaac's passing as I had at Hitomi's. He had lived well into his eighties and had not been denied the chances that she had. His time had come; she had been robbed. And although he knew that he did not want to be buried, he had not said what I should do with the ashes. And unlike the occasion with Hitomi, I knew exactly what I needed to do.

It was late in the year and the sun was not shining as Shane and I walked hand in hand along the dusty trail. It wasn't cold but there was chill enough in the air that we kept up a healthy pace. Shane's vocabulary had expanded considerably and he locked his hand into mine as we walked along, his tiny voice chattering away without any self-consciousness while I watched the path ahead, knowing where my destination lay, my mind lost in thoughts even as I tried to answer the questions he asked me.

He was too young to understand death, of course, and so I didn't bother to explain it to him. Someday, years from now, I thought I would. He wouldn't remember Isaac, of course, but there were things I could tell him about his grandfather that would keep him alive. Stories that might make him wish that he had lived just a few years longer so that they might have got to know each other a little.

'Here we are,' I said finally, just at the point where I thought he was getting ready to start complaining about the length of the walk. 'This is where we need to be.' There was no one else around but Shane pointed in the distance and I stared as a deer appeared from the woods and turned its graceful neck towards us, staring at us indifferently before padding cautiously on its way and out of sight. I looked down at my son who was staring up at me with breathless delight, his face lit up with such wonder and happiness that I felt an urge to pick him up and crush him to me. And so I did.

I opened my haversack and walked to the side of the mountain, taking the lid off the urn. 'What's that?' asked Shane from behind me and I turned to see him

456

pointing towards the headstone marking the grave of his great-great-grandfather, Buffalo Bill Cody.

'That's where my great-grandfather is buried,' I explained to him. 'I thought Isaac would like to be here too.' Then I scattered his ashes over Lookout Mountain and, without waiting around any longer, took a firm hold of my son's hand and turned to leave. We were only there a few moments; there was no need for more.

The House of Special Purpose
John Boyne

'An exciting, fast-paced story . . . absorbing and richly satisfying'
THE TIMES

RUSSIA, 1915: Sixteen-year-old farmer's son Georgy Jachmenev steps in front of an assassin's bullet intended for a senior member of the Russian Imperial Family and is instantly proclaimed a hero. Rewarded with the position of bodyguard to Alexei Romanov, the only son of Tsar Nicholas II, the course of his life is changed for ever.

Privy to the secrets of Nicholas and Alexandra, the machinations of Rasputin and the events which will lead to the final collapse of the autocracy, Georgy is both a witness and participant in a drama that will echo down the century.

Sixty-five years later, visiting his wife Zoya in a London hospital, memories of the life they have lived together flood his mind. And with them, the consequences of the brutal fate of the Romanovs which has hung like a shroud over their marriage . . .

'John Boyne brings a completely fresh eye to the most important stories. He is prepared to look at the dark, yet somehow manages to find whatever light was there in the first place. He guides us through the realm of history and makes the journey substantial, poignant, real. He is one of the great craftsmen in contemporary literature'
Colum McCann

'Boyne writes with consummate ease, and is particularly good at drawing the indecently rich world of the pre-revolutionary Romanovs'
INDEPENDENT

Mutiny on the Bounty
John Boyne

Portsmouth 1787

PICKPOCKET JOHN JACOB TURNSTILE is on his way to be detained at His Majesty's Pleasure when he is offered a lifeline, what seems like a freedom of sorts – the job of personal valet to a departing naval captain. Little does he realize that it is anything but – and by accepting the devil's bargain he will put his life in perilous danger. For the ship is HMS Bounty, his new captain William Bligh and their destination Tahiti.

From the moment the ship leaves port, Turnstile's life is turned upside down, for not only must he put his own demons to rest, but he must also confront the many adversaries he will encounter on the Bounty's extraordinary last voyage. Walking a dangerous line between an unhappy crew and a captain he comes to admire, he finds himself in a no-man's land where the distinction between friend and foe is increasingly difficult to determine . . .

'An excellent story . . . written with a total command of naval expertise, without ever spilling into pedantry, Mutiny on the Bounty is storytelling at its most accomplished'
INDEPENDENT

'A memsmerising tour-de-force . . . this is a remarkable and compelling piece of storytelling'
IRISH TIMES

The Boy in the Striped Pyjamas
John Boyne

'A small wonder of a book . . . a particular historical moment,
one that cannot be told too often'

GUARDIAN

What happens when innocence is confronted by monstrous evil?

NINE YEAR OLD Bruno knows nothing of the Final Solution and the
Holocaust. He is oblivious to the appalling cruelties being inflicted
on the people of Europe by his country. All he knows is that he
has been moved from a comfortable home in Berlin to a house in
a desolate area where there is nothing to do and no-one to play
with. Until he meets Shmuel, a boy who lives a strange parallel
existence on the other side of the adjoining wire fence and who,
like the other people there, wears a uniform of striped pyjamas.

Bruno's friendship with Shmuel will take him from innocence to
revelation. And in exploring what he is unwittingly a part of, he
will inevitably become subsumed by the terrible process.

'The Holocaust as a subject insists on respect, precludes criticism,
prefers silence. One thing is clear: this book
will not go gently into any good night'

OBSERVER

'An extraordinary tale of friendship and the horrors of war . . . raw
literary talent at its best'

IRISH INDEPENDENT

'A book that lingers in the mind for quite some time . . . a subtle,
calculatedly simple and ultimately moving story'

IRISH TIMES

'Simply written and highly memorable. There are no monstrosities on the
page but the true horror is all the more potent for being implicit'

IRELAND ON SUNDAY

'Stays ahead of its readers before delivering its killer-punch final pages'

INDEPENDENT

NOW A MAJOR FILM

The Absolutist
John Boyne

SEPTEMBER 1919: Twenty-year-old Tristan Sadler takes a train from London to Norwich to deliver some letters to Marian Bancroft. Tristan fought alongside Marian's brother Will during the Great War, but in 1917, Will laid down his guns on the battlefield, declared himself a conscientious objector and was shot as a traitor, an act which has brought shame and dishonour on the Bancroft family.

But the letters are not the real reason for Tristan's visit. He holds a secret deep in his soul. One that he is desperate to unburden himself of to Marian, if he can only find the courage.

As he recalls his friendship with Will, from the training ground at Aldershot to the trenches of Northern France, he speaks of how the intensity of their friendship brought him both happiness and self-discovery as well as despair and pain.

The Absolutist is a novel that examines the events of the Great War from the perspective of two young soldiers, both struggling with the complexity of their emotions and the confusion of their friendship.

The Thief of Time
John Boyne

MATTHIEU ZELA HAS lived his life well. In fact, he's lived several lives well. Because Matthieu Zela's life is characterised by one amazing fact: his body stopped ageing before the end of the eighteenth century.

Starting in 1758, a young Matthieu flees Paris after witnessing his mother's brutal murder. His only companions are his younger brother Tomas and one true love, Dominique Sauvet. The story of his life takes us from the French Revolution to 1920s Hollywood, from the Great Exhibition to the Wall Street Crash, and by the end of the twentieth century, Matthieu has been an engineer, a rogue, a movie mogul, a soldier, a financier, a lover to many, a cable TV executive and much more besides.

Brilliantly weaving history and personal experiences, this is a dazzling story of love, murder, missed chances, treachery – and redemption.

'An extraordinary debut'
SUNDAY EXPRESS

'A minor masterpiece'
TIME OUT

'Boyne should be congratulated for his spirited take
on an old theme'
GUARDIAN

'Boyne is a skilful storyteller, expertly weaving
differing stories together'
SUNDAY TRIBUNE

The Heart's Invisible Furies
John Boyne

Cast out from her West Cork village, sixteen years old and pregnant, Catherine Goggin makes her way to Dublin to start afresh. She has no choice but to believe that the nun to whom she entrusts her child will find him a better life.

The baby is named Cyril by his adoptive parents, Charles and Maude Avery, a well-to-do but deeply eccentric couple who treat him more like a curiosity than a son. You're not a proper Avery, they tell him. And perhaps he isn't. But through them he meets Julian Woodbead who, even from childhood, seems destined for an infinitely more glamorous and dangerous life.

And so begins one man's funny and moving search to find his place in a world that seems to delight in gently tormenting him at every turn. Buffeted by circumstance and, at times, the consequences of his own questionable judgement, Cyril must navigate his emotions and desires in a search for that most elemental human need . . . happiness.

'A substantial achievement'
GUARDIAN

'A bold, funny epic'
OBSERVER

'Written with verve, humour and heart . . . at its core,
The Heart's Invisible Furies aspires to be not just the tale
of Cyril Avery, a man buffeted by coincidence and circumstance,
but the story of Ireland itself'
IRISH TIMES

A Ladder to the Sky
John Boyne

You've heard the old proverb about ambition, that it's like setting a ladder to the sky. It can lead to a long and painful fall.

If you look hard enough, you will find stories pretty much anywhere. They don't even have to be your own. Or so would-be-novelist Maurice Swift decides very early on in his career.

A chance encounter in a Berlin hotel with celebrated author Erich Ackerman gives Maurice an opportunity. For Erich is lonely, and he has a story to tell; whether or not he should is another matter.

Once Maurice has made his name, he finds himself in need of a fresh idea. He doesn't care where he finds it, as long as it helps him rise to the top. Stories will make him famous, but they will also make him beg, borrow and steal. They may even make him do worse.